Miss Read, or in real life Mrs Dora Saint, is a teacher by profession who started writing after the Second World War, beginning with light essays written for *Punch* and other journals. She has written on educational and country matters, and worked as a scriptwriter for the BBC. Miss Read is married to a retired schoolmaster and they have one daughter. They live in a tiny Berkshire hamlet. She is a local magistrate and her hobbies are theatregoing, listening to music and reading.

Miss Read is the author of numerous books, which have gained immense popularity for their humorous and honest depictions of English rural life, including, most recently, *Tales from a Village School* and *A Year at Thrush Green*. Many of her books are published by Penguin, together with six omnibus editions. She has also written several books for children, including The Red Bus series for the very young (published in one volume by Puffin as *The Little Red Bus and Other Stories*), a cookery book, *Miss Read's Country Cooking*, and two autobiograpical works, *A Fortunate Grandchild* and *Time Remembered*, also published in one volume as *Early Days*, with a new foreword by the author.

Miss Read

TALES FROM THRUSH GREEN

Illustrated by J. S. Goodall

PENGUIN BOOKS

PENGUIN BOOKS

Published by the Penguin Group
Penguin Books Ltd, 27 Wrights Lane, London W8 5TZ, England
Penguin Books USA Inc., 375 Hudson Street, New York, New York 10014, USA
Penguin Books Australia Ltd, Ringwood, Victoria, Australia
Penguin Books Canada Ltd, 10 Alcorn Avenue, Toronto, Ontario, Canada M4V 3B2
Penguin Books (NZ) Ltd, 182–190 Wairau Road, Auckland 10, New Zealand

Penguin Books Ltd, Registered Offices: Harmondsworth, Middlesex, England

Affairs at Thrush Green first published by Michael Joseph 1983
At Home in Thrush Green first published by Michael Joseph 1985
First published in one volume as *Tales from Thrush Green* by Michael Joseph 1994
Published in Penguin Books 1995
1 3 5 7 9 10 8 6 4 2

Affairs at Thrush Green copyright © Miss Read, 1983
At Home in Thrush Green copyright © Miss Read, 1985
All rights reserved

Printed in England by Clays Ltd, St Ives plc

CONTENTS

AFFAIRS AT THRUSH GREEN

To Jenny
With Love

Contents

1   A Snowy Morning

CHARLES HENSTOCK awoke with a start. He must have overslept, it was so light in the bedroom. He turned his head and squinted sideways at the bedside clock. To his relief, the hands stood at twenty past seven.

Still bemused, he gazed above him, relishing the warmth of his bed and the elegant swags of plasterwork which decorated the vicarage ceiling. Those skilful workers some two hundred years ago certainly knew how to delight the eye, thought the present incumbent of the parish of Lulling.

Not that Lulling was the only parish in his care. A mile to the north lay his old parish of Thrush Green, and north and west of that delectable spot were those of Nidden and Lulling Woods. It was a large area to care for, with four splendid churches, and Charles Henstock constantly prayed that he might fulfil his responsibilities with diligence.

His wife Dimity lay curled beside him, still deep in sleep. They had started their married life together at Thrush Green, in the bleak Victorian rectory which had been burnt to the ground some two years earlier. The general opinion was that the fire was a blessing in disguise. The hideous building had stood out like a sore thumb among the beautiful stone-built Cotswold houses round the green.

But Charles still mourned his old home. He had known

great happiness there, and even now could scarcely bear to look at the empty site where once his home had stood.

A pinkish glow was beginning to spread over the ceiling. The sun must be rising, but still that strange luminosity which had roused him hung about the room. More alert now, the good rector struggled upright, taking care not to disturb his sleeping partner.

The ancient cedar tree was now in sight, its outspread arms holding thick bands of snow. The telephone wire sagged beneath the weight it was bearing, and the window sill was heavily encrusted.

Very carefully the rector slipped out of bed and went to the window to survey the cold February scene. Since his early childhood he had delighted in snow. Now, looking at his transformed garden, his heart beat faster with the old familiar excitement.

The snow covered everything – the paths, the flower-beds, the tiny snowdrops which had so recently braved the bitter winds and tossed their little bells under the hedges. It lay in gentle billows against the summerhouse door and the tall yew hedge.

Beyond the garden, St John's church roof glistened under its snowy canopy against a rose-pink cloud and, high above, the golden weathercock on the steeple caught the first rays of the winter sun.

The beauty of it all enraptured Charles. He caught his breath in wonderment, oblivious of the chilly bedroom and his congealing feet. What enchantment! What purity! An overnight miracle!

'Charles,' said Dimity, 'what has happened?'

'It's been snowing,' said her husband, smiling upon her. 'It's quite deep.'

'Oh dear,' said Dimity, getting out of bed. 'What a blessing I brought the spade indoors last night! No doubt we'll have to dig ourselves out.'

Dimity had always been the practical partner.

Charles Henstock's appointment to the living of Lulling

and its combined parishes, had been welcomed by almost all who knew him.

He was much loved in the district for his modesty, his warm heart, and the willing care he gave to his parishioners. The fire at Thrush Green rectory had shocked the community, and Dimity and Charles received much sympathy. It seemed particularly appropriate that he should now live in the beautiful Queen Anne house and enjoy such pleasant surroundings.

Nevertheless, there were a few people in Lulling who viewed their new pastor with some reserve.

Charles had followed his old friend Anthony Bull who had held the living of Lulling for almost twenty years, and had made his mark in the parish.

Anthony had been the very opposite of Charles Henstock. In appearance he was tall and handsome, with a fine mane of hair which he tossed back from a noble brow with the ready expertise of an actor. Charles was short, tubby and bald, and lacked any sort of dramatic technique in the pulpit.

There were quite a few of Anthony's followers who admitted unashamedly that they had attended St John's for the enjoyment of their vicar's eloquent sermons as much as for the High Church ritual for which the church was noted. Anthony Bull's magnificent vestments were the admiration of all, and particularly of the needlewomen in his flock. The fact that he was fortunate in having a wealthy wife who adored him, and was generous with her money, was one which did not go unnoticed in the parish. Never had Lulling Vicarage been so beautifully furnished, or its gardens kept so immaculately. Mrs Bull, it was common knowledge, was prepared to pay almost twice as much an hour for domestic help as was customary, and there were a number of infuriated housewives who were obliged to see their own charwomen vanish towards the vicarage, or else to pay wages which they could ill afford.

The vicarage was now more sparsely furnished with the few pieces of furniture salvaged from the disastrous Thrush Green fire and some modest articles newly acquired. The Bulls' magnificent Persian rugs had given way to some well worn runners in the hall. The priceless Chinese vase which had held exotic blooms all the year round on the

Jacobean hall chest, was now replaced by a sturdy earthen-ware pitcher holding garden flowers or the silvery moons of locally grown honesty, throughout the winter months.

Nevertheless, Dimity, with help on only two mornings, kept the lovely old house shining, and nothing could detract from the beautifully proportioned rooms with their great windows looking out upon one of the most superb settings in Lulling.

No one expected the Henstocks to attempt the same standard of living as their predecessor. They were less concerned than he with material trappings, and even if they had wanted to keep the house as expensively furnished, their modest income would not allow it.

But everyone agreed, even those who lamented Anthony Bull's departed glory in the church itself, that the welcome to be found now at Lulling Vicarage was warmer than ever. It was good, they told each other, to have such a fine pair living at Lulling.

Some quarter of a mile away in the High Street of Lulling the three Miss Lovelocks were surveying the snow from their front bedroom windows.

The old ladies were still in their night attire. The collars of their warm flannel nightgowns were buttoned modestly around thin scrawny necks. Miss Bertha and Miss Ada were wrapped in ancient camel-coloured Jaeger dressing gowns, and Miss Violet in a voluminous light plaid garment purchased some twenty years earlier on a visit to the Shetland Isles. Bony feet were encased in sheepskin slippers, but even so the old ladies shivered as they surveyed the snowy High Street.

'So unexpected,' said Miss Bertha.

'Not a *word* about it on the weather forecast,' said Miss Ada severely.

'But it's very pretty,' said Miss Violet. 'Just see how lovely it looks caught in the railings!'

They gazed across at the railings outside the Methodist

chapel. There certainly was something attractive about the white thick fur that blurred their usual starkness. In fact, the whole street was transformed in the early sunshine.

The roofs glistened like sugar icing. Doorsteps were hidden under gentle billows, and dark ribbons showed where traffic had trundled by in the road itself, highlighting the vivid whiteness of the rest. The pollarded lime trees along the pavement wore thick caps of snow, and the scarlet pillar box, outside The Fuchsia Bush café next door, was similarly topped.

A small black and white terrier rushed out from a house nearby, barking ecstatically and stirring up a flurry of snow dust in its excitement. Now and again it stopped, head up, pink tongue pulsing, legs quivering and stiff, before dashing off again in another frenzy of delight in this strange element.

'Well,' said Miss Bertha, 'this won't do. We must get dressed and see what's to be done.'

'I think *porridge* for breakfast would be a good idea,' said Miss Violet. 'We don't need much milk if I make it fairly runny.'

'And I really prefer a little salt on mine,' said Miss Bertha. 'So much *cheaper* than sugar.'

'And whoever is down first,' called Miss Ada to her departing sisters, 'switch on the electric fire in the dining room. *One* bar, of course, but I think it's cold enough to indulge ourselves this morning.'

The Misses Lovelock were renowned for quite unnecessary parsimony.

A mile away to the north, the inhabitants of Thrush Green greeted the snow with much the same surprise. The young welcomed it with the same rapture as Charles Henstock's. The old looked upon it with some dismay.

Miss Watson and Miss Fogerty, headmistress and assistant at the village school, discussed this unexpected quirk in the weather as they tackled their boiled eggs.

'I hope Betty remembers to put down newspaper in the lobbies,' said Miss Watson. 'It saves such a lot of mess.'

'I'm sure she will,' responded little Miss Fogerty. 'I only hope the children don't try and make slides in the playground before we go across. So dangerous.'

Miss Watson sighed.

'It's mornings like this that makes me regret staying on here,' she confessed. 'To think we might have been happily settled in dear old Barton. There's probably no snow there at all!'

Miss Fogerty tried to rally her old friend.

'It was not to be, Dorothy dear. I'm sure of that. And after all, we've always been very snug in this school house.'

'Maybe, maybe,' agreed her headmistress, 'but I still wish we could have retired when we had planned to do so. It has been such a disappointment.'

Even Miss Fogerty, devout believer in divine intervention in human affairs, could not help agreeing.

The two old friends had hoped to retire together to a small house at Barton-on-Sea. Property, of the type they wanted, was expensive and scarce. A great many people, it seemed, wanted to live in such a pleasant area. They too wanted a small, easily managed house with only a little land to maintain.

The two ladies had spent several weeks during their holidays in looking for a future home. On more than one occasion they thought they had found it, only to come up against snags. Sometimes the surveys had disclosed faulty drains, crumbling foundations, unaccountable subsidence, dry rot, wet rot, or plain shoddy building. In other cases the owners had backed out at the last minute, unable to buy the property they had hoped to purchase, or suddenly deciding to take their own off the market.

In the meantime Agnes Fogerty's arthritis had become worse and the Thrush Green doctor, John Lovell, had recommended a course of treatment which would spread over some months. Added to this was pressure from the local education office, upon Dorothy Watson, to postpone her retirement.

What with one thing and another the two hard-pressed ladies agreed to stay on in their present circumstances, and great was the relief felt by all their old friends at Thrush Green.

On the whole they had been relieved to have this respite after the frustrations of house-hunting. They both enjoyed their teaching, and had the satisfaction of knowing that their efforts were appreciated. The genuine delight of the parents and friends of the school when they had told them of their decision to stay on, was of great comfort to them, and did much to mitigate the disappointment of failing to find a house.

But this morning, with the snow blanketing all, and with memories of past snowy winters at Thrush Green school, the two friends knew that they must put all those wistful might-have-beens behind them, and face the realities of snow-crazed children, wet floor-boards, clothes drying on the fire-guards and, worst of all, no possible hope of playtime being taken outdoors. The dog-eared comics, the well-worn jigsaw puzzles, the ludo and snakes and ladders boards must emerge from the cupboard which held the wet-playtime equipment, and all one could do was to pray for a rapid thaw.

Dorothy Watson folded her napkin briskly.

'May as well make a start, dear,' she said, rising from her chair. 'And if it's not too slushy at playtime, I propose that we let the children make a snowman.'

'But only those with wellingtons,' Miss Fogerty reminded her.

And with this proviso the two friends prepared to face the day.

Next door, in one of the finest houses on Thrush Green, Harold Shoosmith and his wife Isobel were also at breakfast.

Theirs was a more leisurely affair than that of the two schoolteachers, for Harold had been a retired man for several years, and relished the fact that he could dally over his breakfast coffee.

Isobel had first met him on one of her visits to Thrush Green. She had been at college with little Agnes Fogerty and they had kept up their friendship over the years. It was a great joy to both to find themselves neighbours in middle age.

The shouts of children took Harold to the window, still cradling his coffee cup.

'My word,' he exclaimed, 'they've made the most splendid slide the whole width of the playground!'

'Agnes and Dorothy won't approve,' commented his wife.

'They wouldn't be such spoil sports as to ruin it, surely,' said Harold. 'I wouldn't mind a go on it myself. They're keeping the pot boiling marvellously!'

Isobel joined him at the window which overlooked the playground. Sure enough, the sight was exhilarating. Some dozen or more children, scarves flying, hair on end, were chasing each other in a long line down the twenty-foot slide. Their breath steamed in the frosty air, their faces glowed like winter suns, and the din was appalling.

Rows of smaller, or more timid, children lined the route adding their cheers to the general racket. There was no doubt about it. The slide was a huge success.

Harold, still smiling, looked across the green. The statue of Nathaniel Patten, a zealous missionary of the last century, much admired by Harold who had been instrumental in honouring the old gentleman on his hundredth anniversary, was plentifully daubed with snowy patches. The white cap on his head, and the snowy shawl across his shoulders were deposited naturally from above, but the spattered frock coat showed clearly the results of well-aimed snowballs.

Certainly, the teachers at Thrush Green school were

going to have unusually lively pupils on this winter morning, thought Isobel.

At that moment, Betty Bell appeared, pushing her bicycle
up the path with some difficulty. She had finished her
ministrations at the school next door, remembering to
carpet the lobby with newspapers as Agnes knew she
would. For good measure she had surrounded the fire
guard round the tortoise stove with more newspaper, to
catch stray drips from wet clothing and, her duties there
done, now approached the Shoosmiths' abode.

'Lord!' she puffed, blowing into the kitchen on a gale of
cold air. 'What some weather, eh? Your front path wants
doing, and that's a fact.'

'I'm just off to tackle it,' Harold assured her, putting
down his cup, and going in search of his largest shovel.

There were others already at work when Harold emerged
from his house. At The Two Pheasants, hard by the village
school, Mr Jones the landlord was busy shovelling the
snow away from the door.

His neighbour, Albert Piggott, watched him morosely,
leaning heavily the while upon an upturned broom.

'Time you cleared your own patch,' pointed out Mr
Jones, becoming annoyed at Albert's scrutiny.

'I shan't be doin' much,' growled Albert. 'Jest my bit
round the door. That lazy Cooke article can dig over to the
church. His arms is younger'n mine.'

'Strikes me, young Bob Cooke's doing the lot these
days,' replied the landlord, straightening his aching back
for a moment. 'Can't see you earn your wage, Albert.'

Albert forbore to answer, but shuffled a few paces
nearer his grubby front door, and thrust the broom lan-
guidly this way and that in front of him.

Mr Jones muttered something uncomplimentary under
his breath, seized his spade again, and set to with a will. It
was a sore trial having Albert Piggott as next door neighbour, and he was already regretting his action in getting

the miserable old sexton of St Andrew's to help with the beer crates in the evenings. Half the time he didn't turn up, and the other half he was too muzzy to do the job properly.

Ah well! His mother used to say: 'These little things are sent to try us.'

One thing was certain, Albert Piggott was the most unpopular man in Thrush Green.

Mr Jones scooped up the last shovelful, dumped it neatly on the pile at the corner, waved to Harold and went indoors, ready for opening time.

Across the green the distant sounds of other inhabitants at work carried clearly to Harold. Ella Bembridge was digging a way to her gate from her thatched cottage. She and Dimity Henstock had lived there for years until Charles had whisked Dimity across to the rectory and now to the lovely vicarage at Lulling. A cigarette was clamped to her lower lip, and its blue smoke mingled with the clouds of breath around her.

Somewhere nearer, in the grounds of the most splendid of all the Thrush Green houses, Harold could hear the cheerful cries of children. It was probably Paul Young's half-term holiday, and it sounded as though he had a companion with him. A good deal of spade-clanging was going on, and even more laughter. Clearing the Youngs' drive was going to take some time, Harold surmised, but it was certainly being enjoyed.

He straightened his aching back and looked with pleasure at the clear blue sky. It made a breathtakingly lovely backdrop to the snowy landscape and the grey-golden buildings around the open space. A good spot to live, Harold told himself, for the umpteenth time. He never grew tired of the place.

It was lovely in all the seasons, possibly at its best in autumn, when the avenue of horsechestnut trees glowed with tawny foliage, and drifts of golden leaves crackled underfoot and whispered as the wind played with them.

But nevertheless, this morning's view of Thrush Green took some beating. Even the rough patch of ground left by the cruel removal of Charles's rectory was smoothly beautiful, and the stark shapes of the tombstones in St Andrew's graveyard were softened by snowy drapery.

Three more yards, thought Harold, eyeing his progress, and he would go in for a well-earned cup of coffee.

2   The Rector Goes About His Duties

LATER THAT DAY, in the sunny afternoon, the newly appointed vicar of Lulling and the more familiar rector of Thrush Green, Lulling Woods and Nidden, set out for Thrush Green.

All these important persons, as Pooh-Bah might say, were rolled into the one chubby frame of Charles Henstock. He drove his shabby car very carefully along the High Street, waving, as he made his royal progress, to a number of his parishioners. Occasionally a passing car would hoot, or flash its lights, but Charles Henstock contented himself with a wave of the hand.

'You see,' he explained to Dimity sitting beside him, 'I'm never quite sure what flashing lights mean. There was an excellent letter on the subject in one of the newspapers some time ago.'

'There's Bertha Lovelock!' exclaimed Dimity. Charles waved dutifully, and continued his story.

'The writer said – he was also a man of the cloth, by the way – that he couldn't make out if the driver was telling him his lights were on, or warning him that there was a police trap or an accident or flooding or some other disaster –'

'A police trap isn't a disaster,' objected Dimity. 'Mind that pigeon!'

'Or whether,' continued her husband unperturbed, 'the driver was simply saying: "Good morning, vicar."'

'There's another pigeon,' said Dimity. 'Sometimes I think they're more foolhardy than pheasants about crossing the road.'

The rector changed gear to negotiate the short steep hill which led to Thrush Green. At the summit he pulled into the side of the road for Dimity to get out. She was going to see her old friend Ella Bembridge while Charles set about some sick visiting of his more northerly parishioners.

Dimity picked her way carefully across the snowy road and Charles watched her enter her old home, before driving on.

To his left St Andrew's loomed above its white church-yard. The door of The Two Pheasants was now closed, and Charles guessed that the landlord was having a well-earned snooze in his snug sitting room behind the bar. Smoke curled from most of the chimneys, and he could imagine the cheerful log fires of his friends. It would have been pleasant to call on Harold and Isobel, or Frank and Phyllida Hurst but he had duties to the sick, and his first call must be at the most beautiful house on Thrush Green, where the Youngs lived. Here he must make enquiries about Joan Young's father who lived with his wife in the converted stables. Charles feared that the old man was close to his end, and it would be best to find out first from his daughter if he was up to receiving visitors.

Charles sighed as he turned into the Youngs' gateway. As a staunch Christian he had no doubt of his old friend's future happiness in a life beyond this. But how he would be missed by those he left behind!

Meanwhile, Dimity sat by Ella's fireside and heard the latest news of Thrush Green. Robert Bassett's failing health was the saddest item, and already known to Dimity.

'And it looks as though Percy Hodge's new wife isn't at all happy,' said Ella, puffing at one of her untidy cigarettes which she rolled herself in a slap-happy manner.

'Tell me more,' urged Dimity. It was extremely agreeable to hear all the latest gossip. She considered Charles a perfect husband, but he refused to impart those little snippets of information about his parishioners which his wife would have welcomed. Ella had always been one of the first to hear about her neighbours' affairs, and always enjoyed passing on her knowledge. Dimity realized how much she missed her confidences.

'Percy's fault, I gather. He will keep harking back to his first wife's virtues – particularly her cooking.'

'How very unfair!' cried Dimity. 'I mean, we all know that Gertie was a wonderful cook, but it's so stupid of Percy to expect Doris to be the same.'

'So John Lovell told him, I gather, when Percy called at the surgery to have his ears syringed. "Comparisons are odious", he quoted to him, but I don't suppose Percy took it in. If he's not careful, his Doris will up and leave him, like Albert Piggott's Nelly did.'

'Oh, I do hope not,' said Dimity earnestly.

'Thank God I'm a spinster,' replied Ella. 'I really couldn't be doing with considering a man's feelings day in and day out. Let alone cooking and cleaning for him! As it is, I can make a real meal of a boiled egg and a slice of toast, and am spared spending the best part of the morning scraping vegetables and mucking about with meat.'

'Well, I quite enjoy cooking,' answered Dimity, 'as you know, and it's really a pleasure to cook for Charles, he's so appreciative.'

'As well he might be,' agreed Ella, 'after the terrible stuff that Scots housekeeper of his dished up. I shall never forget seeing an appalling dish of grey tripe with grey dried peas round it, and all swimming in thin grey gravy. She was carrying it in for poor Charles's lunch. My heart bled for him.'

'She married, you know, when she left Charles.'

'I pity her husband,' said Ella. 'Now he *would* have something to complain about, and that's a fact. By the way, I picked up a cookery book at our last jumble sale.'

'Anything useful in it?'

'Not much that we haven't tried, and a very irritating way of explaining things – far too devil-may-care for my taste. You know the sort of thing: "Toss in a handful of chopped walnuts", "Add a dash of tabasco, Worcester sauce, curry or any other personal favourite". I like to know how much of everything. All this airy-fairy stuff annoys me.'

'Quite,' agreed Dimity. 'After all, a handful would vary considerably from person to person, and what's a dash anyway? A teaspoonful or three drops?'

'What's more it gives all the recipes in those vile grammes – and I'm horrified to see that those nice tubs of margarine which one could count on being half a Christian pound are now marked as two hundred and fifty grammes.'

'I expect that's why the cookery book had been sent to the jumble sale,' said Dimity sagaciously. 'Frankly, I just use my old recipes, all full of lovely ozes.'

'We're too old a pair of dogs to learn new tricks,' agreed Ella. 'I must say I'm proud to use our old blue and white jug marked British Imperial Pint. I feel I know where I am.'

At that moment there was a knock on the door, and before Ella could answer it, a voice called:

'Can I come in? I'm taking off my wellingtons.'

'Connie, with the goats' milk,' exclaimed Ella, making her way into the hall. 'Come in by the fire. I didn't expect you to plough up here through this snow.'

Connie entered and greeted Dimity with a kiss.

'Heavens, it's good to see a fire,' she cried, holding out her hands to the blaze. 'I thought I'd come up in good time. It might snow again according to the weather man.'

'Don't suppose he knows any more than we do,' said Ella flatly, 'for all those satellite pictures they dote on, and the rest of the gimmicks. I reckon Albert Piggott does rather better as a weather prophet. His chest and joints are wonderful predictors of climatic conditions.'

'How's Dotty?' enquired Dimity.

'Very well, I'm glad to say. As long as she doesn't do anything silly such as wandering out in the snow to see if Dulcie's all right, and that kind of thing, she's in good trim. But you know dear old Aunt Dot – she likes her own way and I have to watch her.'

'Well, you do it very well, Connie,' said Ella. 'She's lucky to have you there.'

Ella went on to tell Connie about the latest news at Thrush Green, and how the inhabitants were coping with their particular snow problems. Dimity sat back in the old familiar armchair and studied Dotty Harmer's niece.

No one, she decided, could call Connie handsome, but she had fine eyes and her thick auburn hair showed very little grey. She must be in her forties now, strongly built, and with a determined look about her square chin. She needed strength of character to cope with her indomitable aunt, thought Dimity. It said much for her sweet disposition

that she was obviously devoted to the trying old lady, and
had given up her own home to come to her aid. It was to
be hoped that Dotty appreciated Connie's attentions, but
really poor Dotty grew more vague and eccentric as the
years passed and Dimity sometimes wondered if her old
friend really grasped what was happening around her.

'And how has your house stood up to the snow?' she
asked.

'Oh, we're pretty snug,' answered Connie. 'There's nothing like a good thatched roof and thick walls for insulation.
Thank goodness Aunt Dotty always kept the outside in
good repair. The interior, of course, was another matter,
but I'm gradually getting it straight. You'll be glad to
know I've had a marvellous spring-clean of the pantry.'

'And about time too,' said Ella forthrightly. 'Why Dotty
didn't succumb to food poisoning years ago beats me.
Those witches' brews of home-made wine and preserves
made from dubious plants were positively grisly. Dim and
I knew better than to eat any of Dotty's concoctions, but
the doctors around here know jolly well that there is a
local indigestion known as "Dotty's Collywobbles" which
the unwary suffer from if they sample your aunt's potions.'

Connie laughed, and Dimity thought how attractive she
was when animated. It made one realize how young she
was after all.

'The first things to go were half a dozen fearful jars of
fungi swimming in cloudy liquid,' she told them. 'Heaven
alone knows what they were, but I took them down into
Lulling Woods and tipped the contents into a deep hole,
when Aunt Dot was having a nap. I didn't dare bury the
stuff in the garden in case the hens scratched it up.'

'Yes, she gave me a jar,' said Ella. 'It went straight in
the dustbin, but I believe she sent several pots to Lulling
Church Bazaar. Luckily Mrs Bull knew about them, and no
doubt disposed of them safely.'

'One certainly gets some extraordinary things sent in for
the church fund raisers,' commented Dimity. 'Lady Mary

sent six pairs of pink corsets, all rather grubby too which made it worse, and so *vast*, of course, that it was difficult to know what to do with them.'

Connie rose to go, and Ella accompanied her to the door.

'Talking of unwanted gifts,' said Ella, when she returned, 'would that spoilt cat of yours eat hare?'

'There's nothing Tabitha likes more,' Dimity replied. 'She used to get some when we lived here, but somehow nobody leaves a nice hare hanging on the door knob at Lulling vicarage as they did at Thrush Green.'

'Percy Hodge left it in even better shape,' said Ella, 'all skinned and jointed in a plastic bag. Enough for a large family, so come and take your pick, Dim.'

'I'm sorry Percy's not happy,' said Dimity, as Ella wrapped a generous portion of the farmer's largesse for her friend.

'Maybe they'll shake down together. Will you and Charles eat any of this?'

'Indeed we will! It will be a great treat.'

'Good. I should never get through a third of all this. Now shall we have a cup of tea, or wait for Charles?'

'Charles will have had at least six cups by now,' Dimity assured her old friend. 'So let's put on the kettle.'

At that moment Charles was sitting beside his old friend Robert Bassett, having refused all refreshment pressed upon him by hospitable Milly Bassett.

Robert was in his dressing gown sitting near the window with a rug over his knees. Outside, a bird table had been fixed to the window sill, and blue tits and greenfinches squabbled over a net of peanut kernels suspended there, while a bright-eyed robin, ignoring the commotion, pecked busily at some kitchen scraps.

'They must be grateful for all that sustenance,' observed Charles.

'Not half as grateful as I am to them,' responded Robert.

'They are a constant joy. I find I can't read for long, and the television tires my eyes after a time, but I can watch these little beauties for hours on end. Tell me, Charles, how are you enjoying the new living?'

The rector recognized this query as a deliberate attempt to divert attention from his own problems, and told the invalid how much he and Dimity enjoyed their new house and explained their modest plans for the garden.

Milly excused herself and hurried back to the kitchen where she was cooking a splendid Dundee cake. Charles guessed rightly that she was relieved to see her husband happily engaged in conversation, thus relieving her for a short while from her anxious surveillance.

For there was no doubt about it, as Charles knew well as he rambled on gently about his own affairs, that Robert had little time left to him. He had lost a great deal of weight. His complexion had the waxen pallor of the desperately ill, and the bones of his thin fingers showed clearly as he plucked feebly at the rug. But his smile was as sweet as ever, and he listened as courteously as he had always done to Charles's remarks.

At last Charles rose, looking at his watch.

'I must be off, Robert, I've one or two other friends to visit, and it gets dark so confoundedly early still. I'll call in again if I may.'

'Before you go, I've something for you,' said Robert, pointing to a large envelope on his desk.

Charles brought it to him, and his old friend withdrew a beautiful leather-bound book of poems which he gave to the rector.

'James Elroy Flecker,' said Robert. 'A poet I've always loved, and as fond of this country as you and I have been. I should like you to have it.'

Charles was deeply moved.

'I shall always treasure it,' he assured the sick man. 'As a boy I learnt "The Old Ships" at school, and can still quote from it. I share your admiration, Robert, and you couldn't have given me anything more precious.'

He held the thin hand in his for a moment. It felt as frail as a bird's frame.

'I must see Milly before I go,' he said, turning towards the door. 'I'll come again, Robert.'

'You must come soon then,' called Robert after him, as the rector made his way towards the kitchen, blinking tears away before facing brave Milly.

It was past six o'clock before the rector turned his car towards Ella's cottage where Dimity awaited him.

He was, as she had surmised, awash with many cups of tea and had vague indigestion. Beside him lay the beautiful parting present from Robert in company with a large bag full of cooking apples which had been pressed upon him at his final visit in Nidden.

In some ways it had been a sad afternoon, thought the good rector, slowing down to let a pheasant stalk majestically across the lane, and yet there had been beauty too. He remembered Robert's loving look as he had presented him with the book, and the kindly welcome he had received at all the homes he had visited.

He gradually approached Thrush Green. The sun had set, and dusk was falling over the wintry scene.

'"Light thickens,"' said the rector aloud, '"and the crow Makes wing to the rooky wood."'

He savoured the sonority of the phrase. What a comfort it was to have a retentive memory! He corrected himself quickly. His memory, he reminded himself, was certainly not retentive when it came to practical matters, as Dimity frequently told him. Where on earth, for instance, had he left the key to the vestry? And what had he done with that slip for the cleaners which Dimity had given him only that morning?

Nevertheless, he comforted himself, it was a never-failing joy to find a happy phrase surfacing to add to the pleasures of daily life.

He looked approvingly at the white landscape against a

darkening sky. In the distance he caught a glimpse of Lulling Woods, black against a steely-grey background.

'Rooky, indeed!' said the rector aloud. Who but Shakespeare could have thought of a crow making wing to a rooky wood, thus adding blackness to blackness?

He drew up outside Ella's cottage. The light glowed from her windows, shining a welcome, but the good rector sat still for a moment or two remembering his afternoon.

He would visit Robert again within the next day or two. Meanwhile he proposed to read some of the poems, which they both loved, before he slept that night. He wanted his old friend to know how much this last gift had meant to him.

But now he had other duties. He emerged into the chilly owl-light, and hurried up the path to collect his wife.

3 Unknown at The Fuchsia Bush

T HE SNOW LASTED for a full week. For the first
three days the pristine purity which had so delighted
Charles Henstock continued to enchant most of the
inhabitants of Lulling and Thrush Green. The trees glittered in the frosty sunshine. Walls and hedges, capped in
white, reflected the radiance of the clear sky. Underfoot the
snow crunched to hard ice, and skaters were out in force
on the shallow reaches of the River Pleshey and local ponds.

But overnight the weather changed, and by the fourth
day a slow thaw had begun.

Snow fell from the outstretched branches of the vicarage
cedar tree with soft flumps and clouds of snow dust. It
slithered from walls and hedges. It dropped dramatically
from the roofs of the houses and shops in Lulling High
Street, much to the disgust and discomfiture of those
walking below about their proper occasions. Two respectable ladies, about to enter The Fuchsia Bush in search of
morning coffee, were engulfed in a miniature avalanche
which descended from the guttering, and were obliged to
spend their coffee break hatless and coatless as these garments were dried on the café's radiators.

At Thrush Green, Mr Jones's ancient spaniel, dozing
peacefully in its kennel, was completely covered and had to
be rescued by its alarmed owners from a four-foot fall of
snow off an outhouse roof.

In the playground next door little rivulets ran from under the slush, much to the children's pleasure and their teachers' annoyance. Shoes and socks were rapidly soaked, and hardened delinquents of six and seven years of age had to be taken to task for throwing the last of the snowballs at their smaller brethren.

Nathaniel Patten's mantle slipped from his shoulders. The chestnut trees shed their loads, and the cars threw up a shower of watery slush as they passed.

It was, as the landlord of The Two Pheasants remarked to his neighbour, 'a dam' uncomfortable spell of weather.'

'Might freeze,' Albert replied morosely, 'and then we'll all break our legs, I shouldn't wonder.'

'That's right!' commented Mr Jones. 'Cheer us all up!'

And he bustled back into the snugness of the bar.

On that same morning, Charles Henstock planned to visit Robert Bassett but decided that he would telephone Joan Young first to see if a visit would be welcome to the invalid. He had seemed so frail a few days before, and the rector could not help wondering if the doctor might have vetoed any such excitements as visitors.

The bell seemed to ring for an unconscionably long time, and the good rector was filled with the usual doubts of one in his situation. Should he put down the receiver? No doubt, if he did so, then Joan Young would arrive, panting from the garden, just in time to find the instrument silent. On the other hand, the poor girl might be prostrate with a splitting headache, and lying abed praying for the noise to stop, with her hands over her ears. Really, thought Charles, even the simplest operation is fraught with worry, and one could quite understand how nervous people succumbed to all sorts of dreadful mental strain.

He was about to return the telephone to its cradle when Joan spoke.

'My dear,' said the rector, 'I trust I haven't brought you from the garden?'

'No indeed,' she replied. She sounded breathless nevertheless. 'In fact I was about to ring you. About Father.'

A sudden chill gripped Charles.

'How is he?'

'I'm sorry to tell you, Charles, but he has gone. Mother found him only ten minutes ago.'

The rector murmured his sympathy.

'He spoke to my mother about six o'clock when she gave him some tea, and then said he would go off to sleep again.'

The voice, so well-controlled, suddenly broke.

'I'm going to ring off,' said Charles, gently taking command. 'You have enough to do now, but let me help in any way. Who is with you?'

'Ben and Molly are coping,' replied Joan, 'and have gone to fetch John.'

'I'll call again later,' said the rector, adding his sympathy again.

He found that his knees were uncommonly shaky as he made his way to his study. Poor Milly and the family! How Robert would be missed! And how regrettable that he himself had not called to see his old friend yesterday! But there it was. The old sad cry of 'Too late, too late!' with which most mourners scourge themselves, rose to the rector's mind with bitter poignancy.

But such remorse was fruitless. His duty now was to the living who had so much to face at a time when their distress was at its most acute. Thank goodness, thought Charles, that the young Curdles lived in the same house! Both Molly and Ben would be of practical help and inestimable comfort to the Youngs, and to Joan's sister Ruth who was married to Doctor Lovell, and lived nearby.

There was a great deal to be said for living in a close community, mused the good rector. Irritating though it was at times to find that one had little or no privacy, yet when death or disaster struck how comforting to have the support of friends and relations close at hand.

Sighing, Charles went off to break the news to Dimity.

Within a few hours, the news of Robert Bassett's death was general knowledge. Although he had been in ill health for several years, as always the news of his going came as a shock to Thrush Green and Lulling.

His contemporaries remembered him well as a young man at Thrush Green. Joan and Edward Young's fine house had originally been Robert's, but he preferred to live in Ealing where he carried on his furniture business, only visiting his daughters and the lovely Cotswold house two or three times a year.

When at last he had been obliged to retire he and his wife Milly had no desire to turn out the Youngs, nor in fact did they want to cope with such a large establishment. It was then that Edward, a sound architect, had so successfully converted the old coach house in the garden into an attractive bungalow, and where Milly and Robert had spent the last few years very happily.

Winnie Bailey was one of the first to hear. She was the widow of Donald Bailey who had been the senior partner of the Thrush Green practice when young John Lovell had come to join him, had settled in successfully and later found Ruth Bassett for a wife.

It was John who broke the news to Winnie as he left the surgery to hurry across the green to his father-in-law. Winnie watched his departure with a heavy heart. One of the saddest things about growing old was the inevitable loss of contemporaries. It was some comfort to know that Robert's widow was surrounded by her family at this sombre time, but nothing, as Winnie herself knew, could mitigate the loneliness of the partner left behind.

She went into the kitchen to tell Jenny, her maid and friend who lived in the same house. Jenny was busy breaking a handsome cauliflower into its separate florets at the sink when she was told the news.

To Winnie's alarm, her serene Jenny, who always seemed

to face a crisis with exemplary placidity, burst into tears, and sat down heavily on the kitchen chair.

'But Jenny,' said her mistress, much bewildered, 'we all knew the poor man had very little time left. Why are you so upset?'

Jenny raised a wet and woebegone face.

'He was kind to me once. It was when I first came to Lulling as a little girl. I was sent to the big house with a message, and I was a bit scared. Mr Bassett answered the door, and must have seen I was frightened, and he took me round the garden and asked me all about where I was living and that.'

She gave a violent hiccup, and Winnie patted her back as though she were curing a baby of the wind.

'And he picked me a bunch of flowers – pinks and roses, I remember – to take back to the old people, and he gave me a shilling for myself. I never was so rich in my life. And best of all, you see, I had something to give my pa and ma which I'd never had before. They thought the world of those flowers, and I thought the world of Mr Bassett, and always did.'

A mighty sniff terminated the tale, but Winnie could see that the telling of it had eased poor Jenny's grief and that now she would recover her habitual calm.

'That's a very fine memory to have of a very fine man,' she said gently. 'Typical of dear Robert.'

Jenny rose to her feet, and mopped her face vigorously.

'Well, now I must get back to the cooking. Poor old gentleman, but there – it's time the vegetables were put on.'

And Winnie, returning to her own duties, could not help being reminded of one of the entries in James Woodforde's Diary which she had been reading.

'Found the old gentleman almost at his last gasp. Totally senseless with rattlings in his throat. Dinner today boiled beef and Rabbit rosted.'

Life is just such a jumble of tragedy and everyday

chores. Robert himself would have appreciated warmly the confrontation of death and the preparation of Jenny's cauliflower, in the same hour.

The funeral was at St Andrew's church a week later. It was a still day, mild and grey, with only a few tattered shreds of snow under the hedges to remind the mourners of the bitter weather.

The rector took the service for his old friend and gave a short and simple address. The two hymns chosen by the family were Robert's favourites, 'Ye holy angels bright' and 'God be in my head'.

After the service, when the congregation had gone home and Robert rested alone beneath a canopy of bright flowers, Charles and Dimity went with Ella to her nearby cottage and had tea there. Dotty Harmer and her niece Connie had been persuaded to join them.

Naturally, most of those present were in a subdued mood, grateful for the comfort of a bright fire and a cup of tea among friends, on a sad occasion.

Dotty was the exception. She was at her most chirpy, chattering of her memories of Robert in his younger days, and scattering cake crumbs as she waved her claw-like hands about.

'He had a most dreadful old bicycle he kept here in the coach house. D'you remember, Connie? It had an acetylene lamp. So smelly. No, of course, dear, it was before your time. He ran into my father's flower bed with it once. Father was *most upset*.'

'Oh dear!' commented Dimity nervously. Old Mr Harmer had been a fierce martinet, dreaded by all, and such an encounter must have had dire consequences.

'Of course,' went on Dotty, 'Robert had such charming manners, and was so truly contrite, that Father let him off with only a slight kick on the shin. *Very* good of Father, we all thought.'

Charles caught Ella's eye and looked away hastily.

'I liked the hymns, didn't you?' continued Dotty, wiping her fingers on the hem of her skirt. 'He was always musical, and I'm so glad he didn't ask for "ER-bide with me". So lugubrious, don't you think? I mean, if someone is bound straight for heaven, as I'm sure dear Robert is, then why not have something cheerful to speed him on his way?'

'May I have another cup of tea, Ella?' asked Charles, looking a little pinker than usual.

'Personally,' said the irrepressible Dotty, 'I should like the Hallelujah Chorus, though it does take some time to get through, of course, and one would need a full choir. But it's so *rousing*, isn't it? Triumphant, and yet sacred. Do bear it in mind for me, Connie dear. Or failing that I rather like a pretty little song called "I Like Life", but perhaps if one were lying there dead, as presumably one would be if the doctors had examined one efficiently, then to ask for life might be a little presumptuous, in the circumstances. What do you think, Charles?'

The rector put his cup down.

'I think, Dotty, that you should sit back quietly and enjoy Ella's excellent tea. We've all had a sad afternoon, and need a little rest, I'm quite sure.'

'Well,' said Dotty, 'speaking for myself I feel quite perky, but no doubt there is something in what you say.'

And after Charles's gentle chiding she sat back in her chair and sipped her tea like an obedient child, much to the relief of her companions.

The still grey days of February continued. The sky remained overcast. The leafless trees stood with no stirring of branches. It seemed as if all Nature slept.

The roads were damp. The hedges were beaded with minute drops, and even the birds seemed silent.

In Lulling High Street the pavements gleamed wetly. The pollarded lime trees, bristling with leafless twigs, were streaked with lines of moisture. The air was heavy, and

Lulling folk looked across the water meadows of the nearby River Pleshey and longed for relief from this oppressive humidity.

''Tisn't natural,' said one waitress to another in The Fuchsia Bush. 'Not a bit like spring. And as for getting a polish on these tables, well, it's love's labour lost, I say.'

'Never mind, love,' responded her fellow worker, Gloria Williams, who was busy arranging iced buns in a glass cabinet and licking her fingers noisily the while. 'Be March in a day or two, coming in like a lion, no doubt, and we'll have all the old biddies coming in grumbling about their hair being messed up.'

Her companion, Rosa, flicked a duster idly over an improbable collection of plastic flowers with daffodils nuzzling red geraniums above some fiercely autumnal leaves, all set precariously in a tub which had once held margarine.

'I was thinking of giving the windows a clean,' she said, with a yawn. 'But there, old Mrs Peters isn't coming in today, and it don't hardly seem worth it.'

Mrs Peters was the present owner of The Fuchsia Bush, and was possessed of an energy which would galvanize any but such obdurate employees as those at the café into action. When she was present, even the lethargic waitresses were stirred into semi-activity. In her absence, they reverted to their usual apathy.

'I wouldn't trouble,' agreed her colleague. 'Not this weather. Get all smeary, wouldn't they? You take it easy, dear. We'll have the elevenses lot in any minute now, and we'll be fair rushed off our feet.'

The two sat down at a table at the back of the empty room, and Rosa began to tell Gloria about the disco she had attended the night before when the door bell gave its mighty ping, and in came an elderly man. Rosa sighed.

'Here we go, then. I'll take him, dear. You do the next.'

She allowed the stranger to settle at a table near the window where he had a good view of the High Street, and had time to buff her nails on her apron while he studied the menu.

Slowly she approached.

'What can I get you?'

'Some coffee, please. Oh, and one of those iced buns.'

'White or black?'

The stranger look temporarily nonplussed.

'Surely you will bring me a pot of coffee and one of hot milk?'

'It's usually just a cup.'

'Well, today will you please bring me a pot of each, as I have asked you.'

His eyes were very blue, Rosa noted, and flashed when he was cross. Proper old martinet, she reckoned. A general or admiral or something awkward like that, and used to having his own way, that was sure.

'It'll be extra,' she shrugged.

'I've no doubt I can stand the expense,' he said shortly. 'And I'm in a hurry, so look sharp.'

Rosa ambled into the kitchen at the rear.

'Got a right one in there,' she informed the kitchen staff. 'Wants a pot of coffee and one of hot milk. I ask you!'

She cast her eyes aloft as if seeking divine aid for such recalcitrance.

Old Mrs Jefferson, chief cook for many years at The Fuchsia Bush, and a staunch upholder of long-forgotten principles of service, gave one of her famous snorts.

'Then get what he's asked for. It ain't your place to query a customer's order. Do as you're told, and keep a civil tongue in your head.'

'You don't have to face the customers,' grumbled Rosa.

'I have in my time,' reminded Mrs Jefferson, 'and given satisfaction too, my girl, which is a lot more than anyone can say about you. Now, get your tray ready, and see if you can manage a smile on that ugly mug of yours. Enough to turn the milk sour looking like that.'

She whisked back and forth from stove to the central table, nimble as ever despite her impressive bulk.

Rosa took the tray without a word, but if looks could have killed, Mrs Jefferson would have been a substantial corpse on the kitchen floor.

Half an hour or so later, the stranger emerged from The Fuchsia Bush into the muggy air of Lulling High Street.

The shoppers were in action now, and the tall figure had to circumvent perambulators, dogs on leads, and worst of all, two ladies having a lengthy gossip with their baskets on wheels spread behind them across the width of the pavement.

'Excuse me!' said the man firmly, pushing aside one of the baskets with a well-polished brogue.

'Really!' exclaimed one of the ladies. 'What are people coming to? It's a pity if we can't stop to say a civil word to our friends!'

But she waited until the stranger was out of earshot, before making these protestations.

Her companion was gazing after the upright figure making his way up the slight incline towards the market place.

'I believe I've seen him before,' she mused. 'Years ago.'

'Well, I shouldn't bother to resume the acquaintance-ship,' replied her friend. 'A very thrusting sort of individual, I should think.'

They settled back into their former positions and continued their interrupted discussion.

Miss Violet Lovelock was in the market place comparing the price of leeks on each of the vegetable stalls.

It was really outrageous how expensive even the lowliest vegetables were these days, she thought. Perhaps three of Dawson's thick leeks would make enough soup for two meals for the three of them. Plenty of the leek water, of course, and some salt and pepper should eke things out.

She was just putting her parcel in her basket, and endeavouring to avert her eyes from page three of the newspaper in which the leeks were wrapped – what was the world coming to! – when she noticed the figure striding vigorously uphill across the road.

Miss Violet gazed with concentration. She knew that walk. Who was he? If only her sight were keener, but she feared that her sisters were quite right in urging her to get her spectacles changed. Now a lorry was in the way. Now he had stopped to look in Barlow's window, and had his back to her. If only she could place him! There was something familiar about that straight back. Now who could it be?

The figure moved on, and suddenly opened the door of the solicitors, Twitter and Venables. In a trice he had vanished into the murk of that establishment, leaving Miss Violet to ruminate on her way home.

Perhaps she had been mistaken. Perhaps it was a complete stranger going into dear Justin Venables' office on business. Her sight really was getting worse, and it made it quite easy to make mistakes when people were at a distance. She would think no more about it.

And yet – there was *something*! And that something had given her a thrill of pleasure, as though some long-forgotten happiness had been stirred into life again, on that quiet grey morning in the damp Lulling street.

4   Rumours At Thrush Green

MARCH ARRIVED, but there was nothing lion-like about its coming.

The same grey stillness enveloped Lulling and Thrush Green. The same listlessness enveloped the inhabitants. Everyone longed for the clouds to lift, for a great wind to rush gustily through the trees, for the streets to be blown dry and for spirits to feel exhilaration again.

At Lulling vicarage Charles was having a most uncomfortable interview with one of his keenest parishioners. Mrs Thurgood was the widow of a wealthy provision merchant who had supplied a great many first-class Cotswold grocers with such exotic articles as coffee beans, tea, spices, dried fruits and preserved fruits, jars of ginger, toothsome pâtés and a host of other elegant comestibles.

His fleet of dark blue vans, chastely inscribed in gold lettering, were a common sight in the district, and Mrs Thurgood, carrying on the tradition of her husband, was a generous donor to all the church finances, and boasted that she never missed a service.

Anthony Bull had been her idea of the perfect vicar. 'The sort of fellow,' she had been heard to say, 'that one can invite quite safely to the house, no matter who is staying.' She approved of his distinguished looks, his charm of manner and the content of his sermons. She liked the ritual, the robes, the genuflecting, the sonorous chanting, the plethora of descants and the use of the seven-fold Amen. He was, in her eyes, completely satisfactory, and she mourned his promotion to a Kensington living.

She was also making it quite clear that she found Charles Henstock much inferior in every way to his predecessor.

'I can't believe,' she was telling Charles, 'that dear Mr Bull didn't mention this business of new kneelers for the Lady Chapel.'

'He had a great deal to think of, you know,' said Charles, 'before his move. It probably slipped his memory.'

'I doubt it,' replied Mrs Thurgood. 'I spoke to him a few weeks before his departure pointing out the need for a complete new set. He said, I remember, that he would mention it to you, as obviously you would be in charge when the work was undertaken.'

And who could blame Anthony Bull for shelving the problem, thought the rector? But now, it seemed, the birds had come home to roost, and it had become his problem.

'Do we really need new kneelers?' began Charles. 'The present ones seem very attractive, and I fear that we must guard against undue expense.'

'*Of course* we need them! And I made it quite clear to Mr Bull from the outset, that I would be happy to pay for all the materials. It's just a case of getting the Mothers' Union, and the Ladies' Guild, and the Church Flower Ladies to take on the work – one kneeler apiece should be all that is needed – and to get your permission to go ahead.'

At the mention of all the potential kneeler-makers, many of whom Charles found profoundly intimidating, he found his mind turning to the hosts of Midian who prowled and prowled around.

'And, of course,' went on his formidable visitor, 'it would be best to have one person leading the way.'

Like a bull-dozer, thought Charles unhappily.

'To co-ordinate the whole scheme,' said Mrs Thurgood. 'For one thing we must think about Design and Colour.'

'But surely, each lady would choose her own pattern?'

'Good gracious, no! Naturally the main colour must be blue. Soft furnishings in Lady Chapels are traditionally blue. And one must have the kneelers of uniform size. And frankly, I think that they should all be of the same design. Luckily, my daughter Janet, who is exceptionally gifted and has studied Design, Tapestry Work and Embroidery at Art School, has drawn up a charming pattern on squared paper, ready for the project.'

Charles began to feel besieged. The preliminary skirmishes were over. Now the heavy guns were in action.

He looked out at the misty garden, the beaded grass and the cedar tree, darker than ever with moisture. That glimpse of placid unchanging nature gave him the strength to counter-attack.

'It's plain that you have given much thought to the matter,' said Charles kindly. 'And it is most generous of you to offer to face the expense. I shall talk to Dimity about it – she is always so practical – and have a word with my church-wardens. Perhaps I may ring you in a day or two?'

Even the redoubtable Mrs Thurgood realized that she had advanced as far as was possible on the present occasion. Now was the moment to halt and remuster her strength for future assaults.

'Very well,' she agreed, rising from the vicarage sofa. 'Everything is absolutely ready as soon as you give the word. I know,' she added meaningly, as she preceded the vicar of Lulling into the hall, 'that it was a matter very dear to Mr Bull's heart. How we miss him!'

This parting thrust was successfully parried by the genuine sweetness of Charles's smile.

'We do indeed, Mrs Thurgood,' he said. 'But Lulling's loss was Kensington's gain, and I hear he is exceptionally happy in his new parish.'

He watched Mrs Thurgood's ramrod-straight back departing down the drive, and sighed.

The Mothers' Union! The Ladies' Guild! The Church Flower Ladies!

Could he ever hope to gain a victory against such a monstrous regiment of women?

It was Ella Bembridge, Dotty's old friend, who first discovered the identity of the tall stranger in Lulling. Like so many ladies who live alone, Ella had the uncommon knack of assimilating local gossip and, what was even better, of remembering it. It was not that she actively ferreted out information as many of the Thrush Green and Lulling ladies were wont to do. Such obvious seekers after gossip were well-known in the community, and those who met them were on their guard and curbed their tongues.

But Ella was invariably engaged in one of her many crafts, clacking her handloom, knitting or crocheting at incredible speed, or simply rolling one of her deplorable cigarettes, and so appeared to the retailer of local news to be attending principally to the matter in hand. Consequently, much was divulged, and Ella's keen mind retained it.

'Did you know that the Venables have got a visitor?' she asked Charles and Dimity when she called in for the parish magazine one morning.

'Anyone we know?' asked Dimity.

'I shouldn't think so. He's been overseas most of his life, but he was born and brought up here, and went to the grammar school when Dotty's father was headmaster.'

'Poor boy!' exclaimed Dimity. Mr Harmer's idea of corporal punishment would have brought him before any present day court on a charge of battery and assault, if not grievous bodily harm, and the tales of elderly old boys, even though understandably exaggerated, were enough to curdle the blood.

'Kit Armitage. That's his name,' went on Ella, stuffing the parish magazine between a head of celery and her library book in the rather lop-sided basket of her own making. 'I expect Dotty will remember him, and the Love-locks, of course, but before our time here.'

'Is he staying long?'

'I don't think so. He's looking for a small place of his own now that he's retired. Justin's always dealt with the family's legal affairs, and they've kept in touch over the years, and I gather he's just having a week or so with them until he gets settled.'

'Of course, now that Justin has retired he must have plenty of spare time to entertain,' observed the rector. 'I sometimes wonder if he would consent to coming on the Parochial Church Council. He would be such an asset with his grasp of legal and financial affairs.'

'Try him,' advised Ella. 'Besides he might back you up on such knotty problems as the new kneelers.'

'And how on earth do you know about the new kneelers?' asked Charles, looking at Dimity in bewilderment.

'Not from your wife,' responded Ella robustly. 'I've never met such a model of discretion. But Frances Thurgood button-holed me in the butcher's this week, and hoped I would "use my good offices", as she put it, to persuade you to agree.'

'Really!' the rector expostulated.

'Don't worry,' continued Ella. 'I wouldn't support Frances Thurgood on any of her projects, on principle. Of all the bossy, scheming, devious bullies I have met, she takes the biscuit.'

'Ella, please!' protested Charles, holding up a plump hand. 'I don't like to hear you speak so ill of anyone.'

'You wouldn't,' agreed Ella. 'You're far too tolerant. And if you really want me to speak ill, I can do a lot better than that.'

'Not now,' broke in Dimity. 'Sit down, dear, and have a cigarette.'

Ella allowed herself to be persuaded, took a chair, and then produced the battered tobacco tin which was her private cigarette-making factory.

'Don't you give way to her, Charles,' she said, when she had at last got the cigarette going and was wreathed in blue smoke. 'Let her win this round and she'll have you licked for many to come. As for this dreadful plan of using Janet's ghastly design, well, nip it in the bud, is my advice. Have you ever seen any of that girl's work?'

'No,' said Charles and Dimity together.

'Well, you've been spared a very horrific experience. She had a show of her drawings and paintings in the Corn Exchange last autumn. Enough to put your teeth on edge, believe me. Half the time you wondered if they were the right way up, and the other half you were sorry if they were. And all with such pretentious titles! The Reckoning, Meditation, Aspirations, A Theme of Beauty, Transcendental Awakening – all that sort of twaddle. And nothing under eighty quid! As you might imagine, there were mighty few red sales stickers about.'

'She did go to Art College, I understand,' said Dimity timidly.

'I should take that as an excuse rather than a recommendation,' replied Ella. 'No, Charles. Just you watch it! Smite her hip and what-ever-it-is, before she does it to you. And if Justin Venables will come and support you, I should get all the help he can give you. Or perhaps this new chap, Christopher Armitage, will turn out to be a pillar of the Church if he settles here.'

'I certainly miss Harold Shoosmith by my side,' admitted Charles. 'He's still such a help at Thrush Green, but so far I don't seem to have found anyone quite so supporting at Lulling.'

'Keep hoping,' said Ella, stubbing out her untidy cigarette, and collecting her things. 'Must be off. I promised to sit in with Dotty this afternoon, as Connie's off to have her hair permed.'

On the doorstep, she paused and looked skyward.

'Smells different, Charles. Has the wind turned round?'

They both gazed towards St John's weather-vane.

'It has indeed,' cried the rector. 'Let's hope we get a change in this depressing weather. We need something to raise our spirits.'

'Cheer up, Charles,' said Ella, smiting him quite painfully on the shoulder. 'You'll win through whatever the weather. But beware of Frances Thurgood!'

She stumped off towards the High Street on her way to Thrush Green. Dear old Charles! She hoped he would stand firm about those dam' kneelers. And not for worlds would she ever let that saintly man know of the beastly, condescending, cruel remarks which that cat Frances had made about him in her hearing.

Within twenty-four hours the grey clouds had lifted, the welcome sun shone again, and the March wind scoured the streets of Lulling.

Dead leaves frisked about the gutters like kittens. Inn signs creaked, saplings swayed, and the housewives of Lulling and Thrush Green watched with relief the lines of flapping washing billowing in the gardens.

At Thrush Green school the lethargy of the last few weeks had made way for the usual boisterous high spirits which wind invariably engendered. Grateful though little Miss Fogerty and her headmistress were for the change in the weather, nevertheless it brought its problems.

The children were noisy and excited. Doors banged, papers flew from desks, windows burst open, and general disorder prevailed. At break the children rushed screaming around the playground, pushing and romping like so many crazy puppies, clothes flattened against bodies, and hair on end.

Miss Fogerty was quite used to such behaviour. On duty in the playground, a mug of tea in hand, she watched the chaos about her with a benevolent eye, but alert to any particular recklessness which might lead to injury. John Todd, for instance, temporary aeroplane though he was, had no need to zoom quite so menacingly round the unsuspecting infants nearby. Arms outstretched, a mad gleam in his eye, and a terrible puttering noise emerging from his mouth, he constituted a considerable danger to his fellows, and Agnes Fogerty went at once to chide him.

It was because of this, and her subsequent attention to other malefactors crazed with March euphoria, that she failed to notice the two men who were pacing round the empty plot left by the vanished Thrush Green rectory, where Charles and Dimity had been so happy.

It was her companion, Dorothy Watson, who noted their activities and mentioned it when school had finished for the day and the two friends were restoring themselves with a cup of tea and shortbread fingers in the school house.

Even in here the wind made itself felt, singing through the key hole and stirring the curtains. But compared with the upheaval at school, it was remarkably peaceful, and anyway very pleasant to see the branches tossing in the garden, and the grass silvering as the breeze combed it.

'They were surveyors, I imagine,' said Dorothy. 'They

had one of those great tape measures in a leather case. I
think one works for the council. It's strange we haven't
heard anything.'

'We will,' Agnes promised her. 'You know Thrush
Green. The news gets round in no time. And if you
managed to see them, Dorothy, dear, I'm quite sure plenty
of other people did too. More shortbread?'

Miss Fogerty was quite right. Albert Piggott and his
neighbour Mr Jones, landlord of The Two Pheasants, had
also noticed the two men at work.

'Council chaps,' said Mr Jones. 'I did hear from Perce
Hodge that the council had bought the site.'

'What for?' asked Albert, toying with his half-pint of
bitter. 'And how does Perce know? 'E never goes nowhere
to find out. That missus of his keeps him knuckled down,
I hear.'

'You wants to watch your tongue about Percy's Doris,'
warned the landlord. 'It don't do to come between husband
and wife, and their private life's their own, I reckon.'

'What's come over you, turning so righteous?' asked
Albert. 'You was the first to blab about my Nelly when
she left me for that dratted oilman. One thing, he'll have
learnt his mistake by now, I don't doubt. And nothing's
private in Thrush Green, as you knows, and I do too. So
come on, tell us what Perce said about the council.'

Mr Jones polished a tumbler carefully, huffed inside it,
and polished it again before replying.

'Going to build old people's homes, so he said. Heard it
from his cousin who cleans the council offices.'

Albert digested this news with a mouthful of beer to
settle it.

'Ah! I wonder! By rights it should have another rectory
on it. It's church land, ain't it?'

'Not now, boy. The church sold it to the council, and
it's my bet they're looking over plans for these homes and
going to choose the cheapest. I bet Mr Young's put in a

plan. He fair hated that old place, and he always said he'd like to see something worth looking at on the site.'

'Bet that'll be a fine old eye-sore, if his own new offices are anything to go by. I'd a done better myself. No roof hardly, and the windows hanging off of the guttering, and brick as black as your hat. Makes a proper mess of Lulling High Street, I reckons,' said Albert sourly.

At that moment young Ben Curdle, his son-in-law, came in with a basket full of empty bottles.

'Morning, Dad,' he nodded. 'What you having?'

Albert brightened, and pushed his empty glass forward.

'Been talking about these new homes the council's going to build over yonder,' he said. 'I was just wondering who's going to live in 'em.'

'Well, you might be one,' said Ben.

Albert bridled.

'What would I need with a council place?' he asked indignantly. 'I got me own nice little cottage, paid for by the church. I'm not all that old anyway!'

'You will be soon,' replied Ben, with maddening calm. 'And it won't be long before young Cooke is doing all the church caretaking – he does most of it now as far as I can see. Then he'll want a place. Yours would suit him fine one day.'

Albert grew red with wrath, and began to bluster.

'See here, Ben, I still pulls my weight. Why, only yesterday I had all the mats up and swilled over the aisle. Took me best part of two hours, that did.'

'That's what I mean,' said Ben. 'It should only take half an hour at the most. You're gettin' past it, Dad, and you'll have to face it. If you could get one of these new homes, you'd be quids in. I bet there'd be a warden to look after you, and that'd save my Molly working her fingers to the bone for you.'

He picked up his empty basket, nodded pleasantly to the landlord and departed.

'Well I'm blowed!' puffed Albert in disgust. 'That's a

fine way of goin' on, ain't it? Telling me I'm too old to work, and practically handin' over my house to that young lay-about Cooke. Me livin' in an old people's home indeed! I'd watch it.'

Mr Jones let him rumble on crossly. He wiped the counter with a red-checked cloth and then leant across it conspiratorially.

'See here, Albert. You're looking ahead a bit. No one's said anything about you losing your house, and while you're still working it remains yours.'

Albert looked slightly mollified.

'And what's more,' went on his companion, draping the damp cloth over the beer handles to dry, 'no one knows for sure if old people's homes are going up there. Someone once said it might be a clinic or some such.'

'Or a brewery?' queried Albert. 'Now that would be a real good idea, wouldn't it?'

He swilled down the remainder of his glass and hobbled quite briskly to the door.

5 A Visit To Tom Hardy

ONE BLUE AND WHITE day towards the end of March, the rector made his way towards a remote cottage near the River Pleshey.

He walked by the path bordering the river, holding on his hat every now and again as the boisterous wind tried to tear it from his head.

The gentle murmuring of the water was lost in the noise of the wind around him. The pollarded willows along the banks were bristling with young twigs, and the golden-green leaves were beginning to unfurl.

Here and there an ancient willow, spared the woodcutter's attention, trailed branches in the river. As the wind whipped them the long twigs flailed the water creating little whirlpools and eddies.

A moorhen fled squawking as the rector passed by, its feet making a sequinned track on the surface of the stream. A water vole crossed nearby leaving an arrow-shaped wake as it forged towards the safety of the bank.

The rector had an observant eye for such details. They added to the joy of his walk which he had undertaken for just such refreshment. He had felt the need for a little solitude, for time to relish the lovely natural scenes about him, free from the intrusion of fellow humans.

He noted the crinkled bark of the willow trunks, the criss-cross pattern softened by grey-green lichen. He smelt the pungency of water-mint growing in the muddy shallows at the brink of the Pleshey. He heard the plop of small animals making for watery cover as he approached, and he saw the great galleons of white clouds sailing superbly across the blue sky above the water meadows, and felt the wind on his face.

He revelled in his senses which brought to him such richness, and thanked God that he still had health and strength to enjoy all five. This morning walk acted as balm to Charles's spirits, for despite his serene appearance and his gentle courtesy to everyone, he was a secret worrier, and at the moment there was plenty to perplex him.

He had only been at Lulling for a few months and already he knew that he fell short in many ways of the expectations of his new parishioners. It grieved him.

It grieved him, not because he was a vain man eager for the approbation of his fellows, but because he seemed to be causing anxiety to others. Mrs Thurgood's obvious disdain was comparatively easy to bear. Charles was perceptive enough to realize that her adoration of Anthony Bull made her consider any successor inadequate. But she was not alone in her criticism. It was this that perturbed him.

He had known from the start that to follow someone as magnetically outstanding as Anthony Bull would not be easy. He had been a man who engendered strong feelings, particularly in women. Charles recognized that there would be robust loyalty for his predecessor, and he considered it a laudable thing among his flock. What was hard to bear was the simple fact that anyone who succeeded Anthony was bound to be different, and that that particular fact was being ignored by some of his followers.

He had heard comments on his inadequacy, some obviously intended to wound. Several devout ladies had reproached him delicately about the simplicity of his services compared with the more extravagant ritual of Anthony's reign. He did his best to explain his beliefs. Comparisons might be odious, but he had to face them. For all the pinpricks, the petty humiliations, the unnecessary injustices done to him, yet Charles never wavered in his own admiration of Anthony Bull nor in the forbearance with which he faced his critics.

His chief unhappiness was caused by the fact that at least three families had now started to support a neighbouring vicar. This he found extremely upsetting. Only half an hour earlier, outside The Fuchsia Bush on his way to the river, he had run into one of his deserters, Albert Beverley.

'I was hoping to see you,' the rector had said cheerfully. 'We haven't seen much of each other lately.'

Albert Beverley looked about him unhappily.

'Well, you know how it is. The weeks slip by, don't they?'

'Time certainly flies,' agreed the rector. 'Perhaps I shall see you and the family –?'

'Ah!' said Albert hastily, 'must get on. I've promised to meet the wife in here. Late now, I'm afraid. Nice to have seen you.'

And he bolted into the haven of The Fuchsia Bush where, it was quite apparent, no wife was waiting.

It was incidents like this which were so distressing. 'The slings and arrows of outrageous fortune' he could bear for himself, but it was the Church which mattered.

Charles suddenly stood stock still and gazed across the river.

'That's the real trouble,' he said aloud, much to the surprise of a thrush briskly tapping out a snail from its shell on a handy flint. 'It's the Church that matters! I am failing the Church!'

He sighed deeply, clutched his hat, and continued on his errand.

The thrush gobbled down its succulent breakfast, and also went about its daily business.

On that same March morning Justin Venables sat in his usual seat in front of the well-worn desk at Twitter and Venables.

Although he had had his seventieth birthday, Justin was still known in Lulling as 'Young Mr Venables' to distinguish him from his illustrious father, Harvey Venables, who had founded the firm with Basil Twitter when both young men had returned from World War One.

The partnership had flourished, so much so that a third partner, called Adrian Treadgold, had been appointed. It was soon apparent that this latest addition was not of the same solid qualities as Basil Twitter and Harvey Venables, and when he blotted his copybook by running away with the wife of a well-to-do landowner, who was also a much respected client of the firm, then Adrian Treadgold's name was removed from the brass plate, and from all the office stationery.

Young Justin had served with his father until the latter's death. When he attained the age of seventy he made it clear that he was retiring. The whole of Lulling regretted his departure, and the office itself begged him to keep in touch. He was persuaded to keep on a few very old and valued clients, and to this end he was available at the office on Tuesday of each week.

'And don't expect me to do more,' he had told his staff severely. 'You boys are now in your forties and fifties and quite old enough to know your job. I want time for my fishing.'

On this particular Tuesday morning he sat contemplating a cast-iron ash tray bearing the words 'Long Live Victoria 1837–1897' and a colossal inkstand bearing a silver disc which told the world at large that it had been presented to Harvey Venables on the occasion of his silver wedding.

Justin was so used to these historic pieces that he barely noticed them. What he was more interested in was the wall clock which said ten minutes to eleven. His client was already five minutes late, and Justin valued punctuality.

Among the few favoured clients of advanced age whom Justin still attended was Dotty Harmer. Some years earlier he had defended her successfully on a charge of careless driving. He was fond of his eccentric old friend, and glad that he had helped to prove her innocence on that occasion. Nevertheless, wild horses would never have dragged him into any vehicle driven by Dotty. He was relieved when he had heard that she was now without a car, and that her niece Connie acted as chauffeur whenever she was needed.

It was Connie that he awaited now. When she arrived, he would ask Muriel in the outer office, to bring them coffee. He was glad that he had allowed himself to be persuaded to spend this one day a week in his old chair. He did not mind admitting that he missed the office routine, and the company of his staff, and particularly the faithful Muriel who had been with the firm for almost as many years as he had, and knew exactly how he liked his tea and his coffee and kept him supplied with shortbread of her own making. Why, he thought suddenly, she must have made pounds of the stuff over the years! He had never thought of it before. He must make a point of mentioning it to her. She would value such civility, good faithful girl.

It was also some relief, he secretly admitted, to get out of the house regularly and on legitimate business. Much as he appreciated his freedom nowadays, and his escape from the stern limits imposed by the clock and his desk diary, yet there was a certain aimlessness about mornings at home which had become something of a problem to a man accustomed to a rigid timetable.

And then, it was quite apparent that he was something of a nuisance to his wife. She was used to having the house to herself from eight forty-five every morning. The newspaper used to be hers when it was pushed through the letter box at nine o'clock. Now he grabbed it, as his right, and she had pointed this out to him only that week.

Then there were those little visits from neighbours, and the cups of coffee and gossip which he found irksome. Yes, there was no doubt about it, retirement forced one to make adjustments, and he readily admitted that his dear wife probably found difficulties quite as great as his own, in this new situation. Ah well, thank heaven for Tuesdays, he thought gratefully!

The hands of the clock now stood at five to eleven, and Justin was about to check with Muriel about the time of Connie Harmer's appointment when the door opened, and Connie stood, pink and breathless, on the threshold, with Muriel.

'Oh, Mr Venables, I'm so very sorry I'm late –' she began.

'Think nothing of it,' replied Justin. 'Come and sit down, my dear Miss Harmer. Coffee please, Muriel.'

Two miles away, Charles Henstock waited on the doorstep of Tom Hardy's cottage, and admired the tidiness of his little garden.

It had been a water-keeper's house once, but Tom had taken it over when the water board had decided to dispose of the property. Not many of the tenants had been satisfied with the amenities offered, and the board did not feel that the expense of adequate plumbing, new wiring and extensive structural repairs could be undertaken. The water-keeper who looked after the next stretch of the river owned a car, and with an increase in salary was glad to take on the extra work. Tom Hardy, a widower in his late fifties, had been pleased to buy the property for a fairly low sum.

He had once run a haulage business, but had sold it when he came to live at Keeper's Cottage. He was a jack-of-all trades, remaining in touch with many of his business associates, and willing to turn his hand to driving a heavy vehicle, painting and decorating, doing odd-job gardening and even giving a hand with sheep-shearing in the early summer.

He was held in high regard by the inhabitants of Lulling and Thrush Green who appreciated his old-fashioned virtues of patience, honesty and helpfulness. Among his various trades was the felling and chopping of trees, and it was

in his role of a supplier of logs that Charles came to see
him.

He heard footsteps approaching round the side of the
house, and Tom appeared holding a dead rabbit dangling
by the legs.

'Come round the back, sir,' said Tom. 'I thought there
must be someone about. My old Polly growled, but she's
past bothering about stirring herself these days.'

'I can't think why I knocked at the front door,' replied
the rector. 'I usually come to the back one, but I was
thinking of something else.'

'Sunday's sermon, maybe?' Tom smiled, his blue eyes
looking sideways at his visitor.

He led the way into the kitchen, and motioned Charles
to a sturdy wooden armchair by the table.

'Glass of my home-made beer?' asked Tom.

'Thank you. A small one would be very welcome.'

Tom vanished into a larder which ran the length of the
room, and the rector looked about him.

It was a man's room, no doubt about that. Over the
mantelpiece, above the kitchen range, was a gun rack
holding three guns. By the side of the fire-place some large
coat pegs supported a belt of cartridges, a riding crop,
pieces of leather harness and a fishing gaff, and propped in
a corner were a shepherd's crook and a thumb stick cut
from a fine hazel sapling.

On the mantelpiece itself stood a tobacco jar, a large box
of matches, a tin labelled TEA and another labelled SUGAR,
and on the adjacent dresser, in front of the willow-pattern
plates, stood an old-style circular knife cleaner, a wooden
box labelled SALT and a basket of eggs.

There was not a flower or a plant to be seen, not even a
bunch of herbs hanging up to dry. The kitchen table was
bare, though scrubbed very clean. A woman, thought the
rector, would have had a cloth on it, and probably a plant
standing atop, but there was something attractive about
this sparsely accoutred mannish room. He decided that it

must be because everything visible was strictly functional, plainly useful, unadorned. There was a workaday atmosphere here, as honest and unassuming as its owner.

Charles thought of his own drawing room at Lulling vicarage. It was a charming room, beautifully proportioned and filled with all the objects which he and Dimity treasured. There were cushions, pelmets, ornaments of china, brass and silver. There were vases of flowers, pictures, a tapestry fire screen and innumerable rugs.

It was a gracious room, a woman's room, and he loved it. But sitting here, among these stark surroundings, on his hard wooden chair, caressing its well-worn arms and noting that the only picture provided was a corn-chandler's almanack by the door, his own drawing room seemed frivolously cluttered, and these simple surroundings chimed better with his present mood.

Tom returned with two tankards.

'Like to come in the parlour?' he asked, as though suddenly aware of his surroundings.

'No, thank you, Tom,' said the rector. 'I like this room very well.'

'I live here most of the time,' said Tom. 'Mind you, I give the parlour a clean every now and again, and keep the window ajar. But it's full of fal-de-lals, Margaret's best china in a cabinet, and the bird cage she used to keep her budgies in, and the family bible – all that sort of Sunday stuff.'

'Sunday stuff?'

'Well, a few books, you know. The kind of thing you looked at after church on Sundays.'

He laughed rather shame-facedly.

'Not as I go now, as you well know, sir. I'm what I call lapsed C. of E. when I'm asked what religion I am. Still, I could say the Creed to you now, and the Twenty-third Psalm, and sing most of the usual hymns, if need be. It's just I don't feel the need for going to church. I used to go with Margaret. She enjoyed Mr Bull's services, but to tell you the truth, I found him a bit too high-falutin', if you know what I mean?'

A warm pang of happiness made the rector's heart beat more quickly. As quickly, he chided himself for this involuntary response to comfort.

'He's very much missed, I know,' said Charles steadily. He put his tankard carefully on to the bare table top. 'I miss him myself, I don't mind admitting. But what I called for, Tom, was to order some logs and to ask you if you have any idea how many we should need. I believe you supplied Mr Bull in his time?'

'Well, they always kept plenty of fires going, but they'd the two maids living in so that was one extra fire for them. And they liked the hall one going in really cold weather. I don't think you'd need as much as Mr Bull wanted. I'd say two good loads would see you through.'

'I think you used to deliver two to the old rectory at Thrush Green, if I remember aright. The present house is considerably bigger, Tom.'

'And a sight warmer, sir. That old place was pesky cold always, and caught all the winds God sent, specially the north-east. No, your present place is better built, and sheltered too. The church keeps a lot off you in the way of weather. Acts as a protection, you might say.'

The same warm feeling of comfort engulfed Charles. He rose to go.

'I'll take your advice, Tom. Two loads whenever you can manage it, and the old coach house is waiting for the logs. I swept it out myself yesterday.'

'Right!' said Tom, accompanying his guest to the back door. 'And if need be, I'll top you up after Christmas.'

A Welsh collie dog, grey round the muzzle and with one opaque eye, nuzzled the rector's ankles as he gained the path. The rector patted the silky flanks.

'She's a good old girl,' said Tom fondly. 'Rare company! Don't look much, like me and my house, but she suits me.'

'That's all that matters,' the rector assured him.

The wind was behind him as he went homeward, thrusting him so forcefully that now and again he was nudged into a few running steps.

He found himself exhilarated by the boisterous wind. His spirits, so low on the outward journey, had revived. Could it be the exercise and fresh air which had worked this small miracle? Or could the good fellowship of honest Tom, and the glimpse of his simple and uncomplicated way of living, have put his own worries into perspective?

Whatever the reason, Charles felt better able to face his problems. It reaffirmed his belief in sticking to his principles, to do right by all his flock to the best of his ability, to foster patience and forbearance, and to ignore the pinpricks of petty malice.

He remembered suddenly that someone − he rather thought that it was A. P. Herbert of blessed memory − said that he was sustained by four words:

Fear nothing! Thank God!

The first two words took care of the unknown future. The last two covered past mercies received.

The rector turned the four words over in his mind, and was strengthened and comforted.

In Justin's office Connie was about to make her departure. Dotty's business, concerning the deeds of the cottage at Lulling Woods, was over, the coffee drunk, and Justin was ushering her to the door.

'Did you ever meet Christopher Armitage?' he asked her. 'Kit, he's called more generally. I know your aunt would remember him. He was at school when her father was headmaster.'

'And he survived?' laughed Connie.

'Yes, indeed. A resilient fellow, and excellent company. He's just retired and looking about for a house here.'

'No, I haven't come across him, I'm afraid.'

'Well, he's based with us for a little while, but at the moment he is looking up relatives and old friends before

getting down to serious house-hunting. We expect him back in a week or two. No doubt he'll call to see your aunt before long.'

'That will be nice,' said Connie.

They had now reached the open front door. The wind had blown in a few dead leaves from the lime trees. They skittered about the tiled floor like small crabs.

'Well, thank you again,' said Connie, holding out her hand. 'Come and see us when you can. We both enjoy visitors.'

Justin watched her hasten down the street, a trim athletic figure. Dotty was lucky to have her, he thought.

He bent to pick up the dead leaves and put them carefully in the waste paper basket when he returned to his office.

He suddenly remembered the shortbread, and rang for Muriel.

'Yes, Mr Venables?' she asked deferentially.

'Muriel, I should have said this many years ago. The

shortbread is always delicious. Miss Harmer told me to tell you how much she enjoyed it this morning, as I have too hundreds and hundreds of times. Much appreciated, Muriel, believe me.'

'Oh sir!' faltered Muriel, turning pink. 'Thank you. I'm so glad –'

She broke off and hurried from the room, and straight to the privacy of the staff lavatory where she mopped her tears.

Why was it, she thought fiercely, that one could stand any amount of scolding and censure without a qualm, and yet dissolve into tears at a few words of kindness?

She tidied her hair, stuffed her damp handkerchief up her sleeve, and after a colossal sniff, returned to her duties with a gladsome mind.

6 Spring Fevers

THE MISSES LOVELOCK were delighted to hear that
Kit Armitage had returned.

'I thought I recognized that back,' said Violet
triumphantly. 'So upright, still so straight and soldierly!
He always had a most impressive carriage.'

Miss Ada looked at her younger sister with faint dislike.

'I can't recall Kit's back being anything very different
from any of the other young men's.'

'Oh, I always admired his stance when we played tennis,'
said Violet. 'He always threw the ball a tremendous height
in the air when he served. D'you remember, Bertha?'

Bertha nodded. Pencil in hand she was engrossed in the
crossword, but her cheeks were a little flushed. There was
no doubt about it, the return of Christopher Armitage was
causing a stir in this particular household.

'He was always very athletic,' observed Ada. 'Wasn't he
Victor Ludorum one year at the Grammar School? And
once he turned twenty cartwheels at a tennis party here.
Someone said he couldn't – Justin maybe – and I remember
he put down his glass and took off his jacket, and went
over and over all round the lawn.'

'I suspected at the time that he had partaken of too
much punch. If you remember we let that maid we had at
the time mix up a second batch, and she was very free with
the gin.'

'Kit was never the worse for drink,' protested Miss Violet. 'Just high spirits, on that occasion, I feel sure.'

'Well, I don't suppose he turns many cartwheels nowadays,' said Bertha. 'Nor Dotty either. What a dreadful affair that was!'

'She only turned *two*,' Ada pointed out, 'and it was Kit who dared her to. Besides, her bloomers were perfectly respectable and substantial, which was a blessing, I must say, in the circumstances.'

'Well, we were all young then,' said Violet indulgently, 'and what a lot of fun we had in the old days! It will be good to see Kit again and revive happy memories.'

'We must invite him to lunch when he returns,' agreed Ada. 'What a pity he lost his wife so long ago! She was a pretty girl, I remember.'

'I always thought she was rather fast,' commented Miss Bertha. 'A typical Londoner, and she certainly came without her gloves to Sung Eucharist once.'

'Perhaps she forgot them,' said Violet.

'A lady,' replied Bertha severely, 'never forgets her gloves.'

And thus rebuked, her sister fell silent.

The winds of March, which Shakespeare's daffodils enjoyed, was not welcome to Albert Piggott at Thrush Green.

For one thing, they blew an unconscionable number of leaves into the church porch of St Andrew's and needed to be swept out by Albert himself.

When young Cooke had taken on most of the church duties of a heavier nature, digging graves, tending the coke furnace and so on, it had been arranged that Albert would be responsible for sweeping the church floor and the porch. When a really stiff breeze came along, no matter from which quarter of the globe, the leaves managed to eddy in drifts against the church door, under the stone benches which flanked the porch, and often into the church itself. Albert found it all very trying.

March winds also made him cough. Albert's bronchial equipment had always been sub-standard, even Doctor Lovell admitted that, and Albert's habitual dolour exaggerated his condition. He was not given to suffering in silence, and intended to let the landlord of The Two Pheasants have a detailed account of his respiratory ailments as soon as he went in there for his midday meal of a pork pie, pickles and beer.

But that was not all that he had to worry about on this particular morning. For once, Willie Marchant the postman had brought him a letter. It was hand written, and Albert opened it with caution.

The message was short. It was signed 'Charlie Wright' and Albert's face registered disgust, as well as its habitual gloom, as he read.

Dear Albert,

Nelly has had a bad turn and is in hospital here. Thought you ought to know as you are her next-of-kin.

Charlie Wright

'"Next of kin" indeed!' said Albert aloud. 'And a fat lot of good that is!' Didn't he take her on? Didn't this dratted oil-man, this wife-stealer, have first claim on Nelly?

He thrust the letter into his pocket and went across to deal with the dead leaves which were as troublesome as Nelly herself. He felt no stirrings of pity for his ailing wife. She'd chosen her bed, hadn't she? Well, she must lie in it. Let this Charlie do the coping. It was no business of his. He would ignore the letter.

But he found that he could not ignore the matter completely. As he swept morosely, coughing occasionally, and taking a rest every now and again on one or other of the stone benches in the porch, he began to wonder about Charlie's message. Did the fact that he had informed him that he was next-of-kin mean that Nelly was likely to snuff it? In which case, did it mean that any property belonging to her would then come to him?

It was one thing to let the oilman who had lured away his Nelly have the responsibility of looking after her 'in sickness and in health', as it said in the marriage service – not that Nelly and this Charlie had bothered with such niceties – but quite a different kettle of fish if the dratted fellow came into Nelly's bits and pieces, simply because he didn't write back as, he supposed glumly, a husband should.

Sitting, resting his head on the broom handle, Albert pondered this problem. True, Nelly had never had much in the way of possessions, but there had been a gold wrist watch and a brooch from Italy she was fond of, and come to think of it, there was a Post Office savings book that she kept mighty quiet about in her handbag.

On the other hand, if it meant going all the way to
Brighton to see her in hospital, he was inclined to forfeit
her assets and let the pair of them sort out their troubles.
Why should he bother about them? A fat lot they'd troubled about him, that was for sure!

He brushed a spider from his knee and began to sweep
it, with the leaves, into the corner of the porch. Although
he told himself that he would take no action over the
letter, he still suffered a small nagging doubt.

Perhaps old Jones could give him some advice? Two
heads were better than one, they said. Over his pub dinner
he would mention it, in a casual way, to the landlord, and
see what transpired. No need to rush his fences, and if he
had to reply after all, then Molly could give him a hand
with the writing.

Somewhat comforted he fetched a shovel and bucket to
collect the leaves, and even chirruped to a robin who had
come to investigate the activity.

On the Saturday morning following the arrival of Albert's
letter, little Miss Fogerty lay prone on her bedroom floor
at the school house, and conscientiously went through the
exercises prescribed by Doctor Lovell.

He had been sympathetic about her aching joints some
months previously, and had forborn to tell her automatically to lose a stone in weight as he did to three-
quarters of his patients suffering from anything from gout
to gall bladder troubles. Miss Fogerty, who could not
weigh much over six and a half stone, was exempt from
this ritual prescription, but was given some tablets to help
alleviate the pain, and a sheet which set out some simple
exercises for strengthening muscles.

Agnes Fogerty did not like to tell her medical adviser that
the tablets tended to make her head swim, and that she had
cut down the dose privately to half. The exercises, she
believed, were certainly strengthening her legs, although
they seemed to strain something in her back at the same time.

However, she was philosophical about this unwelcome side effect, and after adjusting her lisle stockings, she gazed at the ceiling, and began to raise and lower each leg in turn.

It was extraordinary how similar that damp patch was to the map of Wales! A lovely country, and one she hoped to visit again when at last she and Dorothy retired. She counted to ten, and then resumed the exercise.

Such a pity that retirement had needed to be postponed! Perhaps if she had been at Barton now the good sea air would have put paid to all these aches and pains.

Time for bicycling, and very strenuous it was too. It was all very well for Doctor Lovell, half her age and athletic too, to loll back in his chair at the surgery and issue his instructions, but really it was no joke when one was in one's sixties and with kneecaps cracking like pistol shots!

Puffing heavily, little Miss Fogerty lay still and surveyed the carpet under the bed. Betty Bell kept things beautifully – no dust at all, and only one hair grip which she had lost only two days ago. It was quite interesting seeing the world from a different angle, and rather pleasant lying on the carpet. How nice to be a cat!

She pulled herself together hastily, and set herself to cycle another two minutes before tackling her standing routine.

There, that was done! She scrambled to her feet with the help of the bedstead, and stood quite still until her head had stopped spinning. Then she went close to the wall and kept one steadying hand on it while she rose and fell on her toes. Doctor Lovell had said earnestly that he wanted to restore suppleness, as far as was possible, so that she could run again quite easily.

Agnes had not liked to tell the dear man that she had not run anywhere for the last ten years, and had no intention of starting again now, but she was fond of her adviser and respected his faith in her possible prowess.

She did her exercises zealously, studying a still life in

water colours executed by one of Dorothy's college friends. It depicted a bowl of fruit with a few vegetables lying beside it, and Agnes was not wholly enamoured of it. Certainly, the grapes were superbly done, and the bananas were recognisable, of course, so yellow and curved, as they were, it would be hard to disguise them, but the carrots looked anaemic and those green things which must be artichoke heads were not the right green.

Dipping briskly from left foot to right, Agnes recalled her own efforts at vegetable painting. Cabbages, she remembered, had responded wonderfully to a mixture of veridian green, a spot of crimson lake and a little Chinese white. The result had been a most successful soft colour, and her art teacher had congratulated her on the effect. Very gratifying it had been.

Agnes felt that her legs had suffered quite enough, and began to rotate her arms gently. She wandered to the window, and surveyed the little world of Thrush Green as she worked away.

A stranger was walking purposefully across the grass towards the Youngs' house. He was tall and soldierly. He had no hat and his hair was thick and silvery.

'That must be young Mr Venables' friend,' thought Agnes, now shrugging her shoulders up and down as Exercise Six required. 'What a nice-looking fellow! No arthritis there, I'm sure!'

She finished her twentieth shrug conscientiously, folded the exercise list away in a drawer, tidied her hair and went downstairs to tell Dorothy about the Youngs' visitor.

Kit Armitage was warmly welcomed by Joan and Edward Young and the sherry glasses were soon filled.

After some exchange of news, Kit said how very sorry he had been to hear of the death of Robert Bassett.

'Of course, he was a good deal older than I am, but I was quite often invited to play tennis here and he was always so excessively kind. No bad hand at lobs and volleys either, if I remember rightly.'

'He loved all games, and was very quick on his feet,' agreed Edward. 'I used to dread being asked to partner him. He could beat me hollow at tennis, and although he was the most considerate of partners, I always felt mightily inferior. I was courting Joan at the time and very conscious of the poor figure I was cutting.'

Joan laughed.

'I was so sorry for you, and pity being akin to love I'm sure it helped your cause.'

'And your mother?' asked Kit.

'Pretty shaken, and can't make up her mind if it would be better to stay on in the little house, or move in with Ruth up the road. I tell her not to make any decisions yet. It's too soon after Father's death to make plans.'

'Very wise. Now tell me about the other Thrush Green friends. I gather Dotty is still fighting fit.'

'I don't know about that, but she's jolly well looked after by her niece Connie. Do call and see them. Dotty remembers you well.'

'I'm looking forward to seeing her again.'

He asked after Albert Piggott, the Misses Lovelock, and was told about the disastrous fire which had robbed Charles and Dimity of their home.

'And what's going to be there instead?' he asked.

'Eight homes for old people,' Edward told him. 'I've just put in my plan. We want something easy on the eye this time.'

'I could do with an old people's home myself,' observed Kit. 'Let me know if you hear of a small place anywhere near Lulling or Thrush Green. I'm getting down in earnest now to some house-hunting.'

They took him round the garden and showed him the attractive little house which Edward had designed and converted from the old stable. Mrs Bassett was out, and he promised to call on her another time.

'And whose is this?' he enquired, eyeing the gipsy caravan which had once been the home of Mrs Curdle, Ben's grandmother.

Joan told him about the old lady's death, the sad but necessary sale of the fair, and how glad they were to have Ben and Molly living in the flat at the top of the house.

'Mrs Curdle!' exclaimed Kit. 'May the first! My goodness, that takes me back. What a day that was every year! We used to look forward to that fair day for weeks.'

'We all did, ' said Joan. 'It's lovely to have the caravan here as a reminder. Sometimes Ben's children have a tea party in there with their friends. I don't think Mrs Curdle would have let them make as much noise as we allow them.'

They walked to the gate, and Kit looked at his watch.

'I'll call and see Dotty another time, but do you think Winnie Bailey would remember me?'

'Try her and see,' advised Joan, and they watched him step out across the grass in the direction of the doctor's.

'If your mother does decide to live with Ruth,' said Edward, as they returned to the house, 'I wonder if Kit would want the stable cottage? He'd be a considerate neighbour, that's certain.'

'I've been thinking about it too,' said Joan, 'but I feel we should offer it to Ben and Molly before anyone else. The flat was ideal when they only had George to consider, but now there are two children they are pretty cramped up there. Besides, they need a garden of their own, and those stairs are quite tiring, although Molly never complains.'

'You're right, of course. I hope your mother decides to stay on. She's near enough for us to keep an eye on her, but she can still feel independent with all her own things around her. Let's shelve the problem until further notice.'

And so they left the matter.

Kit found Winnie Bailey in the garden picking daffodils for Ella Bembridge who was with her.

After introductions, Winnie tried to persuade him into the house, but he pleaded shortness of time and promised to call again.

They accompanied him to the gate.

'And we hear you hope to settle here,' said Winnie. 'It will be lovely to have you among us. Do you play bridge still?'

'Yes, and just as badly, but I'll make up a four whenever you like. But not just yet. I'm busy looking for a little house. Two up and two down sort of thing – well, perhaps *three* up and three down, on second thoughts – but something I can cope with alone. Any ideas?'

'None at the moment,' said Winnie slowly. She turned to Ella.

'There's that place near the Cookes along the Nidden road,' said Ella. 'But I doubt if you'd want to be anywhere near that family. And someone told me that there's a flat going over The Fuchsia Bush in Lulling High Street.'

'Terribly noisy,' observed Winnie.

'I think I'd like a little garden,' said Kit, at the same moment.

Anyway, the ladies assured him, they would ask around and let him know if anything cropped up.

'I've got my name down with several agents, of course,' said Kit, 'but I wouldn't mind betting I get something through my friends eventually.'

They waved goodbye to him, and returned to the house to collect the daffodils from the shelter of the porch.

'Tell you what,' said Ella, uttering one of her favourite phrases, 'I'll mention it to Charles and Dimity. Between them they quarter four parishes, and if we can't find something suitable for that nice man, I'll eat my hat.'

Albert Piggott found little comfort in Mr Jones's advice about Nelly's illness.

Having read the letter, which emerged much crumpled from Albert's pocket, he reacted forthrightly.

'If Nelly's in hospital then you should go and see her,' was his edict. 'Oh, I know all about her leaving you, and the rows you had, but that's in the past, Albert, and she's still your wife, you know. You get down to this hospital and see her. It's your duty to stand by her.'

Albert was taken aback by such straight talking.

'I don't know about my duty,' he responded with some heat. 'What about her duty to her lawful wedded husband, eh? What I'm concerned about is this Charlie. I bet he's got his eye on Nelly's bits and pieces, and why should he have 'em?'

Mr Jones looked at him with disgust.

'And you've got your eye on them too, I take it? You makes me puke, Albert, that you do. There's this poor soul – your own flesh and blood –'

'And plenty there was of it too,' interjected Albert morosely, recalling his wife's vast bulk.

'Flesh and blood,' continued the landlord unperturbed, 'dying, from what this chap says, and you think of nothing but what you might get out of it. Finish your beer, Albert, and clear out, will you? I'm fed up with this business. You asked my advice and this is it. Ring up this chap, find out where Nelly is, and get down there pronto to see her.'

At that moment, two men entered the bar and he turned to serve them, still flushed with anger at Albert's behaviour.

Albert took advantage of the interruption to creep away to his house next door.

There was cold comfort there, but at least it was more congenial today than The Two Pheasants.

7 Albert Piggott Under Pressure

T HE AFFAIR OF THE Lady Chapel kneelers still
caused the good rector some unhappy twinges, but
nothing more had been said directly to him by Mrs
Thurgood.

Could she have decided against pursuing the matter? It
seemed unlikely. There was a ruthless tenacity about the
woman which Charles recognized only too well. He quailed
before it, and chided himself for cowardice, but this self-
flagellation did not mitigate his fears.

He had a horrid feeling that Mrs Thurgood was simply
biding her time before returning to the attack. With Dimity
beside him one afternoon, they had examined the present
kneelers minutely, and had put aside any which appeared
to be the worse for wear. Naturally, Mrs Thurgood's own
kneeler was one of the shabbiest as she was such an
outstandingly regular church-goer, and about six or eight
others would benefit from some attention. But on the
whole, Dimity and Charles agreed, the rest of the kneelers
were perfectly capable of fulfilling their function for several
years.

Comforted by this discovery, Charles felt that he could
withstand any onslaught from the doughty Frances Thurgood. It was certainly rather unnerving to find that the
weeks slid by without any further manifestations of the
lady's pugnacity. What lay behind this silence? Had she

decided to give up the fight? Had she simply forgotten about the kneelers? Had she, perhaps, suddenly regretted her offer to pay for the work?

Charles wondered if he would ever learn the answers to these questions. He had not long to wait.

One bright morning he collected the letters from the hall mat and carried them to the breakfast table where Dimity was already buttering her toast. There were half a dozen or so envelopes, but one was immediately noteworthy for its excellent quality and imposing seal at the back.

'From the bishop,' said Charles, opening it first.

Dimity, watching him closely, saw his expression turn from pleasure to dismay. Having read the bishop's letter, he then turned to another enclosed with it, and the dismay upon his chubby countenance was now tinged with indignation.

'Well, *really*!' protested Charles, handing over the letters. 'Now what do you make of that?'

Dimity read rapidly. The bishop's note was kindly and concise. It said that he had received the enclosed letter from Mrs Thurgood to which he had replied. He said that he had every confidence in Charles's decision and urged him not to worry unduly about a matter which was really very trivial. He sent his regards to Dimity and hoped to see them both very soon.

Frances Thurgood's letter was belligerent in comparison. She set forth her own generosity, her anxiety to see the Lady Chapel furnished 'in a God-like manner', and hinted at the regrettable attitude taken up by Anthony Bull's successor both in his services and his dealings with parishioners. She trusted that the bishop would see fit to remind the present incumbent of his duties.

'The *cat*!' fumed Dimity, throwing the letter across the table. 'To go behind your back like that! It is absolutely unforgivable, Charles! What will you do?'

'Nothing in a hurry,' said her husband equably. 'I may say something I should regret later, and I don't want the

dear bishop to be badgered any further with complaints about me.'

'You are far too forgiving,' said Dimity.

'I don't know about that.' He picked up the bishop's letter, and read it again.

'You know, Dimity, it is really uncommonly nice of him to write so warmly. And in his own hand too!'

'He's hardly likely to write in anybody else's,' retorted Dimity, with unusual tartness. She still smarted from the effect of Mrs Thurgood's outrageous behaviour, and was irritated too by Charles's deference, one might almost say *awe*, in his handling of the bishop's letter. In her opinion, Charles was quite as worthy as the bishop himself – probably a better man altogether when you considered his modesty and selflessness – and Dimity felt herself glowing with mingled righteous indignation and wifely devotion.

'Well, I only hope I don't encounter Frances Thurgood in the next day or two,' she exclaimed. 'I don't think I could remain silent about such appalling behaviour.'

The rector looked alarmed.

'Oh, my dear, please don't fan the flames! The bishop is

absolutely right to call this a trivial matter. I will speak to her privately before the week is out, but I beg you to say nothing, if you love me.'

He looked so pink and agitated that Dimity's wrath faded, and she bent across the table to kiss his cheek.

'I will do exactly as you say,' she promised him.

Meanwhile, Albert Piggott had problems of his own.

After his rebuff at the hands of Mr Jones, the landlord, he had almost decided to ignore Charlie's letter, and leave Nelly's future in the hands of the gods.

But he reckoned without the loquacity of The Two Pheasants. It so happened that Ben Curdle called in for a pint soon after his father-in-law had departed.

The landlord, still full of indignation at Albert's callousness, told Ben the story. Ben returned to his flat at the top of the Youngs' house to consult Molly on the matter, and that evening they went together to face the old man.

He was surlier than ever, and obstinate with it.

'She's been no wife to me,' he asserted. 'Why should I put myself out for her?'

'Don't talk so daft!' said his daughter. 'She looked after you all the time she was here, and kept the place lovely. And cooked a treat! And what thanks did she get?'

'She had me company. And me money,' growled Albert.

'You listen to me, dad,' said Ben quietly. 'If anything happens to her you're going to regret it. And what's more, all Thrush Green is going to chuck it in your face. She's your wife, whatever she's done. You'd best get down there as fast as you can.'

'And how am I going to get to Brighton, may I ask? And who pays the fare?'

'We've been looking up ways and means. I can put you and your case on the morning coach at Lulling. It goes right up to Victoria Coach Station, and there's plenty of coaches direct from there to Brighton. You'd be with Nelly in a matter of hours.'

Albert began to look cornered.

'And Ben and I will pay the fare,' Molly promised him. 'We've talked it over, haven't we, Ben?'

Her husband nodded loyally, and Albert looked more hopeful.

'Well, I don't say as it might not be the right thing to do,' he admitted cautiously, 'but she's a fair old trollop, as well you know, and I don't reckon she deserves to see me again.'

Molly privately thought that her father's remark could be construed in two ways, but prudently remained silent.

'That's settled then,' said Ben, standing up. 'I'll pick you up in the van at a quarter past eight tomorrow morning, on my way to work. The coach sets off at eight-thirty, so you'll be all right.'

'And I'll come over tonight and pack one or two things for you,' added Molly swiftly. 'You may want to stay for a while.'

'That'll be the day,' commented Albert bitterly.

But he knew when he was beaten.

In common with most small communities, news in Thrush Green and Lulling has always spread with the rapidity of a forest fire.

Sharp eyes that morning had seen Albert waiting at the coach stop. He was actually wearing a tie as well as his best dark blue suit, the one in which he had married Nelly at St Andrew's. At his feet stood a small case.

Obviously, he was off on his travels, and where would that be? News of Nelly's illness had already gone the rounds, and it did not need much guesswork on the part of his observers to settle his destination.

The coach stop was immediately outside The Fuchsia Bush, and Mrs Peters, the owner of this establishment, noticed Albert as she drove up to open the café. Ten minutes later Gloria Williams arrived on foot, and soon after that her co-worker Rosa entered their place of work.

The coach was late, and Albert was shifting impatiently from one foot to the other.

'No doubt Nelly's took a turn for the worse,' surmised Rosa. 'I did hear she was in the intensive.'

'What's that when it's at home?' queried Gloria, licking her fingers and arranging a curl over one eyebrow.

'It's where they put you when it's touch and go,' Rosa explained. 'You're all wired up to a television thing for the nurses to watch.'

'And Nelly's that bad?'

'I expect so,' said Rosa with evident satisfaction. 'Can't see old Smiley there bothering to go and see her if she was just in an ordinary ward.'

'My mum said no one wasn't allowed to see people when they was wired up like you say.'

Rosa was somewhat put out by this sudden display of medical knowledge from a junior.

'Oh! Know it all, do you?' she enquired, with heavy sarcasm. 'Perhaps you can tell me –'

But at this moment, Mrs Peters came hurrying through from her swift inspection of the kitchen, and the two girls broke off their discussion to collect their overalls and to appear moderately active.

'Come along, girls,' cried their bustling employer. 'No time for gossip! The tables need dusting, and one of you must hurry along to Abbot's. We're nearly out of butter.'

Gloria cast a resigned look at her colleague behind Mrs Peters's back, and at that moment the London coach drew up with a dreadful squealing of brakes.

The door opened automatically. Albert picked up his case and mounted the steps. Within a minute he was on his way, all his movements having been watched by the three ladies behind the window of The Fuchsia Bush.

Betty Bell was full of the drama when she blew into the Shoosmiths' house at Thrush Green 'to put them to rights'.

'Fancy our Albert making such a trip! I bet he wouldn't have gone if he'd been left to himself though. They say Mr Jones gave him the rough side of his tongue, and Ben and Molly put the pressure on too. I'd dearly like to be a fly on the ceiling when he sees his Nelly in hospital. What's the betting he takes her some flowers? Or a bunch of grapes? I don't think! The mean old devil! Want your study done over?'

Harold looked helplessly at his wife. She came swiftly to the rescue, as always.

'Bedrooms today, Betty. I did the study yesterday.'

'Righty-o! I'll lug the vacuum up.'

She made for the kitchen, but lingered in the doorway.

'They say she's pretty bad, you know. Trouble with her breathing. Well, with all that fat and her being so short in the neck it's not surprising. My auntie was the same. Never had a cold but what it was bronchitis. Doctor Lovell took her off butter but it never did any good. Now it's all this fibre nonsense. Everyone comes out of that surgery being told to eat bran these days. Last year it was no animals fats, and the year before that no sugar. I s'pose we'll all be on hay or silage this time next year. Funny folk, doctors, I reckon.'

'Who told you that Mrs Piggott was seriously ill?' said Isobel, trying to stem the tirade against the medical profession.

'Why, Percy Hodge! He was just coming out of The Two Pheasants as I was leaving the school yesterday. Been in to get his courage up to face that Doris of his, I don't doubt. Now, there's a fine how-do-you-do. She's real sharp with poor old Perce. He has to take his shoes off outside the back door, and then she hands him a clothes brush to have a clean-up in case he's got any bits of straw and that on him. You'd hardly credit it, would you? And she once a barmaid.'

'But Nelly —' broke in Isobel.

'Ah yes! Well, Perce said Mr Jones had told him he'd read a letter of Albert's that said she was at her last gasp.'

'Oh dear!'

'One thing, I bet she ain't calling for Albert, ill though she is. And I wonder what she'll say when the old misery turns up at her bedside? Enough to give her a prolapse.'

'I think it's "relapse",' said Harold.

'That as well, I shouldn't wonder,' conceded Betty. 'I'll get that vacuum cleaner. Standing here listening to you running on won't buy the baby a new frock, will it?'

She vanished through the door, and the Shoosmiths exchanged conspiratorial glances.

'I think I could do with a second cup of coffee,' said Harold handing over his cup.

'I'll join you,' said his wife.

April was at its loveliest that year, the first spring that Charles and Dimity had enjoyed in their new home at Lulling.

Charles woke early one April morning and lay quietly watching the changing sky. The first apricot warmth faded slowly to pink and then to a clear shade of lemon yellow.

Charles watched the young leaves fluttering in silhouette against their changing background. A dove cooed. A blackbird poured forth a liquid stream of bird music, and the metallic call of a nearby wren added to the dawn chorus.

As the day brightened into silvery light the birds became more active, swooping from trees to earth, from hedge to further hedge, in their search for food and nesting material. The air seemed full of their activity, and the flutter of wings and the varied cries brought the morning to life.

Charles lay beside his sleeping wife savouring this joyousness of spring. Truly, his lot had been cast in pleasant places, he thought, as he watched the sun burnishing the eastern side of the ancient cedar tree.

It was good to have a quiet contemplative time now and again. He recalled one of Wordsworth's sonnets learnt long ago at school:

> *The world is too much with us: late and soon,*
> *Getting and spending, we lay waste our powers:*
> *Little we see in Nature that is ours;*
> *We have given our hearts away, a sordid boon!*

His own day, Charles knew only too well, was a succession of activities which kept him busy mentally and bodily. Somehow one was always looking ahead, planning the next move, trying to cut down time. And in all this bustle the present was lost. The daisy opened, closed and died. The chaffinch threaded the last shred of moss into its nest before sitting. The sun reached the point in the heavens when the weathercock turned to gold. And all these wonders passed unremarked, because the clock on the mantelpiece gave stern reminder of the service at three-thirty, the visit to a sick parishioner at five o'clock, and the meeting of the Parochial Church Council at eight sharp.

Charles Henstock was the first to honour his duties towards God and his neighbours. But what a bonus it was, he told himself as he stretched his toes luxuriously in the warmth of the bed, to have these precious moments of just *being*, of becoming aware of all the other lives impinging on one's own, and of having time to give thanks for such revelation.

He sat up, being careful not to disturb his wife, and gazed out of the window. There was a heavy dew. It looked more like September than April. The grass shimmered and glittered in the low rays of the rising sun. Each little spear, it seemed to Charles, bore a shining droplet. How many thousands would there be, he wondered, clustered beneath the trees, spreading far and wide, almost to the church itself?

Surrounded by leaves! All sorts of shapes and sizes, large and small, green and gold, smooth and rough, some aromatic, some not, but all breathing entities, as far as the eye could see!

He found the thought strangely moving and comforting. It put his own life into perspective. It made him more sharply aware of his modest place amidst such a wealth of living things. The trees he looked upon now would still be there when he himself had gone. And that little jewelled chaffinch, rose-breasted and blue-capped, which fluttered at the window, would have become a lacework of small ivory bones long before he himself took the same way home.

Dimity stirred.

'Are you all right?' she asked drowsily.

'Everything's all right,' Charles assured her truthfully.

One breezy spring afternoon Connie emerged from Dotty's cottage, milk-can in one hand and Flossie's lead in the other, and made her way to Thrush Green to deliver Ella Bembridge's daily quota of goat's milk.

Albert Piggott had proved surprisingly capable at dealing with Dulcie's bounty while her aunt had been laid up, but once Connie had settled in she assured him that she could manage the animals.

'Well, I don't mind givin' a hand when you're pushed,' said Albert. 'Makes a change from humping a broom round the church or tidying the grave-yard, and old Dulce and me gets on pretty fairish. Goats has got more sense than people, I reckons.'

Connie thanked him sincerely. She knew that by nature he was a gloomy soul, and that he had strangely blossomed in his new role as animal minder. She assured him that she might well need his services if a domestic emergency arose, and he seemed content.

It was as well that she had not relied upon him daily, she thought, following Flossie along the footpath, for she had just heard about his departure to Brighton to visit his wife. As things were, she found looking after Dotty and the many animals well within her capabilities, and enjoyed renewing her friendships in Thrush Green. But just occasionally, when the sun was setting over Lulling Woods and that wistful time between daylight and dark spread its shadows, she mourned the cottage she had left behind in Somerset, and the familiar shapes of hills and trees around it. But it was a momentary sadness, and Connie was able to dismiss it bravely. Aunt Dotty had always been good to her and Connie knew that she was sole heir to her little estate. She was glad to be able to give her a hand now that she needed it. Certainly, no one could have been kinder or more grateful than her eccentric aunt, and what were known in the neighbourhood as 'Dotty's funny little ways' gave Connie no cause for alarm. She was quite used to them, and in any case the affection she felt for this unusual relative was strong enough to over-ride any fears.

Flossie quickened her pace when they reached Thrush Green, and Connie found herself running to keep up. Luckily, the lid of the old-fashioned milk can was well-fitting, but she could hear the liquid splashing about inside.

The children were having games in the playground, and Connie could hear them chanting: I *sent a letter to my love*, while little Miss Fogerty watched carefully from outside the circle to make sure that all the rules of the game were properly kept.

The path to Ella's front door was lined with velvety wallflowers, wine-dark, gold and cream. The scent was delicious, and even Flossie stood still, nose upraised, as if enjoying their fragrance.

No one was in. Connie went into the garden to see if Ella were there; but both back and front doors were locked, and the windows tight shut. Obviously, Ella was out for some time, and now she came to think of it, Connie recalled that she had said something about going to that excellent shop in Ship Street, Oxford, to buy tapestry wools.

'Well, Floss,' said Connie, 'we must just leave the milk in the porch. No biscuit for you today, old girl. We'll see if we can find one at home.'

Flossie was reluctant to leave Ella's abode. It was rarely that she had to return without having consumed one of Ella's wholesome digestive biscuits, but she was a philosophical animal, and at last consented to accompany Connie homeward.

They crossed the green, and now the children were playing 'Twos and Threes', still in their circle, and still being watched indulgently by little Agnes Fogerty.

Connie and Flossie soon entered the narrow footpath beside Albert Piggott's cottage. His windows too were shut, and Connie wondered how he was faring on his travels.

As they emerged into the field leading to Dotty's, Connie became aware of footsteps behind her. She glanced back and saw a tall stranger, with silvery hair, striding along purposefully.

Connie quickened her step. The path was narrow, and unless she stopped to let him pass, there was really nothing else to do. She did not want to be obliged to carry on a conversation with a complete stranger simply because the path forced them to walk closely together.

To her surprise, the footsteps behind her quickened too, and a voice hailed her.

'I say, don't run away! Aren't you Miss Harmer? Miss Connie Harmer?'

She turned to face the oncomer. He really had a fine turn of speed for a man of his age, and a remarkably well-cut tweed jacket and shining brogue shoes.

'My word, you go at a good pace!' he said, smiling at her. 'I'm Kit Armitage, and I was about to call and pay my respects to my old friend Dotty. That is, if she would be willing to see me. How is she?'

'She's getting on well, and will be all the better for a visit from you,' said Connie, holding out her hand.

8   Albert Makes A Journey

ALBERT PIGGOTT ARRIVED at Victoria. Coach Station later in the morning, and his first port of call was a café.

Breakfast time seemed a long way behind him. He sat at a table and waited for someone to serve him.

He was not a lover of London. True, he had only visited the capital about five or six times in his life, and had always thought it noisy and dirty. If anything, it seemed noisier and dirtier than ever.

'Self-service here, love,' said a large woman setting down a tray on his table.

Albert looked bewildered.

'You fetch your own, see? Get a tray and pick out what you want off of the bits and pieces. You get your drink at the end.'

'Thanks,' said Albert, picking up his case.

'You can leave that with me, love. I shan't pinch it.'

Albert shuffled off, collected the tray and, copying the rest of the queue, selected a currant bun and a plastic cup of coffee.

'I takes sugar,' he said to the girl behind the hissing machine.

'On the table,' she told him impatiently. Albert drifted off.

The woman at his table was busy with a large piece of chocolate cake and a cup of tea.

She nodded to him, but he was relieved to find that she seemed quite content to continue her meal in silence. His case was exactly as he left it.

He had over an hour to wait, and killed time over the coffee and a newspaper someone had left on the next table. The woman had departed, without speaking again, long before Albert had finished the sports' pages. It seemed odd to him that one could share a table and yet not pass a common word. Not like Thrush Green, he thought with a pang!

He looked at the crowd about him. He might have been a fly on the ceiling for all the notice they took of him – or anyone else, for that matter. What a way to live!

At length, he picked up his case and set out to track down the bus which would take him to his destination. He was tired already, and looked forward to having a nap as soon as his case was safely stowed on the rack, and he had found a seat.

It was nearly four o'clock when Albert finally arrived at the hospital. The coach had been late in starting, and various road works had delayed them. The hospital was some distance from the town centre and involved a tedious bus journey. Albert, who had grown increasingly anxious about this whole project, now began to wonder just how Nelly would greet him.

He was directed up many flights of stone stairs and along miles of corridors before arriving at Nelly's ward. Other visitors surged along with him, bearing bunches of flowers, boxes of eggs and bundles of clean nighties. Albert began to wonder if he should have splashed out on one of the small bunches of violets being sold at the gate, but it was too late to bother about it now.

He saw Nelly as soon as he entered the long ward. She was easily the largest and most gaudily dressed of the ladies present, and her hair was even brighter than he remembered it.

But there was no smile to match the hair. An expression of intense hostility greeted him, and the ominous words:

'And who told you to come, may I ask?'

Albert put his case by the bedside locker and sat down upon a hard chair.

'Your chap,' he said, still breathless from the stairs and corridors.

'What, my Charlie?'

'That's right. Said you was at death's door, and I was to come.'

'Well, you can go back again for all I care,' said Nelly, pulling her bright pink bed jacket across her splendid bust. 'I told you I never wanted to see you again.'

Albert was silent. For one thing there seemed to be no answer to such remarks, and in any case he was dog-tired.

After some minutes of uneasy silence, Nelly relented a little.

'Well, now you're here you might tell me about that dead and alive hole Thrush Green.'

'It's just the same,' said Albert.

'And them old Lovelocks? Wizened old trout. Never known love, and not many locks between 'em.'

'Don't see much of Lulling folk.'

There was another pause. By the next bed a crowd of exuberant Pakistanis were passing round photographs of a family wedding. They seemed to have plenty to say.

'Well, what are you in for?' said Albert, stirring himself at last. 'Going to be in here long?'

'Another few days. Something to do with my gall bladder, they say, but it's my belief they haven't got a clue. One thing I do know. The food's something chronic. I wouldn't offer it to a dog.'

'Ah!' said Albert, relapsing into silence again.

'You aren't going all the way back tonight, are you?'

'Hadn't thought about it.'

'Well, you'd better think now. You'll never get a coach or train from London as'll get you to Thrush Green today. I'd stay overnight if I was you.'

'Where, may I ask? I ain't sharing a bed with Charlie!' Albert was stung into sarcasm, and the thought of having to spend good money on a night's lodging. It was something he had not thought about seriously, despite the pyjamas and face flannel carefully packed by Molly, 'just in case'.

Nelly bridled.

'Charlie don't want your company, believe me. He comes along after work, by the way, so if you don't want to see him, you'll have to look slippy.'

Albert bent down for his case.

'Brought me a box of chocolates?' asked Nelly, eyes bright with anticipation.

Albert had a sudden brain wave.

'Didn't think they'd allow it, but I've got today's paper.'

He took out the copy which he had picked up at Victoria.

'Better than nothing, I suppose,' said Nelly. 'Have a

word with Sister as you go out. She knows somewhere to stay around here. Won't break the bank either, I gather.'

Albert stood up.

'Well, I hope you'll go on all right.'

'I suppose I ought to say "thank you for coming", but to tell the truth, Albert, I'm blowed if I know why you did. Still, who knows, I might pop back to Thrush Green for a bit of convalescence. How'd you like that? We had some good times now and again after all, didn't we?'

She giggled as she reached for the paper.

Albert wondered if he should kiss her goodbye, but decided that the circumstances did not warrant it. He raised his hand in farewell, and set off down the ward.

At the end he looked back. Nelly was already immersed in the paper.

'Mrs Desmond sometimes obliges,' the nurse had said, and had directed him some quarter of a mile from the hospital gates.

It was already beginning to get overcast, and the tall Victorian house looked particularly gloomy.

He mounted the steps and rang the bell. A buxom woman with grey curly hair opened the door.

'The hospital people –' began Albert.

'Ah! You're looking for a bed for the night. Come in!'

Albert followed her into a bleak hall with black and white tiles on the floor. A massive fern in a brass pot dominated the scene.

Mrs Desmond mounted the stairs and Albert followed in her wake. The carpet was thick and the banisters shining. A strong smell of furniture polish pervaded the place. It was apparent that the owner was house-proud.

'I keep two bedrooms ready for people like yourself,' said Mrs Desmond. 'The hospital works in with me. I don't do meals, except breakfast, and that's Continental.'

Albert wondered if that meant frogs' legs or any other French nonsense.

'But there's a fish and chip shop down the road, or if you want anything rather classier for supper there's a "Little Chef" nearer the sea front. Here's the room.'

She opened a door and stood back for Albert to enter. The room was sparsely furnished, but the linoleum on the floor, and the brass handles on the dressing table, gleamed with daily care.

A gas fire stood in the hearth, its rows of little skulls awaiting ignition. Mrs Desmond waved towards it.

'It takes tenpenny pieces if you want some heat.'

I bet it does, thought Albert grimly. But the bed looked comfortable, and he was dropping with fatigue.

'How much?' he said shortly.

'Seven pounds, for bed and breakfast. Continental, as I said.'

'What's that mean?'

'Tea-or-coffee-rolls-and-butter-and-marmalade,' recited Mrs Desmond. 'And now if you'll excuse me I must go down to the kitchen. I've a piece of bacon on the boil. Are you staying?'

'Yes, please,' replied Albert.

'It's easier if you pay now,' said his new landlady. 'Then you're free to go any time in the morning.'

Albert took out a greasy wallet and extracted seven one pound notes. It seemed a monstrous sum to him. Mrs Desmond took it and stuffed it into her cardigan pocket.

'We lock the front door at eleven-thirty sharp,' she said. 'Give me a call if you need anything. The water's hot if you want a wash.'

She vanished along the landing, and Albert sank down in the wicker chair and contemplated the miniature Golgotha of the gas fire.

Seven pounds! What a day! It seemed to have gone on for ever. And what good had been done? Dam' all, as far as he could see. Sheer waste of time and money, and as like as not Nelly might turn up again at Thrush Green. One tiff with Charlie could easily send her back to her lawful wedded husband. The thought was too horrific to face.

Albert shivered. A few drops of rain spattered at the window, and the room was cold and dark.

A box of matches stood on the mantel shelf and Albert turned the gas tap. There was a welcome hissing noise. The fire popped into life as he applied the light, and the rows of skulls glowed with welcome heat.

Obviously, someone else's tenpenny piece had not run out.

It was the brightest spot of Albert's day.

Later he went out in search of a meal. The fish and chip shop was crowded with young people in studded leather coats, with here and there a head-band or earrings. The deafening noise from a juke-box was a further deterrent for Albert.

The 'Little Chef' was infinitely superior. There were even some flowers on the tables, and the girls were young and pretty.

Albert demolished a plate of bacon and eggs, with baked beans and tomatoes, and a crusty roll to mop up the liquid. He sat back to enjoy a large cup of strong tea with four spoonfuls of sugar in it. Life certainly appeared brighter. His purse was lighter, but he remembered that Molly and Ben had given him two fivers as well as paying his fare. One way and another, he'd be all right.

He wandered back to Mrs Desmond's by way of the sea front, and paused to lean on the sea wall. He had never been over-fond of the sea. Too wet and cold and restless. And too much of it anyway. Give him some nice fields and woods, any day, all round him, not half the view taken up with this heaving monster.

He stayed there for some time until he found his eyes were closing of their own accord.

He roused himself, threaded his way through the streets to Mrs Desmond's, had a perfunctory wash in the corner basin, and undressed.

He clambered into the spotless bed. It creaked alarmingly, but Albert did not care.

Within five minutes he was deep in the sleep of the utterly exhausted.

Nelly's gibe about the Misses Lovelocks' complete ignorance of love was far from the mark.

They had been attractive young women in their time, and the straight-cut boyish fashions of the twenties had suited their sparse figures very well.

Ada and Bertha were some years older than Violet, but all played tennis together at their own home in Lulling High Street, or at friends' and neighbours'.

Justin Venables and his brothers, Dotty Harmer and her brother, had been some of their contemporaries and tennis partners. Ada had been engaged for some months to Justin's elder brother, but he had gone to India and met someone else. The engagement was broken off, but there was soon another admirer to take his place, although marriage, yet again, evaded Ada.

Violet was easily the prettiest of the sisters in their youth. She may not have had the same deadly back-hand of her sister Ada, or the smashing volley of her sister Bertha, but her eyelashes were definitely longer, her hair curlier and her legs more shapely than her sisters!

It was she who nurtured a secret passion for Kit Armitage, then unattached and at his most handsome. The two elder sisters were inclined to be derogatory about her affection.

'Don't throw yourself at him so blatantly,' said Ada primly. 'No man wants to be pursued. You only make yourself cheap.'

'He won't thank you for making him look silly in front of the others,' added Bertha. 'If he wants to be more friendly then he will make the running.'

Violet said little, but privately thought that Ada and Bertha were prompted by feelings of jealousy rather than

sisterly concern. Kit Armitage was easily the most glamor-
ous of their circle, and long after he had left England and
then found a wife abroad, Violet kept a warm place for
him in her heart.

His reappearance had stirred her affections into life
again. True, they were both old people now, but was it
not possible, thought Violet, that they might find a great
deal in common? Kit was now a widower. Might he not
be in need of an understanding companion, much his
age?

She was careful to conceal these slender hopes from her
two sisters, but with memories of Violet's earlier infatua-
tion the older two ladies were on their guard.

However, all agreed that such an old friend should be
welcomed again to Lulling, and much thought went into
the best way to entertain him.

'A tea-party seems rather *feminine*,' announced Ada, 'and
I don't think we are up to a formal dinner party, what with
cleaning all the silver, and getting Mrs Fox in for the
evening to wait at table.'

'Besides the expense,' pointed out Bertha.

'Besides the expense,' agreed Ada.

Violet held her tongue.

'So it boils down to lunch,' said Ada. 'I suggest we ask
Justin and his wife, now he has retired, and Winnie
Bailey.'

'It makes rather a monstrous regiment of women,' protested Bertha, 'with the three of us.'

Ada considered the problem.

'Well, I really can't think of any unattached men whom
we could invite. Men are so thoughtless in the way they
die before their poor wives. For every widower or bachelor
in Thrush Green and Lulling there must be half a dozen
lone women. It really is trying!'

Violet now ventured to speak.

'He won't expect us to have even numbers. After all, he
knows our circumstances. If Justin and Lily are here to

keep us all company, I think it will make a very nice little
party. And you know that six fit very comfortably round
our dining room table.'

Her sisters looked at her with approbation.

'You are quite right, dear. Let's leave it at six, and I'll
send out invitations today. We might think of an easy meal
to serve too. Cold, do you think?'

'Definitely cold,' said Bertha. 'And people can help
themselves. Salad, of course, though lettuces are a terrible
price at the moment.'

'We have our home-made green tomato chutney,' replied
Ada brightening, 'and those spiced pears are perfectly
good if we lift off the mildew at the top.'

'We should have baked potatoes then,' said Violet, assert-
ing herself. 'And soup first. It looks more welcoming, and
our dining room can be very cold, as you know.'

'As you wish, dear,' said Ada with some hauteur.
'Frankly, I see no need for a *feast*, but if you like to make
yourself responsible for the soup course and give an eye to

the baked potatoes in the second, I see no reason to object. Gentlemen do seem to need more than we do.'

'Then I think we should have a fruit tart for pudding,' went on Violet, encouraged by her success. 'A hot apple tart is always popular.'

'I thought of doing one of my cold shapes,' put in Bertha. 'Made with some of our bottled gooseberries it could be quite acceptable.'

'We'll have that as well,' said Violet firmly. 'We shall need a choice.'

Her two sisters exchanged glances. Was Violet going to be silly all over again? And at her age?

Flinging caution to the winds, Violet entered the fray again.

'And we must order some cream,' she added. Ada and Bertha drew in their breath sharply. The expense!

'*Double* cream!' added their renegade sister, pink and reckless.

What was the world coming to?

9   Dotty Harmer Has Visitors

THE INHABITANTS OF Thrush Green awoke on May the first to a morning of such pearly beauty that they remembered, with a lift of the heart, that the loveliest of months had begun.

But there were some among them whose exhilaration was tempered with a certain sadness. These were the people who remembered, with poignant clarity, that May the first, for many years, meant the excitement of old Mrs Curdle's famous fair.

Ben Curdle, her grandson, had particular cause to recall it as he cycled by the green to work on that glistening morning.

It was he who had been forced to sell the business a few years earlier and to leave the nomadic life, which he had always known, for a settled existence at Thrush Green with Molly and the two children.

He did not regret the change. It was a decision which had to be made. The fair was running down after Mrs Curdle's death, beaten by more sophisticated pleasures such as television and bingo.

Ben knew that he was fortunate to sell when he did. The price had been a good one. Molly was glad to be near her father, miserable old curmudgeon that he was, thought Ben privately, and young George Curdle had settled well at Thrush Green village school. The Youngs were the kindest of landlords, and Ben enjoyed the work he had found as a mechanic in the local firm of agricultural engineers.

Nevertheless, as he mounted his bicycle that May morning he felt a pang of nostalgia. He remembered the clopping of hoofs as the old horse-drawn caravan had threaded its way through the deep lanes of southern England. He recalled the thrill of finding satin-skinned mushrooms in the dewy grass, and the smell of them cooking with bacon on Gran's minute stove. He could hear now the small intimate sounds of early morning, the birdsong, the snuffle of the horse at its nosebag, the rattle of the frying pan. Later, the noises would turn to the clamour of the fair; men shouting, swingboats creaking, the raucous music from the roundabouts and the shrill cries of excited children.

And through it all, running like a linking theme through this orchestration, was the low and sometimes harsh voice of his beloved grandmother. She had been a despot, a benevolent one to Ben, but not to any of her employees who shirked hard work.

She was on duty every hour, and expected the same unswerving loyalty from all who travelled with her. It was one of the qualities which had given Curdle's Fair its name for complete reliability. If the Fair was due to arrive on a certain date, then without fail it would be there. Ben could remember floods, breakdowns to the waggons, sudden illnesses and once, between High Wycombe and Marlow, a wicked storm which had sent a jagged fork of lightning upon one man, Jem Murphy, who was leading his frightened horse, and who had to be taken to hospital suffering from shock and burns.

Even so, the Fair had arrived punctually at its next destination, Ben remembered with pride.

Ah! It had been a good life, and a good training for a boy! Old Gran had taught him right from wrong and had set him standards of behaviour which were now standing him in good stead. He could only hope that he could pass on those standards to his own children.

He took a deep breath of fresh morning air, and pedalled energetically towards his work.

No good looking back, he told himself. Times changed, and perhaps for the better. He would buy Molly a box of chocolates on his way home to celebrate the first of May. She would understand.

An hour or two later Winnie Bailey and Jenny, her friend and maid, were recalling Mrs Curdle and the Fair.

'To tell you the truth, Jenny,' said Winnie, busily rolling out pastry at the kitchen table, 'I was about to throw out those bunches of artificial flowers that have been gathering dust on the top shelf of the landing cupboard, but I couldn't bring myself to do it.'

'I should hope not,' replied Jenny. 'Why, Mrs Curdle made them with her own hands! And I bet if you put them in the dustbin George Fry'd pick 'em out and return them to you. He'd know, as a dustman, just where everything came from. You wouldn't get rid of Mrs Curdle's flowers as easy as that!'

'I think I should have burned them,' confessed Winnie. 'They're made of fine wood-shavings, you know. But it wasn't that which held me back. It was just that I remembered how dear old Mrs Curdle looked when she handed over a new bunch every first of May. They'll just have to stay there, I'm afraid. But I wonder what the person will think when he or she comes to clear up this house when I'm gone!'

'No sense in talking like that,' said Jenny sturdily. She mopped the draining board briskly. 'You've years ahead of you yet.'

'I hope so. Especially when it's a morning like this. We'll get our little jobs done quickly today, Jenny, and make sure we get out in the sunshine. I'm going to take some magazines to Miss Harmer this afternoon.'

'Well, I wouldn't stop to tea,' advised Jenny. 'I hear she's taken to making her own bread.'

'Thank you for warning me,' said Winnie.

Winnie Bailey was not the only one making for Dotty Harmer's house near Lulling Woods.

Stepping briskly up the hill to Thrush Green was Kit Armitage, a carrier bag swinging in his hand. He was some ten minutes behind Dr Bailey's widow, and admired, as she so recently had done, the gauzy green of the young leaves in the avenue on Thrush Green, and the pyramids of tight lilac buds to be seen in the gardens.

A robin accompanied him along the path leading from the green to the fields where Dotty's cottage lay snugly embedded. The bird bobbed ahead of him on the dry stone wall, bowing and chirruping. Was he trying to distract his attention from some nearby nest, Kit wondered?

It was good to have this little companion. Kit admired the smooth plumage, the flaming breast, the bead-bright eyes. He, or perhaps she, thought Kit, as somewhere he remembered reading that male and female looked alike, was a fine specimen, and he fell to wondering if a clutch of small pink-spotted eggs was hidden nearby, and hoped that all would turn into splendid replicas of the bird before him.

Dotty's cottage came in sight. He appreciated the way that the grey thatched roof faded into the folds of land around it. Dotty's garden was extensive, and it was adjoined by a paddock of almost two acres. No wonder Dotty in her time had been able to give her love of animals full scope. Ponies, donkeys, goats, pigs and sheep had at one time or another had the paddock as their home, and a small pond at the end of the garden had been a playground for endless generations of ducks and geese.

Nowadays the pond was used by only ten or so ducks. Dulcie, the goat, lived in solitary splendour in the paddock, and had the sturdy goat-house for her sole use. Not that she often deigned to sleep inside. Dulcie preferred the roof of the shed even in snowy weather. She was just as contrary as any other of her species.

A small pebble had found its way into Kit's shoe, and he was obliged to lean against the stone wall and unlace his shoe. Standing there, on one leg, he surveyed Dotty's little estate with an admiring eye.

There was no doubt about it, the house and its acre or two made a very pretty picture. It was what estate agents would call 'a desirable property'. It was remarkably quiet tucked away from Thrush Green, and yet had an entrance on to a side road which led into Lulling and villages further west.

There was a small orchard near the house, just beginning to come into leaf. Soon, Kit surmised, there would be a pink and white froth of blossom to add to the general enchantment.

As he watched, a figure emerged from the door, carrying a bright orange plastic bowl. Although Kit could not see them, he heard the frenzied squawking of hens hurrying towards their meal.

He recognized the figure as his newfound friend Connie, and obviously she was giving the hens an early supper. Perhaps she was going out later, he thought, bending down to lace his shoe. Surely hens were fed about dusk?

Not that he was an expert on such matters, he was the first to admit.

But he hoped suddenly that Connie was expecting to go out. Much as he admired dear crazy old Dotty, he was sorry for this gallant niece who seemed to have very little fun, but who never complained of the lack of it. From the few times he had met her, Connie appeared to him to be completely selfless, and yet at the same time refreshingly free from the solemnity which so often accompanied that saint-like quality.

He liked her laughter, her strong sense of the ridiculous. He liked her gentleness with her odd charge. He liked the way she appreciated the books and records he lent her, and he was sure that those in the carrier bag, now resting on a fine clump of coltsfoot by the wall, would be enthusiastically welcomed.

Altogether, he thought, stamping his foot to make sure the shoe was as it should be, he just liked Connie.

He strode along the path, happy to think that he would be in her company for the next hour or so.

Albert Piggott, upstairs in his bedroom, had noted the passing of Winnie Bailey and then Kit Armitage along the lane that ran beside his cottage.

He was in the act of trying to fit a piece of cardboard into one of the window-panes. A sudden gust of wind had wrenched the window from its shaky fastening one night, and one pane had shattered.

Albert was getting tired of the moaning noise and the fearful draught when he was abed, and at last had decided to do something about it. By rights, he should inform the rector who would see that a proper glazier did the job, and the church would pay the bill, for Albert's cottage was church property.

'But by the time I've been all through that rigmarole,' grumbled Albert to his cronies at The Two Pheasants, 'I'd be down with the pneumonia, and in me grave, dug with me own hands, I don't doubt.'

'Won't hurt you to patch it up,' said the landlord heartlessly. 'See you all right for a bit until the rector can find a proper man for the job.'

'You saying I'm not a proper man?' queried Albert nastily. 'I can keep my place up together as well as the next.'

'Well, it don't look like it did when your Nelly was there,' asserted Mr Jones, unrepentant.

Albert had choked into his beer mug at the mention of his wife's name, and had departed very soon afterwards.

'Proper touchy, old Albert,' said one man to another. 'Don't dare mention his Nelly, that's for sure.'

It was immediately following this conversation that Albert had started his repair work. Now, cardboard still in hand, he crossed the small landing to the back bedroom, now unused, to follow the progress of the travellers towards Lulling Woods.

'Ah!' said Albert to the cat which had followed him upstairs. 'Off to see old Dotty, I'll be bound. I wish 'em joy of her tea table if they stay that long.'

He stood for a few moments watching the scene, and then returned to his own bedroom which looked out upon St Andrew's church. It was there that he and Nelly had wed, worse luck!

A tremor shook him as he thought of the awful possibility of his wife returning. What was the position, he wondered? If she'd left him of her own free will then surely he would not be obliged to have her back? He supposed that, in the eyes of the law, he was still married to the wicked old besom, for that's what she was, he told himself, edging the cardboard gingerly over the damaged glass.

If only it did not cost good money he would go to one of those solicitor fellows like Justin Venables and ask for advice. But then he might suggest a divorce, and though it would be nice to be free again, there'd be the hell of a lot of gossip about it at The Two Pheasants, and the rector might give him a talking-to and tell him to forgive and forget and all that stuff.

Women were kittle-kattle, thought Albert morosely, giving a sharp tap to an awkward corner. A man was better off without them. He wanted no more truck with Nelly, and if she was so bold as to come to Thrush Green again he'd run her out of town, that he would!

Emboldened by this sudden blaze of spirit he gave the cardboard a last shove. There was a sickening crack, and a moment later, the distant tinkle of shattered glass hitting the pavement. At the same time, the cardboard buckled and fell inward upon the grimy bedroom floor.

A stiff breeze blew into the room stirring the net curtains.

'Lord love us!' shouted Albert. 'It's enough to drive a man barmy!'

He stumbled towards the stairs, the cat fleeing from his wrath before him.

He wrenched open the front door, and nearly fell over a diminutive figure about to post a note about the school jumble sale through the letter box. One of Miss Fogerty's more trustworthy pupils gazed at Albert with round blue eyes.

'Mr Piggott, sir! Your top window's bin and fell out,' he announced importantly.

Albert's reply was terse and to the point. When the small boy repeated it to his mother, later that day, he was sent into the scullery to wash out his mouth at the sink, poor child.

At Dotty's cottage the two visitors were prevailed upon to stay to tea.

Kit had accepted the invitation with alacrity. Winnie had begun to demur, Jenny's warnings still in mind.

As if she read her thoughts, Connie said: 'It's all very simple. Just some scones I've just taken out of the oven, and a pot of honey that Dimity gave me.'

'I can't resist hot scones and honey,' said Winnie, settling back in her chair.

She turned to Dotty.

'And are you eating well now? I expect Connie plies you with all sorts of goodies.'

'I've a better appetite now that I can get into the garden,' said Dotty. 'There are some beautiful young nettles in the paddock that I should cook if I could get there, but Connie says the spinach from the freezer has more vitamins, so we had that today.'

'Is that the stuff Popeye the Sailor-man used to eat in our youth?' asked Kit. 'He was welcome, from the look of it.'

Connie laughed.

'Very strengthening, you know. But tell me all the news from your end of Lulling. How are Charles and Dimity?'

'Working too hard as usual, and Charles is still worrying about those confounded kneelers. Some battle-axe –' he stopped suddenly. 'Not a friend of yours, I hope? I'm still putting my foot in it, forgetting how everyone is related in these parts.'

'If you mean Frances Thurgood,' replied Connie with spirit, 'I don't think she has many friends. Not in this house anyway. Aunt Dotty can't bear her ever since she caught her putting poison down by her garage. She said she had rats, but Aunt Dotty ticked her off about other animals picking up the stuff, and there was a right royal battle.'

'How did Dotty come across this scene?'

'She'd been invited to lunch, I gather, but after telling Frances what she thought of her, she stumped off. There's a lot of her father in Dotty, you know.'

'A very strong character,' agreed Kit, looking across the room at the two women engaged in animated chatter. 'You don't find her too demanding?' he asked diffidently.

'I can't deny that she can be very self-willed,' replied Connie, in a low voice, 'but she is very dear to me, and I'd never leave her. We get on well, and I think she realizes that she must have someone at hand, and she would rather have me than anyone else. It's a very pleasant place to live in.'

'I just wondered if you would ever be free to come out with me one evening? I know Charles and Dimity want to ask you too, but to be frank, they asked me to see how you were placed with Dotty-sitters.'

'Betty Bell has obliged, as they say, and although I hesitate to do it too often, I should love to have an evening off some time.'

'Then we'll arrange it,' said Kit cheerfully, and followed his hostess into the kitchen to help her by carrying in the tea things.

Later that night, Lulling Woods and the surrounding fields lay silvered under a full moon.

Connie, in bed, was happily tired. It was good to look forward to a change of scene in the company of kindly Kit Armitage. Aunt Dotty had enjoyed her impromptu tea party, and she felt all the better for the company.

She plumped up her pillow, turned on her side, and was asleep in five minutes.

Next door, Dotty lay awake, but she too was content with her day. It was strange, she thought, surveying her bony hands spread out on the moon-lit quilt, how pleasant life was even though her movements were so restricted.

If anyone had told her a year ago, that she would not be able to walk much farther than the length of her garden, she would have been shocked to the core. But now that it had happened she found that there were compensations.

She studied her small confines with more attention to pleasurable detail. Only this morning she had enjoyed looking at the thrum-eyed and pin-eyed primroses beneath the hedge. She had noted the tight buds of the lilac and the stiff green spears of the iris leaves.

The comings and goings of the garden birds meant more to her now than the flocks of lapwings and rooks which she used to watch on her travels farther afield. The antics of a bumble bee at the window engaged her attention as sharply as Flossie's chasing across Thrush Green had in earlier days.

And there was as much joy to be had from the surprise visit of two old friends, as from all the dozens one used to meet at social gatherings. One had much to be thankful for, thought Dotty.

There was no doubt about it. God tempered the wind to the shorn lamb, as her old father would say. And despite the lack of Mrs Curdle's Fair, she thought inconsequently, it had been a good first of May.

She pulled the bed clothes around her bony shoulders, and went contentedly to sleep.

CHARLES HENSTOCK'S suspicions that the redoubtable Mrs Thurgood would return to her onslaught
on the Lady Chapel kneelers were well-founded.

He had seen very little of the lady for several weeks, and
had noted the empty pew with some misgivings. Had she
taken umbrage and left his church? If so, which one was
she now attending? And had he failed in his duty towards
this parishioner?

His questions were answered when he heard that Mrs
Thurgood and her artistic daughter were enjoying a tour
of Italy, 'taking in,' as one of his congregation put it,
'Rome, Florence and Venice.' It sounded rather indigestible
to Charles who preferred his culture in book form whilst
sitting peacefully in his study.

Nevertheless, he was relieved to hear that the lady had
not swept in dudgeon from St John's for ever. Perhaps she
would return from her travels with a more informed sense
of beauty, and would realize that the kneelers looked very
well as they were in their ancient setting.

On the other hand, thought Charles with a pang of
alarm, the daughter might have decided to copy some
hangings of the Doge or the Borgias and was already
returning with a folio of designs ready sketched out on
graph paper.

Charles chided himself at this point. He was letting Mrs

Thurgood dominate his thoughts, and all to no good. It was no use allowing his imagination to run away with him. No doubt, she would return much refreshed, and in a more amenable state of mind. He resolved to do nothing until Mrs Thurgood raised the matter herself. After all, he and Dimity had given time and attention to the problem, and he knew he was on firm ground.

But these kindly and rational notions were swept away one sunny May afternoon, when the rector was alone in the vestry checking one of the church registers in response to an overseas correspondent who had asked for details of his grandparents' marriage.

It was the sort of job that Charles enjoyed, and he was happily turning the pages at the vestry table, when he became conscious of voices.

Two women were obviously visiting the church and were now in the Lady Chapel. Charles decided to let them continue their tour while he went on with his investigations. If their visit was protracted he proposed to emerge and welcome them, showing them some of the more unusual features of his beautiful church.

But suddenly, the voices became much clearer.

'I shan't leave it at that, you know,' said one woman stoutly. 'You can see for yourself the state they're in. It would never have done for dear Anthony.'

With horror, Charles realized that his adversary was back. Should he declare himself, or hope that they would soon go away?

Before he had time to make a decision, the younger woman spoke.

'You're quite right, mother. But then what can you expect from this Henstock fellow? No idea of how to run things.'

'I agree. No standards at all. A vulgar little man, and a wife to match. Just take a look at this one, dear. Very badly frayed.'

Charles Henstock closed the register, coughed loudly,

and made his way past the organ into the Lady Chapel. To be called 'a vulgar little man' did not upset him. But to hear his adored Dimity spoken of in such scathing terms was more than he could bear.

Nevertheless, his demeanour was calm as he confronted the two women.

Apart from a sharp indrawn breath from Mrs Thurgood, and a certain reddening of her daughter Janet's complexion, the ladies appeared free from any guilty reactions.

'We are just back from Italy,' announced Mrs Thurgood, 'and we are going through the kneelers again. What neglect! The sooner they are replaced the better.'

'Dimity and I spent a good deal of time inspecting them too,' said Charles gently. 'We put aside some half-dozen which we thought needed repair.'

'*Repair*?' boomed Mrs Thurgood. 'They need more than *repair*! This church has never been the same since dear Mr Bull left us. And I said as much when I wrote to the Bishop.'

'I know,' replied Charles. 'I saw the letter.'

At that, even Mrs Thurgood's boldness wavered, but she contented herself with a snort of disgust.

'I don't intend to discuss the matter now in this holy place,' Charles pointed out, 'but if you and Miss Thurgood –'

'Mizz,' broke in Janet. 'I prefer to be known as Mizz, spelled M and S.'

'I beg your pardon?'

'Capital M, small S,' explained Janet.

'Oh!' said the rector, now enlightened, 'like "*manuscript*".'

'Not in the least like "*manuscript*",' exclaimed Mrs Thurgood. 'But to get back to the point.'

'I was about to say,' said Charles, 'that it would be a good idea to step across to the vicarage to discuss this matter. I have a few papers to put together in the vestry, and then I hope you will accompany me there.'

'Have we time, mother?' asked the manuscript.

'Yes, indeed,' said Mrs Thurgood firmly. 'This is something of outstanding importance.'

Within ten minutes, the three were closeted in Charles's study, and the battle began.

Charles, the kindest of men, nevertheless had a streak of steel in him. When his duty had to be done, nothing could make him shirk it.

There were many parishioners who, having mistaken Charles's gentleness for weakness, could remember the shock they had received on facing their rector's uncompromising attitude to wrong-doing. That pink chubby face and kindly smile hid the strongest sense of right and wrong, and when it came to the point Charles feared no man on a matter of principle.

He sat behind his desk, a crucifix on the wall behind him, a beautiful silver and ivory present from Harold and Isobel Shoosmith to replace the one lost in the Thrush

Green fire. The Thurgood ladies sat before him on wooden upright chairs of a somewhat penitential pattern, although to Charles, a man of simple tastes, they seemed perfectly suitable for his study.

'Please let me know what worries you, Mrs Thurgood,' began Charles. 'I thought that we had already settled this affair of the kneelers.'

'You know quite well we haven't,' replied Mrs Thurgood forthrightly. 'I take it as an insult, a rebuff, a slap in the face –'

'What is?' interjected the rector.

'This turning down of my offer to bear the expense of replacing the kneelers.'

'We are not unmindful of your generosity,' said Charles, 'but my wife and I, and the Bishop too, see no reason for a wholesale replacement. As I said, a few need mending, but the others will last for several years. We should all be deeply grateful if you could undertake the repair work, but we do not want to see you put to needless expense.'

'Humph!' snorted the lady, 'I'm willing to face the expense, and I certainly don't think it "*needless*". The fact is, Mr Henstock, the church is being run down. The singing leaves much to be desired, the vestments are shabby, the flowers are not arranged with a quarter of the skill that Mrs Bull brought to the job, and the services are *distinctly low*! I tremble to think what dear Anthony Bull would think should he ever return.'

'I have always had the highest regard for my predecessor,' answered Charles equably. 'He was a devout and conscientious churchman, but his ways were different from mine. I am the first to recognize it. Nevertheless, I am, I trust, equally devout, and attentive to my parochial duties, and the Bishop, I am glad to say, approves of my conduct.'

'You are going to lose your congregation, believe me,' warned Mrs Thurgood. 'There is a great deal of gossip and discontent. Am I to understand then, that you refuse to let me replace the kneelers?'

'That is so. It is quite unnecessary.'

Mrs Thurgood arose and her daugher followed suit.

'Then in that case, sir, we have no alternative but to leave your company and your church.'

She swept towards the door, and Charles was only just in time to open it for her. He accompanied the two ladies to the front door in silence, bowed them out politely, and returned to his study.

He went to the window and took a deep breath of scented air. Tabitha, the cat, was sprawled on her back in the border, comfortably flattening some pinks and warming her stomach in the sunshine.

'I suppose one could say that the powers of evil won that skirmish,' he said, addressing the cat, 'but somehow I feel that right has triumphed, in the whole battle.'

The Misses Lovelocks' lunch party in honour of Kit Armitage took place a few days after Charles Henstock's confrontation with the Thurgood ladies.

Preparations had been lengthy and heart-searching. Violet, still determined to provide something rather better than the usual fare found at the house, had been studying half a dozen recipes for asparagus soup with considerable anxiety. The asparagus bed was already sprouting well in the shelter of the garden wall, and Violet examined it daily.

As she had rashly suggested a fruit tart as well as the 'cold shape' which her sisters considered obligatory at any luncheon, she also had to look out some bottled plums and make some pastry. She had secretly wondered if she could buy some ready-made frozen pastry, and use it while her sisters were out of the kitchen, but even Violet's stout heart quailed at the thought of being discovered in such deceit. She must just do the best she could, she told herself, and if it happened to get a little overdone, as her pastry sometimes did, she would shake plenty of caster sugar over it and put up with Ada's rebukes.

The main course was the one which gave the ladies the most concern.

'Pork is out,' announced Bertha. 'Justin simply can't digest it, I know for a fact.'

'Pork is not in season anyway,' Ada said loftily. 'Not the right thing for a summer luncheon at all.'

'What about chicken?' said Violet.

'One seems to have chicken whenever one goes out to lunch,' observed Bertha.

'Because everyone likes it,' said Violet. 'It's light and easily digested.'

'And cheap,' added Bertha thoughtfully.

'Yes indeed,' said Ada brightening. 'It's certainly cheaper than most meat.'

The three ladies pondered over this happy attribute of chicken in silence. It appealed strongly.

'And it is extremely tasty when cold,' said Ada. 'Shall we slice it in the kitchen and let people help themselves?'

Violet, still strong in her intention to do right by Kit Armitage, was emboldened to say:

'I think we should have *two* chickens, or else a nice piece of cold gammon to go with it.'

Ada and Bertha exchanged glances. What was Violet coming to? It really seemed as if she were as infatuated as she had been all those years ago. What else could have driven her to suggest such unnecessary lavishness? *Two* chickens indeed!

'The men can have a leg apiece,' said Ada brusquely.

'They'll want breast as well,' argued Violet obstinately. 'And they may need second helpings.'

'*Second helpings?*' echoed Bertha, aghast at the thought.

'Men get hungry,' said Violet, sticking to her guns. 'And in any case, we can eat up anything left for the rest of the week.'

'But *two* chickens!' exclaimed Ada. 'I really don't know –'

'And the carcases will make excellent stock,' persisted Violet.

Silence fell again upon the agitated ladies. It was Ada who broke it at last.

'Perhaps a piece of gammon might be a good idea,' she conceded eventually. 'It always looks so pink and pretty garnished with parsley. Yes, *one* chicken, not more than three pounds in weight, should do us all very well if there is boiled bacon to supplement it.'

'Collar or fore-quarter,' said Bertha, 'is much cheaper, you know.'

'Gammon cuts *much* more economically,' Violet put in swiftly.

And there the matter rested.

Kit Armitage, his old friends Mr and Mrs Venables and the three Lovelock sisters fitted very comfortably round the old ladies' beautiful dining table.

In a way it was a pity, thought Justin, who knew a good deal about antique furniture, that its beauty was hidden by an exquisitely laundered damask tablecloth, but his hostesses were of the generation which gave much attention to the drapery of tables, and he had to admit that the pristine whiteness showed up the sparkling glass and old silver very satisfactorily.

Thanks to Violet's persistence the meal was unusually generous by Lovelock standards, and everyone tucked in heartily.

The conversation turned to affairs at Thrush Green and, in particular, to Kit's difficulty in finding suitable property to buy.

'I should really prefer to be high up,' he said. 'Somewhere around Thrush Green would suit me very well, and I'm getting a little bored at The Fleece, kind though they are.'

'You know you can always come back to us,' said Justin.

'Yes, indeed,' echoed his wife valiantly, trying to ignore the unworthy thoughts of extra catering, bed-making, and general entertaining which loomed darkly.

'You've done more than your share for the wanderer,' said Kit, 'and very grateful I am, as you know.'

'What about Mrs Bassett's house?' suggested Ada. 'Has she decided yet to go to Ruth's?'

'I know Joan and Edward are waiting to hear,' said Violet. 'And then, I believe, they propose to offer it to the young Curdles.'

Kit turned to her.

'I'm so glad you told me, because I was wondering if I dare approach them about it, and it might have been awkward for them. Now I shall keep quiet.'

His smile made Violet's heart turn over. It was good to think she had helped him.

'Won't you have another helping of plum tart?' she asked.

'Yes, please. It's quite the best tart I've tasted for years,' he told her. And Violet's happiness was complete.

At the other side of the table Bertha leant across.

'Have you tried Mrs Jenner? The Henstocks had a flat there when the rectory burnt down. It's along the Nidden road. Very light and airy, but you'd have to do for yourself, of course.'

'I believe Charles mentioned it, but there was someone in it at that time. Still, many thanks for the idea. I'll follow it up.'

'Cousins of mine,' said Justin, 'have a mill house farther up the Pleshey, but it has six bedrooms and several outhouses and is horribly damp. They are selling.'

'I don't blame them,' replied Kit, smiling. 'But I think six bedrooms are more than I need.'

'I know poor Isobel Shoosmith scoured the area for months looking for a little place,' put in Ada. 'In the end she married dear Harold, so that solved her problems.'

'Well, I hope mine will be as happily resolved,' said Kit. 'Now, who knows anything about these old people's homes which are going up at Thrush Green? I heard that Edward's plan was successful, and the builders have made a start.'

'I should put your name down for one,' observed Justin. 'You can't start too early for that sort of thing.'

A week passed before Kit decided to call at Mrs Jenner's. Connie had told him that she was pretty sure that her flat was now free. A service couple on leave had had it last, some distant cousins of Mrs Jenner's, so Connie had heard.

Charles and Dimity were enthusiastic about the idea, recalling with pleasure their happy few months there. He heard too, in the roundabout way of all village communication, that Mrs Bassett was now definitely going to make her home with her younger daughter Ruth, the wife of Doctor Lovell, and that Molly and Ben Curdle were to move into the stable house as soon as it had been redecorated.

It seemed to Kit, as he walked along the road to Nidden, that summer had really arrived. A heat haze hung over the valley where Lulling drowsed in the afternoon sunshine. He paused to look down the pathway which led to Connie and Dotty's house, and caught a glimpse of the buttercup-filled meadow which surrounded their garden.

The hawthorn hedge, which bordered the dusty lane, bristled with fresh red sprigs and was laced with sticky young goosegrass clambering up it from the ditch below. A number of black and white cows were clustered by a farm gate and surveyed him pensively from black eyes beneath a fringe of eyelashes. Their jaws worked rhythmically as they chewed the cud, and Kit thought how soporific it all was, the slow movements, the gentle heat on one's back, the fragrance of bruised grass and the distant hills veiled in a blue haze.

For two pins he would have settled himself under a hedge, and had a snooze, but he dismissed the temptation and went dutifully onward.

He found the house, a pleasant square Georgian building which had once been a farmhouse, and knocked at the door. A red admiral butterfly opened and shut its wings on the path beside him, and everywhere was very quiet.

He began to wonder if anyone were at home, or if perhaps he should have gone round to the back door, when he heard sounds within and Mrs Jenner stood before him with a middle-aged man beside her.

'Mrs Jenner? I'm Kit Armitage. The rector suggested you might be able to help me.'

'Please come in,' said Mrs Jenner.

'Well, I'll be off,' said the man.

'Please don't hurry away on my behalf,' began Kit.

'I was just off anyway,' said the man. He waved a general farewell and made for the gate.

'I hope I didn't interrupt,' said Kit, following his hostess into the hall.

'My brother,' explained Mrs Jenner. 'He farms next door. Percy Hodge. Perhaps you've heard of him?'

'I think maybe the rector may have mentioned him.'

'He's going through a bad time at the moment,' confided Mrs Jenner, leading the way upstairs. 'His wife is giving him trouble.'

'I'm sorry to hear that,' said Kit, surprised at such confidences from a stranger.

'Second wife, you know. Not a patch on the first. And a bit flighty between you and me.'

She threw open the door of the main room upstairs, and Kit, like the Henstocks before him, felt a glow of pleasure. Sun streamed through the large sash windows. The fruit trees were in bud below, and the scent of late narcissi from clumps in the orchard wafted about the room.

'What a lovely room!' exclaimed Kit.

'It is nice,' agreed Mrs Jenner equably. 'Gets all the sun that's going. Come and see the bedrooms. One is quite big, next to this room, and there's a smaller one at the back.'

She showed Kit everywhere, even opening cupboards and drawers. Everything shone and Kit wondered if he would ever be able to keep the place in the apple-pie order now before him.

In the kitchen he made a confession.

'I'm not much of a hand at cooking, I'm afraid, Mrs Jenner. I've lived abroad a great deal and been rather spoilt in that direction.'

Mrs Jenner surveyed him kindly and then smiled.

'I could cook you something most evenings, if you like,' she offered. 'Wouldn't be anything special, you understand, and not on Tuesdays or Thursdays when I go to Choral and Bingo, but we could come to some arrangement, I feel sure.'

Kit, much touched, began to thank her. But she cut him short.

'Any friend of the Henstocks is a friend of mine, Mr Armitage. That man is a born saint, and I've just been telling Perce to go and have a talk with him about his married troubles.'

Poor Charles, thought Kit. Still, no doubt he was accustomed to such problems.

'Well,' he began diffidently, 'if you'll have me, Mrs Jenner?'

'With all the pleasure in the world,' said his new landlady.

As the weeks passed, and high summer embraced Lulling and Thrush Green, Albert Piggott's fears of the return of his Nelly grew less painful.

He regretted the journey to see her. It had been a complete waste of time and money, in his opinion, and it looked as though that confounded Charlie Wright still reigned supreme in his wife's fickle heart.

She must have been out of hospital for weeks now, he told himself with some relief, and that silly threat of hers to spend her convalescence at Thrush Green could safely be ignored.

In fact, Albert was living in a fool's paradise, and things were far from harmonious at Nelly's present address.

It was true that the lady had recovered with remarkable rapidity from the operation, although the surgeon had been quite ferocious about Nelly's superfluous fat and had practically ordered her to lose three stones in weight as soon as she had come round from the anaesthetic. He gave her to understand that it was only his consummate skill which had enabled him to get to the vital parts on this occasion.

Nelly, too weak to argue, agreed to take home a diet sheet which she had no intention of reading, and there the matter rested.

Charlie had called regularly at the hospital, and Nelly had looked forward eagerly to returning home. She could hardly wait to get back to a bed without a horrible piece of plastic sheeting over the mattress, and to some windows which she could have open all night instead of enduring the enveloping hot stuffiness of the ward throughout the hours of darkness.

Charlie took her home and she went straight to bed. In the days that followed, she got up for a few hours and enjoyed cooking Charlie's evening meal and cleaning the house again.

In the midst of her relief at being at large again, she hardly noticed that Charlie was somewhat subdued.

He came home later than usual too, and one evening smelt strongly of chypre perfume. It was a cloying scent that Nelly had always disliked, being an eau-de-Cologne woman herself, and she was alert at once. However, she had the sense to say nothing.

When Charlie had driven to work the next day in his oil van, Nelly began a systematic search through Charlie's drawers and the small desk where he kept his papers. She found nothing, but the smell of the chypre was faintly on the air when she came to the wardrobe.

Only Charlie's clothes hung there. Nelly had appropriated the bedroom cupboard on her arrival, and had little occasion to open the wardrobe. When she did, on this day, she went swiftly through all the pockets, and found a crumpled note in the jacket of his best blue serge suit. It said:

'Will be at the usual 6.30. If you can't make it, give the Grand a ring. 2946.

Best love –
Gladys'

Nelly knew at once who was this correspondent. Gladys and her husband Norman were a couple who lived on the other side of town and whom they met frequently at various pubs where small, but incredibly noisy, bands played, and the customers joined in hearty singing which grew louder as the air grew bluer with cigarette smoke and dubious stories.

It came back to Nelly now, that chypre was the perfume which always engulfed Gladys. Her mouth grew grim as she folded the note and put it into her handbag as evidence of Charlie's misdoings.

Strangely enough, although she was angry at this deceit, she felt sorrier for Norman than she did for herself. He was a poor fool, she had always thought, no match for his boisterous wife with her thick lipstick and over-blacked eye-lashes. Still, despite being something of an old stick, Nelly had found him very polite and always thoughtful for his wife's welfare. It was a rotten trick to play on poor old Norman, to carry on with Charlie like this.

Not that she imagined that Gladys was solely to blame. Nelly knew her Charlie's winning ways all too well. Six of one and half a dozen of the other, she told herself, whirling furiously about the house with a duster.

She would tackle him the minute he had finished the plate of bacon and liver prepared for him. No point in wasting that. Food was important to Nelly. And as soon as he'd apologised properly she would let him understand that it was never to occur again. She would leave it to him to inform Gladys that all was off. And naturally, there could be no more convivial evenings at the pub with that pair. No, forgive and forget would be the best way to tackle this problem, she decided, but Charlie must eat humble pie first.

The possibility of any other reaction on Charlie's part did not occur to Nelly, strangely enough. It was all the more shocking that evening when the note was smoothed out beside Charlie's empty plate, and Nelly stood, arms akimbo, awaiting his apologies and explanations.

'Oh, tumbled to it at last, have you?' said Charlie, grinning maddeningly. 'Well, now you know, what are you going to do about it?'

Nelly's wrath rose.

'It's what *you* are going to do about it that matters! You can tell that Jezebel to clear off pronto.'

'And suppose I don't intend to?'

'Then you can do without me.'

'Too right I can,' responded Charlie with spirit. 'I reckon I took you in when you'd fallen out with that misery Albert, and now it's time you went back.'

Nelly was flabbergasted. For two minutes she stood there, the superfluous fat so denigrated by her surgeon, quivering with rage and shock. Things were not turning out at all well. She decided to change her tactics.

'And what if I tell Norman what's going on behind his back?'

'You needn't try. He knows all right, and he won't stand in Gladys's way.'

'But what about me?' Nelly wailed, becoming tearful. 'What about all I've done for you, looking after this place, and cooking meal after meal? Haven't you got a shred of decent feeling left?'

'Now look here,' said Charlie pushing her down into a chair and facing her across the table. 'Let's get this straight. You came here of your own accord. Well, I was sorry for you, and let you come. Now it's my turn to want a change. Gladys is coming here any day now, so you've got notice to quit.'

'But where shall I go?' cried Nelly, now sobbing noisily. 'You know I haven't got no money, and there's no one round here I know well enough to take me in.'

'Look, girl! You've got Albert. He's still your husband. You may not get on like a house on fire, but my advice to you is to go back, and try and make a go of it this time. I warn you, there's no room for you here now. Gladys and I are going to marry as soon as we can. Norman's agreeable – well, perhaps *agreeable* ain't the right word – but he says it suits him.'

At this, Nelly put her head down upon the table by the greasy liver-and-bacon plate, and howled alarmingly.

Charlie, a kindly man at heart, patted the massive heaving shoulders comfortingly.

'Oh, come on! Don't take on so! You knew it wouldn't last. You go and have a good wash and go to bed early. You'll feel better then, and I'll bring you a nice cup of tea in bed. How's that?'

After some minutes, Nelly rose, snuffling heavily, and made her way to the bathroom. She was speechless with shock at the way things had turned out, and numbed with misery.

True to his word, Charlie brought in a cup of tea. He was wearing his outdoor jacket.

'I'm off to Gladys's. See you first thing before I go off to work.'

'Oh Charlie!' wailed Nelly, the tears beginning again.

'Cheer up,' said her faithless lover. 'I'll give you a hand with your packing tomorrow.'

And he vanished before Nelly had time no answer.

Nelly was not alone in her matrimonial troubles. Percy Hodge was equally unhappy. His second wife, Doris, who had seemed the ideal companion when he had wooed her at The Drovers' Arms at Lulling Woods, had changed considerably after becoming his wife.

He thought of his dear Gertie, now dead some three years. What a hand with pastry! What a manager on the five pounds a week he had allowed her for housekeeping! How he missed her.

Well, they said: 'Marry in haste and repent at leisure.' Not that he had rushed into this second marriage. He had courted Mrs Bailey's Jenny long enough before approaching Doris, but she'd refused him. Strange, thought Percy, straightening his back from hoeing between the rows of peas. You would have thought she would have been pleased to exchange domestic service for married bliss, and after all, he was still an attractive chap, he believed, otherwise why had Doris snatched at his offer?

Women were odd creatures. The smell of pastry burning floated from the back door. His Doris was no hand at cooking, that was a fact. When he thought of the meals that Gertie used to cook, and the stuff that his present wife put before him, he grieved afresh. If only he had been able to persuade Jenny to share his hearth and home!

There was no doubt about it. Marriage to Doris had been a sore mistake. Without the company of The Drovers' Arms crowd, she had grown peevish. Occasionally, she took herself off to Bingo with his sister Mrs Jenner, but that was only because she was pressed to go.

There were constant rows, mainly about money. As Percy told her often enough, Gertie had managed for years on five pounds a week, and he did not see why Doris could be the same. Farmers weren't made of money, he had said only that morning.

And what answer had he had? A stream of abuse which had shocked him. She must have picked up such language from The Drovers' Arms. Not from Ted and Bessie Allen, who had run it for years now, but there were some pretty rough types that came into the public bar of an evening and were too free with their expressions. Percy had been forced to walk out of the kitchen in the face of such a verbal assault.

The thing was what to do about it all? They couldn't go on like this. Let's face it, he had tried time and time again to make the woman see reason, but she simply enjoyed being awkward. Why, she'd even asked for a *private allowance*! Percy shuddered at the very remembrance.

When he had pointed out the rank impossibility of such a measure, she had said that, in that case, she proposed to look for work and if it were far from Thrush Green that would suit her very well.

On that belligerent note the two had parted. Percy had gone into the garden and Doris had set about the pastry with such ferocity that Percy foresaw an even tougher meal than ever ahead.

Ah well, he sighed! Time alone would tell how things would work out. If only it had been Jenny in his kitchen!

Someone had said those two words 'If only' were the saddest in the language.

Percy, resting on his hoe, agreed wholeheartedly.

Little Agnes Fogerty was sitting in a deckchair in the garden of the school house, relishing the warmth of the June sunshine.

School was over, and Dorothy Watson was in the kitchen preparing their simple tea, which they proposed to have outdoors.

Miss Fogerty was looking forward to her cup of tea and one biscuit, with more than usual relish. She was on a strict diet, and quite frankly, she felt all the worse for it.

Loyal though she was to dear Doctor Lovell, she could not help feeling that it was a pity he ever went on that course about the Place of Diet in Arthritis and Allied Diseases. He had talked of nothing else since his return, and those of his patients who had creaked and hobbled about Thrush Green for years, were now enduring a most uncomfortable time.

All meat was banned, all white bread, and sugar of any colour whatsoever. Anything made with flour was out, and dairy products were forbidden.

'It doesn't leave much,' Miss Fogerty had protested, but was quickly told about the advantages of fruit and vegetables, on which, it appeared, she would have to exist for the foreseeable future.

'Boiled water only for the first two days,' John Lovell had said, his eyes alight with a fanatical gleam. 'Then citrus fruits for three days, and after that perhaps a small apple. Then we can get you on to vegetables, particularly pulses. Pulses are absolutely essential to counteract any acid in the system.'

'But I shall be absolutely bursting with acid if I'm on citrus fruit for days,' exclaimed Agnes. 'I really cannot take

lemon juice or grapefruit in any quantity. Even oranges upset me.'

Doctor Lovell, in the thrall of his latest obsession, hardly listened. Consequently, poor Agnes had braved the boiled water for two days and was now struggling through the three devoted to citrus fruits. Frankly, she was starving, and dizzy with weakness.

Doctor Lovell was going to be forgotten while she drank a cup of tea, complete with forbidden milk, and munched the digestive biscuit which Dorothy had insisted she should eat.

'I should take that diet of John Lovell's with a pinch of salt,' she said, arriving with the tea tray, and setting it down on a stool between them.

'Salt's forbidden,' said Agnes.

'What isn't?' replied Dorothy tartly, pouring the tea.

'How marvellous that smells,' said little Miss Fogerty. Her small stomach gave a thunderous rumble, as she reached for her cup and the tempting biscuit.

'It should taste even better than it smells,' Dorothy assured her with a smile.

'"Forbidden fruits are sweet,"' quoted Agnes.

'I wouldn't mind betting,' said Dorothy, 'that John Lovell is settling down to buttered toast and doughnuts at this very minute.'

'Oh *don't*!' begged Agnes in anguish.

And Dorothy apologised.

Charles Henstock was also in his garden on that warm June day.

The grounds of Lulling vicarage were extensive, and by tradition had always been opened for any parish activity.

They were not as immaculate these days as they had been when Anthony Bull and his wife had employed a man full time to keep the place aglow with flowers and the lawns velvety smooth.

The same man came now, but Caleb was getting old, and he only attended to the garden on one day a week.

He combined this work with his job as sexton to St John's, and on the whole did his chores very well if rather slowly. Charles and he were fond of each other, and Caleb found his new master far less demanding than the old one.

They were working together on a long border when Charles heard the wrought-iron gate clang and saw his old friend Harold Shoosmith from Thrush Green approaching.

'Harold!' cried the rector, dusting his palms down the side of his trousers. 'How good to see you! Come and sit down in the shade.'

They retired to a garden seat under the ancient cedar tree.

Harold waved to Caleb in the distance.

'Am I interrupting anything?'

'No, no. We were just tidying up. Caleb's having a bonfire this evening in the churchyard, and we thought our little bits could go on it.'

'This is bliss,' said Harold leaning back. 'Wish my news were too.'

'Oh dear!' said Charles. 'Trouble in Thrush Green?'

He thought sadly that really he had enough of that commodity in Lulling alone, let alone his other three parishes. Mrs Thurgood and her daughter had never appeared again in his church, and one or two other ladies seem to have taken her part, and were not attending St John's. Could he be failing in his duties? He was most unhappy about it.

'Well, I think you should know that the Hodges are pretty acrimonious, and as far as I can see there's going to be a break-up in that marriage.'

'I do hope not,' said the rector alarmed. 'Percy will keep harking back to his first wife. I told him, at the time, he must look ahead not backward. I don't think that poor little Doris has had a chance.'

'Poor little Doris,' Harold observed, 'is somewhat of a virago.' He had knocked about the world rather more than the good rector, and was well acquainted with the diversity of human nature.

'Really? I've always found her a nice little thing.'

'She probably is with you. She's not with Percy.'

'I'll try to have a word with them. Separately, I think.'

'A good idea. They ought to be able to make a go of it. Otherwise I foresee that he'll be badgering Jenny again.'

'But he's *married* now!' cried the rector.

'Infidelity has been known,' pointed out his friend. 'Not that Jenny would encourage him, but on the other hand why should she be pestered?'

'Quite. I will try and call on Percy in the next day or two.'

He watched Caleb wheel the barrow towards the church-yard. It was very peaceful under the tree. A bee investigated a clover flower which had escaped the mower, and a thrush ran about the border with an eye cocked for any passing worm.

' "And only man is vile," ' sighed the rector.

'It does seem so, on a day like this,' agreed Harold.

'And how's dear Isobel?'

'Shopping. I'm picking her up in a quarter of an hour outside The Fuchsia Bush. Oh, and there's another thing, I should mention.'

'And what's that?'

'Nelly Piggott's back.'

'Oh no! Not again!' cried Charles. 'Whatever will Albert say?'

'I shouldn't enquire,' advised Harold. 'I hear he's absolutely furious, but she's refusing to go, and if it comes to a physical battle I'd back Nelly any day. Weight alone would settle that.'

Charles shook his head sadly.

'Another call to make, I can see.'

The two men sat in silence for, a few minutes, but the peace was soon broken by the return of Caleb, hurrying towards them.

'Sir! Come quick, sir! Someone's been at the poor box. It's all smashed in, and not a penny to be seen.'

'My God!' said Harold. 'We'd better get the police. Shall I ring them for you?

'Please do,' said Charles. 'I'll go over to the church with Caleb to see if anything else has been touched.'

And the two friends hurried in opposite directions.

That evening Dimity looked across at Charles who lay with his eyes closed in the armchair.

'Do you know, my dear, it is the longest day today?'

'I'm not at all surprised,' said Charles.

12   A Question Of Housing

KIT ARMITAGE, happily settled at Mrs Jenner's, was still searching vainly for a suitable house of his own.

He realized that his present conditions were so pleasant that he was in danger of giving up the search altogether. It was good to have no responsibilities except such minor ones as getting his hair cut, paying his bills and cooking his own breakfast.

He had time to wander about the summer countryside looking up old friends. His Thrush Green neighbours were ever welcoming, and he called often upon Dotty and Connie.

He was on his way there one afternoon when he saw Edward Young looking over the old people's homes which were being constructed to his specification.

Kit walked over to talk to him.

'How is it going?'

'With any luck, we'll have them ready by Christmas,' responded Edward. 'What do you think of them?'

He smiled fondly at the muddle of planks, bricks, cement-mixers, wheelbarrows, drain-pipes and bulging sacks which littered the site. To Kit's untutored eye it simply looked an unholy mess.

'How many homes will there be?' he asked, playing for safety.

'Eight in all. Five along this south-facing aspect, and three at right angles. You can see by the footings.'

Kit tried to look appreciative.

'Later, of course, we may add three or four more, changing this L shape to an open E, so to speak.'

'Ah, yes,' replied Kit, nodding sagely.

'But that all depends on the money, of course. It really does look splendid, doesn't it? Such an improvement on that awful rectory. My blood pressure went up every time I looked at it. Now we shall be able to look out on these eight little one-storey poppets.'

He smiled fondly upon the chaos surrounding him, and Kit envied him the inward eye which transformed this muddle into a vista of domestic beauty.

'Got your name down for one?' asked Edward jocularly.

'I'm seriously thinking of it,' replied Kit. 'I'm not getting much farther with my efforts.'

'I'd forget them for a bit,' advised his friend, stepping over a squashed bucket as he accompanied Kit to the safety of Thrush Green's grass. 'Go and have a break somewhere.'

'As a matter of fact,' Kit told him, 'I may well do that. An old school friend has invited me to a spell of fishing, and I'm sorely tempted.'

'An excellent idea! This weather's too good to waste on duties.'

He waved goodbye, and Kit noticed that he returned to his own duties with the greatest enthusiasm.

Connie agreed with Edward when Kit told her later.

'Something will turn up, probably when you are least expecting it,' she told him. 'Go and enjoy this break. It sounds just what you need, and you know you can always come back to Mrs Jenner. I gather you are her star lodger to date.'

'She's certainly my star landlady,' said Kit. 'Well, I'll look forward to seeing you both on my return.'

'Those Armitages were always charming,' said Dotty, when Kit had departed. 'His mother was a raving beauty. Such a pity the boy doesn't take after her.'

'I think Kit is very handsome himself,' said Connie defensively.

Dotty looked at her with unusual shrewdness.

'Yes, you probably do, dear. They say that beauty is in the eye of the beholder. And as a *young* man he was very much sought after. Those Lovelock girls made a dead set at him, and Justin's wife would have had him if he would have had her, if you follow me, but he was not keen – anyone could see that – and so she settled for Justin. A nice fellow, but very much second-best, we all thought.'

Connie did not reply. She could hardly imagine Dotty and the Lovelocks and the Venables as young people, and in any case, they all seemed so very much *older* than dear Kit.

The phrase 'dear Kit' echoed in her mind, and she was honest enough to admit now that he was indeed, in her own estimation, very much 'dear Kit'.

She checked her thoughts sharply. This would not do. She had dear old Aunt Dotty to think about, and that was quite enough to engage her attention at the moment.

Some two or three days later Connie and the faithful Flossie met Ella Bembridge on Thrush Green. Both women were going to post letters at the box on the corner near Tullivers, and Connie was carrying the milk can.

'Glad I've seen you,' hailed Ella. 'I've got a glut of early lettuces and was about to bring you some and save you a journey with the milk. Have you got a minute to spare?'

'I've got plenty of minutes to spare,' smiled Connie. 'Life at Thrush Green is delightfully leisurely, I find.'

They walked back to Ella's snug cottage to collect the lettuces. A fine row of tight little Tom Thumb variety stood ready to be picked. Connie voiced her admiration.

'Best sort to grow,' Ella told her, moving along the row, and puffing as she bent double to her task.

'Quick growing, and all heart. That's how I like 'em,
nice and crisp. And not too big for a woman alone like me.
Five do you?'

She straightened up, the pale green rosettes clutched
together in her two hands.

'Can you spare all those?' said Connie. 'Really two
would be ample.'

'Take 'em! Take 'em!' replied Ella, stuffing them in the
girl's arms. 'You might get somebody calling in at supper
time. Kit Armitage, say.'

Connie was a little taken aback at this assumption that
Kit was a regular visitor, and was stumped for words.

'I forgot,' went on Ella, 'he's just gone off to Wales to
fish with the Olivers. Have you met them? They come up
here occasionally to see the Lovelocks.'

'No, I don't know them. I've heard Kit mention Peter
Oliver but I haven't met his wife.'

'He hasn't got one. It's his sister he lives with – or rather she's living with Peter since her husband died. Pretty woman. She'll be married again before she can turn round, you mark my words.'

She led the way to the garden seat, and began to roll one of her untidy cigarettes. Connie sat nursing the lapful of lettuces, and Flossie settled with a sigh, in the shade.

'We all thought she might be tempted by Kit Armitage. I gather she was a gorgeous looking girl in her youth. A proper raving beauty.'

'So was Kit's mother, I gather from Aunt Dotty.'

'Yes, I believe she was, but I never knew her, of course. Thrush Green seems to produce quite a few raving beauties. Perhaps Kit's gone down to see if she's just as attractive.'

Ella puffed away blissfully. Connie felt suddenly irritated, and longed to be on her own.

'Well, I must get back,' she said, rising briskly. 'Many thanks for the lettuces. I know Aunt Dotty will be delighted.'

She set off for the gate, and Ella accompanied her. Flossie straggled behind, disappointed at the brevity of her rest.

'Give her my love,' called Ella to Connie's departing back. Really, the girl walked at an enormous pace!

Connie, unusually disturbed, made her way swiftly past Albert's cottage and gained the comfort of the lonely lane.

'To my mind,' she told the lagging Flossie, 'there are far too many raving beauties connected with Thrush Green. And alas, I'm not one of them!'

Nelly Piggott, busy scrubbing Albert's badly stained wooden draining board with hot soda water, watched Connie as she passed the window.

'Dotty's niece,' she told the cat, 'and single what's more. Some women have all the luck!'

She paused for a moment from her labours, and sat down on a kitchen chair to get back her breath. Say what you like about doctors, thought Nelly, they may do a good job on one bit of you, but that anaesthetic and the stitches and whatnot fair played up the rest of you. She felt as weak as a baby these days.

Albert was out. He was over in St Andrew's, supposed to be tidying up, but Nelly guessed correctly that he was simply keeping out of her way. Give him his due he'd behaved remarkably well considering the shock she had given him on her return.

The house had been empty when she had arrived in the early evening, and Albert was next door at The Two Pheasants.

Swiftly she had unpacked, putting her things in the spare bedroom, and making up the bed with the deplorable linen from the landing cupboard, before Albert's return.

Downstairs she washed up the mounds of dirty crockery and cooking pans, and put some pork sausages in the frying pan over a low heat. Who knows? Their fragrance might mitigate her husband's fury. To tell the truth, Nelly was remarkably apprehensive about this meeting. If Albert took it into his head to push her out and lock the door, there was little she could do.

She had a few pounds in her purse, and that was all, hardly enough to give her a bed for the night and certainly not enough to keep her going for a week. Her heart jumped when she heard Albert at the door, but she stood and faced him steadily in the last rays of the evening sun.

It was quite apparent that he was fuddled with drink.

'What you doin' 'ere?' he growled, his speech slurred.

Nelly decided to speak the truth.

'I've left Charlie. He don't want me any more.'

'Don't blame 'im,' said Alert, making unsteadily towards a chair. 'Can't say I want you neither.'

Nelly advanced towards the sausages and turned up the heat. She began stabbing the sausages with a fork, and they hissed cheerfully.

She was very near to tears. It had been a long day, and

she was exhausted with travelling, worry, and the after-effects of her operation.

'Just cooked us a bit of supper,' she said. 'I know you like sausages, and I've had nothing all day.'

She was surprised at Albert's lack of response. She had fully expected a stream of abuse, and perhaps physical violence. This moody sulkiness was unexpected. She did not know if it boded ill or good.

The fact was that Albert was too dazed with drink to take it all in. He was also ravenously hungry, he realized, and the thought of pork sausages, cooked to a turn by Nelly, had a mellowing effect.

They ate them at the kitchen table. Little conversation passed between them until Albert had mopped the grease from his plate with a crust of bread, and then leant back to survey his wife.

'You ain't stoppin' you know,' he told her. 'Sausages or no sausages.'

'Just tonight,' pleaded Nelly. 'I'm all in, and that's the truth. Let's talk about it in the morning. I've made up the bed in the back room.'

'So I should hope,' said Albert nastily.

Nelly packed the dirty dishes in the sink and filled them with water.

'I'll do those in the morning,' she said wearily. 'I'm off to bed now, Albert.'

'And don't *snore*,' shouted Albert after her, as she mounted the stairs.

Ever since then an uneasy truce had been the order of the day.

Nelly had remained subdued, conscious that she was at Thrush Green on sufferance. She cleaned the house from top to bottom, cooked for the two of them, and took gentle walks in the neighbourhood mainly to keep out of Albert's way.

He, for his part, was secretly relieved to have his meals

cooked and his house cleaned. As long as Nelly behaved with her present politeness he was prepared to let her stay.

Of course, he put a good front on his attitude when teased by his cronies in The Two Pheasants.

'Let her try any of her old tricks,' he told them, 'and she knows she's shown the door. But she's been in hospital and I'm not one to turn an invalid out, as well you know.'

His listeners certainly knew him well, and guessed correctly that the present state of affairs suited Albert nicely. No one in Thrush Green thought otherwise, and many went so far as to say that he was a lucky man to have his wife back.

Betty Bell was the most outspoken.

'I don't know how that Nelly Piggott can face coming back to that pig-hole of a place! She must've been hard up to come to stay with Albert. He's in clover, all right. Lovely smell of stew as I passed. Keeping him sweet, I suppose. How she can!'

'Well,' said Harold Shoosmith, putting down his cup, 'I suppose it's best for them both. Perhaps they'll make a go of it this time. I've always rather liked Nelly Piggott.'

'Good heavens!' exclaimed Isobel. 'Why?'

'I rather admire plump women,' smiled Harold, looking at his wife's slim figure.

'I'll do my best to put on a stone,' she told him.

Across the green, Winnie Bailey discussed the matter with Jenny.

'D'you think it will last?'

'It might this time,' answered Jenny. 'They're both that much older, and neither of 'em too well. If Nelly got a job, they might settle down quite comfortably together. But she'd need to get out of that house for part of the day, and earn some money of her own.'

'You've been giving it some thought,' observed Winnie.

'Well, to tell the truth, I've been thinking about Doris and Percy. She's in such a state she's threatening to leave him. I met her in Lulling yesterday and we walked back together.'

'Does she want a job?'

'Not really. I think if Percy was a chap who went out to work regular, like Ben Curdle, and wasn't just a farmer in and out of the house and under your feet all day, she'd settle all right. I told her to get something herself, and have a change of surroundings, but there's not a lot of work going, as you know.'

'What about Ted and Bessie Allen at The Drovers' Arms? She seemed to enjoy her time there.'

'She told me she'd asked them, but they're well suited and I think they're a bit chary of coming between husband and wife. It would be all over Thrush Green and Lulling if they took sides, wouldn't it?'

And Winnie Bailey agreed.

Dimity Henstock was walking from Lulling vicarage to St John's while Winnie and Jenny were happily discussing Doris Hodge's affairs.

She carried a trug filled with roses, pinks and peonies having offered to arrange the flowers whilst several of the regular flower ladies of the church were disporting themselves on holiday.

The sun was warm. The church clock showed her that she had plenty of time to spare. Lunch was cold today, and she succumbed to the silent welcome of a garden seat placed in the shelter of the south side of the church.

She placed the basket under the seat, in the shade, and prepared to enjoy her solitude.

Not that one felt alone in a churchyard, she told herself. She had never understood the feeling of fear which so many people confessed to about churchyards. After all, one was so often among old friends who were at rest beneath their grassy mounds.

She read the inscriptions near at hand. 'Eulalia Phipps', for instance. Now there was a name to enchant one! And it was good to know that she had been a devoted wife and loving mother to her nine sorrowing children.

Close by was Amos Enderby enclosed in iron railings and with the top of his tomb a little askew. He had been a Justice of the Peace, a Benefactor to the Town and a Much Respected Citizen. He had died of a Seizure at the age of forty-eight to the Great Distress of his Family and Friends.

The only sad thing, Dimity mused, was the thought of all the talents buried in Lulling's earth. Over there, was the grave of Lucy Bennet whom she well remembered as a superb needlewoman and cook. Her grandchildren had always been exquisitely dressed in handmade frocks with intricate smocking, topped by knitted cardigans made by their loving grandmother.

And nearby was Tom Carter who had been renowned for his skill in layering a hedge. While close beside him rested his old friend Dick who had been a fine cabinet maker. His work stood in many a Lulling home as a reminder of his craftmanship.

What a wealth of skills lay buried here, thought Dimity. She feared that her own accomplishments were small in comparison. She was really no hand at flower-arranging, for instance, when she thought of the expertise of the local Guild of Flower Ladies.

Reminded of her duties, she pulled out the trug and made her way towards the cool shadows of the church.

Perhaps, though, she comforted herself, she might be remembered, if not as a loving mother of nine children, then surely as a devoted wife?

Taking heart, she set off to collect suitable vases for her modest arrangements.

On the next Sunday Charles Henstock celebrated Holy Communion at eight o'clock at his old church in Thrush Green.

The attendance was small, but this was usual. Most people came to matins at ten-thirty, and only a few of the faithful came to the eight o'clock service. Isobel and Harold were among them, and Charles went back with them to the corner house for a cup of coffee.

'I can't tell you how relieved I am to hear that Albert and his wife seem to have settled down again together. I very much dislike having to interfere in domestic matters, as you know.'

'Early days yet,' commented Harold, 'but we're all keeping our fingers crossed. I don't think Percy Hodge is faring so well though.'

'Oh dear,' said Charles, setting down his cup. 'I'm sorry to hear that. I haven't called, partly because I rather shirked it, and also because that old saying "Least said, soonest mended" is often quite right.'

'We heard yesterday that Doris has gone to stay with a sister. Of course, it may be just a genuine visit, but the old boys at The Two Pheasants reckon she's gone for good.'

'You shouldn't listen to gossip,' declared Isobel. 'And you know how things get exaggerated, especially after a pint or two.'

'It might be a good thing,' said Charles thoughtfully, 'if Doris has this little break. She may come back in a happier state of mind.'

'You were always an optimist, Charles,' smiled Harold. 'Have some more coffee while it's hot.'

13   A Job At The Fuchsia Bush

O<small>N</small> W<small>EDNESDAYS</small> Lulling was at its busiest. It was market day, and people from the surrounding villages joined the local residents in their hunt for bargains.

For many people it was the only day of the week when a local bus ran. There were threats too of even that meagre service being abandoned, and for those without cars it was a bleak outlook.

Lulling market is set up early each Wednesday morning hard by the ancient Butter Cross where a miniature square gives room for a number of stalls. As the market has grown over the centuries, a few stalls have been allowed to straggle up the road towards St John's church, and the pens where sheep used to be kept have been moved to a quieter place near the Corn Exchange, making more space for stall holders.

Traffic congestion on market day is quite a problem, and the prudent driver leaves his car in one of the many public house car parks or in the new car park situated behind The Fuchsia Bush in the High Street. Woe betide those foolish enough to park near the market square! Joe Higgins, the local traffic warden, has an eye like a hawk, and enjoys nothing more than slapping a ticket on a windscreen in the course of his duties.

Local people had always found it worth their while to

visit the weekly market. The produce was always fresh, and there were all sorts of choice things to be found, particularly on the Women's Institute stall where home-made cakes, jams and honey, stood beside trays of fresh brown eggs and baskets of apples and plums. Such rare treasures as yellow quinces, field mushrooms or a green-house melon can be found at the appropriate season, cheek by jowl with more homely fare such as crisp cabbages and great marrows striped like tigers.

Some of the stalls sported gay canvas awnings, yellow, green and red, greatly adding to the colourful scene. Some-times an old lady, with dozens of balloons for sale, sat on a chair at the corner nearest to the Butter Cross. The fat balloons of every possible shape and colour, bobbed above her grey head, tugging at their strings as the wind caught them and squeaking as they rubbed against each other. Naturally, she was the magnet for hordes of children, and it was an exhilarating sight on 'Balloon Lady's Day' to see single balloons bobbing along the High Street, clutched in young hands, or tied to the handles of prams or bicycles.

The public houses did brisk business on market days. As well as extra beer and spirits there were many more dishes to choose from on a Wednesday menu, and trade flourished. Here old friends met to exchange news or to do business, and most people returned home from the market at Lulling with heavy baskets and, even more satisfying, a store of news and gossip to keep them happy until the next week.

Ever since Charles and Dimity had gone to live at Lulling, Ella and her old friend met on a Wednesday at The Fuchsia Bush to enjoy a cup of coffee after their marketing. Sometimes they encountered each other at the Women's Institute stall, for Dimity had a standing order for a dozen brown eggs, and Ella always made a bee-line there to buy any particular item that took her fancy before the stall was sold out.

On this particular Wednesday Ella was at The Fuchsia Bush first and managed to find a corner table near the doors to the kitchen.

It was not her favourite spot. She much preferred to be near the window where one could see the life of Lulling passing by. However, on a Wednesday the place was crowded, and she was lucky to get a table at all, as well she knew.

She had just unearthed her cigarette-making equipment when Dimity appeared, much encumbered by a large basket and an armful of single summer chrysanthemums.

'What a crush!' she said, depositing her burdens on the floor. 'I couldn't resist these chrysanths. Such a delicate pink.'

'Very pretty,' agreed Ella, putting away the battered tobacco tin, 'but I don't like to see them as early as this. Makes me think of autumn, and that comes soon enough these days.'

'Have you ordered?'

'Well, no. No one's been along yet. The service gets worse in this dump. I reckon we'd do better at The Fleece.'

'Oh, Ella,' cried Dimity, rather agitated, 'I really don't think Charles would like me to be seen frequenting The Fleece.'

'Why on earth not? It's a perfectly respectable hotel, and in any case we should only order coffee, shouldn't we?'

'Yes, I know all about that, but I'm old-fashioned enough to *mind* about women going to pubs alone.'

'You wouldn't be,' pointed out her friend, 'I'd be there.'

Dimity tut-tutted with exasperation.

'You know what I mean. Without a man to escort her.'

'Probably be strong drink then,' commented Ella. 'Ah! Here's Mrs Peters.'

The owner of The Fuchsia Bush, looking somewhat harassed, came to the table.

'I'm so sorry to keep you waiting. We've trouble in the kitchen, and we're short-handed.'

'I'm sorry to hear that,' said Dimity. 'Someone ill?'

'Just coffee, please, and some of your shortbread,' said Ella.

'No shortbread I'm sorry to say. Mrs Jefferson isn't here to make it.'

'Is she the one who is ill?'

'She fell down a flight of steps at a neighbour's house, and has broken a leg and two ribs.'

'The poor dear,' cried Dimity, genuinely distressed.

'Well, she would go and take some tea into this next door friend who was in bed with a new baby, and she couldn't see where she was going because of the tray, and down she tumbled.'

Mrs Peters spoke as though this was only what could be expected if one were so foolhardy as to minister to neighbours. There was definitely a note of censure in her remarks.

'So we're run off our feet, and I shall have to advertise for another cook while she's laid up. Meanwhile, we're struggling as best we can. Will digestive suit you?'

Taking this to mean that digestive biscuits were being offered instead of the usual delectable home-made shortbread, the ladies assented, and Mrs Peters bustled back to the kitchen.

'A broken leg,' mused Dimity.

'And two ribs,' added Ella. 'Not funny. A long job, I should think.'

'Weeks,' agreed Dimity. 'I must let Charles know. He will want to visit her.'

Ella took out a cigarette paper and began to fill it with tobacco. She rolled it thoughtfully, licked the edge and stuck it together. Dimity watched resignedly.

Ella lit up and then gave vent to her favourite phrase.

'Tell you what, Dim. What price that Nelly Piggott in the kitchen here? She's bored to tears I hear, and a first-rate cook. Shall I have a word with Mrs Peters now?'

Dimity smiled across the cloud of blue smoke.

'Why not?' she said.

That same evening, as soon as The Fuchsia Bush closed,

weary Mrs Peters climbed into her little car and turned its nose towards Thrush Green.

She had spent the day trying to deputise for the absent Mrs Jefferson, and at the same time attempting to galvanise her lethargic staff to greater efforts.

Really, thought Mrs Peters, it was much simpler to do the job oneself rather than urge such lumps as Rosa and Gloria to give a hand. Mrs Jefferson had been one of the old school, punctual, hard-working and taking a pride in all her kitchen creations.

The two women had much in common and had grown to admire and respect each other. Both were widows, and both had been obliged to work to bring up their children single-handed. They were equally energetic, willing to put in many hours of work, and both deplored the slackness of the younger generation.

Mrs Peters drove up the steep hill to Thrush Green, mourning the temporary loss of her old colleague. She did not know Nelly Piggott, as far as she could recall, but it was worth seeing her from what Miss Bembridge and Mrs Henstock had said, although she was not particularly hopeful.

She drew up outside Albert's cottage, much to the interest of the clients in The Two Pheasants who gazed unashamedly as she waited on the doorstep next door.

The step, she noticed, was freshly whitened, and the windows gleamed. It boded well, thought Mrs Peters.

The door opened and Nelly stood before her looking a little puzzled. As soon as she saw her Mrs Peters realized that this was the fat lady who at one time had attended the Misses Lovelock as a char, and whom she had seen passing The Fuchsia Bush. She remembered now that she *cleaned*, but did she *cook*? She only had the two ladies' word for it.

'I'm from The Fuchsia Bush,' began its owner. 'I wondered if you could help me. Miss Bembridge mentioned you to me this morning.'

'Come in,' said Nelly.

The kitchen shone as cleanly as the doorstep, noticed Mrs Peters with pleasure. She took the chair offered her, and put her gloves and handbag on the checked tablecloth. A bunch of pinks, in an old-fashioned earthenware honey pot, scented the air. Mrs Peters had not seen such a honey pot since she was a child, and felt a warm glow of nostalgia for such a homely vessel.

Albert was out at his church duties with his young assistant, and Nelly had obviously been knitting a jumper so vast it could only have been for herself. A delicious smell of cooking mingled with the scent from the pinks.

'You said something about help,' said Nelly, tidying away the knitting.

Mrs Peters told the sad tale of Mrs Jefferson, and Nelly listened attentively. Her spirits rose with the unfolding of the story, but she tried to hide her excitement. It all sounded too good to be true.

'Well, I've never done cooking for *numbers*, if you follow

me,' she said, 'and I always believe in having the very best ingredients. No substitutes or made-up stuff, I mean.'

'We only use the best at The Fuchsia Bush,' her prospective employer told her, with a touch of hauteur. 'I have my reputation to consider.'

'Oh, I only mentioned it,' replied Nelly hastily, 'because I occasionally cooked a meal for them Lovelocks, and the food wasn't what I've been used to at all.'

Mrs Peters unbent at once. The Misses Lovelocks' cuisine was a by-word in Lulling. Her heart warmed towards Nelly.

'I'm sure you would soon get the hang of coping with numbers,' she assured her, 'and of course I should be there to help you. It's mainly small cakes and biscuits, and at midday we offer a cold buffet or one hot dish, something simple like curried lamb and rice, or cottage pie. And there's always soup. We keep a very good stock pot.'

At the thought of a very good stock pot Nelly was quite won over. It would be lovely to play in a really properly equipped kitchen, instead of this poky little place of Albert's. And she would be free of him for best part of the day, and what's more earning some money of her own.

'What wages were you offering?' she asked.

Mrs Peters mentioned a sum which seemed extremely large and generous.

'Well, if you think I can do it,' said Nelly diffidently, 'I'm willing to try my hand with you.'

Something sizzled in the oven, and Nelly excused herself as she bent to open the oven door. A gust of delicious cooking odours blew into the room, reminding Mrs Peters how famished she was.

Nelly bore a magnificent pie to the end of the table where a wooden mat was waiting. The crust was golden brown and neatly indented round the edge. Four beautiful leaves splayed across the top, glossy with egg-yolk gilding. From the centre where the pie-funnel stood, came a little plume of fragrant steam. It was a vision of beauty. It was quite enough to convince that connoisseur of pies, Mrs Peters, that here was a mistress of her craft.

'Steak and kidney,' said Nelly. 'I like a bit of puff for that. Lighter than shortcrust, I always think, and my husband suffers with his stomach, so I have to be careful what I put in front of him. Personally, I enjoy making a nice raised pork pie, but it's too rich for him these days.'

'A raised pork pie,' echoed Mrs Peters, quite faint now with hunger. 'Perhaps you would like to make a really large one for the cold table when you come?'

'Nothing I'd enjoy more,' Nelly assured her. 'And when would you like me to start, ma'am?'

Now that she was engaged, Nelly started as she meant to go on, with due respect. Who knows? She might be taken on permanently if she proved satisfactory.

'You couldn't manage tomorrow, I suppose?' ventured Mrs Peters, her eyes still on the masterpiece before her.

'I'd just love to,' said Nelly sincerely, and stood up as her visitor rose.

'I'm so grateful,' said Mrs Peters. 'Tomorrow then at nine, or eight-thirty if you can manage it.'

'Eight-thirty, ma'am,' promised Nelly.

And with a last look of longing at Nelly's pie, Mrs Peters went to her car, her stomach rumbling protestingly at being denied its rights.

Within a few days the news of Nelly's new job had flashed round Thrush Green.

Nelly had told no one but Albert, who seemed to be little interested. When asked outright by the landlord of The Two Pheasants he admitted grudgingly that the news was correct.

'Give her something to do,' added Albert, 'and the money'll come in useful. Suits me to have a bit of time to meself.'

Certainly Albert's usual dour demeanour remained unchanged by Nelly's good fortune. The truth was that as long as his food was provided, and Nelly kept a civil tongue in her head, he was quite content to let things drift on as they had done since her return.

Dotty Harmer and Connie heard about it when they went to tea with Winnie Bailey one hot afternoon.

Connie took her aunt for a drive after her rest, and they trundled through nearby villages and enjoyed the leafy beauty of the country lanes. Honeysuckle scented the air, and a few late dog roses starred the hedges. The blackberry flowers, pale pinky-mauve, were prolific, and promised a bumper crop later on.

Dotty's spirits were high. She was enjoying her outing and looking forward to tea at Winnie's.

She rattled on in her usual inconsequent vein, and Connie, immersed in her own thoughts, hardly heard her, until she realized that her aunt was busily discussing the old people's homes being erected at Thrush Green.

'But, you see,' rambled Dotty, 'I don't think I should care to be on one floor. One really *should* go upstairs to bed, don't you agree? It's not only the *rightness* of mounting steps to one's bedroom, but the fact that *anyone* could look in as they passed on foot. Friends of my dear father's retired to a bungalow, and she had the most dreadful shock when she realized that the baker was looking in as she was standing in her stays. Very upsetting. She took to dressing in the bathroom, I remember, at least up to her petticoat, and as that was always Vedonis and lock-knit, it was *perfectly* respectable.'

'You're surely not considering applying for one of the houses?' queried Connie, slightly bewildered. A sudden thought struck her. 'You haven't already applied for one?' Dotty was quite capable of doing such a thing, Connie was well aware.

'Oh, no, no, no!' tutted Dotty. 'I shouldn't dream of it. As I was saying, I like to go *upstairs* to sleep, and in any case I have no intention of leaving my own dear house.'

'Thank heaven for that!' said Connie. She turned the car

in the direction of Thrush Green. They were in comfortable time for Winnie's tea party.

'I can't think why you thought I wanted to live in one of Edward Young's little places,' went on Dotty. 'Do you think I ought to apply? Are you finding me too much of a problem, Connie dear? I should hate to *exploit* you. Perhaps I do? Oh, dear, I should have realized I am very demanding. And of course the cottage is rather small. Only three bedrooms, and perhaps you find it *cramped* with us both in it? As you know, it will be yours one day, and if you feel like taking it over *now* instead of *later*, I should readily agree to any arrangements you might like to make –'

Dotty's voice had risen in her agitation, and she sounded slightly tearful. Connie drew in at a convenient field gate and switched off the engine. It was unthinkable to let poor old Dotty work herself into such a state. If she were not careful she would be arriving at Winnie's red-eyed and sniffing.

She turned to face the old lady and smiled at her.

'You've got it all wrong, Aunt Dot. The last thing I want is to turn you out of your home. You know that. You are *no bother at all* to me. Just the opposite. I love you dearly, and enjoy living with you. And I hope we'll have many years of life together. Now, is that better?'

Dotty took a long breath, and found a beautifully folded handkerchief in her pocket. She dabbed her eyes and returned it.

'That's all right then. As long as you are happy, dear, I am too. Did you notice the rather nice scent on my handkerchief? Winnie Bailey gave it to me last Christmas, and I thought it would be a gesture to use it today. And have you noticed, dear, in books and plays, that the heroine never seems to have a handkerchief *at all*, and is obliged to borrow one from the hero? I mean, who on earth ever goes out *without* a handkerchief? It's quite unthinkable. Although I once knew two sisters who *shared* one. At parties you heard them say to each other: "Have you got The Handkerchief?" So insanitary, we always thought. They were odd girls.'

Not the only ones, was Connie's private comment as they mounted the hill to Thrush Green. Dear old Dotty, she needed more attention daily, thought Connie indulgently, and she would make sure that she had it.

Winnie Bailey apologised for it being what she called 'a hen party' in her drawing room. Ella Bembridge and Dimity Henstock were there and Phyllida Hurst from Tullivers next door.

'You wouldn't have kept Frank away,' said the latter, 'if he had been at home. The poor dear's at a publishers' conference in Leamington.'

'And Charles,' added Dimity, as the only other married woman present, 'is at a diocesan conference. Do you think men like conferences, or do they just enjoy getting away on their own now and again?'

'I've never liked to enquire,' replied Phyllida. 'Have you heard about Nelly Piggott?'

An animated discussion followed, and the general feeling was that such employment might be the making of Albert's rather shaky marriage.

'Perhaps,' ventured Dimity, 'Doris Hodge would be happier with a nice little job.'

'The worst of it is,' said Ella, 'that nice little jobs are jolly hard to come by. I met that objectionable Frances Thurgood this week, and she was telling me that Janet is getting quite desperate searching for some employment.'

'Can she do anything?' asked Connie.

'Nothing as useful as Nelly Piggott, but she's got strings of art qualifications for what they're worth. What about Doris? Any hope as a barmaid again?'

'I gather not,' said Winnie. 'I agree that they are thrown too much together, and Percy is a difficult man, you know. His first wife thoroughly spoilt him, and Doris doesn't. It's as simple as that.'

Later that day, when all the ladies had departed and Winnie and Jenny were clearing up in the kitchen, the subject was raised again.

'How are things going at the Hodges'?' asked Winnie, cake tin in hand.

'Haven't you heard?' replied Jenny. 'He had a letter this week, so Mrs Jenner told me, to say Doris is not coming back.'

'Oh Jenny!' sighed Winnie. 'I am sorry.'

'Not as sorry as I am,' said Jenny grimly. 'I only hope he doesn't try his tricks here again.'

And Winnie was relieved to see that her brave Jenny was prepared to repulse any invaders of her territory.

14   Thundery Conditions

THE SUMMER WEEKS slipped by. The honeysuckle flowers had fallen and clusters of garnet berries took their place. Hard little knobs of green replaced the bramble blossom, and the wild late summer flowers, knapweed, agrimony and scabious, enlivened the verges.

Everything was beginning to look shabby. The grass was turning brown. A few leaves were already floating down from the trees. The combine harvesters were at work in the fields, and the lucky people with greenhouses were enjoying a bumper crop of tomatoes.

In the vicarage garden at Lulling Charles Henstock and Caleb were busy.

Caleb was pushing the lawn mower at a leisurely pace, and the smell of freshly cut grass floated pleasantly about the place. Charles was engaged in trimming the edges of the flower beds with his long-handled shears, given to him by Dimity on his last birthday. They were, he noted with infinite satisfaction, a great advance on the old pair of hand shears with which he used to tackle this job. What was even more pleasing was the fact that he didn't get the knees of his trousers stained crawling on the grass.

The air was warm and sultry, and there was no sunshine. Hordes of minute insects, called thunder flies by Lulling folk, filled the garden, tickling Caleb and Charles as they worked. Every now and again the sound of a slap and a vexed exclamation disturbed the peace, as the two men tried to displace their ubiquitous adversaries.

Despite these interruptions, Charles's flow of thought continued. He was in a philosophic mood, brought about, no doubt, by the rhythmic nature of his present labours and the soporific atmosphere of a warm August afternoon. He had put aside, as best he could, his earlier worries. Mrs Thurgood's absence from church could not be helped, sad though it was. It was true that several families had transferred their presence to other establishments, but on the other hand Charles had welcomed several newcomers.

The person who had rifled the poor box, or rather the box asking for help with the fabric of St John's church, had not been found. The police had strongly suspected a young man who lived in one of the riverside cottages by the Pleshey, but he was able to prove that he had been practising his bowling at the nets on the local sports' ground when the felony occurred, and the police were obliged to look fruitlessly elsewhere. Charles had long ago put the matter behind him. A stronger box had been put in its place, and the alms were collected nightly by the rector himself. One could do no more.

On the whole, as the months passed, he began to feel more at ease, although he was still deeply conscious of his own shortcomings when he compared himself with Anthony Bull. But there it was. Anthony was Anthony, charming, a trifle flamboyant, able to talk and laugh easily with all and sundry, an inspiring orator and as handsome as a matinée idol.

He could not hope, nor did he wish, to compete. He could only pray that his parishioners would recognize his own sincerity, his loving care of them and his desire to serve them well. He wanted to be accepted as himself, and not constantly compared to his predecessor. Only time, Charles sighed to himself, scratching his tormented neck, could put that right, he feared. Patience was all.

He straightened up, and saw Dimity approaching with the tea tray. He hurried to help her.

'I thought it would be nice to have it out here,' said Dimity.

'Perfect, my dear. Although there are no end of those horrible little thunder flies.'

'They're worse in the house,' Dimity told him, lifting the milk jug. 'Quite static in there, like veils of treacle.'

' "Veils of treacle",' echoed Charles. 'Can you have veils –?'

'You know what I mean,' said Dimity. 'One has to *push* through them. Out here they do at least move about a bit. Call Caleb, would you? I'm sure he's as parched as we are.'

And still pondering on his wife's extraordinary description, Charles went across the newly-striped lawn to fetch Caleb to the feast.

Some half a mile away, in the kitchen of The Fuchsia Bush, Nelly Piggott found the thunder flies as irritating as the rest of Lulling.

She had just spread coffee-flavoured water icing carefully over a large square of spongecake, and was now placing halved walnuts at equal distances on the sticky surface. Her intention was to cut the whole into twenty squares, each suitable for a delectable portion to be eaten with coffee or tea by the lucky customers.

The thunder flies seemed bent on committing suicide upon Nelly's masterpiece. She moved it from the kitchen table into the larder, but there seemed to be no escape from the maddening little midges.

'Nothing for it but to pick 'em off with a knife point,' said Nelly to Mrs Peters when she came into the kitchen. 'I'd best open that extra tin of home-made biscuits, ma'am, for this afternoon.'

'Yes, that would be best,' agreed her employer, looking doubtfully at Nelly's icing. 'With any luck these wretched midges should clear away as soon as a storm comes, and I think that's on the way already.'

She vanished again into the shop and Nelly was left to her own devices.

She had not been so happy in years, thought Nelly, putting out biscuits. Albert, although no ray of sunshine, was comparatively good tempered, and certainly did not upbraid her about her absence with the oil man, which she fully expected from him. Perhaps he was mellowing with age? Perhaps he felt, as she did since her time in hospital, that peace at any price was the best guideline? No one could call Albert's cottage a love nest, but at least it was a port in a storm.

The main thing was that she was really blissfully happy whilst at work, and she was in The Fuchsia Bush's kitchen promptly at eight-thirty each morning and content to stay there for as long as Mrs Peters needed her. The café closed when afternoon teas were over, and the arrangement had been that Nelly could leave as soon as the cakes and sandwiches were ready, and the kettles on the stove, sometime before four o'clock. Two part-time kitchen helpers came from one o'clock until five-thirty, so that there was no need for Nelly to remain, but more often than not it was nearer five when she departed.

It seemed to suit Albert too. One of Nelly's perks in the new job was a certain amount of spare food which Mrs Peters allowed her to take home. Very often Nelly had no need to cook a meal for Albert on her return, and for this she was grateful, for a long stint in the kitchen, much as she enjoyed it, and the walk up the steep hill to crown the day, did seem to take its toll of Nelly's strength, and made her realize that she had still not fully recovered from the operation.

Her one fear was that as soon as Mrs Jefferson reappeared then her job would come to an end. So far, Mrs Jefferson's injuries had taken their time in mending. 'It's an ill wind that blows nobody any good,' Nelly had quoted silently to herself, when she heard how slowly her predecessor was recovering. The broken ribs had led later to bronchitis, and this in its turn to a troublesome and painful cough. It was obvious that the patient could not expect to return to her duties, and lifting heavy objects and other arduous kitchen duties were going to be beyond her for some time.

Mrs Peters considered herself extremely fortunate in having Nelly in the kitchen, and never ceased to be grateful to Ella and Dimity for suggesting her.

There was no doubt about it, Nelly was superior in every way to Mrs Jefferson, but Mrs Peters had no intention of depriving her old friend of the job and would welcome her back just as soon as she was fit.

If only, thought The Fuchsia Bush's owner, she could employ them both. But would the business stand it? And would the two ladies work together in harmony?

Well, time enough to worry when her former cook returned, she told herself. Something would turn up, no doubt. It generally did.

Kit Armitage returned from his visit to Wales looking remarkably refreshed.

Mrs Jenner was delighted to welcome him back, but within half an hour of his home-coming she had poured out the story of her sister-in-law Doris's perfidy.

'But surely she'll come back?' said Kit. 'Isn't it just a little tiff?'

'To my mind, she's finished with Perce. I can't make up my mind if he wants her back or not. He misses his comforts, that I do know, and asked me if I'd take him in. He's fond of my cooking.'

'And are you going to have him here?' asked Kit, feeling some alarm.

'Dear me, no! I'm in my seventies, and I'm not taking on a silly chap like Percy, brother or no brother. He's old enough and ugly enough to look after his own affairs, as our mother used to say, God rest her. I've never worried Perce with my troubles, and apart from offering him a meal if he blows in at the right time, I'm not making a rod for my back.'

Kit heartily approved of this downright approach to the problem, and said so.

'So you see,' went on his landlady, 'this will make no difference to your arrangements. I only hope you'll be able to stay for a long time to come. You've been the Perfect Lodger, if I may say so.'

'You're very kind,' replied Kit, 'and you make me so comfortable I could easily be persuaded to stay for ever. But I really must find myself a house. Prices go up every month, and I'm determined to put my shoulder to the wheel now, and get settled.'

'Well, don't hurry on my account,' said Mrs Jenner.

There was the sound of someone wiping feet on the door scraper at the back door.

'I'd better go. Probably Perce with some vegetables. He's just in time for a cup of coffee. It's my belief he keeps one eye on the clock.'

And downstairs she went to greet the grass widower.

Kit's first port of call was to see Connie and Dotty.

He found the two ladies shelling peas in the garden, with Flossie at their feet eagerly snatching up any stray pea and munching it with enjoyment.

'That's an odd taste for a dog, isn't it?' he asked, when he had greeted the ladies and was settled in a decidedly rickety deckchair.

'That's nothing,' Dotty told him. 'We had a sweet little cat once who enjoyed peppermints. Not the really strong ones that Papa had for his indigestion, but the mild sort. Sometimes I made her peppermint creams, for a treat. Quite simple, you know, just icing sugar and a few drops of peppermint essence. No doubt you made them yourself as a child.'

Kit confessed that he had never tried his hand at peppermint creams.

'But I did make Everton toffee once,' he said, 'and ruined the saucepan. It went black before my very eyes.'

'Tell us about Wales,' said Connie. His appearance had given her so much delight that she had felt herself blushing, much to her horror. It was really absurd at her age, she scolded herself, to behave like someone of sixteen, and she could only hope that he put her rosiness down to the sun. With any luck, he had not noticed, but men, usually obtuse, were often disconcertingly sharp, just when one would rather they were not.

Kit launched into an animated account of his holiday, and fished from his pocket a folder of photographs.

The colander of peas was set aside, under the seat in the shade, as the two ladies studied them in turn.

'This is the River Dovey,' he explained, 'and this is one of the tributaries where we did most of our fishing. Here's the Olivers' house. Here's the church. And this is Diana.'

Was it just Connie's imagination, or did his voice sound particularly loving as he handed over the last photograph? The subject was certainly stunningly attractive. Connie noted ruefully the excellent figure, the smooth dark hair and the enchanting smile.

'She looks lovely,' commented Connie.

'She is,' agreed Kit, tucking the photographs back in the folder.

'And when are you off next?' enquired Connie.

'I'm not,' he assured her. 'I'm now applying myself whole-heartedly to finding a house. There are two in this week's paper which sound hopeful, and I believe the agent has another two possibilities. And Justin has heard of a place south of Lulling, so that gives me plenty to be going on with.'

He hesitated for a moment.

'If it's not too much to ask, would you like to help me? Both of you, of course. I'd be glad of a second opinion.'

'I should love to,' said Connie.

'Well, I won't promise,' said Dotty. 'I'm making our bread now, you know, and it all takes time. And the early plums need bottling. But, thank you for the invitation. If my duties allow, I should be delighted.'

'Then that's settled,' said Kit, throwing himself back in the chair. A terrible rending sound followed, and Kit gradually subsided through the worn canvas amidst cries of distress from the ladies.

'Are you hurt? That wretched chair! It should have been thrown away years ago,' cried Connie, bending over her laughing visitor who was struggling to rise from the débris.

'No harm done, but look at your peas,' said Kit, standing upright.

The colander was on its side. At least half the peas had gone, and the back view of Flossie, with her tail between her legs, was vanishing through the hedge.

'We asked for that,' commented Connie.

'Excellent roughage for her,' said Dotty indulgently. 'Dear little Floss! So intelligent!'

Kit was folding up the tattered chair.

'You know, the frame's perfectly sound,' he said, studying it. 'I'll get some more canvas and mend it for you.'

They began to protest.

'No, I'd like to. I may not be a dab hand at peppermint creams,' he told Dotty, 'but I can mend deckchairs as well as the next.'

'In that case,' said Connie, 'I'll bring out the other three for your attention. They are all at that stage, believe me.'

The prolonged absence of Percy Hodge's wife made itself felt in places farther afield than Mrs Jenner's.

The example of one stone thrown into a pool creating ripples far around it, is nowhere more to the point than in a small community.

Winnie Bailey, and more particularly, Jenny, were both on guard against any unwelcome intrusions by a would-be suitor.

The regulars at The Two Pheasants discussed the affair avidly, and Albert, as a once-deserted husband, had plenty to say.

'She'll come back all right,' he told his listeners. 'Mine did, didn't she? I just bided my time. Acted dignified. Never run after her. She come back, and now she knows when she's well off.'

'You went down to see her in hospital,' put in the landlord. 'As I remember, you was shamed into it.'

Albert feigned deafness. That was the worst of village life, he mused. No one ever forgot any little mistakes you made. You could slip up perhaps twenty years ago, and some know-all would remind you of it.

He button-holed a woe-begone Percy one day and enlarged on the theme of wife-management.

'You mark my words, she'll come to her senses in time! Just don't give way, Percy my boy. Once she sees you can manage all right without her, she'll come running back. Women is awkward creatures. Like to think they can manage without us. But they can't, of course.'

'I don't know as I wholly *want* her back,' said Percy. 'She's led me a proper dance, and spends money like water.

I never had that trouble with my dear Gertie. And her cooking was streets ahead. Marriage is a lottery, Albert, and that's a fact.'

'Don't I know it!' commiserated Albert. 'I've had my share of trouble, and that's why I'm giving you my advice. You let things ride for a bit. You may feel different if she comes back all humble-pie. On the other hand, if you finds you don't want her you could set about a divorce one day.'

Percy started as if stung by a wasp.

'Divorce? But that costs money!'

'Ah!' agreed Albert morosely. 'But anything worthwhile does, don't it?'

They turned over this sad fact in unhappy silence.

'What about half a pint?' said the sorrowing widower at last.

And together they entered The Two Pheasants.

Even as far away as Lulling, Percy Hodge's troubles were causing ripples. Charles Henstock, who had been relieved to find that Nelly had returned to the marital home and had understood that Doris's absence was simply a visit to her sister, was now dismayed to find that pressure was being exerted, yet again, for his ministrations.

'I'm really most reluctant to interfere in any little upset between husband and wife,' he told Ella when she brought up the matter. 'Ten chances to one it will all blow over, and I shall simply appear as a meddler.'

'Well, I can't see it would do any harm,' said Ella forthrightly, 'if you told Percy to fetch her back. And another thing, you could let him know he's a fool to keep throwing Gertie in Doris's face. What second wife is going to stand for that? I ask you!'

'It would only add fuel to the fire,' exclaimed Dimity, rushing to her husband's support. 'You must see that it can only put Charles in a most difficult position. If Percy comes to him for advice, that's quite a different proposition, but I'm sure it's a case of "Least said, soonest mended" here.'

'Well, I don't know,' protested Ella. 'If you've joined them together in holy matrimony I should have thought a bit of adhesive is needed if they come unstuck. Still, no doubt the bishop gives you guidance on this sort of thing.'

Charles laughed.

'He will if it ever gets to that stage, I'm sure. But at the moment I think we'll simply hope for the best.'

'The best being Doris's return, I suppose? I'll tell you what. Poor Jenny will be jolly relieved if she does deign to come back.'

As it happened, poor Jenny was destined to confront Percy within a day or two of this conversation.

She had walked across to the post box at the corner of Thrush Green, and then decided to take a short walk along the Nidden road.

The recent thunderstorm had cleared the air, and there was a freshness in the breeze that held a hint of early autumn. There were dahlias out in the gardens, great shaggy ones like floor mops, spiky ones of every hue from pale lemon to dark crimson, and dozens of the gay little pompom variety which Jenny loved best.

She was admiring them in a cottage garden when she became conscious of Percy emerging from a field gate.

It was too late to flee. Jenny stood her ground, as Percy approached.

'Nice day, Percy,' she said civilly.

'Would be if things was a bit different,' was his melancholy reply.

Jenny scented danger and took evasive action.

'Well, we'd all like some things different, I daresay,' she began briskly. 'Can't stop, Percy. I've got my ironing to do before tea.'

She turned and set off at a smart pace towards her home. To her dismay she found Percy at her elbow, pouring forth a stream of self-pity.

The well-worn phrases of 'never-understood-me', 'I-was-too-hasty-in-marrying-again' and 'I-always-tried-to-please-her' flowed like water off a duck's back as Jenny hastened along.

But when Percy was rash enough to puff explosively, for their pace was punishing: 'It was always you I wanted, as you well knows, Jenny,' she stopped, so suddenly that Percy nearly tripped over her.

Jenny faced him furiously.

'Stop that, Percy Hodge!' she cried. 'You're a married man and I won't hear no more. Any more of this nonsense and I'll set the police on you, and that's flat.'

Percy's mouth dropped open. The movement seemed to rouse Jenny to still greater heights of fury.

'And take that to be going on with!' she added, giving a resounding slap to her suitor's cheek. It was delivered with such wholesale venom that Percy stumbled into the verge, and while he was recovering his balance, Jenny marched away in triumph.

15 Under Doctor's Orders

THE NEW SCHOOL YEAR was a few weeks old when little Miss Fogerty was taken ill.

For the last two or three months she had diligently done her exercises, and tried to keep to Doctor Lovell's arduous diet.

'I really think that my *muscles* have toned up very well,' she told Dorothy Watson. 'It's just that I seem to get so *tired* these days, and I have lost so much weight that my skirts are slipping down.'

'You know what I think,' responded her friend. 'You are half-starved, my dear, and it's time John Lovell noticed it.'

'But I see him regularly every six weeks,' protested Agnes, 'and he is delighted with my arthritis. He says my blood is very much purer than it was, and I'm making excellent progress.'

'Towards the grave, at this rate,' commented Dorothy tartly. 'I really think you should go and see him. You're right down to skin and bone, Agnes, and far too pale.'

'Well, I'm due to see him again in a fortnight's time. We'll see what he thinks then.'

But it was in the same week, a golden one of mellow September sunshine, that little Miss Fogerty gave a small cry, rather like a kitten's, and slid to the floor from the breakfast table.

Dorothy Watson was much alarmed. She knelt beside her unconscious friend and tried to remember all the right things to do to resuscitate the fainting.

She had a fleeting memory of a railway poster seen in childhood of how to cope with those electrocuted. It showed a railwayman, complete with splendid moustaches, lying comatose, whilst another in gold braid – presumably the station master – was loosening the patient's collar as shown in Figure One.

Agnes's collar did not need loosening, and Dorothy was just about to put a cushion under her head when Miss Fogerty opened her eyes and said quite lucidly:

'It must be time for school.'

'That can wait,' replied Miss Watson. 'You lie there, my dear, while I fetch a rug.'

'Thank you,' agreed Agnes, with such docility that Dorothy's alarm grew.

She hurried upstairs for a travelling rug and took the opportunity of looking from the bedroom window across to John Lovell's surgery. It was with relief that she saw his car was already there, but Miss Pick's, his secretary's, was not.

Miss Pick, although an excellent secretary, was over-anxious to spare her employer, so she frequently kept patients from talking to him on the telephone. It did not endear her to those in emergencies such as the one now confronting Dorothy.

Agnes appeared to be dozing when she returned. She tucked the rug round her, closed the door carefully, and made her way to the telephone in the hall. She did not want Agnes to hear the conversation.

John Lovell answered himself.

'I'll bob over now,' he said, 'before surgery. I'll leave a note for Miss Pick, but no doubt I'll be back before she arrives. Just keep her warm and lying down.'

He was heartily reassuring after examining the patient, and accompanied her upstairs to her bedroom.

'Bed for the rest of the day,' he told her, 'and I'll be over this evening.'

Dorothy followed him downstairs. She was fond of this conscientious doctor, and grateful for his prompt arrival, but this was not going to deter her from speaking her mind.

'I can't help thinking, you know, that this results from that diet you prescribed. She seems to have been taken off all really nourishing food. She's lost far more than a woman of her size can stand, and her job is *most* demanding. I put this collapse down to weakness and anaemia.'

John Lovell smiled indulgently.

'Well, we'll see later. She seems to have been making pretty good progress so far under my treatment.'

Miss Watson curbed any further comment. It could wait until Agnes was seen again this evening.

She mounted the stairs again to see that her old friend had all that was needed for the next hour or so. The school bell was now ringing, and Agnes would be anxious.

*

Miss Watson explained what had happened to the only other member of staff at Thrush Green School.

She was a fresh-faced young woman in her probationary year, and listened to her headmistress with some concern.

She was genuinely fond of little Miss Fogerty and sad to hear of her sudden illness, but she felt even more anxious about her own ability to cope with the infants' class in her absence.

'I shall take your class and mine together,' Miss Watson told her, 'until I can get the office to send me a supply. I know that Mrs Billing is free at the moment, and perhaps we can persuade Mrs Trent, who is due here for the half-day tomorrow, to stay on.'

She went with her young assistant to see her settled in at the new classroom across the playground where Agnes usually held sway.

The children seemed awed by the news of Miss Fogerty's indisposition, but considerably elated at having a new teacher.

They began to converge upon her desk, full of news about their own illnesses, but Miss Watson soon put a stop to that.

'You must stay in your desks until Miss Potter tells you to come out,' she commanded. 'I shall want to hear what good children you have been at the end of the day.'

'I was sick last night,' announced a smug six-year-old in the front row. 'All over the clean counterpane. My mum said a swear word.'

Miss Watson leant towards Miss Potter.

'Keep them busy, dear,' she whispered. 'That's the secret.'

She departed towards her own quarters, checked that her double class was obediently reading in semi-silence, and went to the school telephone in her own tiny office.

She rang Isobel Shoosmith, her good next door neighbour, and told her what had happened to her old college friend.

'To be frank, I'm not surprised,' said Isobel. 'She's been looking pretty groggy for weeks. At least this will make her rest. Don't worry. I'll go and see her now, and I can stay with her until you get over at playtime. Betty Bell's here, and Harold is about too, so don't worry if you are held up.'

Much relieved, Dorothy Watson put down the receiver, and went to resume her duties.

True to his word, Doctor Lovell came again before evening surgery and spent a quarter of an hour with his patient. At Agnes's request, Dorothy waited below until he had finished.

'Well, how is she?' she asked anxiously, when he appeared in the sitting room.

'Nothing that a rest and good food won't cure,' he told her. 'She's very run down, and needs fattening up. I think perhap's she's been more than usually conscientious about her diet.'

'Agnes is always conscientious,' said Dorothy. She could have added a great deal more, but was wise enough to refrain.

'And I want her to take some iron tablets. Here's the prescription. And of course, no going to work for a week at least.'

'What about the diet? Should she try and keep to it?'

'Well, no. I'd see she has plenty of milk, and a good light diet – eggs, fish, that sort of thing. I'll keep in touch.'

Miss Watson, with commendable restraint, made no comment on this complete reversal of Agnes's treatment, and saw him to the door with sincere thanks for his help.

'As I thought,' she said aloud, as she straightened the sitting room curtains, 'half-starved and anaemic! Poor little Agnes!'

The warm September sunshine continued, and Agnes was soon able to sit out in the garden and enjoy her much-needed rest.

It was during this fine week that Charles Henstock found himself the bewildered owner of a dog.

It all began with the arrival of the milkman bearing a pint of gold top Jersey milk and an urgent message from Tom Hardy of the water-keeper's cottage.

'He's ill abed, sir,' said the milkman, 'and says could you come? He said something about hospital tomorrow, but I couldn't hear it all, him speaking so low and that river fair rushing by. I said I'd tell you. He don't write all that well, and of course there's no telephone.'

'Don't worry,' said the rector. 'I've a short service to take in half an hour and I'll go down there immediately after.'

The milkman departed, and Charles told Dimity about it.

'Probably wants a lift to the hospital tomorrow,' said Dimity. 'Are you free?'

'I'm sure I can manage it,' answered the rector. 'I shall be glad to help old Tom in any way.'

He was at the cottage by eleven o'clock. It meant leaving the car a little distance away, and walking across the spongy turf to Tom's door.

This time he did not bother to knock, but entered by the back door, and began to mount the stairs.

'You there, Tom? I'm coming up.'

A grey muzzle pushed its way through the banister railings. Polly made no noise, but her plumed tail wagged in greeting.

'In here, sir,' called Tom.

He was propped up on pillows and looked unusually sallow.

'And what have you been up to?' enquired Charles, drawing a chair to the bedside and sitting down. The Welsh collie put her head on his knee, and he stroked her silky neck automatically as he studied the dog's master.

'Doctor wants me to have some tests in hospital. Something in my stomach, he says. Probably have to have it out, I shouldn't wonder.'

'And you want a lift? I'm quite free to take you.'

'No, no. That's all arranged for me. It's Polly.'

'Polly?'

The dog looked up with her one bright eye and one opaque, and wagged her tail on hearing her name.

'My neighbour, Mrs Johnson, she's been seeing to me, and she was going to have Poll, but her bitch had six pups yesterday, and she'd go for Poll and anyone else she thought'd upset the pups, so the only person I could think of was you, rector. Polly's always taken to you, and she's a good obedient animal. I dare not leave her here, she'd fret so, even if she was fed regular, and I don't hold with kennels. She'd pine away there, that I do know.'

Charles saw, with great pity, that tears were rolling down poor Tom's furrowed cheeks. He was obviously very weak and the anxiety about the dog was more than he could bear.

Charles patted Tom's hand.

'Of course I'll have her,' he said heartily, 'and for as long as you like. Dimity loves dogs as much as I do, and we'll take the greatest care of her. I take it as an honour to have been asked.'

Tom gave a great sigh of relief.

'Well, I don't mind now what they do to me. As long as old Polly's in safe hands, I'm content. You know, sir, you truly are a man of God.'

'I should like to think I was,' said the rector humbly. 'Now, Tom, I'm going to get us both a cup of tea. I can find my way round your kitchen. I know everything's clearly labelled. Then you can tell me what I should know about Polly's diet and her routine before I take her off.'

'You stay here, Poll,' said Tom. He was calmer now. The tears still glistened on his face, and he made no attempt to dry them.

Charles went downstairs and waited for the kettle to boil. He admired again the simple, purely functional, fur- nishings. The tea pot stood by the kettle. The canisters on the mantelpiece were clearly labelled. A few plates, a mug or two and a cup and saucer were lodged on the rack over the sink. The drawer of the scrubbed kitchen table held a few knives, forks and spoons. Life could not be simpler, thought Charles, and found the place deeply tranquil.

The milk was still on the step, and Charles poured it into the two mugs straight from the bottle.

'Sugar?' he called up the stairs.

'Not for me,' came the reply.

He mounted carefully, a mug in each hand.

They sipped in silence. Outside the River Pleshey splashed and gurgled. A blackbird chattered, and in the distance could be heard a pheasant's sharp croak.

'My, that does you a power of good,' said Tom, putting his mug carefully on the stool by the bed. 'And now I'll tell you what Poll likes. Best of all she likes company, and that's why I couldn't leave her alone, for all Mrs Johnson promised to feed her. She eats anything you've got, scraps and that, and there's a sack of biscuits and some tins in the cupboard downstairs. I'd be obliged if you'd take 'em, sir. I'd feel better if you did.'

'I'll do that willingly,' said Charles. 'What about exercise?'

'She don't need much these days, like me,' replied Tom. 'If she can potter about after you in the garden, she won't hurt. And you'd best take her lead. It's hanging on the kitchen door.'

He fondled the dog's ears.

'I do hope she won't be a bother. If I tell her you're her master for a bit she'll understand.'

'I'll go and get the lead and take the mugs down,' said Charles, deeming it best to leave the two old friends together for a few minutes. 'Anything else I can get you?'

'No, thank you all the same, sir. Mrs Johnson will be down in an hour, and she's coming with me to the hospital tomorrow.'

'I'll come and see you as soon as they'll let me,' promised Charles, setting off with the mugs.

He rinsed them at the sink, and replaced them on the rack. There was no sign of food anywhere for Tom, and he presumed that Mrs Johnson would be bringing him a light meal.

He found the dog food and the lead and took the latter upstairs.

Tom fastened it to Polly's collar.

'Now you do as I told you,' he said earnestly. 'You're Mr Henstock's dog till I come back.'

Much to Charles's relief Tom seemed quite calm, and Polly came with him without any fuss.

'Good luck, Tom. I'll ring the hospital tomorrow and tell you how Polly's settled in.'

'She'll be safe enough with you. I know that, and bless you I do, sir, with all my heart.'

Polly led the way downstairs, across the grass and waited by the car door while Charles opened it.

Without any demur, she jumped in and lay down on the back seat.

Charles drove off gently. What would Dimity say, he wondered, when she saw their new visitor?

He need not have worried. Dimity was overjoyed to have the quiet old creature, and the cat, after a preliminary hiss, decided to ignore the interloper.

Charles was astonished and greatly touched by Polly's docility and ready obedience. As Tom had said, she liked company, and the only time she seemed at all disturbed was when a door opened. Then she looked up eagerly, as if expecting her old master, and when she found that he had not come back, she sighed, and drooped her head once more in resignation.

It almost broke Charles's heart.

The fine spell came to an end with a week of high winds and rain.

Work was at a standstill on Edward Young's new project. The children at the village school could not get rid of their high spirits in the playground, and Miss Watson was greatly relieved to have a supply teacher allotted to her by a sympathetic education office. Mrs Trent, who came occasionally each week, to help with what Miss Watson in her young days called 'backward children', now came full time while Miss Fogerty was recovering.

'They were always called "less able children" in my time,' she told Miss Watson. 'What is the latest term?'

'I've an idea it's "disadvantaged",' replied Dorothy, somewhat impatiently, 'but don't ask me why. I only know the present-day inspectors talk about "remedial classes" when I used to know them as "backward classes". It's all very silly, to my mind.'

Mrs Trent agreed, and asked if Miss Fogerty would soon be back.

'I very much hope so, but I'm insisting on her getting really fit again. It will take her some time to get over the doctor's treatment.'

It was Isobel Shoosmith who put forward a plan with which Dorothy readily agreed.

'Let me take Agnes to the sea for a few days. I've talked it over with Harold who entirely agrees.'

'To Barton-on-Sea?' enquired Dorothy. Barton was her idea of Paradise.

'Well, no. Harold suggested the east coast. So bracing, you know. But I pointed out that it is so wickedly cold at times, and what Agnes needed was lots of *warm* sea air. Winnie Bailey and Jenny went to a very nice quiet hotel at Torquay, and it sounds ideal.'

Agnes, as was to be expected, was unhappy about postponing her return to school, but was soon over-powered by the determination of Isobel and Dorothy, backed by Doctor Lovell's blessing.

'Very well,' she said at last, looking at the driving rain lashing across Thrush Green. 'If you all think a holiday will do me good.'

'Of course it will,' they chorused. 'And the weather will be quite different in Torquay!'

A particularly vicious squall had removed Justin Venables' hat in Lulling High Street, and sent it bowling along the pavement outside the Georgian front of the Lovelocks' fine house.

Justin dodged between lowered umbrellas and wellingtons to try and retrieve it. It seemed as if the gods were intent on teasing him, for as fast as he pursued it the faster it went, ricocheting off wet lime trees and railings, being run over by the odd pram, and generally behaving as if it had a life of its own, and a very mischievous one at that.

Luckily, the fishmonger fielded it for him, and Justin, breathless with the chase, thanked him sincerely.

'Not that it's going to be much improved after that,' observed Justin, turning the wet object in his hands. 'I can see I shall have to fork out for another one.'

He retraced his steps, facing the gale again, and heard a peremptory rapping at the Misses Lovelocks' window. Miss Ada was beckoning him in, and Justin knew better than to ignore this command.

'We saw you in trouble,' said Ada at the front door. 'Now you must come in and get dry. What brought you out in such a storm?'

'Business,' replied Justin, handing over his wet coat and hat. 'But it can wait a minute.'

Violet and Bertha now appeared.

'Let us get you some coffee,' said Bertha.

Justin refused politely. He knew the Lovelocks' coffee of old. It took at least half an hour to prepare and was atrociously weak after that.

He was ushered into the chilly drawing room, and the four old friends settled down for a gossip.

'I'm sure I'm keeping you from your affairs,' protested Justin.

'Not at all. Luncheon is cold today,' said Ada.

'Corned beef and a hard-boiled egg,' added Bertha.

'And some very good lettuce,' finished Violet.

'It sounds delicious,' lied Justin bravely.

'And do you ever patronise The Fuchsia Bush? It's so handy, and I hear the new cook is a great asset,' asked Ada.

Amazingly, Justin had not heard about Nelly Piggott's new post, and the ladies were happy to enlighten him.

'We found her a little *extravagant* when she cooked once or twice for us,' commented Bertha. 'Inclined to put *butter* in the mashed potato, and once went so far as to beat in *an egg* as well! Of course, we soon put a stop to that!'

'Naturally,' said Justin solemnly.

'But I must say she has got an excellent reputation with Mrs Peters. Of course, with a *business* one can afford to be rather more lavish than in a private establishment.'

Bertha then told him about Isobel and Agnes's proposed holiday, Ella Bembridge's nasty cold, Percy Hodge's truanting wife and Kit Armitage's fruitless house-hunting.

'Something will turn up, I'm sure,' said Justin. 'I wish he would get married again. I must admit that I had hopes of his recent meeting with Diana Oliver, but there you are. One can never plan for others.'

To his surprise Miss Violet had turned very pink, and her sisters were exchanging meaning glances.

'Well, I must get on,' he said rising. 'The rain has eased a little. It was so kind of you to take pity on me.'

The three ladies helped him on with his coat, and lent him an umbrella. The battered hat was rammed into his pocket.

'That, I fear, is done for,' he said ruefully.

'When it is dry, Justin, do please put it aside for our next Jumble Sale,' begged Ada.

'I won't forget,' promised Justin, and went off with plenty of thoughts in his bare head.

16   House-Hunting

ELLA BEMBRIDGE'S COLD persisted. She was as slack as Dotty Harmer in looking after herself, and Dimity was much alarmed.

'I'm sound as a bell,' Ella said, her gruff voice belying the statement. 'Just a bit thick in the clear. Nothing to worry about.'

'Well, I hope you are not going out in this rough weather. You know I can do any shopping that's needed.'

'There's just one thing,' said Ella, blowing her nose with the sound of the last trump. 'I promised to take my weaving and canework over to John's gallery for the exhibition. It's all ready in a couple of boxes. Do you think Charles would mind taking it over?'

'Of course not. Let me have it now.'

'Too much for you, Dim. Tell you what, ask Charles if he'd pick it up next time he's by. The stuff's supposed to be over there next week, but I don't suppose it matters if it's a day or so late. That young John Fairbrother, who's taken over, is such a worry-pants he always wants everything far too early to my mind.'

Dimity secretly had every sympathy with the nervous young gallery-owner who had to deal with a number of dilatory artists and craftsmen like Ella.

'Don't worry. We'll take it willingly. I always enjoy browsing round his things. I might even find a few Christmas presents.'

'Good grief, Dim! Don't start thinking of that yet. We're hardly into autumn.'

'It tends to sneak up,' Dimity pointed out, as she made her farewells.

The rain had ceased when Charles and Dimity set out in the car to collect Ella's handiwork.

Lulling High Street was busy, and Dimity waved to a dozen or more friends. By The Fuchsia Bush she noticed Janet Thurgood, an unattractive figure in a long bedraggled skirt and a number of shabby garments overlapping each other on her upper half. She wore a rather grubby scarf tied round her hair, and a pair of broken-down sandals on her bare feet. Altogether she looked the Complete Artist. Dimity did not wave to her, but snorted her disgust.

'Sorry?' queried Charles.

'Just saw that dreadful Thurgood girl. She could do with a bath.'

'I'm rather sorry for her,' said Charles, stopping suddenly to allow a dignified Labrador to cross the road. 'With that *mother*, I mean, and no job to do, or so I hear. Life must be rather wretched for her.'

'Well, they both make life wretched enough for other people,' replied Dimity trenchantly, 'and so they must expect a taste of their own medicine now and again.'

Charles said nothing, and Dimity knew that he was sad to hear her make such a remark. What a difficult thing it was to live with a saint! In many ways, life with Ella had been much simpler.

The boxes were packed into the back seat and off they went. The gallery was some five or six miles south of Lulling in a converted barn. A small cottage adjoining it was the home of John Fairbrother, a clever but timid young man, who worked extremely hard at running the gallery.

He was busy setting out pottery on some low shelves when they arrived, and was delighted to have Ella's work.

'I was beginning to wonder if I should ring her to remind her about it. It's so easy to put off a job, and I'm afraid several of the contributors had quite forgotten about the exhibition.'

He waved towards the pottery.

'Isn't this delightful? Three young men have just set up together and I think we shall get plenty of customers for their work.'

Dimity privately was doubtful. It was thick and of a dreary porridge colour. One of the tankards must have been uncomfortably heavy to lift when empty. When full of beer or cider it must have needed the strength often to lift it from the table, thought Dimity.

Charles had drifted to the wall and was surveying some pretty miniatures of wild flowers. He suddenly turned to the owner.

'Do you know Janet Thurgood?' he asked.

The effect of this question was remarkable. A look of awe transfixed the young man's face.

'You mean the abstract artist?'

'Well, yes. I suppose she is best known for that sort of work. Does she ever exhibit here?'

'No, I'm afraid not. And I should never dare to ask her. She would ask far more than my clients could afford. She is very well thought of in artistic circles.'

'You don't want any help in arranging the exhibition, I suppose, or manning it while it's in progress? I happen to know she is free at the moment. I just wondered if you would like me to speak to her.'

The young man turned quite pale at the thought.

'I certainly do want someone, and there's a notice on the door advertising for temporary help, but I doubt if such an eminent artist as Janet Thurgood would even consider such a post. The pay is very small for one thing.'

'Would you like me to approach her? I've a feeling she would love to help, if you are willing.'

'I'd be more than grateful. In fact, I'd be downright

honoured,' admitted young Mr Fairbrother, and there the
matter was left.

Dimity managed to escape from the pottery, but salved
her conscience by buying some tiny straw figures which
would look attractive on the Christmas tree when the time
came.

'Are you really going to bother with that wretched girl?'
she asked as they drove home to get Polly's tea-time
biscuits and Tabitha's saucer of milk.

'I am,' said Charles firmly. 'You call her a wretched girl,
Dimity, and I fear, from the glimpse I had of her this
afternoon, that is exactly what she is. Simply wretched!'

It so happened, that while Charles and Dimity had been
engaged in the gallery, Kit Armitage and Connie had been
less than a mile away looking at one of the houses on Kit's list.

It had been built in the thirties, so that the garden was
mature if rather small. It had three bedrooms looking out
to the rolling countryside, and faced south.

Connie liked it. Her only private sorrow was that it was some way from Thrush Green, and it meant that she would see less of Kit. She admitted to herself how fond she was of him, and the pangs of jealousy she felt when considering the distant Diana Oliver were so completely foreign to her nature that she was obliged to face the fact that she was fast falling in love with the man. It was all delightful, but rather disconcerting, she found, for a sensible woman in her forties.

'Not much ground,' was Kit's comment. 'What do you think?'

'Do you need a lot? The garden's very pretty, and private too. I should have thought it would be big enough to keep you busy.'

'But not big enough for animals,' objected Kit.

This was a new idea altogether, and Connie felt puzzled.

'I didn't know you proposed to keep any animals,' she replied.

'Oh, just a few hens and things,' he said vaguely, and went to investigate a small greenhouse built at the side of the house.

They toured the rooms again. It seemed an ideal house for a bachelor, to Connie's mind, compact, light and easy to run. One of the bedrooms was small, but Connie was old-fashioned enough to think that every house should have a boxroom, and this would make a splendid place for all those things like trunks, odd chairs, fire screens, boxes of spare curtains and such like which need a space to jostle in.

This would leave a large bedroom for Kit and an equally large one for his spare room. However, it was apparent that he had taken a dislike to the place, for some reason best known to himself, so Connie kept her thoughts to herself.

'Well, shall we push off? Let's have tea at The Fuchsia Bush. You aren't in a desperate hurry to get back?'

'No. I'd love that. Aunt Dotty's not expecting me till

six, and Albert is milking Dulcie, so she'll have company too. The Fuchsia Bush has some splendid scones these days, thanks to our Nelly. I'm glad she came back to Thrush Green.'

'Sensible woman,' commented Kit. 'Can't beat Thrush Green. This place is too far from it for my liking.'

His spirits seemed to have recovered, and they drove back to Lulling gossiping cheerfully. Tea was as delicious as ever under Mrs Peters's indulgent eye, and the two returned to Dotty's in great heart.

'No luck?' queried Dotty.

'Too far away,' said Kit.

'Well, you both look all the better for your outing,' said Dotty, 'and I've had a most interesting talk with Albert. Do you know his mother gave him a fried mouse to eat when he had whooping cough as a child? And he used to clean his teeth with sage leaves.'

'No wonder they've dropped out,' was Kit's comment.

Tom Hardy made good progress in Lulling Cottage Hospital, and was always eager to hear about Polly when Charles visited him.

'I've got another favour to ask of you, sir,' he said one afternoon. 'It seems I can go out from here if there's someone to look after me.'

Charles began to rack his brain for some willing neighbour who was free to oblige. The sad thing was that it seemed that everyone was out at work. Where had all those nice single aunts gone? They had been the mainstay of family crises in the rector's own childhood.

'Well, I can't go home, that's flat,' continued the patient. 'But they can fix me up at a convalescent home down Cheltenham way till I'm up and about again. The thing is, of course, old Poll.'

'You needn't worry on her account,' the rector assured him. 'We both love her, and she is the best-behaved dog I've ever come across. We'll keep her with us until you are well enough to have her.'

The old man gave a gusty sigh of relief.

'That's a weight off my mind. I tell 'em here I'll be doing for myself again in a week or two's time.'

But as the good rector returned home, he began to wonder if old Tom would ever be able to look after himself again.

And then the thought of Edward's old people's homes came to him, and he decided to see what could be done about one for his old friend, if the need arose. The biggest snag, of course, would be Tom himself. He loved his simple quiet home, with only the joyous sound of the river splashing alongside for company. How would he feel about neighbours living so close to him, and the sound of traffic nearby? There was no doubt about it, one's home meant so much. He recalled talking to Isobel Shoosmith when she had been house-hunting, and more recently he recalled Kit Armitage's comments.

They had all agreed that each house had an aura about it, and one which was quickly recognized.

'Some really welcomed you,' Isobel had said. 'You felt that the people who had lived there before had loved the place and been happy there. I felt it at once in our present home.'

'I felt it too at Lulling Vicarage,' agreed the rector, 'although I believe there have been some pretty rum incumbents over the centuries.'

'I definitely loathed one cottage I looked at beyond Nidden,' chimed in Kit. 'Couldn't think why. Roses round the door, south facing, sheltered by a little hill, it seemed perfect, but there was something sinister about it. I'm the last chap to claim to be psychic, but I wasn't a bit surprised to hear from Mrs Jenner that a couple lived there at the turn of the century who neglected their six children so appallingly that two of them died. It was a pitiful tale. The squalor alone was enough to curdle you, let alone the cruelty. There's a lot that goes on in the country that is hidden by pretty thatch and leaded windows.'

'I'm afraid you're right,' said the rector nodding sadly.

In the evening of the day they visited the gallery Charles rang Mrs Thurgood's number. He had not been in touch with that formidable woman since the disastrous meeting in the church which had led to her departure from his congregation.

A lesser man might have shirked the job, and been content to write a note to Miss Thurgood herself. But Charles had never lacked courage in a tight place, and he was confident that it would be better to explain matters over the telephone to Janet and to be prepared to answer any questions.

Luckily, it was she who answered the call. On hearing who it was on the other end of the wire her voice became somewhat cool, but Charles was not deterred.

He explained about their visit, the advertisement on the door, and the real need of the young gallery-owner to have help.

She listened attentively and sounded thoughtful when she spoke.

'I should like to help him. Should I write, do you think?'

She sounded more friendly after hearing the news, and Charles was relieved.

'I must stress that John was most reluctant to worry you. He has a great regard for your work, and thought you might be too busy with your own painting to bother with other people's efforts. He is refreshingly modest, I may say, and did remark about it being an honour if you felt you could help at the exhibition.'

'Really? How very kind!' exclaimed Janet, sounding quite enthusiastic. 'I think I will ring him now and find out more about it.'

'An excellent idea,' agreed Charles. 'And I hope you don't think me impertinent for mentioning your name to him.'

'Far from it. It was excessively kind of you. Especially in the – er – circumstances.'

'Not at all.'

'Well, a thousand thanks, anyway. I'm really rather at a loose end, and it will be lovely to have something useful to do. I'll let you know what happens.'

'Thank you,' said Charles. 'I should be interested.'

He rang off, and bent to stroke Polly.

'And how is the wretched girl?' asked Dimity, with a smile.

'Not quite so wretched,' Charles told her.

The days of early autumn were warm and cloudless. The tractors were busy in the fields turning over the golden stubble in long chocolate-coloured furrows.

The sun was still pleasantly warm. The plums and apples were ripening, and prudent housewives were busy storing the last of the runner beans and late peas in readiness for the winter.

Agnes Fogerty, greatly rejuvenated by her few days at Torquay, was now back in the classroom, and Mrs Trent reverted to her half-day's remedial work with backward, or possibly less-able, children.

Edward Young was now at the interesting stage of deciding on the best colours for interior and exterior decoration of his masterpiece. There was still plenty to be done for, as is usual during building operations, it seemed that one operator was always waiting for another to do something before the former could begin. The plasterer waited for the plumber. The plumber waited for the electrician. The electrician waited for the electricity board to supply the correct poles and wires, and so the merry-go-round went on.

'Some time,' cried Edward to Harold Shoosmith, 'I suppose it will get done. In the meantime, I'm trying to visualize what yellow walls would look like in the kitchens.'

'Depends on your mood,' observed Harold. 'They might make you feel sunny or bilious. I suppose the homes have all been allotted by now?'

'I wouldn't know, but I think it's likely. The council copes with that, and I don't envy it the job. I've heard they could be filled five times over.'

'You'll be getting on with the next few then, I take it?'

'Oh well,' said Edward cheerfully, 'these will change hands quite quickly, what with the "natural wastage" as it's so prettily expressed.'

'Deaths, do you mean?'

'That's right. Let's face it, Harold, most of them are on their last legs when they get one of these. However, it's jolly good luck for those on the waiting list, isn't it?'

He smiled brightly at his friend and mounted a ladder nimbly to inspect some guttering.

'It's strange, isn't it,' said Harold to Isobel later, 'how differently people look at life? Or death, for that matter.'

That afternoon Dimity was sitting in her drawing room mending her own and Charles's underclothes.

It was a job which she did not enjoy, and one which she had put off for so long that the pile beside her on the sofa was now formidable.

Polly lay beside her on the floor, thumping her fringed tail whenever Dimity spoke to her. Dimity often wondered what thoughts lay behind those odd eyes and the satiny head. Did she think of Tom? Did she secretly pine for him? Or was she as contented as she seemed to be, staying at the vicarage?

Dimity was a great animal lover, and secretly thought the idea, held by some people, that animals' spirits did not survive death, was desperately wrong. If goodness were anything to go by, there were a dozen or more cats and dogs known to her who had far more noble qualities than their owners. She dare not tell Charles of her beliefs, although she suspected that he felt as she did.

She put down the petticoat she was mending and gazed about her. Everything came to its end at a different age. Look at that lampshade, for instance, made by dear Ella for her last birthday, and already unravelling at the seams. And yet the chest it stood on had been her grandmother's, and had been made between 1780 and 1800 according to an expert in such matters. That surely would survive for another hundred years or so.

Or take Polly. She stroked the smooth head, and the dog thumped her tail with pleasure. Her end must come within the next two or three years. The roses on the table would be over in two or three days. It was an interesting thought.

At that moment, the telephone rang and Dimity put aside the petticoat.

A girl's voice spoke.

'Is your husband at hand, Mrs Henstock? It's Janet here.'

'Janet?' queried Dimity. She found it difficult to recognize voices on the telephone, and she knew three Janets.

'Janet Thurgood,' said the girl.

'No, I'm afraid he's visiting,' said Dimity, trying to disguise the coldness in her tone. 'Can I take a message for him? He will be back for tea.'

'It's just that I have started work at the gallery, and simply love it. John Fairbrother is such a dear, and I haven't been so happy for months. And it's all thanks to your kind husband. Please tell him.'

Dimity thawed at once. Praise of Charles was the surest way to her heart.

'He'll be delighted to hear it,' she said warmly. 'And so am I.'

17   Future Plans

IT WAS BY MEANS of the competent bush telegraph of Thrush Green and Lulling that Nelly Piggott first heard of the probable return of Mrs Jefferson to her kitchen duties at The Fuchsia Bush.

Albert had heard the news in The Two Pheasants. His informant was his young assistant Cooke, and he had heard it from Betty Bell who had heard it from the postman, Willie Bond, who was her cousin. Regretfully, no one seemed to know who had told Willie.

How much the tale had been embellished or confirmed in its roundabout journey, Nelly could not say, but she did know that quite often a rumour ran about several weeks before the fact emerged. She was very upset, but did her best to disguise it.

'I'd have thought Mrs Peters would have said something if that's true,' she told Albert. 'Always been straight with me. I bet this is some barmy idea one of your friends next door has thought up when he was half-seas-over.'

'Well, you wait and see,' replied Albert, nettled at the response to his bit of news.

She did not have to wait long. Mrs Peters met her in the kitchen of The Fuchsia Bush a few days later. It was the first thing in the morning, and they were alone.

The owner came to the point at once. She had been giving a good deal of thought to this tricky problem, but was determined to try to keep Nelly if she could. The sales of home-made cakes, at which Nelly excelled, had risen sharply since her arrival in the kitchen.

'If you would be willing to take sole charge of the cake side,' said Mrs Peters, 'I'm sure Mrs Jefferson will be able to cope with the rest. She will be coming in at ten o'clock for a little while, just to see how things go. That would help over the lunch time, and once that was cleared away she would go home. The new kitchen maids seem capable girls.'

Nelly agreed to all these plans with fervour. It meant that she would have the kitchen to herself for the first hour or so of the day, and this she relished. It also seemed that she could fit the afternoon hours to please herself.

'Take two afternoons off,' said her employer. 'We may be able to work out something half-time for you and for Mrs Jefferson, but we'll have to see how things go for the time being.'

When Nelly told Albert about these temporary arrangements he was somewhat smug.

'What'd I tell you? Now the old girl's back, same as we was told. Two afternoons off a week's not bad going either. You thinking of taking another little job?'

'No, I'm not,' responded Nelly flatly. 'I might spend one evening at Bingo. Must have a bit of fun now and again, and Mrs Jenner mentioned it to me the other day. She goes regular. Sees a bit of life there, she says.'

Which made it plain that Nelly was beginning to find her usual form.

'Well, I only hopes you keep the housekeeping money separate from your own bit,' replied Albert, damping down any unnecessary revival of spirits.

It was about this time that Charles Henstock heard that Tom Hardy was back at home and asking to see him. He was quite fit enough to manage to cope with Polly, was the message, and would take it kindly if the reverend could bring her home one day.

Dimity said farewell to her charge with real regret. She patted the docile old lady as she sat meekly on the back seat of the car.

'Take these too, dear,' said Dimity handing over a basket. 'They will save Tom bothering with catering for a day or two.'

Charles drove circumspectly towards the river. The willow trees were pale gold in the autumn sunshine. Soon they would be stripped bare by the first winds of winter. Already there were drifts of crisp leaves beneath the beech and horse chestnut trees, and chrysanthemums and dahlias outnumbered the roses in Lulling's front gardens.

There was already a chill in the air at dawn and dusk. Dimity had lit the fire in the drawing room on several recent evenings. Far too soon the curtains would be drawn at tea time, and the long dark nights would be upon them.

Not that Charles was wholly sad at the prospect. There was something remarkably satisfying about the domestic side of winter. He enjoyed splitting the logs that Tom had supplied earlier in the year, before his illness had struck him down. He liked piling them in the hearth, ready for the evening's comfort. He relished the long hours of reading or listening to his beloved Mozart on their ancient record player.

Secretly too, he was relieved to see the garden at rest for a few months. He knew quite well that such a vast expanse would benefit from the attention of a full-time gardener, if not two, but Charles's salary would not rise to it. He was lucky to have Caleb's help and advice, but it was evident that the garden was not kept in the pristine state it had been during Anthony Bull's incumbency.

In the winter, with the curtains safely drawn across, the garden was hidden from Charles's eyes, and his self-reproach was lessened.

But although he relished the snugness of his new house and rejoiced to see Dimity so happy in it, the winter brought hardship outside. Despite the blessings of a welfare state, which Charles was the first to acknowledge, there were still families among his parishioners who were short of the basic needs of shelter, food and fuel. There were animals too who suffered, and this grieved the good rector sorely.

The wild birds who flocked around his bird table, the stray cat who came nightly from a neighbouring barn, were given his bounty and his blessing. But there were one or two dogs, chained to kennels, and a few poor farms where the sheep and cattle never seemed adequately fed and housed which touched Charles's tender heart. He spoke his mind to the owners of these unhappy creatures, for when his duty was clear Charles shirked nothing. Sometimes matters improved, sometimes not, and for all his flock, both human and animal, Charles knew that winter could be a cruel season.

As he approached Tom's cottage, basking in the thin sunshine, Polly began to show signs of excitement. She stood up on the seat, her nose pressed to the side window, and began to make curious little growling sounds which were new to Charles.

'Nearly home, Poll,' he told her. 'Soon see your master. Soon see old Tom, Poll.'

He drew into the grass verge, and fastened Polly's lead. The dog was now quivering with excitement and leapt from the car with more energy than Charles had ever seen.

She tugged so strongly that the rector was almost pulled off his feet. She began to bark, high frantic yelps of rapture, and at that moment the door opened and Tom stood there his arms wide in welcome.

Charles let go of the lead, and Polly raced across the gap between them, still yelping hysterically.

'Poll! Poll!' called Tom.

The old dog leapt upon him, almost knocking him down. Tom stooped to caress her, and she licked his face with her large pink tongue, making ecstatic little cries, and dancing on her back legs. Charles was much moved by this reunion.

'Well, Tom old boy, she knows who is her true master, doesn't she?'

'Ah! I knew she wouldn't forget. How's she behaved? Any trouble?'

'None at all,' Charles assured him, 'and we're both sorry to lose her.'

He paused on the threshold. The cottage was as spruce as ever, and Tom seemed quite strong, if somewhat thinner.

'I forgot the basket,' confessed Charles. 'You go in out of the wind, while I fetch it.'

By the time he returned, the old man was sitting in his wooden armchair with his feet propped up on a stool. Polly lay across his lap, almost covering him, with her head resting on his shoulder.

'You'll have to stay there for the rest of the day,' said Charles. 'It's quite apparent she's not going to let you get away again.'

'And I'm not going, sir, that's a fact. I'm managing well,

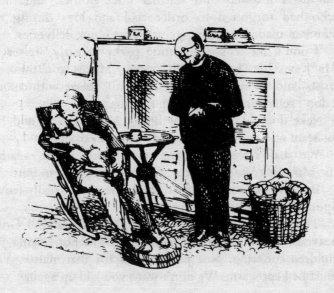

and my good neighbour keeps things up together for me, and does a bit of shopping. I'll be all right now.'

Charles wondered if he should broach the subject of one of the new homes on Thrush Green, but felt that the matter could wait. He turned his attention to unpacking the basket instead.

Dimity had sent a home-made cake, some eggs and rashers and some kedgeree in a screw-top jar. There was also a packet of dog biscuits and the bone which Charles recognized as the residue from yesterday's leg of lamb.

'It seems you've both been provided for,' he said, setting out the provender. 'Now what can I do for you while I'm here? Do you want coal brought in, or anything fetched?'

'No indeed, sir. But if you like to put on the kettle, I'd be pleased to make you a cup of tea when I can get out from under this great silly of a dog.'

And the rector gladly obeyed.

The equinoctial gales came with unusual force, and the leaves came tumbling down. Housewives began looking out extra blankets and warmer underclothes, and those who had forgotten to order coal and logs during the summer, made hasty arrangements for quick deliveries.

'I don't like to see it getting parky so early,' observed Mr Jones of The Two Pheasants. 'Makes you think of frosts, and my hanging baskets are still ablaze with colour. I don't relish bringing them in so soon.'

Next door at the school house Miss Watson and her assistant also deplored the sudden cold weather.

'We shall have to get the stove going if the weather stays like this,' said Dorothy. 'I must mention it to Betty.'

'But what about the office? You know they really frown upon the stoves being lit too early.'

'The office can lump it,' said Dorothy tartly. 'Good heavens, it's October this week, and I'm not having the children suffering. Nor you, Agnes, for that matter. You must be kept warm. We don't want you laid up again.'

'Oh, I shall be all right. My arthritis is really so much better since I've been doing my exercises.'

'Since you've been eating properly,' her friend corrected her. 'Which reminds me. I must leave those beef bones to simmer for stock before we go across to school. This weather makes one think of soup.'

Some half mile away, at Dotty Harmer's, Connie too was dealing with stock and was busy dicing vegetables to put in with a chicken carcase in Dotty's largest saucepan.

Kit had asked her to go with him to see yet another house, this time quite close at Nidden. He had arranged to pick her up at half past two. Dotty had declined the invitation, and said she preferred to take a nap but would see them at tea time.

As Connie chopped carrots and onions her spirits were high. She cherished this friendship with Kit, and knew it was something more than that on her part. As for Kit, who could say? He was cheerful, kindly, attentive and perceptive. She suspected, and hoped, that he too felt as she did. Farther than that she would not go in her thoughts, as things were at present.

One thing bothered her considerably. Why were the houses that he went to see so much too large for a bachelor? And why did he consider that so much garden was essential? Even if he proposed to marry again – and here Connie resolutely put aside the memory of the delectable Diana – there would be no children presumably. And he was not an avid gardener, nor a man who would consider keeping animals. Connie did not like to broach the subject, but it did perplex her.

Squalls of rain were veiling Lulling Woods when Kit arrived, and Dotty, snuggled under the eiderdown, was glad that she was not facing the elements.

'Something smells good,' commented Kit.

'Only stock,' Connie told him. 'I often think it smells better than a whole dinner cooking.'

'Mrs Jenner cooks a great saucepan of odds and ends for

her chickens,' Kit remarked. 'The most delicious scent floats up to my flat. Makes me quite hungry. She mixes in some sort of stuff called "Karswood". I tell her she ought to dish it up for us, it must be good enough.'

He held her mackintosh while she put it on, and they set out to the car through the blustery weather.

Mr Jones's hanging baskets were swinging in the wind outside the pub. A window was banging at Albert Piggott's, and the playground of Thrush Green school was awash with puddles.

'What a beast of a day! I was hoping to show you this latest house in brilliant sunshine.'

'Is it a large house?'

'Four bedrooms. Two bathrooms, and just over an acre of ground. The paddock next to it is up for sale too.'

Connie could keep silence no longer.

'Do you really need anything so big?'

There was silence for a few moments, and Connie wondered if he were offended. His face was serious.

'No,' he said. 'I don't need anything as big. Not for myself.'

A most unwelcome vision of Diana Oliver floated momentarily before Connie's inward eye, blotting out the flicking windscreen wipers and the view beyond.

The road widened here, and a fine beech tree towered on the left hand side. Russet leaves eddied beneath it in the whirling rain.

Kit drew up beneath it and turned to face Connie.

'I should have said all this long before. I wanted you to see the houses because I hoped – I dared to hope, let's say – that I might persuade you to live there with me. And Dotty too, of course.'

'Oh Kit!' said Connie, with a most unromantic hiccup. 'But what about Diana?'

'What Diana?' replied Kit, too much taken aback to bother about correct grammar.

'Diana Oliver,' said Connie, now hiccuping with unbecoming regularity.

'Good God!' cried Kit. 'She doesn't come into it! Anyway, she got married a month ago. I forgot to tell you.'

'I'm glad to hear it,' said Connie. She took a deep breath in order to quell the hiccups.

'Well, my dear, I am trying to ask you if you would think of marrying me. You must have known. I've been trying to say it for weeks!'

Connie looked at him, scarlet in the face from holding her breath. She let it go with a crescendo of hiccups.

'Think of it?' echoed Connie. 'I've thought of nothing else ever since we met.'

A hiccup interrupted her.

'Is that hopelessly unmaidenly? And don't worry about these damned hiccups. I always get them when I'm suddenly happy.'

Kit put his arms around her.

'There's nothing I like more than a hopelessly unmaidenly woman. And what you need is a lump of sugar. I shall carry some in my pocket for the rest of my days.'

Mrs Cooke, pedalling against the wind on her bicycle, was intensely interested in the sight of Mrs Jenner's respectable lodger locked in a close embrace with Dotty Harmer's niece.

'Fine goings-on,' she muttered to herself, as she struggled past the car. 'And both old enough to know better.'

She felt obliged to express her displeasure at the scene when she met Betty Bell on her way to her duties at the school. It was hardly surprising that the famous bush telegraph was humming before many hours had passed.

Bemused, the two elderly lovers drove to the house and followed its owner from one room to the next with unseeing eyes. They nodded vaguely at the conservatory ('very large'), the larder ('north-facing – always cool'), the four bedrooms ('all doubles, if the bed isn't too big') and the monkey-puzzle tree in the garden ('such a feature of the place').

The seller was surprised at their lack of interest, and even more surprised to see them holding hands.

'I take it you are married,' she said at last.

'Not yet,' replied Kit, with such a doting look at his companion, who occasionally emitted a hiccup, that their guide was quite scandalised.

They promised to let her know their decision in a day or two. She showed them to the front door with alacrity, and watched them battle through the rain to their car.

'Well!' she exclaimed as she shut the door. 'They talk about the young ones' behaviour! But what do you think about that?'

Before they reached home, Connie bade Kit stop the car. Reason was beginning to return and almost succeeding in routing the bliss in which she was engulfed.

'We must talk before we go back to Aunt Dotty. You see, it's really out of the question for me to leave her.'

'I know that. That's why I've wanted plenty of ground for the animals, and a big enough place for her to have a room or two of her own.'

'Yes, I see it all now, and love you even more because of it. But still, it would never do, Kit.'

'Why on earth not?'

'I can't ask her to leave her own house. It would be like prising a snail's shell from its back. She's lived there for years now. She couldn't bear to be uprooted.'

Kit gazed at his affianced's troubled face. At least the return of reason, however damping, had stopped the hiccups. He thought she looked prettier than ever.

'Well, don't worry about that now. Let's ask her before you upset yourself. She may jump at the chance to move. You never know.'

'I don't think she will. You see, she's so old and quite groggy. I simply must stay with her. I'd marry you tomorrow, but do you really want to have us *both* on your hands?'

'Try me and see,' said Kit.

Betty Bell, vigorously scouring the school wash basins, turned over Mrs Cooke's disclosure with much pleasure.

It certainly would be nice for Miss Connie to be married, and that Mr Armitage seemed a good sort of fellow. Bit long in the tooth, perhaps, and set in his ways, but *very clean*, and had been quite handsome years ago, so she'd heard. And come to think of it, he had plenty of money, and that was always half the battle in marriage. Mrs Jenner had said that he always paid in advance, and gave her extra for doing his smalls, though she'd never expected it. Yes, one way or another, Miss Connie should be all right.

She paused from her scouring to fish up some extraneous matter from the plug hole. It felt like bubble gum, and when she held it to the light she saw that that was exactly what it was. Children! A good thing Miss Connie was past having any, decided Betty, depositing the revolting pellet in her bucket.

At that moment, another thought struck her. What about Dotty? Surely Miss Connie wouldn't abandon her?

Perhaps they would all move to one of these places Mr Armitage had been viewing. But would Dotty go?

Just then Miss Watson appeared, and broached the subject of the stove. What did Betty think?

'You're right, miss. I'll put a match to it first thing tomorrow. This place is getting proper clammy.'

Miss Watson agreed.

Betty wrung out her cloth and spread it out to dry.

'I've just heard a piece of good news,' said Betty. 'Seems as Romance has come to Miss Harmer and Mr Armitage.'

'Miss *Dotty* Harmer?' queried Dorothy, in stupefaction.

'No, no, no! *Young* Miss Harmer!'

'Well, how very nice! I'm delighted to hear of it. Who told you?'

'Mrs Cooke.'

Dorothy Watson's face dropped. Mrs Cooke had been a thorn in her side, both as mother of many of her pupils and one-time temporary – and most unsatisfactory – school cleaner.

'Oh indeed!' she said frostily. 'I should advise you, Betty, not to repeat the news to *anyone*. We both know how unreliable that lady can be. I shall keep the news to myself – much as I hope that it is true – until I have it confirmed.'

Betty Bell, bursting to confide in all and sundry, nevertheless saw the wisdom of Miss Watson's remarks, and sighed.

'I reckon you're right, miss. But isn't it *romantic* if it's true?'

And Dorothy Watson conceded graciously that it certainly was.

18 Charles Is Melancholy

WHEN KIT AND Connie returned they found Dotty cutting bread and butter. The loaf was of her own making, slightly burnt on top, craggy, and remarkably resistant to the knife.

The slices, when Dotty had managed to hack them from their source, were of the doorstep variety. Kit wondered if he should ever be able to work his way through one.

'You must be starved,' said Dotty, busy with the butter. 'I thought we'd have some of my bramble jelly with this. Full of all the vitamins you need to face the winter.'

Connie made the tea, and it was not until they were settled by the fire that she felt she could tell Dotty their news. But Dotty got in first.

'I had the most peculiar dream,' said Dotty, trying to spread runny jelly. 'I thought I was swimming with dear Papa, and he somehow got out of his depth and was about to drown. And do you know, I was *hesitating*, about rescuing him!'

Very Freudian, was Kit's private thought. From all he remembered of Dotty's formidable parent, drowning seemed a relatively painless demise for one so sadistic.

'I can't remember now if I did or not,' went on Dotty, sucking a sticky finger, 'but the odd thing was the water was warm. How extraordinary things are. And how was the house?'

'Not very suitable,' said Kit, putting down his slice of bread and determined not to pick it up again. 'As a matter of fact, we've wonderful news for you.'

'You've found a better place?'

'No, not that. But Connie has been persuaded to marry me.'

If the happy pair had been expecting any excitement from Dotty at this stupendous news, they were disappointed. Dotty replied in a very matter-of-fact tone of voice.

'Well, I'm so glad to hear it. You've both looked so sheep's-eyed for weeks, I wondered when it would happen. I'm never wrong over these things. I've seen it hundreds of times, you know, with Dulcie and Flossie, not to mention the poultry, though with all those feathers one doesn't get quite the same clarity of facial expression, if you follow me.'

'But you're pleased, Aunt Dotty?' said Connie, with some anxiety. It was not exactly flattering that she had looked like a love-sick female goat, dog, or hen, for some time, but knowing her aunt's little ways she could ignore any such pinpricks.

'Well, of course I'm pleased,' cried Dotty. 'And when's the marriage?'

'We haven't got that far,' said Kit. 'Being engaged is quite enough for today. Could I have some more tea? I find that all this excitement makes me terribly thirsty.'

'Very natural,' said Dotty approvingly.

'It's something to do with the hormones, I believe. I must look it up in my veterinary encyclopedia.'

Dotty poured his tea, and under cover of her preoccupation with the tea pot, Kit smuggled the revolting remains of his bread to the attentive Flossie, who took it, and with commendable intelligence, hid it under the sofa.

Local reaction to the news was predictable and congratulatory. Harold Shoosmith, who had also made a late marriage, was particularly delighted.

'I wonder you didn't tell us, Betty,' he said to her when she was trundling the vacuum cleaner along the hall. 'Miss Harmer rang herself to tell us, but I wouldn't mind betting you knew about it long ago.'

Betty Bell looked smug.

'To tell the truth I heard a couple of days ago, but as it was from that Mrs Cooke, I never said nothing to nobody. I'm not a one for idle gossip, as you know.'

Harold, if asked, would have said quite the opposite. Most of their local intelligence came from Betty. However, it was plain that she was enjoying the fruits of unaccustomed prudence on this occasion, and Harold was quick to commend her for her virtue.

'I wonder if Miss Connie will have a white wedding? Look lovely, wouldn't she? I mean, even if you are past your best there's something dignified about a long white frock.'

Most of the ladies at Thrush Green were also interested in Connie's wedding attire, but the general vote seemed to go to a suit or a frock and jacket.

'Much more sensible,' said Jenny to Winnie Bailey. 'Be

able to wear it afterwards. After all, when can you get the wear out of a wedding dress? Most of 'em end up cut down for a christening robe, and I shouldn't think Miss Connie would need to do that.'

Winnie managed to evade comment, but was amused to find that Connie's age was a cause for discussion among her friends.

'Won't be bothered with the patter of tiny feet, anyway,' was Ella Bembridge's comment.

Phyllida Hurst confessed herself rather sad at the thought of no children.

'Although there was that woman in the Old Testament who had a child when she was about eighty. But of course, they reckoned their ages differently. In cubits or something,' she added vaguely.

Isobel Shoosmith, happily married for the second time, gave whole-hearted support to the proposed union and declared that age had nothing to do with the case, while at Lulling Charles and Dimity rejoiced, and Justin Venables in his office wrote a most beautiful epistle in his best copperplate, and sent Muriel out specially to catch the next post.

The three Misses Lovelock heard the news by telephone from Dotty herself. Miss Ada had answered the telephone in the hall, and Bertha and Violet hovered nearby anxious to be told the message.

'Good gracious!' said Ada. 'Well of course, I am delighted. So will my sisters be. We shall write at once. How nice of you to ring, Dotty. Do give Connie our love and congratulations.'

She replaced the receiver carefully.

'How is Dotty?' asked Bertha.

'Like a cat with two tails. Connie's engaged. You can guess who to.'

Violet was white, and seemed unable to speak.

'Kit?' queried Bertha.

'Yes, Kit Armitage. She's a lucky girl. I'm sure they will be admirably suited.'

'I think I will see if I have closed my bedroom window,' said Violet faintly, making for the stairs.

Bertha and Ada exchanged looks. Bertha began to follow Violet, but Ada shook her head violently.

Violet mounted alone.

Once in the sanctuary of her bedroom, she sank down upon the stool before the dressing table, and gazed at her reflection with unseeing eyes.

So that was that! It was only to be expected, of course, but it made the blow no less painful. She had always known that she could never hope to become Kit's wife, but she had enjoyed such pleasure in these last few months of dallying with the idea of love.

When she had caught a glimpse of Kit striding up the High Street, or he had waved to her from his car, her heart had quickened as if she were still a young girl. His many kindnesses had warmed her. She recalled the little complements, the appreciation of her plum tart, his gratitude on being told about Mrs Bassett's house, and she felt both loved and loving. Now all the daydreams must end.

For they were only daydreams, she knew full well. It was not so much that she had lost Kit, for in her heart she knew she had never been able to call him her own. It was as inescapable fact that this was the end of all hope of love, and that she must resign herself to being one of the three old Lovelock sisters until the day she died.

She became conscious of her reflection in the mirror. Her hair was still thick and wavy, but wholly silver in colour. Her neck was scrawny, her mouth had little lines radiating from it, and two tears shone on her papery cheeks. The hand she lifted to wipe them away, was bent and bony, old and claw-like. There she was, an ancient crone becoming more fragile and forgetful every year. This was the sad truth which she must face. Those last youthful flutterings were now stilled for ever, and had vanished with the once-golden hair, the round pink cheeks and the smiling red mouth.

She rose from the seat and went to look out of the window. The life of Lulling flowed by unheedingly. The dustman was humping a dustbin from The Fushsia Bush. The greengrocer across the road was holding out a cauli- flower for young Mrs Hurts's inspection. The black and white dog, who had so enjoyed the snow earlier in the year, was now sniffing along the railings by his house, and in the distance the church clock struck ten from St Mary's tower.

'Well,' said Violet, stuffing her damp handkerchief into her pocket, 'that's all behind me! Now to work!'

She made for the door, but stopped abruptly by a fine mahogany chest of drawers. On it stood a faded snapshot in a silver frame.

It showed half a dozen young people in the tennis clothes of the late twenties. Among them, taller and hand- somer than any, smiled Kit.

Violet swallowed hard. She put the photograph into the top drawer and went resolutely downstairs to face her sisters.

'I think,' she said, to forestall any comments, 'that I have a cold coming.'

'You must take things gently then, my dear,' said Bertha kindly.

'Why not lie down for an hour or two?' suggested Ada. 'We can bring you up some soup at lunch time. It's no bother, Violet dear.'

'You don't want to start a cold so early. Time enough for that after Christmas. Would an aspirin help?' asked Bertha solicitously.

'The thing that would help most,' said Violet steadily, 'is to carry on as usual. It's my day to make the pudding, I believe. Would you both like trifle?'

'Delicious, Violet,' said Ada.

'Nothing better,' agreed Bertha.

Sisters, although often maddening, can be of great com- fort at times, thought Violet, on her way to the kitchen.

*

The blustery weather continued, and it became much colder.

'Very unseasonable weather,' commented one of the customers in The Two Pheasants.

'Means a hard winter,' prophesied Percy Hodge morosely. His wife was still absent from home, and any hope of her returning grew dimmer as the weeks passed. Percy was much cast down.

'Well, that's healthier than weather that's too muggy,' Albert told him. 'Doctor Lovell told me once he'd sooner see some good sharp frosts than a mild winter. Unhealthy, see? Frost kills the germs. He told me that when I went about my last operation. Did I tell you, Perce?'

'Time and time again,' growled Percy, putting his beer mug on the counter. 'I know more about your inside than me own, and that's a fact.'

'All right, all right!' cried Albert. 'You wants to keep a check on your temper. I don't wonder your Doris left home.'

There was a sudden silence. Percy stood up slowly and menacingly. Albert realized that he had gone too far.

'Sorry, Perce, sorry! Forget it.'

'I don't know as I want to,' said Percy dangerously.

Mr Jones bustled round from the other side of the bar.

'Now, now, gentlemen! We don't want no silly talk in here. You sit down again, Percy, and have the other half. It's on the house.'

'Oh, it is, is it?' said Albert nastily.

'And I hope you'll have a half pint too,' said Mr Jones, with hasty diplomacy. 'Come on, boys! Sit down again.'

The two men obeyed with some reluctance. The beer was put before them, and they acknowledged the gift with nods.

The mugs were half empty before Percy spoke, after wiping his frothy mouth with the back of his hand.

'She ain't ever coming back, you know,' he said at last to Albert. 'All that advice you give me about being dignified and that, and then she'd come back! Well, it don't work, Albert. I wrote to her a week ago, and I had a letter this morning. She's got a job at Marks and Sparks. Likes it too, and her sister's putting her up. I reckon I made a fool of meself there, Albert.'

The beer was beginning to make him maudlin.

Albert did his best to be a comforter.

'I reckon you're better off without her, Perce. She don't know when she's well off. A good chap like you – she must be off her rocker to throw you over. Forget her, is my advice.'

'It's all right for you,' grumbled the abandoned husband. 'You've got your Nelly back safe and sound.'

'Well, to tell the truth, that ain't all beer and skittles by a long chalk. She's taken up Bingo twice a week, and I gets cold supper them nights. And what she's spending I dursen't think.'

Percy nodded sadly.

'Women is nothing but trouble,' he sighed. 'Well, Albert, best get back to work, I suppose.'

He linked his arm in Albert's, and the two set off rather unsteadily to the door.

Mr Jones watched their departure with infinite relief.

On one of the cold windy evenings, Charles Henstock made his way from the vicarage to St John's church.

He had arranged to meet the organist there to decide on the music for a recital to raise money for the Church Fabric Fund. Raising money had never come easily to the good rector, and now that he had four churches under his care he found the upkeep of them a formidable problem.

The loss of the fund's box had been a setback, although Charles realized, since he had made a point of emptying the new one daily, that contributions were very small indeed.

He did not blame people. He knew only too keenly how short of money so many families were these days. He too denied himself in many things, and was glad to do so,

embarrassed at times by the multitude of expensive gimmicks he found in the homes of some of his parishioners.

He was beginning to realize too that Anthony Bull and
his wealthy and generous wife gave readily to St John's,
something which he could not do in his more humble circumstances.

The rector pondered on these things as he sat in his
accustomed place in the chancel, awaiting the arrival of Bill
Mitchell.

The church was cavernous and dark. Only the chancel
light was on. It was also bone-chillingly cold, and Charles
wished that he had put on a thicker coat.

It had been a sad day. The post had brought a letter
from a friend of his schooldays to tell him of the death
from leukemia of their only son. Charles had been the
boy's godfather.

The sense of shock had remained with him throughout
the day. The death of one's parents' generation one could
accept, albeit with sadness.

When the time of life came, as it had to Charles, that his
own contemporaries were common in the obituary col-
umns, it was always a severe shock. But when, as today,
one heard of the young, the children, the rising generation
going untimely to the grave, it was enough to break one's
heart.

He had gone about his duties all day with a shattering
sense of loss. He normally enjoyed robust health. Today he
suddenly realized how fragile and empty he felt, as vulner-
able as a wounded bird, or a broken sapling. How rapidly,
it seemed, one could change from a strong being to an
invalid. It was a sharp lesson on the frailty of life.

The weather had done nothing to raise his spirits. Mist
had risen from the river and engulfed the little town.
People moved like ghosts, emerging from greyness to
vanish again within yards. No wonder the Americans
called this the fall of the year, ruminated Charles, sitting in
his chilly church. It was not just the falling of the leaves, it

was the decline of abounding life everywhere, the quiet slide from summer's joy towards winter's death.

He stirred himself and peered at his wrist watch. What could have happened to the organist? Bill Mitchell was always so punctual, and now he was ten minutes overdue.

He traversed the long aisle, and opened the south door. Dead leaves had gathered in the porch, and rustled as he walked through them. He made his way to the wrought iron gate. The bulk of his own vicarage loomed dimly through the mist.

Nearer at hand, beyond the graves, were six ancient almshouses. The lights shone mutedly in the mist. Waiting by the gate, his hand on the clammy metal, Charles saw one of the doors open. The clinking of bottles made him aware of the milk bottles being put out on the stone doorstep, ready for the morning.

The radio was on quite loudly, and a violin sobbed across the gloom. It had a haunting sound, 'a dying fall', which affected Charles with unaccustomed melancholy. He was glad when the door slammed, and he heard it no more.

The trees dripped dismally. There were puddles in the path. Really, thought Charles, all the approaches to the church needed fresh gravel. There was so much to do, and at times he felt that it was all beyond him. He mourned his loss of physical strength, his lost youth and vigour, his lost companions. Perhaps the succession of pinpricks, the criticisms, the petty comparisons with Anthony's ministrations, the departure of people like Mrs Thurgood from his flock, had contributed to his present low spirits. But the overwhelming feeling was this poignant one of loss.

Even dear old Polly had now gone, he remembered with a pang. And his old rectory was no more. He had been happy there, and had grieved far more keenly than his wife and friends over the charred remains. There were still precious objects which he missed. His old crucifix was one, a Bible given to him at his confirmation, a letter-opener he had made as a child, and innumerable dearly-loved books which could never be replaced.

Charles sighed. He was about to retrace his steps when a car skidded to a halt in the road, a door slammed, and Bill Mitchell ran towards him.

'I'm so *very* sorry,' he cried. 'Some poor chap had crashed his lorry and blocked the road. It was full of bottles of tomato ketchup, so the place looked like a battle field, besides bristling with glass.'

'No one hurt, I hope?'

'Only Constable Darwin who slipped up in the mess and sat down. But he's quite all right. Directed us all round the houses, which is why I'm so late.'

They entered by the south door, which the rector locked behind him. In the light of the chancel Bill Mitchell looked at the rector.

'Are you all right? You look as though you might have a chill.'

'No, no,' protested Charles, touched by this solicitude. 'I find this weather a little depressing, but that's all.'

'Good! Well, let's get down to the music. That will cheer us up. Music always does.'

'You are quite right, Bill,' agreed Charles, rubbing his cold hands briskly. 'Music always does!'

19 Marriage Plans

THE ENGAGEMENT OF Kit and Connie afforded general satisfaction to their friends in Lulling and Thrush Green, but after the congratulations came two questions.

The first was: 'Where would they live?' The second was: 'Would Dotty live with them?'

Connie had been the first to pose them, and it was she who insisted that she would broach the subject with Dotty when they were alone.

'It's the best way,' she told Kit. 'If she's willing to move and come with us to a new place, then that settles it. But, if she won't, and I think that's more likely, we shall just have to think again.'

Kit agreed, and Connie awaited a suitable opportunity. It did not arise until two or three days after the engagement.

The two women were sitting by the fire, Dotty engrossed in brushing Flossie, and Connie trying to do the crossword. Kit was calling at half past three, and Connie decided that this was the moment to grasp the nettle.

'Where would I live?' queried Dotty, pausing momentarily from her work. 'The point is where are you deciding to live?'

'As you know, Aunt Dotty, Kit hasn't found anything yet. We must know if you would be willing to make a new home with us. One thing's certain. I shan't leave you, and Kit knows it, and approves.'

'That dratted dog!' exclaimed Dotty, as Flossie made her escape and went to ground under the sofa.

'Well, dear,' continued Dotty, putting down the brush. 'I've been giving a lot of thought to this matter ever since Kit appeared on the scene, and it was as plain as a pike staff to me that he had his eye on you.'

'You make me sound like a bargain!' protested Connie.

'And so you are. Now, I can't think why you keep fussing about looking at houses when you know this one is yours. I know it's not all that commodious, but you could always build on. Edward Young could probably run you up a nice little annexe. He's quite intelligent, and those homes of his are really very pleasant for people who don't want to go upstairs to bed.'

'But its *your* house, not mine!'

'It's left to you, as you know, and I shall be in Thrush Green churchyard before long,' said Dotty cheerfully. 'And I only hope that Albert Piggott will have gone too by then. Such a muddler at his work. I still think they would have been better advised to let my goats crop the grass there. The mowing is deplorable.'

Connie sat pondering on this development. Dotty was quite right. There was plenty of space round the cottage on which to build. It would solve the problem too of Dotty's future.

The only thing was how would Kit feel about settling at such close quarters with this dear, but slightly mad, relative?

As if reading her thoughts, Dotty rambled on.

'You see, there are *three* bedrooms after all, which would make one apiece. Though, of course, when you are married it would be quite in order, dear, for you to share one room.'

'I had realized that,' said Connie.

'And it would be a very good thing to be on the

premises when the builders were working. Some of these fellows can be very dilatory, and I know for a fact that the men who renovated Tullivers, for the Hursts, were not above sitting down and *playing cards*!'

Dotty made it sound like one of the deadly sins.

'I said to them often: "This wouldn't do for my father, you know. You would have got short shrift had he been employing you!" They were quite impertinent, I remember.'

Dotty grew quite pink at the memory.

'Very naughty of them,' agreed Connie, wishing she had been on the scene at the time. 'Well, Aunt Dot, it's a marvellous offer, and I shall tell Kit about it. But could you bear to share your house?'

'It's *your* house! And there's nothing I should enjoy more than having you both under this roof. I could keep an eye on you, and make sure that Kit treated you properly.'

'I don't think he will turn out a wife-beater,' said Connie.

'You never can tell,' replied Dotty. 'Do bend down, dear, and fetch Flossie out. She badly needs kempting.'

'Kempting?' echoed Connie.

'Well, if she's *unkempt*, which she most certainly is, then she should be made the opposite. Now, where did I put that brush?'

Walking into Lulling with Kit that afternoon, Connie told him of Dotty's plans.

'There's a lot to be said for it,' he agreed. 'It settles Aunt Dotty's future, and I honestly think we could have a lovely house there if it were sensibly enlarged. The site is perfect and I shouldn't think there would be any planning difficulties. If you like the idea, I'll have a word with Edward, and see what he thinks about the possibilities.'

'I'm all for it,' said Connie, 'but are you truly happy about these arrangements? I can see some men refusing

point blank, and I shouldn't blame them. Aunt Dotty's not everybody's idea of a close companion.'

'My dear girl, I know quite well I shall never get you to leave her, and I respect you for it. Therefore, if I want you – and God knows I do – then I'm more than happy to take on dear old Dotty as well. I think she's being uncommonly generous in making the offer. Let's jolly well enjoy it. We ought to have a lot of fun planning the new building.'

'It's an enormous weight off my mind,' confessed Connie. 'Let's have a cup of tea at The Fuchsia Bush to celebrate.'

Kit's landlady, Mrs Jenner, was delighted on her lodger's account to know of the forthcoming marriage, but told him frankly that she hardly dared to hope that she would ever get such a paragon again in her upstairs flat.

'Nonsense!' Kit said. 'You wait and see. There'll be a queue from here to Nidden when the word goes round that there's a flat here to let. You'll be able to pick and choose, and state any rent you like.'

'I'm not sure I shall let at all,' said Mrs Jenner. 'Percy

keeps badgering me to have him here for good. I've said to him, time and time again: "Look here, Perce! I don't want you, so stop asking!" But, you know, he won't take a hint.'

Some hint, thought Kit privately! It sounded a straight-forward ultimatum from sister to brother to him. He hoped that Mrs Jenner would not weaken. It was time she had life a little easier, and Percy could look after himself quite well, if he would get over his self-pity.

'I tell him,' went on his landlady, 'that I want the place to myself now and again. Percy would expect a cooked dinner prompt at twelve o'clock, meat and two veg and a proper pudding. Well, I'm not starting. A boiled egg and a slice of toast does me, and I've had my fill of cooking over the years. Besides, I'm enjoying getting out of an evening now. I like my choral nights, and Bingo.'

'Have you won anything?' asked Kit.

'Well, I once won eighty pence, but you'll never believe this! Nelly Piggott won fifty pounds last week. Think of it! But don't breathe a word, will you?'

'Of course not. But surely there were dozens of people present who know all about it?'

'Maybe, but Nelly doesn't want Albert to hear of it. She's putting by as much as she can in case he ever throws her out again.'

This was news to Kit, who had always understood that it was Nelly who deserted Albert, not the other way about.

'She's a good sort,' went on Mrs Jenner, 'and a real hard worker. They say The Fuchsia Bush is coining money since she started cooking there. I've got quite fond of her over the last few months, and I reckon she's had a hard time.'

'Well, you can count on me,' Kit assured her. 'I shan't say anything about her winnings. But I hope their marriage won't break up again.'

'Well, marriage is a proper lottery, isn't it? And when's yours to be?'

'Soon after Christmas. There's quite a bit to be arranged.

I must sort out some of my furniture still in store for one thing.'

'And it will take some time to get the plans passed for the new wing on Miss Harmer's place, won't it?' said Mrs Jenner conversationally.

As neither Kit himself nor Connie had breathed a word of their hopes to anyone, he realized that this was just another prize example of rural communication at work.

'That's quite right,' he agreed resignedly.

As Dimity had remarked to Ella on an earlier occasion, Christmas seemed to have sneaked up on Lulling and Thrush Green, and no doubt on the rest of the British Isles as well.

At Thrush Green School Miss Fogerty had set her children to making Christmas cards and calendars already. Miss Potter's slightly older children were promoted to book-marks with tassels, knitted string dish cloths and covers for the *Radio Times* and *TV Times*, in crash embroidered with lazy daisy stitch.

Miss Watson's class, as befitted the most experienced and talented members of the school, were engaged on such heady projects as tea-cosies, handerkchief sachets, decorated boxes and tea pot stands.

As well as all this handicraft activity, Christmas carols were being practised and plans were afoot for a Christmas party. Anything more ambitious had been vetoed this year after much earnest discussion in the school house.

'I really don't think I can face another nativity play,' confessed Miss Watson. 'I know the mothers are marvellous in getting the costumes done and helping with the make-up, but there's always some crisis or other. Do you remember when the three wise men all wore dreadful robes which clashed terribly? And then John Todd's mother was so difficult about providing a beard for Joseph? And really the floorboards are far too splintery for all that kneeling, and I do detest taking my rug over for the front of the manger. In any case, I don't think Axminster looks reverent enough.'

'A nativity play certainly makes a lot of work,' agreed Agnes. 'And the one pantomime we tried years ago was a little amateurish, I felt.'

'To be honest,' said Dorothy, 'I suppose we are getting past all the effort. But after all, if things had been as we wanted we should be retired by now. I really don't think we need to feel too guilty, at our age, for making Christmas simpler.'

'In any case,' pointed out Agnes, 'we are having the carol service in the church this year, instead of at the school. It should be a very impressive afternoon, and I'm sure the parents will appreciate it.'

'Mrs Todd won't. She's staunch Plymouth Brethren, and is refusing to let John set foot in St Andrew's.'

'Sometimes one wonders if church unity will ever be realized,' said Agnes, shaking her head.

'Well, I've a scheme which I think ought to be realized,' said Dorothy, changing the subject. 'As soon as term ends, I propose that we spend Christmas at Barton and have a thorough rest.'

'What a wonderful idea! But can we afford it?'

'We're going to,' said Dorothy firmly. 'You are not really fit yet, and my leg is still a nuisance. I think it would do us both a world of good to have a week by the sea, and to let other people wait on us. What's more, we might even hear of a little house for sale while we're down there.'

'But what about the parties we usually go to? And the Christmas Day service at St Andrew's?'

'They'll have to do without our presence for once. No, Agnes, my mind's made up. No bothering with Christmas catering, no standing about at cocktail parties drinking stuff you don't want while your headache gets worse, no last-minute presents to deliver. We're going to have a very quiet, lazy week indulging ourselves. And surely, Agnes, at our age, we deserve it?'

'Indeed we do, indeed we do!' agreed little Miss Fogerty.

Across the green, Christmas preparations were also going on. Jenny was surveying a splendidly rich fruit cake, and deciding on its future icing. Ella Bembridge was sorting out scarves and ties of her own weaving for the unfortunate recipients of her bounty. Joan and Edward Young were trying to fix a convenient date to have a mammoth Christmas shopping spree, and in every house where there were children notes were being sent up the chimney to Santa Claus, most of them asking for presents of such magnitude and expense that parents' hearts quailed.

At Lulling the pace was even faster. The shops were beginning their pre-Christmas fever, and the council men were threading the lime trees with coloured lights.

The Fuchsia Bush had a mouth-watering display of Christmas cakes, boxes of home-made sweets and short-bread, most of them made by Nelly Piggott and her helpers. Mrs Peters was looking forward to a bumper Christmas this year, and congratulated herself on being able to keep Nelly in her employ as well as Mrs Jefferson.

Next door, the three Lovelock sisters were already going through the little gifts which had been put aside throughout the year. Some had been bought at local bazaars or coffee mornings. Some had been given to them and were un-wanted. This useful store was now being allotted to various friends, many of whom would recognize the gift, when the time came, as something they had given to one of the sisters on an earlier occasion. It was all part of the fun. One particular vase, of hideous shape and unsteady on its base, had been bandied about the Lovelock circle for more years than could be recalled, and was looked upon as a peripatetic old friend. People had been known to say with pride: 'I've got the vase this year!'

It was early in December that Charles and Dimity had unexpected visitors.

The morning was clear and cold, the grass glittering with hoar frost. At Dimity's bird table greenfinches, tits and chaffinches squabbled for the nuts and fat, and on this sharp morning even the rooks from the trees in the church-yard had flown down for Dimity's largesse.

Charles was in the greenhouse picking dead leaves from his geranium cuttings, and doing a little watering. He found the brilliant morning a comfort to his spirits, for he had been unable to throw off entirely the unusual melancholy which seemed to envelop him.

He had said nothing about it to Dimity. The feeling was nebulous, and Charles chided himself for harbouring these unwanted spells of sadness. They would pass. He did not intend to burden anyone, and certainly not his dear wife, with such vague twinges of discomfort.

Working among his plants, ministering to their needs in peaceful warmth, the good rector felt calmed and useful. He set about repotting some penstemon cuttings, enjoying the feeling of the moist compost in his hands, and the sight of tiny white roots thrusting bravely into the world.

He was so engrossed in his job, cares forgotten for a while, that he was surprised to find that his wrist watch said eleven o'clock. Dimity would be brewing coffee, and he dusted his hands, and went off to the house.

The frost still furred the grass, and there was ice on the bird bath. But the sun was beginning to shed warmth, and the sky was a brilliant blue.

Hurrying to the front door, Charles was surprised to see a large shining car there, and recognized it as Anthony Bull's.

He and his wife had just arrived and Dimity was taking their coats. Her face was alight with joy.

'Isn't this marvellous?' she said. 'I was just going to send a search party for you.'

The Bulls were equally pleased at this reunion.

'We are on our way to Cirencester,' Anthony said, 'to deliver Christmas presents to an aged uncle of mine, and we couldn't resist dropping in. Have we interrupted anything vital?'

'Nothing!' Charles assured him.

The two women went out to the kitchen to superintend the coffee making.

'It all looks splendid,' said Anthony, gazing across the garden to his former church. 'And how are things going?'

'I love the place,' said Charles, 'and so does Dimity. And I have had the greatest kindness from so many people.'

'From *all*, from what I hear.'

'I'm afraid not *all*, Anthony. You know, you were a difficult man to follow. I lack so many fine qualities which you possess, and which, I think, my congregation misses.'

'Rubbish!' exclaimed Anthony. 'You must not belittle yourself, Charles. You have got a wonderful reputation in the parish – in all four parishes – and the Bishop has told me several times how highly he thinks of you.'

Charles looked at his friend in amazement.

'We see quite a bit of him. He stays with us if he has a meeting in London. He's pretty shrewd, and has his ear to the ground. He's told me about a score of happenings here which have warmed his heart. And mine too, for that matter. There's no doubt about it, Charles, you are a far more conscientious parish priest than ever I was.'

'I don't believe it,' protested Charles.

'It wasn't all plain sailing for me, you know. Every clergyman has to face criticism from some quarter. I may have given satisfaction to those who enjoy a good sermon and a well-decorated church. I hope I did. But I faced quite a bit if suspicion from others. I think they resented the fact that my wife is a wealthy woman. The less generous of them were inclined to sneer at "too much display", as I heard one call it. I often thought about the camel and the eye of the needle, Charles, and I came to the conclusion that you simply can't please all the people all the time. So one just gets on with the job, as best one can, and that's it.'

Charles felt much comforted by this sound reasoning.

'But I can't believe that you ever met such slights. I've only heard good of you, Anthony.'

'You only hear from those who are articulate. There are plenty in Lulling who say little to one's face, but who make their feelings known to their friends. Take heart, Charles! What does it matter in the end? We are both doing our humble best. Let the Almighty judge our endeavours.'

Charles smiled at his old friend.

'You've done me a power of good. And you're quite right. Ah! I hear the coffee arriving.'

And he bustled across to open the door.

Three Christmas Visitors

THE WEDDING OF Kit and Connie was arranged for the first week in January, and the banns were read at St Andrew's church.

It was to be a quiet affair. Apart from her aunt Dotty, Connie had few relatives, and Kit was similarly placed. Some old friends from Thrush Green and Lulling were invited, and the service was to be at eleven o'clock. Joan and Edward Young insisted on the wedding breakfast being held in their house.

'It will be a buffet affair,' Joan said. 'Kit and Connie are off to Heathrow before two, but it will give us time for wishing them well.'

The honeymoon was to be spent in Madeira, and they were not returning until the end of January. The fact that they had this opportunity to spend over three weeks in the sunshine was due mainly to Winnie Bailey's insistence.

As soon as she had heard the wedding plans she called to see Connie whilst Dotty was aloft having her afternoon nap.

'Let her come to stay with me, Connie. Jenny and I would love it, and we have plenty of room. It would never do to leave her here, even if she had someone living in. You know full well she would be out in the garden, and coping with the animals, whatever the weather. And she really would revert to her catering ways – an apple in her hand as she wandered about, and nothing cooked.'

'I know exactly what you mean,' said Connie. 'I was going to ask Mrs Jenner if she could have Kit's old room while we're away. I know she would care for her, but it hardly seemed fair to expect her to take responsibility for dear old Dotty. She is rather a handful.'

Winnie thought that this was the understatement of the year, but not the moment to say so.

'I know Mrs Jenner goes out on some evenings,' said Winnie, 'and really Dotty shouldn't be alone in the house. If she were with us there would be two of us to care for her, and also she wouldn't be tempted to potter out to see to things as I know she would if she were here, or even at Mrs Jenner's. Do think it over, Connie, and say "Yes".'

And so it had been arranged. Albert Piggott had jumped at the chance of looking after the animals, night and morning, and of taking complete charge of the goat Dulcie on whom he doted. Betty Bell would continue her ministrations twice a week. All the post would be delivered to Winnie Bailey's address, and far more important than any of these plans was the enthusiastic agreement of Dotty herself.

Kit and Connie approached Edward Young with their ideas for the enlargement of Dotty's cottage, and the three of them spent many hours discussing possibilities.

It was only a few days before Christmas when they agreed Edward's final design which he promised to submit to the local planning committee.

'And I don't think there should be any difficulty,' he assured them. 'You've got a marvellous site there, and whatever is built is not going to affect anyone nearby. Everything's there already in the way of drainage, electricity and so on, and there's easy access for the builders so that they will have no excuse for uprooting hedges and chopping down trees when no one's looking. Leave it all with me, my children, and go and enjoy yourselves.'

'We intend to,' said Kit. 'But none of it would have been possible without friends in Thrush Green.'

Matters at the Piggott household continued to run with unaccustomed harmony. Nelly, still happy in her job at The Fuchsia Bush, was made still happier when she discovered that she had lost almost a stone in weight and felt all the better for it.

It was not lack of food. She usually had a substantial lunch provided by The Fuchsia Bush, but there was no doubt that the semi-run downhill to Lulling, and the arduous plod back after work, were giving the lady much-needed exercise.

Better still, from Nelly's point of view, was the healthy state of her Post Office savings' account. It now stood at one hundred and seventy five pounds, boosted most satisfactorily by the fifty-pound Bingo winnings.

All in all, Nelly found life at Thrush Green much pleasanter than she had expected on her nervous return from the perfidious Charlie. Of him, she had heard nothing. She assumed that his entanglement with his new love still engrossed him. They were both welcome, Nelly told herself. She had had quite enough of love. Good health, a nice job and money behind her really provided a much more satisfactory state of mind, and she said as much to her new friend, Mrs Jenner, as they puffed uphill one evening from a Bingo session.

'You're quite right, Nelly,' said Mrs Jenner. 'I know Albert's behaving himself very well at the moment, and looking forward to spending time with Dulcie, so he's in good spirits, but you watch your step, my dear! Put as much in your account as you can. There's nothing like a bit of money behind you. That way you can be independent, and I don't care what all the book-writers say about love and marriage. To my mind, you can't trust men.'

And with this sentiment Nelly heartily agreed.

*

The visit of Anthony Bull had done much to comfort Charles. To be told that he was considered by his Bishop to be a conscientious parish priest made Charles feel humble as well as proud.

He treasured too, Anthony's own kindly comments, and only hoped that they were not exaggerated. It was amazing to Charles to learn that there had ever been any adverse criticism of his predecessor, although he realized now that, as Anthony had pointed out, no man in the public eye could expect to be free of censure in some form or other. Those few exchanges with Anthony had put matters into perspective for Charles, and he felt greatly heartened.

Dimity was much relieved to see this improvement in his spirits. She had grieved to see him cast down during the past few weeks, and guessed the cause. Primarily, she blamed Mrs Thurgood. Charles had taken her wounding remarks much to heart, Dimity considered, and she could never forgive her for making her dear husband so unhappy.

Charles, of course, would have none of it, brushing aside Dimity's queries, and insisting that he was in perfect health and spirits. Now it really seemed that the doldrums were over, and Dimity rejoiced.

A week or two before Christmas she left him immediately after lunch to spend the afternoon at an old people's Christmas party in Lulling.

It was bitterly cold, with a cruel northerly wind sweeping the High Street, as she made her way to the hall at the other end of the town.

The shops were gaily decked for Christmas, and a fine Christmas tree was being put in place in the little square by the Butter Market. Dimity, ignoring the wind, thought it all looked remarkably gay.

Across the road she saw old Tom Hardy with a large parcel under his arm. Polly was on a lead, trotting quite briskly, and although Dimity waved to him, he did not see her, and continued steadily up the street towards Lulling church. He was certainly walking well, thought Dimity, and it was good to see the two old friends united again.

It was some minutes later that Charles went to the back door. There stood Tom and Polly.

'Come in! Come in, out of this dreadful wind,' cried the rector, ushering them in. 'It's good to see you both.'

Polly's tail wagged in greeting, and she moved towards the study where she guessed correctly that the rector had a fire.

Tom carried the parcel with him and settled in an arm chair.

'I've brought you and Mrs Henstock a little Christmas present,' he said, pushing the parcel across the rector's desk. 'It's not much, but I made it myself.'

'May I undo it?'

'Of course, sir. Tell me if you think it'll do.'

Charles unwrapped it carefully. The old man had done it up beautifully, and the parcel was stoutly secured with string. It took some time to get the present free, but at last it was revealed.

Tom had made a fine sturdy birds' nesting box with a cleverly thatched roof.

'It's superb!' the rector told him. 'A marvellous piece of work! Dimity will be delighted.'

'Well, I know she's one for the birds, and I thought it would give you both pleasure. It's just a little return for all your kindness to me and Polly.'

The dog, hearing her name, thumped her tail on the hearth rug.

'I wish my wife were here to thank you too,' said Charles. 'She will be sorry to have missed you. I can assure you, Tom, you couldn't have given us anything more welcome. Now, let me get you a drink.'

'No, no, I won't if you don't mind, sir. I've another call to make, and then I'll get back before it's dark.'

He stood up briskly, and Charles was pleased to see how much stronger he seemed.

'Then I won't keep you, but thank you again for a perfect present. Come out this way, Tom, it's quicker for you.'

He led the way to the front door, shook hands with the old man and patted Polly.

He watched the two setting off down the drive. They had reached the gate when a car turned in.

To Charles's dismay, he recognized it as the one belonging to Mrs Thurgood.

'Will you come into my study? I'm afraid the drawing room fire isn't alight yet. Dimity is out this afternoon.'

'No doubt about her good works,' said Mrs Thurgood, graciously accepting a seat.

Her eye alighted on Tom's nesting box.

'What an attractive object!' Charles found Mrs Thurgood's smile almost as disconcerting as her withering tongue, but at least it seemed that she was in a pleasant mood.

'Tom Hardy made it,' said he. 'It's an early Christmas present. I'm looking forward to showing it to my wife.'

'Yes, I've heard about your kindness to that old fellow,' replied Mrs Thurgood. 'One of your *many* kindnesses, let me add, which is why I have called.'

Charles was nonplussed. This complete change of attitude was puzzling enough, but he could not recall any particular favour he had given Mrs Thurgood. Their paths had not crossed since their last stormy meeting.

'I wanted you to know that Janet is going to be married shortly, and you were the person who introduced her to her future husband, John Fairbrother.'

'I'm delighted to know,' said Charles. 'He seemed a very pleasant young man, and much admired your daughter's work, I remember.'

'Yes, he really does recognize her remarkable artistic ability, I'm happy to say. Of course, he has very little money, and is rather shy in manner, but he is *very well-connected*. The Shropshire Fairbrothers, you know.'

'Indeed,' said Charles. The phrase, 'very well-connected' was one which the good rector heard often from the lips of his more socially-conscious parishioners. He had once overheard: 'I know that he is seriously addicted to drugs, and has spent several months in prison, but he is *very well-connected*.' It seemed to excuse all.

'We should so much like the wedding here at St John's,' went on Mrs Thurgood, coming to the point, 'probably just before Easter. Such a pretty time of year with all the daffodils out. And, of course, I do so hope that you will agree to take the service. Having introduced them, you know, so very fitting.'

Mrs Thurgood gave the rector another unnerving smile. He rallied his strength.

'I shall be delighted to officiate,' he assured her. 'It will be a pleasure as well as a duty. With so much in common, they should be a very happy pair.'

Mrs Thurgood gave a little sigh of relief. It was plain to the rector that this confrontation had needed courage, and his tender heart was touched.

Mrs Thurgood rose to go.

'I am so glad that you will take the service. I was afraid that perhaps you might dislike the idea. My daughter and I have sometimes felt that we were a little – how shall I put it?'

'Don't attempt to put it,' said Charles impulsively. 'Let bygones be bygones. There are no hard feelings on my side, I promise you, and I very much appreciate your coming here today.'

He opened the study door and accompanied his visitor down the hall.

'Ah! Just one moment,' she said, rummaging in her large crocodile-skin handbag. 'Open it when you are alone,' she ordered him, thrusting an envelope into his hand.

'Thank you,' said Charles, somewhat bemused, but imagining that this was a Christmas card which she was very sensibly delivering by hand to save postage.

'Well, this is the season of giving and goodwill, isn't it?' said Mrs Thurgood, climbing into her car. 'Very glad that we are friends again.'

She waved, and drove off.

Charles returned to his fireside and opened the envelope. It did indeed contain a handsome card depicting the nativity. But within that was a folded cheque.

It was made out to St John's Church Fabric Fund, and had more noughts on it than Charles had ever seen on a cheque before.

He had to sit down suddenly to recover from the shock.

By the time Christmas arrived most of the inhabitants of Lulling and Thrush Green were quite exhausted with all the many preparations, and were looking forward to having a rest as soon as possible.

The weather had turned mild and tranquil, as is so often the case at this time, making a mockery of the Christmas card scenes of stage coaches in deep snow, children constructing snowmen and winter landscapes complete with skaters.

In Lulling gardens a few tattered roses still clung to unpruned bushes, and one or two early crocuses and snowdrops were thrusting through the damp soil. The more morose inhabitants, such as Albert Piggott, reminded each other of the old saying that a green Christmas meant a full churchyard.

But on the whole, people rejoiced in the mild spell, and among them was Charles Henstock. He had been able to go about his visiting, and to attend the plethora of pre Christmas festivities, unencumbered by slippery roads and snow drifts.

On the morning of the great day he awoke early as usual. Dimity was still deep in sleep, and the rector thought of the duties before him with real pleasure.

It would be a busy day. He was to go to Thrush Green first, to take Holy Communion at eight o'clock in the church he loved so well. At eleven he would officiate at Morning Service at St John's, and at three-thirty he was due at his most distant church at Lulling Woods for Evensong.

Today, he knew, those churches would be full and he would have the joy of seeing almost all his flock.

He looked forward keenly to his Christmas Day. It was still dark, but by the illuminated dial of the bedside clock he saw that he must rise if he wished to be in good time.

He smiled in the darkness. How lucky he was to have work that he relished! How lucky to have escaped from the gloomy valley he had been transversing, and to have entered the sunny uplands again!

He edged gently out of bed, hoping not to disturb his wife, but she stirred as he moved.

'Happy Christmas!' she murmured, her eyes still closed.

'It will be,' said the rector, with conviction.

AT HOME IN THRUSH GREEN

AT HOME THRUSH

For
Nina and Bill
With Love

Among new men, strange faces, other minds.
Tennyson (1809–1892)

The house of every one is the him as his castle and fortress.
Sir Edward Coke (1552–1634)

Contents

PART THREE
Getting Settled

PART ONE
Work in Progress

1   June Afternoon

'**I** MUST PAY A visit to Thrush Green this afternoon,' said Dimity Henstock to her husband Charles.

They were breakfasting in the kitchen of Lulling Vicarage. Charles buttered a slice of toast carefully.

'I can drive you there before two, my dear, but I have this meeting in Oxford at three.'

'Don't worry, I shall walk. Ella is clean out of light blue tapestry wool for her lovers' knots, and I have some here.'

'Her lovers' knots?' echoed Charles, toast poised.

'Round the edge of the chair seat,' explained Dimity.

She rose and began to clear the table. Charles, still looking bewildered, chewed the last mouthful of toast.

'I must get on, dear,' said Dimity. 'Mrs Allen comes today, and I like to get things cleared up.'

'I always thought that we employed Mrs Allen for the express purpose of clearing up for us.'

'Yes, one would think that in theory, but in practice, of course, it really makes more work to do.'

'Then I will go and water the greenhouse,' said the vicar of Lulling, rector of Thrush Green, and general priest in charge of Lulling Woods and Nidden – otherwise Charles Henstock.

He stepped out of the back door into the dewy freshness of a fine June morning, and made his way happily through the vicarage garden.

*

As he tended his seedlings in the pleasantly humid atmosphere of the greenhouse, Charles pondered on the felicity of his life in Lulling.

His present vicarage and its garden were both mellow and beautiful, owing much to the care given by his immediate predecessor, Anthony Bull, who now had a living in Kensington, where his good looks and slightly dramatic sermons were as much admired there as they had been at Lulling. Charles and he remained staunch friends.

Charles had been twice married, and after the untimely death of his first wife life had been bleak. Soon after, he had been appointed to the living of Thrush Green, where he dwelt in the ugliest and coldest house there. Most of the dwellings round the large triangle of grass which gave the place its name, were built of Cotswold stone and tiled to match. Why a Victorian builder had ever been allowed to erect the gloomy pile which had been Charles's home for so many years, remained a mystery.

The good rector, the humblest and most hard-working of men, seemed oblivious of the draughts, the murkiness, and the sheer discomfort of his home. When he married his second wife, Dimity, who had shared a cottage with her friend Ella Bembridge nearby, he was perplexed to hear her complaints about her new abode, and did his best to help her to render the rectory more comfortable.

In fact, it was a losing battle. The house faced northeast, was shoddily built, and had a long corridor, leading from the front door to the back, which acted as an efficient wind tunnel and chilled the atmosphere whenever either door was opened.

Two or three years before the present June morning, the whole place had been consumed by fire, and very few local people regretted its passing.

Charles himself was devastated. He and Dimity had been away from home on the night of the fire, but he knew that he could never forget the sight of the smoking ruins which greeted him on his return.

He shuddered now at the remembrance, standing upright, a minute seedling of Cos lettuce held between thumb and forefinger, and his gaze fixed, unseeing, upon the present splendour of his Lulling garden beyond the greenhouse glass. His mind's eye saw again the blackened heap, the drifting smoke, and the pathetic huddle of his salvaged possessions at some distance on the green.

And then he remembered his neighbours, the comforting arm about his shoulder, the stricken looks of those who mourned with him, their blackened hands offering mugs of steaming tea, their eyes reddened with the acrid smoke. It was their sympathy and practical help which had supported him and Dimity through the weeks that followed. He would never forget.

A sneeze shook him back into the present. With infinite care he lowered the threadlike roots of the seedling into its tiny home, and gently made it secure.

Dimity set out for Thrush Green as soon as lunch was over, leaving her husband sorting out the papers he would need for the afternoon's meeting at Oxford.

It was a time of day that Dimity always enjoyed, the slack period when most people were digesting their midday meal, the streets were quiet, and an air of torpor hung over the little town.

Most of the Lulling shops still closed for an hour or more. Old customs die hard in this part of the Cotswolds, and some shopkeepers still lived above their businesses, or near enough to go home to a midday meal. Dimity approved of this sensible practice, and did not rail, as many of her friends did, about the difficulty of shopping in the middle of the day.

The two modern supermarkets, made hideous with garish window stickers, seemed to be the only places open, as Dimity made her way along the High Street. Even they appeared remarkably quiet, she noticed. So far, Lulling folk seemed to keep to their usual ways, and would not be emerging from their rest until the older shops turned the CLOSED notice to OPEN, unlocked their doors, and pulled out the awnings to shade their wares should the sun have arrived.

Dimity did not hurry. The sun was warm, and she was pleasantly conscious of its comfort on her back as she admired, yet again, the honey-coloured stone of the buildings, the fresh green of the lime trees, and the plumes of lilac, white and purple, which nodded from the front gardens, and scented the warm air.

A tabby cat was stretched across the sunny doorstep of the draper's shop. Dimity bent to stroke it, and it acknowledged her attentions with a little chirruping sound and a luxurious flexing of its striped legs. Hard by, in the dusty gutter, a bevy of sparrows bathed noisily, but the cat was too lethargic to stir itself into action in the present warmth.

Dimity made her way through the somnolent town, crossed the murmuring River Pleshey, pausing to watch its eddies and dimples for a few minutes, and then faced the steep hill which led to Thrush Green and her friend Ella Bembridge.

Ella was one of those squarely-built, gruff ladies of mannish appearance whose looks belie their gentleness.

Her large hands, rough and brown from gardening, were equally at home with weaving, smocking, embroidery and tapestry work. Those hands had also tackled pottery, carpentry, painting and metalwork in their time, but now that Ella lived alone she preferred to enjoy the handiwork which she could do in her own home, without the complications of potter's wheels, lathes, soldering irons and the like.

She and Dimity had spent several happy years together. Though different in looks and temperament the one had complemented the other. When Dimity had been carried off by Charles, first to the rectory across the way at Thrush

Green, and later to the vicarage at Lulling, Ella had missed her old friend, but rejoiced in her good fortune.

She was not one to pine, and her innumerable projects kept Ella busy and cheerful. It was lucky that Dimity lived so near, and that the two could see each other frequently.

As Dimity was puffing her way uphill, Ella was kneeling in the front garden of their home planting out a row of pansies, a cigarette dangling from her lips. She looked up as the latch of the gate clicked.

'What a nice surprise!' she exclaimed, scrambling to her feet, and wiping her hands energetically down her skirt.

'I told you I'd bring the wool,' replied Dimity. 'On the phone.'

'Well, I didn't cotton on that you'd come this afternoon. To be honest, Dim, I believe I'm getting deaf. Don't hear half people say on the blower.'

'Probably only wax,' said Dimity, sitting down exhaustedly on a rustic seat under the eaves of the thatch. 'Get John Lovell to squish it out.'

'He'd perforate my ear drums, more like,' commented Ella. Her opinion of medical practitioners was low. Good health had kept her largely from their clutches, and she was suspicious of their professional activities.

'Want a cuppa?' she continued. 'You look whacked.'

'No, no. It's only walking up the hill. Don't let me stop you working. Can I help?'

'No, I've only a few more to bung in. You sit there and tell me all the news. How's Charles?'

'He's off to Oxford for a meeting.'

'Poor thing! Rather him than me. What on earth do clergymen do at these meetings? Do a bit of re-editing of *Hymns Ancient and Modern*? Make a list of their fellow priests who need censuring? Or defrocking?'

'Oh, nothing like that, I'm sure,' replied Dimity, somewhat shocked. 'I think it's more to do with money. Upkeep of the church property, allocation of funds, that sort of thing. Though I must admit that Charles never talks about

church matters to me, and I'm very glad he doesn't. One can so easily let out something innocently that is supposed to be private.'

'Your Charles is a wise old bird. If you don't want a thing known, say nowt to anyone. I can't abide people who tell you some titbit and then add: "But don't say a word. You are the only person I've told!" You can bet your bottom dollar she's said the same to a dozen others before telling you.'

She rammed home the last pansy plant, and came to sit beside Dimity in the sun. Out from her skirt pocket came the battered tin which Dimity knew so well, and Ella began to roll one of her pungent and untidy cigarettes.

The two old friends sat in silence. They were both drowsy and pleasantly tired from their recent exercise. A chaffinch pottered busily in the garden bed, occasionally giving a satisfied chirrup, and a light breeze rustled the budding may bush by the gate.

In the distance, they could hear the school children at play across the green, and the rumble of traffic from the main road at the foot of the hill. It was all very soporific and the ladies could easily have dropped off. But suddenly the rattling of machinery close at hand made them alert.

'That dratted cement mixer,' said Ella. 'They're still mucking about with those new houses. Putting in steps, or a terrace, or some such, the foreman told me.'

Dimity stood up to see what was happening across the road, on the very site of her demolished old home.

Eight one-storey houses in the form of a south-facing L were being built for old people, designed by the local architect Edward Young, who lived close by in what was readily acknowledged as the handsomest house on Thrush Green.

'What a time they're taking!' commented Dimity. 'They were started ages ago.'

'Poor old Edward's having the deuce of a time with some of his suppliers, I gather. He's having handles fixed to the baths, and rails by the loos, and they had to be sent back because they weren't to his specification. Then he'd planned underfloor heating, and it was practically complete when another chap told him that some old people had complained of foot trouble after some time in a place in Northamptonshire. So off he went to investigate, and decided to rip it out and start again.'

'When does he hope to have them ready?'

'You tell me! One thing, there are plenty of people around with their names on the list. Is Charles mixed up with this?'

'He's on the committee, I know.'

'Well, he's got my sympathy when it comes to selecting eight deserving cases from the roll. The fur will fly for some time, is my guess. Why, even Percy Hodge has put his name down.'

'Percy Hodge?' echoed Dimity. 'But he's already got a house! And a wife to look after him!'

'Not now he hasn't. She's left him for good, has our Doris.'

'But he can only be sixty at the outside,' expostulated Dimity. 'That's not old by today's standards.'

'True enough, but he's not the only sixty-year-old to try it on. I hear Mrs Cooke at Nidden's applied too, and those mercenary old twins at Nod whose name I can never remember.'

'But Mrs Cooke has heaps of children to look after her, and those Bellamy twins have pots of money, and a bungalow of their own!'

'We all know that. All I'm saying is, Charles will have his work cut out when he's one of the panel trying to make a choice.'

Dimity looked troubled as she gazed across the hedge to the new buildings.

'Well, at this rate he won't be making any decisions yet a while,' she said at last. 'Maybe things will be easier when the time comes.'

To Ella's mind, this was a forlorn hope. But, for once, she forbore to say so.

'You don't have to hurry back, do you, Dim? Stop and have a cup of tea.'

'I'd love to. Charles won't be home before six, I imagine.'

'Good, then we'll go down to Dotty's to collect the milk. It will save Connie a trip. Incidentally, Dotty sent me some biscuits she'd made. Shall we try them at tea time?'

Dimity laughed.

'You can, I shan't! I had a fine bout of Dotty's Collywobbles when I went there last.'

Ella smiled behind her cigarette smoke.

'Don't worry. I was only teasing. They went out to the birds within half an hour, and I can't say they were too keen either.'

Later the two ladies crossed the green and entered the narrow lane that led across fields to Dotty Harmer's cottage, and then on to Lulling Woods.

The cement mixer by the new buildings was now at rest, and the site deserted. The low terrace of houses was going to be very attractive once the builders' mess was removed, lawns and shrubs planted, and the final lick of paint applied.

'Almost makes you think of putting your name on the list,' commented Ella as they walked on. 'Not that I'd stand a chance, and in any case I should hate to leave our little place.'

At Dotty's there was evidence of building too. Their eccentric old friend had lived there for many years with numerous animals and a large garden erratically tended. She had been the only daughter of the headmaster of the local grammar school. He had had a fearsome reputation for stern discipline, and grown men in Lulling still quailed at the mention of his name.

On his death, marked by a packed church at his memorial service ('Relief rather than respect!' as some wag remarked later), Dotty had moved to her present abode and enjoyed her freedom. As well as caring for her animals with passionate devotion, she experimented with the bounty of the fields and hedgerows, making chutneys and preserves of dubious plants and berries which she pressed upon her apprehensive friends. John Lovell, the Thrush Green doctor, was well aware of the local stomach trouble known as Dotty's Collywobbles, and it was the first question he asked of his suffering patients before turning to more orthodox complaints.

Dotty's own health was the concern of her friends for several years, but when her niece Connie came to take charge they breathed a sigh of relief. Now Connie had married Kit Armitage, a handsome widower, who once had attended Lulling's grammar school and known Dotty's ferocious father only too well for comfort. The enlargement of Dotty's thatched cottage was the result of their marriage.

It was Connie who opened the door to Ella and Dimity, and greeted them with affection.

'Do come in. Aunt Dotty's in the sitting room. Kit's shopping in Lulling. Have you had tea?'

They assured her on this point and went through the hall to see Dotty. They found her semi-prone on a sofa, a tapestry frame lodged on her stomach, and mounds of wool scattered around her.

'Don't get up!' exclaimed Ella, as Dotty began to thrash about. 'What are you making?'

She gazed with an expert eye at Dotty's efforts.

'A cushion cover, so the pattern says,' replied Dotty. 'It's called Florentine stitch, and supposed to be quite simple.'

'It is,' said Ella. 'Let's have a look.'

She removed the frame from Dotty's stomach, tightened some nuts, and then studied the work closely, back and front.

'You've missed a whole row of holes in some places,' she said at last. 'See these white lines? That's the canvas showing through.'

'Oh really?' said Dotty, yawning. 'Does it matter?'

'It does if you want the work to look well done,' said Ella with spirit. 'Tell you what, I'll take it home and put it right for you.'

Dotty lowered her skinny legs to the ground, and pulled up her wrinkled stockings.

'Oh, don't bother, Ella dear. I quite like the white lines. Rather a pretty effect. In any case, I'm rather busy sorting out a drawerful of old photos at the moment, and I think I'll put this work aside till the winter.'

'She took possession of the frame and thrust it under the sofa. There was a yelp, and Flossie the spaniel emerged, looking hurt.

'Oh, my poor love!' cried Dotty. 'I had no idea you were there! Let me find you a biscuit as a peace offering.'

She scrabbled behind a cushion on the sofa head and produced a crumpled paper bag. From it she withdrew a piece of Rich Tea biscuit, and offered it to the dog. It was warmly received.

'Now,' said Dotty, rising to her feet and wiping her hands down her skirt. 'Come and see the new building.'

'Aunt Dotty,' protested Connie, now entering the room, 'there's nothing to see yet. Let Ella and Dimity have a rest after their walk.'

'No, let's see it,' said Ella, stumping along behind Dotty. 'How long have the men been here?'

The four women surveyed the piles of building material scattered about the garden. Dimity thought the sight depressing. Planks were propped against the fruit trees. Piles of bricks lurched drunkenly on what was once a lawn. Buckets, wheelbarrows, hods and spades all jostled together, and the inevitable cement mixer lurked behind the lilac bushes which were already covered in white dust

'Full of hope, isn't it?' cried Dotty, eyes shining through her spectacles. 'Of course, there will be rather a mess when the thatcher comes. All that straw, you know, and his little hazel spars. I'm so looking forward to that. I shall have a chair out here and watch him at work. I think it must be rather a lonely job up on a roof. A little conversation should help him along.'

No one dared to comment on this appalling plan, but Connie hastily blew her nose, and looked towards the distant Lulling Woods.

'And when do you hope to see it complete?' asked Dimity.

'Edward says it should be ready by the winter,' replied Dotty. 'It's not a very big project, after all. The garage will be there.' She pointed to the powdered lilac bushes. 'And behind that will be a sitting room, or is it the larder, Connie dear?'

'The sitting room. And a bedroom above with a bathroom.'

'For Kit and Connie,' explained Dotty. 'A *large* bedroom,

you understand. I think married people should have plenty of *air* at night. Two of them, in one room, you see. Now I only need that *small* room of mine. Plenty of cubic space for one sleeper. If ever I married, of course, I should have the wall knocked down between the two small rooms at the other end of the house.'

The hope of matrimony for dear old Dotty, now in her eighties, seemed so remote to all three ladies that they made no comment upon these wild conjectures, but contented themselves with picking their way among the muddle, and making polite noises.

'We really came to collect the milk,' said Ella at last, tired of stepping round piles of bricks, and circumventing wheelbarrows.

'It's all ready,' said Connie, turning towards the kitchen door.

Ella and Dotty followed the younger woman, but Dimity lingered in the garden.

The air was warm, and heavy with the scent of hay lying in the field beyond Dotty's hedge. Soon the baler would be thumping the crop into neat oblongs, grass and flowers and aromatic leaves compacted together, to carry the smell and comfort of summer into the winter byres where the cattle store stood, or to the snowy fields and the hungry sheep.

Of all the seasons, summer was the one that Dimity loved best. Thin and frail, she dreaded the cold Cotswold winter which dragged on, more often than not, into a chilling April. But a sunny June, with its many blessings of roses, hayfields, strawberries and long warm evenings, raised Dimity's spirits to near ecstasy.

She sighed with deep contentment, and made her way after the others. It was good to live in the country. It was good to have so many friends. It was good to feel warm and in splendid health.

She paused by the kitchen door to pick the bright bud of an Albertine rose to thread in her buttonhole.

'Perfect!' said Dimity, entering the house.

2   Problems at Thrush Green

T HE HAWTHORN BLOSSOM along the hedges gave way to the showy cream plates of elder flowers, and sprays of wild roses, pink and frail as sea shells.

The gardens of Thrush Green were bright with irises and peonies, and the air was murmurous with the sound of lawn mowers.

But not all was idyllic.

Albert Piggott, caretaker, sexton, and erstwhile grave-digger at St Andrew's, found the June heat a sore trial, his nature being inclined to melancholy and excessive self-pity. But it was the mowing which gave him his present reason for complaint.

Some years earlier, Charles Henstock had decided that the tombstones of the Thrush Green forefathers should be moved, with due reverence, to the edge of the graveyard, and the turf flattened, so that a mower could keep the area tidy with the minimum of effort.

For too long it had been an eyesore. Albert, whose job it had been to scythe the grass over and around the mounds, was clearly beyond the work, and it seemed impossible to get a replacement.

There was some opposition to the good rector's pro-posal, but eventually it was accepted, and now, years later, it was generally agreed that the churchyard of St Andrew's

was an exceptionally pleasant place, and the change had
been quite successful.

Albert did not agree, as he told his long-suffering neighbour, Mr Jones of The Two Pheasants, one bright morning
as soon as the pub was open.

'Them dratted tombstones was put too close to the
outside wall when they done the job.'

He took a noisy slurp of his beer.

'Young Cooke,' he went on, replacing the dripping glass
on Mr Jones's carefully polished bar counter, 'can't get the
mower between them and the wall.'

'Oh-ah!' replied Mr Jones without much interest. Albert
and his young assistant had been at loggerheads for years
now. The publican had heard both sides of the many
arguments between the two, and for far too long.

'Means as I has to get down on me hands and knees
with the bill-hook, round the back, like. Not that easy at
my age. Not after me Operation.'

A shadow fell across the sunlit floor. Percy Hodge, a
farmer from the Nidden road hard by, was seeking
refreshment.

'You ain't still on about your innards, are you?' he
queried. 'I reckon all Thrush Green knows about them
tubes of yours. And fair sick of 'em too. Half a pint,
please.'

Albert's face grew even more morose.

'All right for you. Never had a day's illness in your life!'

'Ah! But I got my troubles.'

He pulled some coins across the counter and settled on
the next stool to Albert.

'Oh? Your Doris come back?'

Percy drew in his breath noisily.

'Now, Albert,' began Mr Jones. 'We don't want no
trouble between old friends.'

'Who's talking about old friends?' enquired Albert nastily. Percy's breathing became heavier.

'You keep Doris's name out of this,' he said. 'I don't

keep on about your Nelly, though we all know what she is!'

'*Gentlemen!*' cried Mr Jones in alarm.

Percy and Albert fell silent, and turned their attention to their glasses. A distant clanking sound, followed by a steady chugging, proclaimed that the cement mixer was at work.

'By the time them places is finished,' said Albert, 'our lot'll all be in the graveyard. Be about ready for young Cooke, I reckon.'

'Wonder who they'll choose?' asked Percy, secretly glad to pick up this olive branch. 'You put your name down?'

'What, with my Nelly to look after me? And my girl Molly across the green at the Youngs? No point in me havin' a try. They'll be looking for old folk on their own.'

'Well, I've put my name forward,' said Percy. 'I'm old, and on my own.'

His listeners seemed taken aback. Albert was trying to work out how much younger Percy was than he himself. Mr Jones was shocked at the cheek of a man who was only middle-aged, and had a house and a living, in applying for one of the new homes. But he forbore to comment. He did not want any trouble in his respectable hostelry, and both customers were touchy.

'You'll be lucky!' commented Albert at last, putting his empty glass down. 'Must get back to my bill-hook. I'd like to meet the chap as set them tombstones round the wall. I'd give him a piece of me mind.'

'He got hurt in a car crash, other side of Oxford,' volunteered Percy. 'My cousin told me. Broke his arm, he said.'

'No more'n he deserved,' said Albert heartlessly, and hobbled back to his duties.

Later that morning, as the church clock struck twelve, the noise of the cement mixer growled into silence.

Two of the workmen appeared, hot and dusty, and ordered pints of bitter across the counter.

'And how's it going?' asked Mr Jones.

'Not bad,' said the one in a blue shirt.

'Just doin' the steps,' said the other, who sported a black singlet.

'*Steps*?' echoed Mr Jones. 'I should've thought there'd be no steps at all in a place for old people. Bit of a hazard, surely?'

'That's what the orders are,' said Blue Shirt.

'Only three of them,' said the second man. 'Shaller ones too.'

'And a rail to hang on to,' chimed in Blue Shirt. 'You'll be safe enough, Dad, when you move over there!' He winked at his companion.

Mr Jones smiled a shade frostily. If he had spoken to his elders in such a way, when he was young, his father would have boxed his ears for him.

'Well, I'm sure Mr Young knows best,' he said diplomatically. 'He's reckoned to be a top-notch architect.'

But privately, the good publican found the thought of steps, no matter how shallow, and even when accompanied by a rail, a somewhat disconcerting feature of an old people's home.

'Could lead to trouble,' he confided to his wife that afternoon when the pub door was closed.

He was to recall his misgivings later.

Almost facing The Two Pheasants across Thrush Green stood the house where Winnie Bailey and her maid Jenny lived.

Adjoining it was John Lovell's surgery. Old Doctor Bailey had died a year or two earlier, and sorely did his younger partner miss the wisdom and local knowledge of his senior.

The practice was a busy one. John had two junior partners, both keen young men well up in modern medicine. The older folk in Thrush Green still viewed them with some suspicion, and tended to hark back to 'good old

Doctor Bailey' and his methods. But gradually the newcomers were beginning to be recognized, much to John Lovell's relief.

He himself was glad to have Winnie Bailey at hand. Her memory was prodigious, and she could frequently give him a brief history of a family which he found enormously helpful.

He was now very much a part of Thrush Green. As a junior partner to Donald Bailey, he had met and married Ruth Bassett, sister to Joan Young, the architect's wife. They lived some half a mile or so from the green itself, and as well as their own two young children they cared for old Mrs Bassett who had made her home with them since the death of her husband.

John was a serious and conscientious man, deeply appreciative of his good fortune in having such a settled marriage and a rewarding job. He enjoyed his trips to outlying villages, for he had a great love of country life and was knowledgeable about flowers and birds. These interests were of particular value to him for they helped him to relax.

His wife Ruth knew that if his nature had a flaw at all – which she would have denied hotly, if challenged – it was in the very seriousness which his patients found so reassuring. She did her best to lighten his load, but books, music and theatre, in which she had always delighted, could not engage his attention for any length of time.

'You are always telling your patients,' she said, 'that they must have a few hobbies to relieve any tension, but you don't take your own advice.'

'Doctors never do,' he told her.

It was with Winnie Bailey, as much as anyone, that John Lovell really found some relief from the pressures of his practice.

As soon as surgery was over, on this sunny June morning, he saw Winnie in her garden picking the dead heads from the roses.

'I was coming to get some directions from you, Winnie,' he called, putting his case in the back of the car.

'Come in and have a cup of coffee. I know Jenny's just getting some ready.'

'I dare not stop, many thanks.'

He walked across the lawn.

'I've had a call from a Leys Farm. Do you know it? Somewhere off the road to Oxford, I gather.'

'Who lives there?'

'That's what all my patients asked,' said John smiling.

'Why is it in the country that we know the names of the people and never the names of their houses?'

Winnie laughed.

'I don't think I ever heard of Leys Farm, and I'm sure Donald never mentioned it. Could the owners have re-named it?'

'Quite likely. One of my patients said it was once known as Trotters. Does that mean anything?'

'Yes, indeed. A large family used to live at Trotters. They were Bells. Some vague relation of Betty Bell who cleans the school, you know?'

'And where is it?'

'Now you're asking! If you go about two miles out of Lulling on the Oxford road you will come to a narrow lane on the left. There used to be a fir tree there.'

'No gate? No sign?'

'Nothing. It's just a rough track. Heaven help you if you meet a tractor, John. But it's about another two miles to the house. I went there once with Donald.'

'Well, many thanks, Winnie dear. I'll go and blaze a trail to Leys-Farm-once-Trotters, and what's more I'll tell you the name of the people who live there now, when I get back.'

'*If* you get back,' replied Winnie. 'It's that sort of place if I remember it aright.'

He waved, and departed on his mission.

Winnie had her coffee with Jenny in the kitchen. The room was warm and peaceful, and filled with the mixed scents of Jenny's cooking preparations.

At one end of the scrubbed table was the chopping board with mint awaiting the attention of Jenny's knife. Beside it stood a punnet of strawberries.

'Percy Hodge brought 'em,' said Jenny. 'His first picking, so he said.'

'He's not courting you again, Jenny? I thought you had nipped that little affair in the bud.'

'He knows my feelings right enough,' replied Jenny. 'But I didn't see any harm in turning down some good strawberries, even if his Doris has left him. Anyway, he knows there's no chance here for him.'

'So we can eat his strawberries with an easy conscience, can we, Jenny?'

'Why not?'

'I had a letter this morning from Richard,' said Winnie, changing the subject.

'Coming to stay, is he?'

'He doesn't say so. He'll be in the area next week and invites himself to lunch or tea. I have a phone number. Tea, I think, it's simpler for us.'

'Good. I'll make him some of my cheese scones. Men always like 'em.'

'I'm sure Richard will too, but don't expect extravagant thanks from him,' warned Winnie. 'He's inclined to take everything for granted, I'm sorry to say.'

She rinsed her cup and went upstairs to dust the bedrooms, her mind busy with thoughts of this, her least favourite, nephew.

Donald had always said: 'The boy's head's all right, but he has no heart.' Certainly, he had done brilliantly in his career as a physicist, and was acknowledged as supreme in his particular field. He spent much of his time lecturing abroad on subjects with such abstruse titles as: 'Molecular structures in relation to nuclear principles'. In fact, thought Winnie, that would probably be one of his elementary lectures, for she remembered seeing one listed which had a title four lines long. Richard's world was a vast unknown to his aunt.

She had not seen him since Donald's death, which had occurred while the young man was in America. To give him his due, he had written a very kind letter, expressing sympathy, which had touched Winnie.

For Richard, she had to admit, was quite the most self-centred individual she had ever come across. Perhaps that was why, she surmised, dusting the windowsill, he had never married, although he was now in his forties.

She ceased her work for a moment and gazed across the sunlit garden. It was true that years before he had expressed a fondness for Winnie's neighbour Phyllida, then a young widow, but she had turned him down, as gently as could be managed, and within a few weeks she was married to Frank Hurst.

'I shouldn't think that dented Richard's armour very much,' commented Winnie to a surprised chaffinch on a nearby twig.

No, Richard would not have changed much, if she knew anything about him. Probably the same old hypochondriac too, everlastingly fussing with his diet and his bodily functions. Well, she would see him before long, and it would be interesting to see if he appreciated Jenny's cheese scones as richly as they deserved.

Time alone would tell.

John Lovell, driving along the busy road to Oxford, was too engrossed in dodging lorries, queuing up behind tractors laden with bales of hay, and trying to look out for the turning to his new patient's, to turn his mind to any Thrush Green problems.

As it was, he overshot the turning, for he had been looking out for the fir tree mentioned by Winnie, but evidently it had been felled since her visit, for nothing marked the entrance to the farm track.

He managed to execute a neat U-turn in a lull in the traffic, and then was compelled to wait while yet another tractor, and its tail of fuming motorists, held up his right-hand entry into the lane.

It certainly was narrow, as Winnie had warned him, and the surface was gritty. Banks of nettles and seeding cow parsley brushed the sides of the car, and here and there the vivid blue of cranesbill made splashes of colour among the tall grass. With the eye of a born naturalist John noted the variety of butterflies and birds that frequented such richness.

The hedges were high on each side and badly in need of trimming, but John looked approvingly at the cascading wild roses, the brambles and the goosegrass which clambered from the ditch to drape its sticky shoots across the stronger twigs above. Plenty of good forage there for all manner of insect life, he thought.

Now that he was free of traffic he turned his mind to another topic. Soon the new homes for old people would be allotted, and he had been asked to join the committee and to give his advice on the applicants.

It was going to be a problem. As far as he could gather from the local grapevine, there would be no shortage of people applying for the houses. Some could be rejected pretty swiftly.

Some, like Percy Hodge, were too well placed with a house and help already. Some were already so old and helpless that they really needed hospital care which the new homes could not provide. It was striking the balance which was going to be the main difficulty.

He knew at least twenty people who would benefit from being rehoused. His work took him into some pathetically inadequate homes, many of them of picture-book prettiness outside. But under many a quaint thatched roof were damp walls, with fungus growth, and the stains of years. Windows were tiny, stairs crooked and uneven, and a menace to aging limbs. There were still cottages with oil lamps and candles, and John Lovell had seen and treated the outcome of three fires in such premises, all lived in by frail old people who should have had accommodation in just the sort of homes so soon to be allotted.

He jammed on his brakes as a covey of young partridges ran from the overgrown verge. They took off with a whirring of wings and flew over the hedge.

Shelving his future responsibilities, John continued on his way to the distant farmhouse.

While John Lovell was driving cautiously along the neglected track, the subject which had been occupying his thoughts was also under discussion at Dotty Harmer's.

She, with Kit and Connie, sat at the side of the cottage farthest from the noise of the workmen, mugs in hand.

'Joan Young tells me that Edward is quite distraught with all the delays to those dear little houses of his.'

Dotty always spoke of the old people's homes as though Edward owned the lot.

'We're in the same boat,' commented Kit. 'They've just told me that the plumber has been taken to hospital.'

'Oh no!' cried Connie.

'Well, surely,' said Dotty reasonably, 'the plumber has a deputy? When my father was taken ill, the Second Master stepped into the breach, and simply adjusted the timetable.'

'I've no doubt that things were rather better organized at Lulling Grammar School,' said Kit. 'As far as I can see, the work will be put back until Fred's on his feet again.'

'What's the matter with him?' asked Connie.

'Tummy pains. If it's appendicitis he'll be out in a few days. May not be too long.'

'A dear friend of mine,' mused Dotty, 'who nursed at Edinburgh Infirmary told me that one of her appendectomy patients cycled from there to Glasgow, or Perth, or perhaps Leith – I can't quite recall now – but some distance away, only *four* days after the operation. Wasn't that marvellous?'

'I can't see our Fred returning after four days,' commented Kit, 'even by ambulance, let alone a bike. Still, we aren't quite as desperate as poor old Edward, who is supposed to have all ship-shape and Bristol-fashion by October, I'm told.'

'Winnie tells me that they are going to be quite charming,' said Dotty. She bent down to stroke her spaniel's silky ears. 'But there's a rumour that animals won't be allowed. I shouldn't like that.'

Connie and Kit exchanged glances.

'You aren't still wondering about applying, are you, Aunt Dot?'

'Well, no,' replied Dotty, sounding alarmingly doubtful.

Kit took charge, as he did so often and so admirably.

'Dotty dear, we've had this all out time and time again. You are staying here *for ever*. Understand? You can have all the animals you like. We are here to look after you, and even if you wanted one of Edward's homes, which you know you don't, you wouldn't get one for all those reasons.'

'You don't really want to leave here, do you?' Connie pleaded, taking one of Dotty's skinny paws in her own. 'This is your home, and has been for years. You know you would hate to make a change, and we want you with us.'

'Yes, yes,' agreed Dotty, much agitated, 'I know all that, and I know that's why we are building on, but sometimes I wonder if I shall be a nuisance to you. All young things should start married life on their own.'

'I feel flattered,' said Kit, patting Dotty's bony shoulder, 'to be called "a young thing" when I'm in my sixties. Now, snap out of it, Dotty. We three aging bodies will settle happily under this one roof. That is, if ever it gets round to being thatched, which I'm beginning to doubt.'

'There you are!' cried Connie. 'So stop harking back to those new homes. Your home is here.'

'Tell you what,' said Kit, echoing Ella Bembridge, whose favourite phrase this was, 'if our builders get on at this rate we could probably all move into one of Edward's abodes for our last declining years.'

'I shan't come,' said Dotty decidedly. 'They haven't got any upstairs. Very upsetting to have no upstairs. We're better off here.'

'That's what we've been telling you,' said Kit, smiling at his wife.

3 Market Day at Lulling

ON WEDNESDAY MORNINGS throughout the year, unless illness, catastrophic weather or matters of extreme urgency cropped up, Ella Bembridge descended the steep hill from Thrush Green to Lulling.

She carried a large basket, for it was market day in the little Cotswold town, and Ella always made a bee-line for the Women's Institute stall where she could be sure of beautiful fresh eggs, crisp vegetables, home-grown fruit and mouth-watering homemade cakes and scones.

Business done she met her old friend Dimity at The Fuchsia Bush, and over a cup of coffee they exchanged news in the company of many other ladies and, very occasionally, one or two gentlemen.

On this particular morning, Ella was carrying a raincoat as well as her laden basket. The morning was warm and humid, the sky overcast, and the weather prophets had forecast heavy rain.

'Not that they know any more than my strip of seaweed outside the back door,' pronounced Ella, in ringing tones. Dimity hoped that none of those present had close relations at the Weather Centre, although over the years she had become less sensitive to the reaction of others when confronted by Ella's trenchant remarks.

'We could do with it,' replied Dimity. 'The vicarage lawns are terribly parched, and Charles won't use the sprinkler. He says it sets a bad example, when we've been asked to save water.'

'I can't think why these whizz kids of science can't manage to store some of the water we get too much of half the year. One week we're sloshing abut in our wellies, and then after a fortnight's sunshine we are looked upon as criminals if we take a can of water to the carrots.'

'Try one of these sponge fingers,' said Dimity placatingly. 'They melt in the mouth. I expect Nelly made them.'

She pushed the plate across to her friend.

'I reckon we did The Fuchsia Bush a good turn when we suggested that Nelly Piggott might help out in the kitchen,' observed Ella, spurning the excellent sponge fingers, but producing her cigarette-making equipment.

'By the way,' she continued, dropping tobacco flakes on to the cigarette paper, the tabletop and the floor, 'I think the Youngs may get Mrs Peters and the rest of the staff here to make some of the goodies for this lunch do.'

'What lunch do?'

'I thought you knew. They are having a fund-raising effort, half the proceeds to St Andrew's roof fund and the rest to Hearts and Chests, or Ears, Noses and Throats. Can't remember exactly, but it's medically inclined, and to do with *tubes*, not *limbs*.'

'A coffee morning, you mean?'

'More ambitious than that. Joan said a buffet lunch one Saturday should bring in much more cash. We shall have a few stalls, jam and cakes, you know, and I've promised some weaving and canework.'

'It sounds marvellous,' said Dimity, trying to appear enthusiastic. 'When's it to be?'

'End of July, I think. I'll tell you when I know definitely. And Joan asked me to tell the Lovelock girls, so I'll bob in as soon as we've paid the bill.'

'The Lovelock girls' lived almost next door to The Fuchsia

Bush, in one of the pleasant Georgian houses which are dotted along Lulling's High Street.

The three sisters were far from girlhood, their average age being closer to eighty than eighteen. They were a formidable trio, and had lived all their lives in the same house.

Ada, Bertha and Violet had been left comfortably provided for by a wealthy and indulgent father. But they were renowned throughout Lulling and its environs for parsimony of an extreme kind. Visitors, bidden to lunch at the house, prudently had a snack beforehand, knowing that in winter they might be lucky enough to get one small chop from the neck end of lamb, with a spoonful of potato and half a dozen peas.

If it were a summer lunch party the fare would be even more spartan. Miss Ada had been known to count the rounds of beetroot as she allotted them to the plates, and as the eyesight of all three sisters was now less than perfect, the lettuce was inclined to be crunchy with particles of garden soil.

However, the linen was always snowy, the glass crystal clear, even if it only held tap water at the meal, and the ancient heavy silver beautifully polished.

When Dimity and Ella entered the house the ladies greeted them effusively.

'How lovely to see you!' cried Miss Ada.

'Come through to the kitchen!' called Miss Bertha. 'We are just preparing lunch. Will you stay?'

The two visitors, long familiar with meals here, made hasty apologies.

Miss Violet was putting the finishing touches to the first course. Six slices of corned beef lay along an oblong dish, flanked with parsley at each corner. A few lettuce leaves, and one tomato, cut into four, seemed to constitute the accompanying dish.

Ella wondered idly who would be so bold as to have the quarter of tomato left over. She hoped that there would not be an ugly fight.

Bertha was concocting a small trifle from two slices of stale sponge cake, half a dozen strawberries cut into pieces and a spoonful of runny jam of indeterminate variety.

Dimity and Ella looked upon these preparations as politely as they could.

'I've only to moisten this with the top of the milk,' said Bertha happily, 'and then we can go into the drawing room.'

That done, they did indeed traverse the hall again, and settle in the beautiful room which looked out into Lulling High Street.

The drawing room was crowded with old and lovely articles. The sisters still lived in Edwardian style, with a number of small tables dotted here and there on the Chinese carpet, each laden with photographs in silver frames, tiny pieces of exquisite china, and other knick-knacks. The thought of the wreckage one small child or an exuberant dog could cause did not bear contemplating.

An enormous bronze jug stood in the hearth containing the silver pennies of dried honesty, and the blue and green sheen of long peacock feathers. Dark brown velvet curtains were looped back from the windows, and the pictures were by some of the pre-Raphaelites. It was indeed a real period piece, thought Ella, seated uncomfortably, for one of her bulk, on a spindly mahogany chair decorated with fine marquetry work.

'A cup of coffee?' asked Bertha.

'No, many thanks,' said Ella. 'We've just had some next door.'

'Ah! Mrs Peters makes excellent coffee,' commented Violet. 'And seems to be doing very well now that she has Mrs Jefferson and that rather vulgar Nelly Piggott to help her.'

'I don't think,' said Bertha frostily, 'that there was any need for "*rather vulgar*", Violet. She seems a good enough woman of her type.'

Violet looked abashed at this rebuke from her older sister.

'She always cleaned our silver very well,' put in Ada. 'It was the *cooking* which we found disappointing. Not that she did very much here, but we found her very extravagant. Particularly with butter and eggs.'

'Nevertheless,' said Violet, striking a blow for justice, 'her food was delicious, you know. And they say that The Fuchsia Bush is packed every lunch time.'

'So we hear,' said Ella. 'It's partly because of that that Joan Young thought she might ask Mrs Peters to make up a few cold dishes. Pies and quiches and salads, you know.'

She proceeded to outline the plan for raising money by a buffet lunch at Thrush Green. The sisters, Dimity noted, grew steadily more apprehensive. Obviously, the thought of having to spend money was daunting.

Nevertheless, Ella ploughed on with her task.

'I'll let you know the date, and the price of the tickets and so on, as soon as things are settled,' she promised.

'There will be a bring and buy stall too, of course, and probably a raffle.'

The expressions on the three wrinkled visages became more relaxed.

'Oh, I'm sure we can find something suitable for the stall or the raffle, even if we can't fit in the lunch party with our other duties,' said Ada.

'Those ear-muffs I knitted, and the brooches made of beech husks should be quite acceptable,' agreed Bertha, 'and Violet made some excellent elderberry wine last autumn. Not all the corks blew out, if I remember rightly, and I'm sure there are a few bottles left.'

'Well, we'll keep in touch about it,' replied Ella, with rare diplomacy, and she and Dimity rose to depart. The ladies of the house followed them to the front door.

The pavement was now spotted with rain, and Ella began to struggle into her raincoat. Dimity, less well protected, looked dismayed, but turned up the collar of her summer suit.

'You simply must borrow Father's umbrella,' fluttered

Miss Violet, darting to a cylindrical vessel, decorated with improbable bulrushes, which stood in the corner of the hall. 'It was a present from the lodge of his Freemasons. He valued it highly, and we always lend it to our friends on just such an occasion as this.'

It was certainly a handsome object, made of heavy black silk, with a splendid malacca handle embellished with a gold ring.

'I hardly like to take charge of it,' admitted Dimity. But the umbrella was already being opened above the three steps leading down to the pavement, the rain was increasing every minute, and she accepted the umbrella's protection gratefully.

The three sisters waved goodbye, and then retired behind the front door, no doubt to discuss the dreadful possibility of having to purchase tickets for Joan's buffet lunch.

'Well, thank God we weren't staying to lunch,' said Ella when they were safely out of earshot. 'I'm going back to eggs and bacon. Like to join me?'

'I mustn't, Ella, many thanks. Charles and I are having some chicken in a casserole, and I've a horrid feeling I forgot to switch on the oven before coming out.'

'You'd better drop into lunch with the Lovelocks,' said Ella, 'if that's the case.'

And the two friends departed cheerfully.

The rain grew heavier, and by midday the gutters were gurgling, the thatched eaves were dripping, and the puddles in Thrush Green's school playground grew larger every minute.

Miss Watson, the headmistress, and her devoted assistant Agnes Fogerty surveyed the scene anxiously.

'You would think,' said Miss Watson tartly, 'that parents would have the sense to provide their children with mackintoshes, especially when the weather man specifically forecast rain in the south.'

'He's often wrong,' protested Agnes.

Miss Watson gave one of her famous snorts, much mimicked by the naughtier of the pupils.

'Well, it can't be helped. Those who go home to dinner must hurry along as best they can. Obviously, this has set in for the day.'

Little Miss Fogerty supervised the departure of the few children who went home for their meal, organizing the sharing of umbrellas, buttoning the raincoats of those prudent enough to sport them and exhorting her charges to: 'Hurry home, and keep out of the puddles,' a forlorn hope, as well she knew. Meanwhile, Miss Watson and the remaining assistant attended to the distribution of school dinner.

It was impossible for the children to take their break in the playground after the meal, and conditions were just as bad when afternoon playtime came. Out came the dog-eared comics, the jigsaw puzzles, the dominoes and draughts which featured so monotonously in the winter. The past spell of fine weather had made both staff and pupils forget the frustration of wet days indoors.

Miss Watson and Miss Fogerty were quite out of sorts at the end of the afternoon session, and thankful to return to the peace of the schoolhouse which they shared.

'Well, I'm glad to be home,' said Dorothy Watson, kicking off her shoes and putting up her feet on the settee.

'Me too,' agreed Agnes. 'I'll put on the kettle.'

'No, no!' protested Dorothy, not stirring. 'I will get tea in a moment.'

'You will stay there, and rest your poor hip,' responded Agnes firmly. She looked like a mouse trying to be ferocious.

'You spoil me,' murmured her headmistress, and closed her eyes.

The rattle of the tea things brought her back to consciousness. She lowered her legs to the floor, and sat up with a sigh.

'Oh, Agnes, what should I do without you?'

'Manage very well, I'm sure, just as you did when you were here on your own,' Agnes reassured her.

'It has just occurred to me,' said Dorothy, accepting her cup of tea, 'that it is Ray and Kathleen's wedding anniversary the day after tomorrow. I always sent them a card, but since their last dreadful visit here I haven't done so. Their behaviour was so appalling, I really haven't felt inclined to get in touch, but now – well, I don't know –'. Her voice trailed away into silence.

Little Miss Fogerty broke it with unaccustomed energy.

'I should send a card, Dorothy dear. After all, he is your only brother, and we are getting too old, all of us, to harbour hard feelings. I'm sure he and Kathleen would be very touched to have a generous gesture made to them.'

Miss Watson still looked doubtful. The 'last dreadful visit' she spoke of had taken place in this very room, when Ray and Kathleen had been invited to tea, had been particularly trying, in Miss Watson's view, and had, more-over, brought in their large and obstreperous dog which capsized the tea table, wrecked the drawing room and frightened everyone.

Tempers had risen, harsh words had been spoken, Ray and Kathleen had flounced off, vowing never to return, and Dorothy had told them flatly that the arrangement suited her perfectly.

Agnes, whose heart was more tender, had grieved over the rift and was delighted to see that Dorothy too was beginning to be willing to offer the olive branch.

Things had been strained between Ray and Dorothy for some time, and the open quarrel was only the culmination of two or three years' coolness. The headmistress had broken her hip in a fall in the playground, and after the operation had expected to recuperate with Ray, but no invitation had been forthcoming, much to her shocked amazement. Little Miss Fogerty, then living in lodgings, had offered to take up temporary abode at the schoolhouse, for a few weeks, until Dorothy was more mobile.

The offer was gratefully accepted, and when Dorothy realized how well the two got on together, she suggested that Agnes settled in permanently. The arrangement worked perfectly, but it meant that there was now no spare bedroom at the schoolhouse. In the past, Ray had often dropped in, and expected to stay overnight. Now he was offered the sofa, or directed to Lulling's premier hostelry, The Fleece. Looking back, Agnes feared that she had unwittingly been the means of upsetting Ray.

'Write a card now,' urged Agnes, 'and I will run across to catch the five-thirty collection. Even with the post as it is, it should get there on Friday.'

'I suppose so.'

'And I'm sure they would appreciate such a *gracious* act,' pursued Agnes. 'They must know they were in the wrong bringing that poor animal – Harrison, was it? – into this house uninvited. I'm sure they've often felt guilty about it.'

Dorothy had her doubts about that, but the idea of appearing gracious and forgiving appealed to her. And, in any case, as dear Agnes pointed out, they were all getting too old to continue a silly quarrel.

She rose to get her writing case, and scrabbled busily among its contents.

'I know I have some National Trust cards here somewhere.'

She withdrew a folder and spread out the contents on the sofa.

'Now which do you think, Agnes? Bodiam Castle or Mottisfont Abbey? Perhaps Bodiam. All that water round it is so attractive.'

She opened the card, and began to write. Agnes looked on with immense satisfaction, and sipped her tea. After five minutes the card was ready for the post, and Dorothy passed her cup for refilling.

'Well, I hope I've done the right thing. I simply said: "Happy remembrances. Hope all goes well with you both. Agnes joins me in sending love".'

'Perfect,' said her friend. 'I'll go over with it at once. Willie Marchant has been known to collect a few minutes early.' Willie Marchant was Thrush Green's thin postman. Willie Bond was the fat one.

'Still pouring, Agnes dear. Put on your raincoat. And a thousand thanks. I'll clear away the tea things.'

Agnes hurried off, and a minute later Dorothy saw her scurrying across the wet grass to the post box on the corner of Thrush Green.

Had she been wise to write? Would she hear from Ray and Kathleen? Come to that, did she really want to?

Of course she did, she told herself briskly, packing the tray carefully. They were her own flesh and blood after all.

But the response to her gracious gesture was to be rather more overwhelming than Dorothy envisaged.

As the wet day turned into an equally wet and dreary

evening, Winnie Bailey across the green was talking to her nephew Richard on the telephone.

Could he drop in for tea on Friday, he asked? He was only in the area for another week, and was hard pressed for time.

'It will suit us perfectly, Richard,' replied Winnie. 'About four?'

'Yes, yes. I'm sure I can get there by then. Don't worry if I'm a little late. And by the way, I have some exciting news for you.'

'What is it?'

'I'm married.'

'Good heavens, Richard! You've taken my breath away! Do bring her with you on Friday!'

'Can't be done. She's in London, but I'll tell you all about it when I see you. I've been run off my feet with these lectures, some in Birmingham, a couple at the University of Buckingham, and two more here in Oxford.'

'You do work hard,' said Winnie.

The pips went before she could say more.

'Till Friday,' cried Richard, and rang off.

Winnie returned to her sitting room still bemused. What staggering news! And how long had they been married? And why hadn't he told anybody?

What an odd fellow he was! Donald had always said so, and added that he was the most self-centred young man he had ever come across. She was afraid that this was quite true.

She fell to speculating about the new bride. Would she be a quiet submissive little thing, dazzled by Richard's undoubted eminence in his field, and willing to sacrifice her life to his? Or perhaps she had a job, equally important? The fact that she was remaining in London while Richard was on this lecture tour might mean that she too was busy with her own career. Richard would probably choose someone with plenty of brains as a partner.

What amazingly clever children they might have,

thought Winnie, her thoughts racing several years ahead. She recalled spending a short holiday, as a young woman, with a dear friend who lived in Sedley Taylor road in Cambridge. A good many of the houses were lived in then by newly-married university men, and the roads were busy with young children on tricycles and what were known then as fairy cycles. All seemed to be wiry, energetic infants, with spectacles and sandals, and their vocabularies appeared to Winnie to be much in advance of their tender years. Privately, she referred to any precocious children she met later as 'tiddly-widdly children'. Richard had always been one of them, to her, from the time he first sat up in his pram.

When Jenny put her head round the door to say goodnight, Winnie told her that Richard would be coming to tea on Friday.

'And Jenny, some terrific news! He's married.'

Jenny looked suitably astonished.

'Well, I never! I wonder what she's like, poor thing?'

She vanished before Winnie could reply, but as she rolled up her knitting and switched off the lights, Winnie could not help feeling that Jenny probably shared Donald's opinion of the bridegroom.

The upstairs lights went on one by one as Thrush Green prepared for bed.

Winnie undressed, still excited by the news of Richard's marriage. Jenny was wondering if she had enough cheese in the larder for the cheese scones she planned to make.

Edward Young tossed and turned, fuming at the weather which was holding up the steps, the ramp and the little paved terrace of the old people's abode.

Nelly Piggott, dropping off to sleep in the back bedroom, and ignoring Albert's snores from the next room, congratulated herself on now having three hundred pounds tucked away in her Post Office savings book. With a chap like Albert as poor provider it was a comfort to have a secret nest egg, she told herself.

At the schoolhouse, little Miss Fogerty put her book-mark in the novel she was reading, and closed it thought-fully. Did she really want to go on with this story, and were the characters typical of young people today? In this book not one appeared to have a normal home, parents appeared to be non-existent, marital arrangements much to be deplored, and drug-taking the accepted thing. No one, it seemed, wanted to work either. It was all extremely depressing.

She turned out the light. sighed heavily, and snuggled into her pillow for comfort.

In the next room, Dorothy Watson began to drift into sleep, serene in her belief that she had been forgiving, generous and – what had Agnes said? Ah yes, of course! *Gracious*, was the word.

She was asleep in five minutes.

4   Family Demands

THURSDAY WAS AS WET as the day before. The summer flowers were flattened in the gardens, the chestnut avenue outside the Youngs' gate dripped steadily, and the puddles grew apace.

But, on Friday, Thrush Green woke to blue skies and a freshly washed world. Spirits rose, and Betty Bell, always cheerful, was more exuberant than ever as she wheeled her bicycle from the school to Harold and Isobel Shoosmiths' house next door.

She 'put the school to rights' each morning, and on two days a week she worked as well at the Shoosmiths' home. When Harold Shoosmith had arrived in Thrush Green as a single man some years earlier, Betty had looked after the cleaning and also did some cooking, but since he had married, Isobel undertook most of the household work, and Betty's duties were much reduced.

She espied Willie Bond, the fat postman, ploughing his way towards her, and waited to see if he had any post for the Shoosmiths.

'How's tricks then, Willie? Got any letters for us? I'll save you a few steps maybe.'

Willie dismounted heavily, and fumbled in his canvas bag.

'Two from abroad it seems, and one of them bingo nonsenses as says you're going to win half a million what you never do.'

Betty accepted them.

'And how's auntie?'

Willie Bond and Betty Bell were first cousins.

'Worriting, as usual. Reckons the price of things is enough to give her the dumps. She's wondering whether to apply for one of these 'ere houses, but I don't reckon she'd like it.'

'Well, let's face it, Willie, she never liked anything much. Always a moaner, your mum.'

Willie sighed.

'True enough, Bet my girl. Well, I'd best be speeding off.'

He clambered again on to his bicycle and weaved his way to deliver letters at the schoolhouse.

'At least there are no bills this morning,' said Harold to Isobel, across the breakfast table. Upstairs the hum of the vacuum cleaner joined Betty Bell's voice uplifted in song.

'All's right with the world then,' commented Isobel, looking out at the sunshine, as Harold read his letters.

They had both found a perfect place for retirement, she thought yet again. It was good to be part of the small community of Thrush Green, and she was particularly fortunate to have made such a happy second marriage. She relished, too, the friendship and nearness of Agnes Fogerty, who was a staunch companion from college days.

'Which reminds me,' she said to her husband. 'I've promised to look out some jumble for the school sale at the end of term. I must do it this weekend.'

Harold passed over the two letters.

'They sound happy enough in Africa, although there seems to be quite a lot of opening doors to find chaps waiting there with pangas at the ready. All in all, I'd sooner be at Thrush Green, wouldn't you?'

'Without a doubt,' responded his wife.

Next door, little Miss Fogerty and Miss Watson were preparing to go across the playground to their school duties.

The breakfast things had been washed, beds made and dusting done, for both ladies were early risers, as school-teachers need to be, and were quick with their daily routine. Now they were on their way.

'I do so hope that Ray and Kathleen got their card this morning,' said Dorothy, still glowing with the thought of her forgiving gesture.

'Bound to have done,' Agnes assured her. 'It caught the afternoon post and had a first-class stamp on it.'

George Curdle, aged six, and one of her most promising pupils, now approached and presented her with a splendid posy of sweet peas.

'Why, thank you, George! How lovely! Did your father grow them?'

The child nodded, conscious of Miss Fogerty's sincere pleasure, and the gracious smiles of his headmistress.

'Tell him I am very pleased indeed with them,' said Agnes, passing on.

'Ben Curdle,' observed Dorothy, 'could always do anything. Took after his dear grandmother, no doubt. I still miss the May Day fair she used to bring here yearly.'

'So do I,' agreed her assistant, 'but it is much more peaceful teaching without it.'

'Well, we should have a peaceful enough day today, Agnes. The children will be able to play outside, and we shall get a little rest.'

It was not to last long.

Later that morning, across the green, the appetising smell of cheese scones scented Jenny's kitchen. They had turned out perfectly, nicely risen and gilded with egg yolk. Jenny admired them as they aired on the wire rack. Richard should enjoy those, she thought. A pity his wife could not sample them too.

After lunch Winnie Bailey fell asleep in her chair, and woke to find it almost three o'clock. Perhaps a good thing to have had a nap, she told herself. Richard's company was always exhausting, no matter how pleased one was to welcome him.

By half past four the trolley was ready in the kitchen, and the kettle was filled. Jenny hovered anxiously, one eye on the clock.

'If he's not here by five,' said Winnie, 'we'll have ours.'

But at ten to the hour, Richard arrived, tea was made, the trolley trundled into the sitting room, and Winnie awaited the details of his marriage.

He certainly looked very fit. He still had a good head of fair hair when so many of his contemporaries were losing theirs. His blue eyes, behind the spectacles which he had worn since childhood, were as bright as ever. His appetite too was keen, and he demolished five of Jenny's scones before Winnie had started her first.

Winnie had half-hoped that he would make some complimentary remark about the scones which she could have passed on to Jenny, to that lady's pleasure, but he appeared to demolish his tea simply to satisfy the inner man.

'Do you still follow your friend Otto's diet?' asked Winnie, remembering earlier visits when the dining room table had bristled with Richard's bottles of pills.

'No. I'm afraid he was exposed as something of a charlatan. His pills were mostly sugar with a mild opiate added. If he had been on any medical register he would have been struck off. A great pity about Otto. Quite gifted in some ways.'

Winnie remembered some trenchant remarks of her husband's about Otto and his products, but forbore to tell them to Richard.

'Now, please, I'm all agog. Tell me, when was the wedding?'

'Three weeks ago, Aunt Win. Very quiet affair at our local registry office. We both wanted that.'

'And her name?'

'Fenella. We met about two years ago at a party. She runs an art gallery with a distant cousin of hers. Quite lucrative.'

He helped himself to a slice of fruit cake, and munched busily.

'So will you live in London?'

'Oh yes, when I'm there. There's a flat of sorts over the shop, so to speak. Not very big, but as I'm away such a lot it should do us quite well. Fenella's lived there ever since she started at the gallery.'

'So that's why she couldn't come with you today, I suppose, with the gallery to see to?'

'Well, partly. At the moment she's not too fit.'

'Oh dear,' cried Winnie, envisaging some frail creature lying on a sofa with a severe headache, 'nothing serious, I hope?'

'No, nothing serious,' replied Richard, dusting cake

crumbs briskly from his knees to the carpet. 'But our baby's due next month, and she finds the stairs rather trying.'

Winnie, who had been brought up in the days when one's baby did not appear for at least nine months from the wedding day, adjusted herself to this news whilst refilling Richard's cup.

'Which is really why I wanted to come today,' continued Richard.

'I rather hoped you might want to see me,' smiled Winnie.

'Oh well, of course it is always nice to see you,' replied the young man, looking bewildered, 'but it was Fenella I was worrying about. You see, she will be having the baby at our local hospital, but no doubt will be sent out on the third day, if not earlier.'

He paused to take a gulp of tea.

Winnie's heart sank. If she were to be asked to travel to London to look after a nursing mother and new baby, for which she had no qualifications, she would have to refuse. And the stairs sounded daunting too, at her time of life.

'My suggestion is that she comes straight down here, if you could put her up. It's so quiet and peaceful, and the air would do her good.'

'But has she nowhere else to go?' asked Winnie.

'Her mother lives at Wimbledon, but they don't hit it off together awfully well, and in any case she's getting on. She must be well into her fifties.'

'And I'm well into my seventies,' said Winnie, with some asperity. She was about to remonstrate further when Richard spoke again.

'Of course, Timothy might be a problem. He'd have to come with Fenella.'

'Timothy?'

'Yes, he's four now. By Fenella's first husband. Full of life, is Timothy.'

Winnie began to feel slightly dizzy.

'But where will you be, Richard, when this child is born?'

'Oh, that's the point! I have to do a tour of Australia in about three weeks' time, so that's why I'm trying to get things settled before I go. I talked it over with Fenella, and I told her that you had Jenny to help in the house, and John Lovell practically on the premises if anything went wrong, and it all seemed ideal to us.'

Maybe, thought Winnie, with growing astonishment at these plans, but far from ideal for Jenny and for me! How right Donald had been when he described Richard as the most self-centred individual he had ever met! His calm assumption that two elderly ladies would disrupt their lives to accommodate his wife and two children, while he left all his responsibilities behind, astounded her.

She put down her cup very carefully, and took a deep breath.

'Richard, Fenella and the new baby, and the little boy, are your responsibility. You must have known about this situation for months, and should have made plans properly. To my mind, you should have cancelled the Australian trip, and been with them at this time.'

'But that would have been quite impossible, auntie. The contract was signed a year ago. Besides, I wanted to go.'

There speaks Richard, thought Winnie.

'In any case, it is impossible for me to take on your responsibilities. Now that Jenny lives here, we have only one spare bedroom, and really no facilities for coping with a mother and new baby, let alone Timothy.'

'Well,' said Richard, looking much taken aback, 'I really didn't foresee this!'

'Then you should have done. I am in my seventies, and Jenny not much less. I look forward to meeting Fenella and the family before long, but to expect us to cope with the present problem is remarkably naïve of you and – I must say it, Richard – uncommonly selfish too.'

'Then what am I to do?'

'You must make arrangements for a younger and better qualified woman than I am, to care for your family, if you must go on with this tour, which I consider ill-advised and again extremely selfish. Suppose something goes awry with the birth? How are people to get in touch with you? How will Fenella feel, trying to cope with everything? I'm getting crosser every minute with you, Richard. Have another cup of tea.'

He passed his cup in silence. Winnie found herself breathing heavily. All this was most upsetting. It was against her kindly nature to refuse help at such a time, but the facts were as she stated, and Richard was putting her into an impossible situation.

'So you won't have them?'

'I *can't* have them, and that's top and bottom of it. It would have been more thoughtful of you to have broached this subject months ago. I could have told you then, as I've told you now, that Jenny and I are beyond it, and you would have had more time to make other plans.'

'I'm very disappointed. I shall have to think again.'

'You most certainly will,' agreed Winnie, with some spirit. 'I advise you to try and get someone to live in for a month or so to look after things. No doubt the local district nurse will call as often as she can, but there should be somebody there – you, preferably – to cope with the day-to-day running of the household.'

Richard began to look sulky, reminding Winnie of the time when he had been refused a sixth chocolate biscuit at the age of five. He did not seem to have matured much in some ways.

'You've made things very awkward for me, Aunt Win. I really don't know what to do next.'

'There are plenty of agencies in your part of London,' Winnie told him, 'who will be only too pleased to send you someone who can cope with the nursing and the housework. I remember going to Kensington with my mother years ago when we needed a cook-general.'

'But it will cost money,' protested Richard.

'Naturally,' agreed Winnie. 'If you are expecting skilled and reliable service you must be prepared to pay well. Personally, I should have thought it a small price to pay for help in the circumstances.'

Richard looked at his watch.

'Too late to do anything today, I suppose. I think I'd better get back to town and discuss things with Fenella. I'm afraid she will be as disappointed as I am. I know she was very much looking forward to a week or two here to recuperate.'

Winnie refused to be browbeaten.

'I'm quite sure she will understand, Richard. Are you driving straight home?'

'Yes, of course. My lecture tomorrow isn't until the evening.'

'Then, in that case, I will pick her some roses. They are particularly fine this year. And you must wait while I write a note to go with them.'

Richard followed her into the garden as she snipped among the rosebeds. He still seemed upset, but Winnie ignored his restless pacing to and fro.

A quarter of an hour later, he was in the car, the roses, beautifully shrouded in tissue paper, on the back seat, and Winnie's letter in his pocket.

'I've no idea how to set about finding a suitable agency,' complained Richard, fastening his seat belt.

'Just look in the yellow pages, dear,' advised his aunt, and waved him farewell.

She returned to the kitchen where Jenny was busy washing up the tea things.

'My scones went down well evidently,' she said with satisfaction.

'They did indeed,' her mistress assured her. She went on to explain Richard's mission, and Jenny's eyes grew wider every minute.

When, at last, Winnie reached the end of her tale, Jenny

summed up the whole proceedings in one succinct word.

'Cheek!' she said.

Nelly Piggott, toiling up the hill from Lulling to Thrush Green after her day at The Fuchsia Bush, noticed Richard's car, which was waiting to enter the busy road to Oxford.

The roses caught her eye first, and then the particularly sulky look on the driver's face.

'Proper nasty tempered, that one,' thought Nelly. 'Wonder what he's doing in these parts? A rep, no doubt, and with them flowers in the back probably no better than he should be.'

She paused to get her breath halfway up the hill, and remembered her faithless Charlie who had so cruelly turned her out of home when his roving eye had lit upon another woman more to his liking. She dwelt on his infamy with martyred pleasure. The fact that he had taken her in when she had left Albert, her husband, some months earlier, she chose to forget.

All in all, she supposed, both men had treated her fairly well, and Albert had been remarkably amiable when she had returned to him. She would enjoy frying the chops for him which were in her basket. Cooking was the true joy of Nelly's life.

As she reached the top of the hill she could see Edward and Jean Young's fine house beyond the chestnut trees, and recalled the earnest discussion she and Mrs Peters had had that afternoon about veal and ham pie, salmon mousse, roast turkey, spiced beef and a score of other dishes suitable for a particularly select cold buffet. She was going to enjoy getting that lot ready!

Crossing behind the old people's homes, and now mercifully on the flat, Nelly came face to face with her husband's old friend Percy Hodge, who farmed a mile or so northwards off the Nidden road.

'Wotcher, Perce? Nice drop of rain yesterday. Do your crops good.'

'Done the potatoes a bit of good, I suppose, but too late for the wheat and barley. Be a poor yield, I shouldn't wonder.'

'You farmers never stop grumbling,' said Nelly. 'I'm glad I'm not married to one.'

She stopped hastily, remembering the truant Doris. Perhaps she'd said something to upset poor old Perce?

Had she known, he was thinking that Albert did his share of grumbling too, and a fine bonny woman like Nelly might have been better off with a farmer after all.

'Well, I must get on,' said Nelly, somewhat flustered. 'Albert's waiting for his tea.'

'He's a lucky chap to have someone to cook it for him,' replied Percy. 'Some of us have to cook our own.'

Nelly felt that the conversation was taking a dangerous turn. Percy Hodge was full of self-pity, and she didn't want any attentions from him. He'd been enough nuisance to that poor Jenny of Mrs Bailey's until she'd boxed his ears.

What a tiresome lot men were, thought Nelly, approaching her door. It made you wonder why they had been put into the world in the first place. If she'd had any hand in arranging matters at the Creation, she would have made sure that there would have been only one sex. Life would have been much simpler.

'And about time!' said Albert, when she closed the door behind her. 'I was getting fair weak with hunger.'

Nelly managed to stay silent, but she banged the frying pan viciously on to the stove to relieve her feelings.

Before Albert's chops were done, an upsetting telephone call came to the schoolhouse a few yards away.

Agnes and Dorothy were enjoying the newspapers, and the comfortable thought that it was Friday evening, and the much-blest weekend stretched ahead, when the telephone rang.

Dorothy answered it, and a few stray phrases were heard by Agnes.

'How serious is it? . . . Well, *of course*, we were in school. You must have known, Kathleen! . . . Which hospital? . . . Most inconvenient . . . Yes, of course, I shall go. I shall set off tomorrow morning . . . No, no, don't put yourself to any trouble. I can find a room.'

She came back, pink and flustered.

'Oh, what a kettle of fish! Really, Kathleen gets more impossible yearly! She's complaining because she's tried to ring us twice today, once at ten and then again at two o'clock. *Of course* we were in school, and no one but Kathleen would be so woolly-headed as to forget it.'

'But what's happened?'

'Oh, Ray has had an accident with the car,' said Dorothy, in what to anxious little Miss Fogerty seemed a remarkably off-hand manner.

Her hands fluttered to her face.

'But Dorothy, how dreadful! Is he badly hurt?'

'No, no! Kathleen said he has concussion, and probably a broken arm. The hospital people are keeping him in for a day or two.'

'I heard you say you would visit him. Shall I come with you?'

'No, Agnes. I shall catch the morning coach to London, and then take a taxi. Kathleen offered to put me up if I wanted to stay the night. In rather a *grudging* tone of voice, I thought. But I shall come back during the evening. Really, it is dreadfully annoying. I intended to wash my new cardigan tomorrow.'

'I will do that willingly.'

'It can wait until another day,' said Miss Watson firmly. 'We are going to get in a flummox over Ray's foolishness.'

'But what happened? Did Kathleen say?'

'I think he swerved into one of those islands with bollards in the middle of the road, but Kathleen didn't say what caused it. Fortunately, no one else was involved.'

'What a blessing!'

'Now one thing I must see to,' said Dorothy, reaching

for her handbag. 'Of course, the wretched banks will be closed tomorrow, but I think I have enough money to pay my way. In any case, I can use my Post Office book to withdraw some cash. I must say, my Post Office book is a real friend in need.'

'I have ten pounds put by,' said Agnes, 'in my stocking drawer.'

'Thank you, dear, but there is no need. I shall be all right. I'm meeting Kathleen at the hospital, so I shall know more then.'

'Did she get your card?' Agnes asked.

'She did indeed, and sounded very gratified. In fact, she said if it hadn't been for my kind message she wouldn't have liked to worry me about Ray's accident.'

'Now, isn't that nice!' cried little Miss Fogerty, aglow with noble feelings.

Dorothy gave one of her resounding snorts.

'I'm beginning to wonder,' she said.

5 The Longest Day

NELLY PIGGOTT, hurrying to work on the Saturday morning, remembered that today was the longest day of the year.

'June nearly on its way out,' thought Nelly, 'and them blankets not washed yet for the winter. Not that Albert'd notice.'

As she reached the bottom of the hill she noticed Miss Watson, stick in one hand, and a crocodile-skin handbag in the other, waiting to cross the road. Why was she out so early, wondered Nelly? Looked very smart too. A wedding perhaps?

Although she was not averse to making the occasional derisive remark about her two schoolteacher neighbours, secretly Nelly felt great respect for them. The school which Nelly had attended as a child, put discipline at the head of its priorities.

None of the staff could have held a candle to Dotty Harmer's tyrant of a father, but nevertheless due respect to teachers by pupils was expected, and punishment was severe if it was not forthcoming. Nelly herself could remember standing on her chair, a figure of shame before her contemporaries, enduring the while the lash of her teacher's tongue.

'Good morning, Miss Watson,' she said deferentially.

'Ah! Good morning, Mrs Piggott,' replied Dorothy. 'Are we in for a fine day, do you think?'

'I hope so. I only do the morning at The Fuchsia Bush on a Saturday, and I thought I might wash a few blankets this afternoon.'

Dorothy nodded vaguely. She had never washed a blanket in her life. Surely one would need something bigger than the sink for that? Luckily, the laundry took care of their blankets.

Nelly slackened her pace, to keep in step with her companion.

'Please don't let me hold you up,' said Dorothy. 'I'm rather slow these days.'

'No hurry for me now, we're nearly there,' Nelly assured her.

'I'm catching the coach,' said Dorothy. 'Rather bad news about my brother.'

Nelly was agog. A little drama is always welcome.

'I'm sorry to hear that.'

'A car accident. I don't think he is badly hurt, but I'm going to the hospital to make sure.'

'Oh, of course! Blood's thicker than water, I always say. Have you got far to go?'

'No, it's one of the London hospitals. I can visit any time this afternoon.'

'Then you'll be in nice time,' commented Nelly, wondering why Miss Watson should be making such an early start.

As if reading her thoughts. Dorothy replied.

'I propose to do a little shopping while I'm in town. Selfridge's and John Lewis's are so satisfactory.'

They were now at the coach stop outside The Fuchsia Bush.

'Well, I hope you find your brother pretty well,' said Nelly politely, and departed to her day's work.

Really a very nice woman, thought Dorothy, watching her go. Not many of that calibre about these days. Hardworking, well-mannered, kindly – Albert hardly deserved anyone so worthwhile.

On the other hand, of course, one had heard things about Nelly's moral standards.

But before she could dwell on the baser and more interesting side of Nelly's character, the coach arrived, mercifully half empty, and Miss Watson mounted the steps to choose her seat for the journey.

Winnie Bailey had had a troubled night after her encounter with Richard. She did not regret her refusal to take on Fenella and her two children, but she was annoyed with Richard for suggesting it.

And yet she was fond of her nephew, despite his irritating ways, and hoped that he would not have a prolonged fit of the sulks, and cut her out of his life. She was getting too old to cope with harboured grudges, and would like to see Richard, and his wife and family, as she had said.

Well, time would show, she thought philosophically, putting out the milk bottles on the front step.

John Lovell, on his way to morning surgery, hurried across to speak to her.

'Did you ever find that farm, John?' she asked him.

'After a false start or two. The fir tree's gone now, but the house is still there, and the farm buildings, though everything's a bit run down.'

'Who lives there now?'

'At Trotters? Leys Farm, I mean.'

'Yes. Which do they call it, by the way?'

'Leys Farm. Though an old boy on the road knew it as Trotters, as you do.'

'Nice family?'

'Two middle-aged brothers, and a youngster, a nephew, I gathered. It was he who was groggy. Some tummy bug or other. Violent D. and V. but he had responded well to antibiotics when I called again, so I shan't need to make another visit, unless they ring.'

'No women?'

'Not in evidence. They looked a pretty scruffy lot,

despite half a dozen expensive-looking cars in the yard. How are things with you?'

'Fine, John.'

She was half-inclined to tell him of Richard's visit, but already a few patients were entering his waiting room, and Winnie, as a doctor's wife, knew better than to keep him from his work.

She might tell him later, she decided, watching him cross to the surgery. Perhaps she might feel less worried about the affair as time passed.

Downhill at Lulling, the rector decided to take advantage of the sunshine to walk along the tow path of the River Pleshey.

The exercise would do him good, Dimity told him, as she set about preparing a lamb casserole.

'And it might clear my brain,' added Charles. 'Tomorrow's sermon doesn't read very well, I must admit. Perhaps I shall get some flashes of inspiration.'

He always enjoyed this quiet pathway. The willows shimmered their grey green leaves above the water. Their rustling, and the river's rippling, made a tranquil background to the rector's thoughts, and he walked rather farther than he first intended, until he found himself within sight of the cottage which had once belonged to the water keeper, and now housed his old friend Tom Hardy and his equally ancient dog, Polly.

He decided to call on them, and crossed the wooden footbridge to the house. As was his wont, he went to the back door, and there discovered Tom chopping up wood on the doorstep. Polly was lying nearby in the sun, but came to greet him, tail wagging.

'She remembers you, sir,' said Tom, straightening his back slowly. 'This is a nice surprise, I must say. Come into the kitchen.'

A bench stood against the wall, hard by the back door.

'Let's sit here,' said the rector. 'Too good to go inside.'

The old man sat down heavily with a sigh.

'Who'd have thought choppin' a few sticks would wind you? It does though.'

'Do you need them in this weather?'

'Well, no. I don't light my kitchen stove much come the summer, but I suppose it's going most of the year, and I likes to have plenty of firing put by.'

'It must make quite a bit of work, Tom. Clearing out the ashes and so on.'

'Ah! But it's company. And the kettle's always on, and the oven stays nice and hot. I puts in a chop, or some sausages in a little old tin, and a rice pudden for afters. That cooks lovely that old stove, and in the evening I opens the little door, and Poll and me enjoys the firelight and the warmth on us.'

Charles Henstock recalled the massive black hod which

held the fuel for Tom's stove, and wondered how he could lift it nowadays. He had never completely regained his strength after his sojourn in the local hospital, when Polly had been a welcome guest at Lulling Vicarage in her master's absence.

'Do you get anybody to help you in the house?' asked Charles.

'Well, my good neighbour comes now and again, but she's a busy soul. But that reminds me, sir, she brought a form for me to write on to see if I could have a home help once or twice a week.'

'That's a splendid idea.'

'Yes, I s'pose so. But I'm no hand at forms. Would you be so good as to help me with it? It's upstairs.'

'Willingly, Tom. Let's fetch it.'

Tom led the way through the kitchen which Charles always admired for its practicality and bare, but beautiful, simplicity. It was as tidy as ever, the table top scrubbed white, the now cold stove black and shining.

The staircase opened from this room, and Charles watched Tom mount the steep flight with shaky steps. The rope banister against the wall was the only support, and Charles watched his old friend's progress with mounting anxiety.

'Shall I come up, Tom?'

'No, sir,' wheezed Tom, 'I'll bring it down.'

Charles waited at the foot of the staircase, listening to the old man opening drawers and shifting furniture. A print of a moonlight steeplechase hung on the wall, foxed with age and damp, but the intrepid riders in their white night shirts could still be descried, if one peered closely. It seemed to be the only picture in the house, and hanging in such a murky place, it obviously did not gain much attention.

Tom reappeared, letter in hand, and descended carefully.

'Let's spread it out on the kitchen table,' said Charles, and was relieved when the two of them were sitting on sturdy wooden chairs with their task before them.

The rector filled in the data as Tom answered his questions, and in ten minutes the form was ready and signed in Tom's quavering hand.

'I'll post it for you with my letters,' said Charles. 'I have to go to the Post Office this afternoon.'

'Then I'll give you the stamp money,' said the old man, pulling out the drawer of the table and taking out an old tobacco tin.

'No need for that, Tom.'

The old man looked stubborn.

'I won't be beholden,' he said.

'Very well,' replied the rector amiably. 'If you insist. Second class will do, I'm sure.'

Tom handed over the coins, and gave a great smile.

'That's a weight off my chest. How about some tea?'

'I'd better not, Tom. I've got to eat a meal when I get back. But let's have a few minutes outside in the sun.'

He stayed for half an hour, relishing the old man's company, and the affection displayed by Polly to them both. She and Tom were a devoted pair, and enjoyed each other's tranquil companionship.

On his way back, the rector thought seriously about Tom's future. Here, surely, was an absolutely suitable person for one of Thrush Green's new homes. He would not have to negotiate those dangerous stairs, or chop sticks, or handle that hefty coal hod. He could have a meal brought to him, if need be, and although the rice pudding might not be as good as those he cooked himself, the rector felt sure that Tom would appreciate it in time.

But even if a place were allotted to Tom, would he want to move? He loved his cottage hard by the river, his little garden, filled with old-fashioned flowers, pansies, a musk rose and mignonette.

And most of all he loved his independence. He could be obstinate. Charles recalled the tight lips and stern eyes when he had attempted to wave aside the stamp money. No, it would not be easy to move Tom should the need arise.

And Polly? What about Polly? He would never leave her, that was certain. They were as close as mother and child, or husband and wife.

Charles stood stock still for a moment, taken aback by this problem. A moorhen, scared at the intrusion, fluttered squawking from the reeds, and crossed the stream with trailing legs that scattered diamond-bright drops.

'We must cross that bridge when we come to it,' Charles told the bird, and continued on his way to attack tomorrow's sermon once more.

Little Miss Fogerty spent the morning doing the usual Saturday chores, the personal washing, including Dorothy's cardigan which received particular care, a thorough dusting and carpet-sweeping which was done sketchily on workdays, and sorting out the bedlinen ready for the laundryman on Tuesday.

The evening meal was to be cold chicken and salad, and Agnes went down the garden to pull a fine lettuce and some radishes to wash.

Her college friend Isobel was in her garden next door.

'Agnes dear, could I bring the jumble stuff round this afternoon?'

'Any time, Isobel. I am on my own all day.'

She explained about Dorothy's absence, and knew that her headmistress would not mind Isobel hearing about Ray's accident. Normally, at Thrush Green, one needed to filter one's thoughts before speaking and getting a name for being a gossip, but the two neighbours relied on each other's discretion, and knew that they could discuss matters unguardedly.

'Why don't you come to lunch with Harold and me? Come and take pot luck. We'd love it.'

'I won't, dear, many thanks. I'm having a clearing-up day. But I'll look forward to seeing you with the jumble.'

Agnes partook of a lightly-boiled egg for lunch, and a cup of coffee, had a brief snooze with her feet up on the string stool Dorothy had made at last winter's evening class in Lulling, and was alert when Isobel arrived, and ready for the exchange of news.

As always, Isobel looked pretty in a blue linen frock and white sandals. Agnes secretly admired her unblemished brown bare legs, and thought ruefully of her own heavily veined ones. Ah well! Isobel had not had to stand so many hours before a class, thought Agnes without envy, and it was a pleasure to see how young and healthy she looked, despite being almost exactly her own age.

In the evening, Agnes set the table and then made her way down the hill to meet Dorothy at the London coach stop in the High Street.

It was a golden evening. A glimpse of a cornfield in the distance showed the crop already looking a pale gold in the low rays of the sinking sun. A nearby row of trees had their trunks turned to bronze on their north-west side. It was going to be a spectacular sunset, thought Agnes, and was reminded of a reverberating phrase in her ancient copy of *A Handbook for Teachers*, which exhorted all those who had to teach in dismal towns to 'direct the pupils' attention to the ever-changing panorama of the heavens', if there were nothing else of natural beauty to be seen.

Agnes thought how fortunate she was to have her lot cast at Thrush Green which had such splendid walks suitable for the young. She made a mental note to take her class to see the beauties of the June hedgerows on the road to Nidden. The elder flowers were magnificent at the moment, and the wild roses at their best.

With any luck, they might see a nest, but really it might be wiser not to disclose such treasures. The girls would relish the secret, no doubt, but one really could not trust *all* the boys to be quite so gentle. That youngest Cooke boy, for instance, had a truly barbaric streak in him, sad to say.

By this time, Agnes had reached the coach stop. The High Street was pleasantly quiet, and the lime trees already showing pale flowers. The coach was late, and Agnes found a low wall near The Fuchsia Bush for a comfortable seat. She was observed there by the three Miss Lovelock sisters who peered from time to time from their drawing room window to make sure that nothing of note escaped them.

Agnes was unaware of their scrutiny, but was turning over in her mind certain plans for her winter wardrobe. Her camel coat should do another season. Such a useful garment, and equally wearable with black or brown. On the other hand, she rather favoured a green hat for formal wear, and wondered if it would go well with her new black suit and the camel colour? Of course, there were always *scarves*, Agnes mused, and at that moment the coach arrived, and Dorothy descended the stairs carefully.

'Agnes, how *nice* of you to come! No, no, I can quite well manage the parcels. They are very light, just a few little things for the winter, though why we should be dwelling on that on this gorgeous summer's day, I really don't know.'

'And how did you find Ray?'

'Very little amiss. But I'll tell you all when we are home. This hill takes all one's breath, doesn't it?'

And Agnes could not help but agree, despite her eagerness to hear Dorothy's news.

After the chicken and salad had been enjoyed, Dorothy kicked off her shoes and settled back on the sofa with a sigh.

'Delicious, Agnes! I feel quite restored. How people can think of a day in London as a *treat* beats me! I find it an endurance test, I must say, although as a girl I really enjoyed pottering round Liberty's or dear old Heal's, and then going to a matinée or an exhibition after that. What resilience we used to have!'

'But Ray?' pressed Agnes. 'How was he?'

'In bed, of course, and he had a bandage round his head

which made him look rather worse than he was. His forehead evidently had a nasty gash from the windscreen. It was quite shattered.'

'*His forehead*?' exclaimed Agnes aghast.

'No, no, dear. The windscreen. I heard the whole story in bits and pieces between the two of them.'

'So you met Kathleen there?'

'Yes, as I told you, at two-thirty.'

Agnes forbore to point out that Dorothy had told her nothing of the sort, but awaited enlightenment.

'As a matter of fact, I very much doubt if Ray would have told me much at all – certainly not about the dog – if Kathleen hadn't blurted it out.'

'The dog? What was its name now?'

'Harrison, of all the stupid names. Called after their butcher or some such whimsical nonsense. I do dislike animals referred to as Miss Poppet or Mr Thompson. One is misled into thinking they are lodgers at first hearing. What's wrong with Rover or Pip or Towser? Though, come to think of it, I haven't come across a Towser for years. My Uncle Tom had a Towser, a most intelligent mongrel.'

'But Ray's accident,' prodded Agnes, who felt that Dorothy's digressions from the main subject were more infuriating than usual.

Miss Watson sat up, and began to look more attentive.

'Well, I met Kathleen as arranged, although, of course, she was ten minutes overdue, as one would expect. She referred again to my anniversary card, and they both gave me a warm welcome which was gratifying.'

'Yes, indeed. Bygones must be bygones.'

'She had brought a great sheaf of irises for Ray, and the nurse looked a bit taken aback, as well she might, for the ward was not very well furnished for bouquets which would have been more suitable in a cathedral. I took three bunches of violets, incidentally.'

'Ray would like those, I'm sure.'

'The first thing he did was to enquire after the dog, which I thought rather absurd, until Kathleen replied that he was recovering well and had eaten some minced beef and four beaten eggs in milk.'

'How *expensive*!' commented frugal little Miss Fogerty.

'Exactly. I asked if the dog were seriously ill, and do you know what Kathleen said?'

'How *could* I know?' answered Agnes reasonably, but with a touch of impatience. Would the story never end? It reminded her of *Tristram Shandy*, read long ago at college.

' "Not seriously ill, but still a little upset by the accident." I ask you!'

'So the dog was in the car too?'

'It was indeed, and it transpires that it was the cause of the accident. Evidently, Ray was driving alone, with the animal sitting in the back, when it saw a cat on the pavement, went berserk, leapt into the front seat and created pandemonium. Just as it did at our tea party, you remember.'

'I do indeed. What a dreadful thing! And so Ray swerved, I suppose?'

'Right into one of those islands, and at some speed. The windscreen shattered, and the side of the car was pushed in. It's a wonder poor Ray wasn't killed. They had to cut part of the car away to get him out.'

'Is he badly cut about?'

'Only his forehead, and he has two cracked ribs and a broken arm. Nothing to worry about,' said Dorothy with sisterly casualness. 'The concussion seems to have been very slight. He should be out in a day or two.'

'Well, it was right to go and see him,' said Agnes. 'And it is a blessing he is not worse, poor fellow. And I'm glad the dog is well. They are so devoted to it.'

'Much *too* devoted, if you ask me,' said Dorothy, with asperity. 'I very nearly told them what I thought of their foolish indulgence of that disgustingly behaved animal, but it didn't seem quite the time and place for a bit of plain speaking. It might have started Kathleen off on one of her hysterical fits, and I didn't think the other patients in the ward should be subjected to that. After all, they all had enough to put up with, Ray included.'

'That was thoughtful of you,' agreed Agnes, who knew how easily her friend was stirred to outspokenness, sometimes with disastrous and embarrassing results.

'Do you know, Agnes, I should really enjoy a cup of coffee. It's been a long day.'

'The longest of the year,' said Agnes, pointing to the calendar. 'Stay there, my dear, and I'll go and make the coffee.'

The two ladies went to bed early. Little Miss Fogerty had also found it a long and tiring day, but was relieved to have Dorothy back safe and sound, and to know that her brother was making steady progress. There was much to be thankful for, she thought, gazing out of her bedroom window across Thrush Green.

It was still light, although the little travelling clock on the bedroom mantelpiece said ten o'clock. The statue of Nathaniel Patten shone in the rosy light of a spectacular sunset, now beginning to fade into shades of pink and mauve.

The air was still. Far away, a distant train hooted at Lulling station, a pigeon clattered homeward, and a small black shadow crossed the road below Miss Fogerty's window. Albert Piggott's cat was about its night time business.

'Time for bed,' yawned little Miss Fogerty.

It really had been an exceptionally long day.

6 The Fuchsia Bush to the Rescue

THROUGHOUT JULY WORK went on steadily at the old people's homes. The weather was kind, and the outside painting went ahead without disruption. Edward Young was relieved to see such progress, and optimistic about its opening in the autumn.

He said as much to his wife Joan, one breakfast time.

'I only hope the weather will hold up for my lunch party,' she replied. 'I've made plans to hustle everything under cover if need be, but it would be splendid if people could picnic on the lawn.'

'Of course it will stay fine,' Edward said robustly. 'Looks settled for weeks. Mark my words, things will go without a hitch!'

But he was wrong. Later that morning she answered the telephone to find that it was her sister Ruth speaking, sounding much agitated.

'It's mother, Joan. I went in just now to see if she were needing help in dressing, and found her on the floor.'

'Oh no! Heart again?'

'There's no saying. I've got her into bed, but John's on his rounds, of course. I've left a message.'

'I'll come straightaway.'

Molly Curdle was in the kitchen, at her morning duties. She and her husband Ben now lived in the converted stable where Joan and Ruth's mother had lived until recently.

Joan explained briefly what had happened, and left Molly troubled in mind. She had known the Bassetts, Joan's parents, ever since she was a child, and the death of the old man had grieved her. Was his wife to follow him so soon? Ben, now busy at work in Lulling, would be as upset as she was.

Joan found her mother barely conscious, but the old lady managed to smile at the two anxious faces bending over her.

'John's just rung,' whispered Ruth. 'He's coming straight back from Lulling. Miss Pick caught him at the Venables', luckily.'

Mrs Bassett's eyes were now closed, but she seemed to be breathing normally.

Ruth smoothed the bedclothes, nodded to her sister, and the two tiptoed from the room.

Agnes Fogerty, with a straggling crocodile of small children behind her, recognized Joan Young's car outside her sister's. It was nice to see how devoted the two were, she thought fondly. So many sisters did not get on well. Families could be quite sorely divided. Look at Dorothy and Ray, for instance.

'John Todd,' called little Miss Fogerty, temporarily diverted from her musings on the variability of family relationships, 'throw that nettle away, and if I see you tormenting George Curdle again I *shall send you to Miss Watson.*'

This appalling threat succeeded in frightening John Todd, a hardened criminal of six years old, into temporary good behaviour, and the observation of the Thrush Green hedgerows continued.

There was plenty to be seen. On the grass verges the pink trumpets of mallow bloomed. Nearer the edge grew the shorter white yarrow, with its darker foliage and tough stems, and in the dust of the gutter, pink and white striped bindweed showed its trumpets against a mat of flat leaves, as pretty as marshmallows, thought Agnes.

Nearby was yellow silverweed with its feathery foliage, almost hidden by a mass of dog daisies, as the children called them. In the sunshine their pungent scent was almost overpowering, but three small brown and orange butterflies were giving the plants their attention, and the children were excited.

'My grandpa,' said John Todd, anxious to reinstate himself in Miss Fogerty's good books, 'has got six drawers in a cabinet, full of butterflies with pins through 'em.'

Some of the girls gave squeaks of disgust, and little Miss Fogerty herself inwardly recoiled from the picture this evoked.

'They're dead all right,' John Todd said hastily. 'He done 'em in in a bottle. Years ago, it was.'

'Very interesting,' commented Agnes primly. One could not always believe John Todd's stories, and even if this one happened to be true, good manners forbade one to criticise the child's grandfather.

'Now we will stop under this tree for a moment,' said Agnes, diverting the children's attention, and remembering 'the ever-changing panorama of the heavens' phrase of long ago. 'You may sit on the grass as it is quite dry, and I want you to notice the lovely creamy flowers hanging down. This is a lime tree, and if you breathe in you can smell the beautiful fragrance of the flowers.'

Some unnecessarily squelchy indrawing of breath made Miss Fogerty clap her hands sharply.

'Perhaps we will have a little nose-blowing first,' she said firmly. 'Hold up your hankies!'

There were times, thought Agnes, trying to recapture the heady bliss of breathing in the perfume of flowering lime, when children were excessively tiresome.

It was a good thing that Miss Fogerty had taken her children on the nature walk when she did, for a rainy spell of weather set in, when mackintoshes were the rule, and many of the fragrant lime flowers fell wetly to the ground beneath the downpour.

The gardeners of Lulling and Thrush Green welcomed

the rain. The broad beans plumped out, the raspberries flourished, red flowers burst out on the runner bean plants, and the thirsty flowers everywhere revived.

Joan Young viewed the wet garden with less enthusiasm. In a week's time the buffet lunch was to take place, and that morning before breakfast, she had made a decision. She must ask Mrs Peters of The Fuchsia Bush if she could cope with the waiting on her guests, and with the main bulk of the catering.

Her mother was still in a precarious state, needing to be in bed for most of the day, and Ruth, with two young children, was hard-pressed.

Joan and Edward's only child, Paul, was away at school, and Joan was sharing the nursing duties as often as she could, but the extra work of the lunch party was beginning to worry her enormously.

'If The Fuchsia Bush could take it off my shoulders,' she said to Edward, as they dressed, 'it would make it so much easier. You see, I had planned to collect plates and cutlery from no end of people, and napkins and serving bowls for the salads and trifles and whatnot.'

'What about glasses?' asked Edward, putting first things first.

'Oh, that's simple. The wine people are coping with that anyway. But with mother as she is, I want to feel I could slip away, if need be, without disrupting anything.'

'You bob down to Lulling, and see Mrs Peters,' advised Edward, fighting his way into his pullover. He tugged it down, and went to look at his latest project through the streaming windowpane.

'They really look splendid, don't they?' he said with satisfaction. 'A great improvement on Charles's ghastly abode.'

'Will this weather hold up the work?'

'Not greatly. There's plenty to finish off inside.'

He put his arm round his wife, and gave her a kiss.

She was glad his work was nearly over. Hers, it seemed, was about to begin.

When Nelly Piggott entered The Fuchsia Bush the next morning, she found Mrs Peters sitting at the vast table in the quiet kitchen. She was busy making a list, and looked up as Nelly entered.

'Such news, Nelly,' she cried. 'Come and sit down.'

Nelly took off her wet mackintosh, hung it in the passage, and flopped down thankfully on the chair opposite her employer.

'I had a visit from Mrs Young last night,' she began. 'She's in rather a state about this lunch party of hers.'

She went on to explain Joan's needs, and her own plans to help her in this emergency. Nelly listened enthralled. Here was a challenge indeed!

'But can we do it?' she asked at length. 'What about

getting the food up there? And the plates and dishes? And who's going to look after this place? After all, Saturdays are always busy.'

'I rang Bunnings about transport and they'll ferry everything. The Wine Bar's coping with the drink and glasses. We can take most of our own crockery and silver, and I intend to ask Mrs Jefferson, if she would take charge here until we are back.'

Mrs Jefferson had been at The Fuchsia Bush for many years, but ill health had meant that she now only came part time. But, as Nelly knew, she was quite capable of holding the fort for a day in an emergency. Really, thought Nelly, it was all very exciting!

'How many of us will you need?' she asked.

'Well, you'll be my chief assistant, Nelly, if you feel you can undertake it.'

Nelly beamed. 'I'll thoroughly enjoy myself,' she assured her employer. 'What's the plan of campaign?'

'We'll take up the plates and things on the Friday evening when we're closed. I'm sure I can get all we need in the car. Then the food can go up with Bunning on Saturday morning. People will help themselves. It's just a case of us slicing the meat and the pies and quiches. We'll get the various salads ready here.'

'Just the two of us?' asked Nelly enthusiastically.

'Well, no. I'll see if Gloria and Rosa will come too. We shall want a few more hands, and though they leave much to be desired, at least they can stack plates, and put the dirty cutlery in a bucket to bring back here.'

Nelly thought swiftly.

'So really we'll be busy from Friday night till Saturday night?'

Mrs Peters looked suddenly anxious and careworn, and Nelly's kind heart was stirred.

'Yes, that's about it, Nelly. How do you feel?'

'Dead keen!' that lady told her energetically, and meant it.

*

Albert Piggott was remarkably docile when Nelly told him the great news.

'As long as I gets my tea as usual, it's all the same to me,' he said, pushing aside the plate which had been filled with oxtail stew ten minutes earlier.

'It might have to be cold that day,' his wife warned him.

'Then make a decent bit of pie,' said Albert. 'That brawn you brought back from the shop hadn't got no staying power in it for a hardworking chap.'

Nelly forbore to comment, but set about clearing the table with her customary energy.

While she was thus engaged a knock came at the door, and Albert, heaving himself from the armchair with a sigh, went to answer it.

To his amazement, Percy Hodge stood on the doorstep holding a bunch of roses. Percy himself looked equally taken aback.

'What the hell do you want?' asked Albert of his drinking companion.

'I thought this was your evening over the churchyard,' spluttered Percy.

'Well, it ain't. Young Cooke's wasting his time there tonight.'

He peered at the roses with dislike. Nelly, secretly nettled at this unwanted attention, came forward, drying her hands on a teacloth.

'Good evening, Percy,' she said primly.

'I was wondering,' said Percy, who had been thinking as quickly as his slow brain would allow, 'if Mrs Peters down the shop would like these roses for the tea tables. Maybe you'd be kind enough to take 'em down in the morning.'

'I'm sure she'd be pleased,' said Nelly. 'Won't you come in?'

'Just going next door,' said Percy hastily, thrusting the bouquet into Nelly's arms, to her discomfort. 'You coming for a pint, Albert?'

'No, I ain't,' said Albert grimly, and slammed the door.

'Well,' said Nelly, much flustered, 'I'd better put these in a bucket overnight.'

'Best place for them,' responded Albert sourly, 'is the dustbin. And how long, may I ask, has all this been going on?'

At the village school, end of term was bringing its usual flurry of activity, and Miss Watson and her staff were looking forward to the final day with ever-increasing exhaustion.

'Sometimes I wonder if it is practicable to have Sports Day and the Annual Outing and the Parents' Fête and the Leavers' Service, all in the last month when we are so busy with reports and all these wretched returns to the office,' sighed Dorothy, as she walked homeward across the playground.

'But we couldn't really arrange things very well for the end of any of the other terms,' pointed out little Miss Fogerty. 'Christmas is hectic as it is, and anyway most of the activities are out of door ones. They must be held in the summer.'

'Yes, dear, I know. But it doesn't make things any easier.'

There was a letter on the door mat which Dorothy picked up.

'Kathleen's writing. Now I wonder what she wants?'

The two ladies made their way to the sitting room, and sat down with sighs of relief. Agnes closed her eyes, listening to the rustle of Kathleen's letter, as Dorothy read it with an occasional snort.

'Well, it appears that we can expect a visitation from them soon. Ray is getting so bored with being unable to do much, and a neighbour has offered to take them for a drive. Why Kathleen has never had the commonsense to learn to drive, *I do not know*. Scatterbrained, I know she is, and completely lacking in mechanical skills, but sillier people than she drive cars after all, and it would have been a help to Ray now and again.'

'Are they coming soon?'

'It's left to us. I suppose we'd better say they're welcome.'

Dorothy's voice sounded anything but welcoming.

'But not until we've broken up,' she said firmly. 'One thing, this neighbour refuses to have the dog in his car, sensible fellow, so we shan't have a repetition of their last disastrous visit.'

She rose from her chair.

'I shall make tea today, Agnes, you look tired. Shall we have Earl Grey for a change? So refreshing.'

'That would be lovely, Dorothy,' replied Agnes.

Nelly Piggott descended the hill the next morning with the roses in her basket.

There had been a few harsh words between herself and Albert after Percy's departure, but nothing seriously amiss. Nelly's conscience was clear, and she told Albert so in plain terms.

Albert, knowing Percy, guessed that for once Nelly was telling the truth about this unwelcome admirer, and after ten minutes of bickering the quarrel petered out.

Nelly was extremely cross with Percy but had no intention of confronting him. Better to tell his sister, Mrs Jenner, with whom she went to bingo occasionally, and let her pass on the message to silly old Percy.

Nevertheless, it was rather a comfort to Nelly to know that she could still inspire devotion. She had always had admirers, and was romantic by nature. She passed over the roses to Mrs Peters with a twinge of regret.

That lady was far too engrossed with the plans for Joan Young's buffet lunch to do anything but accept them with perfunctory thanks, and Nelly was not called upon to give any explanation of her gift.

The roses were put into a copper pitcher and had pride of place in the front window of The Fuchsia Bush for two days, where they were much admired by the customers.

Meanwhile, preparations proceeded apace. Mrs Peters was a born organizer, Nelly an enthusiastic supporter, and the two waitresses were sufficiently stirred by this change in routine to agree to don clean overalls and welcoming smiles for their part in the project. All that everyone prayed for now was a fine day.

The weather forecast was equivocal. There might be showers, there was a chance of sunshine, it would probably be overcast, temperatures would be normal for the time of year, winds would be light.

The morning dawned grey and still. Joan Young, a bundle of nerves, could only manage a cup of coffee for breakfast, and was soon outside surveying the preparations.

Molly and Ben Curdle had cleared their garage so that the produce stall and the plants could be displayed under cover. The gipsy caravan, which had once been Ben's grandmother's home, now stood nearby in the orchard, and this today housed the white elephant stall, including some of Ella's handiwork.

The dining room and drawing room were given over to the food, to be spread on long tables for the visitors to help themselves. Both rooms had french windows opening to the lawn and it was Joan's earnest hope that the weather would allow her patrons to sit outside, balancing plates and glasses, and dropping crumbs at their will. All the garden chairs which could be mustered were disposed under trees or near the small ornamental pool, and very pretty and welcoming it all looked.

She could do no more. Now it was over to Mrs Peters, as yet untried, and the Wine Bar in whom she had confidence from past experience.

Edward had volunteered to take the money at the gate and to collect the tickets of those who had gallantly bought them beforehand. At twelve o'clock, he was ensconced before his card table, while Mrs Peters, Nelly, Gloria, Rosa, Joan Young and Molly Curdle were hard at it in the kitchen, dining room and drawing room.

A hazy sun began to shine and everyone's spirits lifted as the first few friends came up the drive, and were directed to the paddock, today the car park, by Ben Curdle.

They had catered for one hundred guests. All seemed to have excellent appetites, and to intend to eat their three pounds-worth of the delicious offerings set before them. Nelly was gratified to receive compliments on her veal and ham pie, the quiches, the spiced beef and other delicacies. Mrs Peters, flushed and happy, watched the delectable trifles, mousses and flans vanish gardenwards.

A good many people had come from Lulling in a coach organized by Mrs Thurgood, a wealthy widow and a regular churchgoer at St John's.

It was she who had fallen out with poor Charles Henstock, soon after his induction, over the kneelers which she was determined to replace against all opposition. Luckily, the quarrel was in the past, and now she and Charles were the best of friends, the relationship being cemented by the marriage of her daughter Jane to a young man, John Fairbrother, to whom Charles had introduced the girl.

Mrs Thurgood insisted on inspecting the kitchen, much to Joan Young's and Mrs Peters' annoyance, but the lady was renowned for her autocratic ways and allowed to snoop without comment, at least of an audible nature, but meaning glances were exchanged behind the lady's back, and later Joan told Edward just what she thought of such behaviour.

Trade was brisk at the stalls. Ella was delighted to find that almost all her weaving and wickerwork had been bought, and even the wispiest geraniums seemed to be snapped up at the plant stall.

At the end of the day, Edward counted his money, and that taken at the stalls, and added it to the ticket money already banked. To everyone's amazement and gratification it came to nine hundred and seventy four pounds and a halfpenny.

After paying Mrs Peters and the Wine Bar there would still be a handsome profit.

'Well,' said Joan, when everyone had gone home and she was sitting on the sofa with her shoes off, 'that's a good beginning for the Heart Appeal and the Church Roof Fund.'

It was the beginning of much more, if she had only known.

7 Summer visitors

WORK ON THE NEW homes was almost finished, and Edward Young was proud of his handiwork. After the rectory fire, there was much conjecture about possible purchasers of the site. Eventually, an old-established charity, which owned similar sheltered accommodation elsewhere, bought it, and worthy local people were appointed trustees.

The vicar of the parish was one, and as for many years Mrs Thurgood's husband had been a generous benefactor to the foundation, it was thought proper to appoint his widow as another at Thrush Green. Justin Venables was another of the trustees.

John Lovell also took a keen interest in the project, for he was one of the trustees who would not only help to select the first lucky residents, but would keep an eye on their health. After much discussion, it had been decided to call the new homes Rectory Cottages.

There would be seven houses to allot, for the end house was reserved for the warden and his, or her, spouse. Applicants for this joint post were to be interviewed very soon, and already some twenty hopeful couples had sent in their application forms. It could be a pleasant job for the right people, but the trustees had agreed from the start that they must look for a couple who were energetic and healthy and particularly sympathetic to the needs of the elderly people in their care.

By the time the closing date had arrived, the trustees met to go through the list in order to whittle it down to four, or possibly five, applicants.

It had not been easy. There were one or two couples who could be eliminated from the start, either because of age, or because one or other would be of no use in a post which demanded the help of both partners. One likely woman, who had trained as a nurse and had a good deal of experience in old people's welfare, had a husband who almost seemed to boast, on the application form, that he had no idea how to fit a tap washer, mend a fuse, or mow a lawn. He added that he had spent most of his life in India and expected such things to be done for him.

In another case, the man seemed an intelligent handyman, but the wife admitted to prostrating attacks of migraine and crippling arthritis. In the end, the trustees sent out four letter to couples they would like to interview, and seventeen to the unsuccessful applicants.

The plan was to install the wardens first before the residents arrived. It looked now as though all should be in readiness by the first of October when, with any luck, the weather would be pleasant enough to see everybody settled comfortably before the onset of a Cotswold winter.

The rector, who was one of the trustees, was particularly interested in one couple who were going to be interviewed. She was the daughter of his old friend Mrs Jenner who lived along the Nidden road, and her husband was an ex-policeman.

The couple had married before Charles Henstock's time, and he had never met them, but Mrs Jenner had often talked about them when he and Dimity had lodged in her comfortable farmhouse after the devastating fire which had made them homeless.

He spoke to John Lovell about them after the meeting.

'Well, I never met the girl,' said John, 'but I remember Donald Bailey speaking highly of her when she was nursing at the Cottage Hospital. She became a sister there, and then got this post in Yorkshire where she met her husband. If she's anything like her mother, she'd be ideal.'

'She would indeed,' agreed Charles, remembering the cheerful manner, the down-to-earth commonsense, and the never-failing kindness of his one-time landlady. 'Nevertheless,' he went on, 'one really must try and keep an open mind. We may find that the other couples are even more satisfactory. I must say, some of their qualifications make excellent reading.'

'You can't believe all you see on paper,' observed John. 'I know half a dozen chaps, in my line, with strings of letters after their names. I wouldn't trust 'em with my patients, and that's flat.'

He climbed into his car, hooted cheerfully, and drove home.

The visit of Ray and Kathleen was planned for the last week in August.

'It had better be lunch, I suppose,' said Dorothy resignedly. 'And of course the neighbour who is driving them must come too. Cold, do you think, or something in a casserole, Agnes? You know how unpunctual they are. It's hopeless to expect them to arrive on the dot.'

'I think a casserole would be best,' replied Agnes. 'It may be a miserable day, and in any case you don't want to be mixing mayonnaise or white sauce last thing. A casserole is so good-tempered. It won't spoil if they are a little late.'

'Then we'll make a steak and kidney one,' decided Dorothy. 'Men always like that. It was my dear father's favourite dish. And could you make one of your delicious raspberry trifles?'

And so the menu was half settled, and the ladies were prepared when the day came.

It was a morning of drizzle and mist, a foretaste of autumn. Dorothy congratulated herself upon the provision of such a comforting dish as stewed steak and kidney, as Agnes decorated the trifle with a few raspberries.

Much to their surprise, the car arrived promptly at

twelve o'clock. Evidently the kind driver was a punctual individual. The two ladies hastily doffed their aprons and hurried to greet their guests.

Ray appeared to be very cheerful, the only visible sign of the accident being the sling supporting his broken arm. But he was rather pale, and Agnes, ever-solicitous, thought he had lost weight.

Kathleen said that the country was looking lovely, but she always suffered with her head, even on the shortest drive, and would they mind if she took one of her pills?

'Not in the least,' said Dorothy briskly. 'Anything to put you right, Kathleen. Would you like a glass of sherry to go with it?'

Kathleen closed her eyes and looked pained.

Dorothy busied herself with pouring drinks, and ignored what she privately designated 'Kathleen's vapours'. The good Samaritan who had driven all the way was called George White, and was a quiet fellow who commended himself to the two ladies by admiring the schoolhouse garden, and asking to be shown around it later on.

This they did after the lunch had been enjoyed by all, except Kathleen, who had been obliged to leave most of her helping on the plate, in deference to her headache. Ray managed his lunch most competently, and congratulated his sister on supplying the sort of meal with which a one-armed man could cope easily.

Dorothy led the way round the garden with a man on each side. Agnes followed more slowly with Kathleen, who said that the air might do her good if she could manage to totter a few steps.

'Perhaps you would like to sit down for a minute or two,' said Agnes, pausing by the garden seat.

Kathleen sank down with a sigh. Agnes was greatly perturbed on their guest's account. Surely, she could not be feigning illness? Dorothy was always so *trenchant* in her remarks about Kathleen's health, but Agnes, much softer in heart, felt sure that something must ail the poor woman.

She was somewhat surprised therefore when Kathleen spoke with undue firmness.

'About Ray, Agnes. He needs a change badly. And so do I, for that matter. Nursing is so debilitating.'

'I can quite imagine it is,' agreed Agnes.

'I thought perhaps Dorothy would like to have us here for a week or so. The air at Thrush Green is so refreshing. It would do us both a world of good.'

'What, now?' squeaked Agnes, envisaging vast trunks already packed in the boot of the neighbour's car. What would Dorothy say? And in any case where could they sleep? There were only two bedrooms at the schoolhouse, and one could hardly expect a one-armed invalid to cope with a sleeping bag, even if he had had the forethought to pack one. And the thought of Kathleen in anything less than a luxurious double bed was not to be contemplated.

Recovering quickly from this mental battering Agnes had the sense to answer diplomatically.

'You must discuss it with Dorothy, of course. As you know, term starts very soon and accommodation here is rather limited. Still, I'm sure that a change of some sort would do you both a lot of good. Shall we go and have a look at the vegetable plot?'

The advance party was already admiring the shallots and some splendid feathery carrot tops. Agnes, much agitated, trusted that Kathleen would not choose the present moment to broach the subject of a holiday at the school-house. Dorothy's reaction might well be forceful, and it seemed a pity to involve the innocent Mr White in a family fracas.

Luckily, Dorothy herself solved the problem by taking Kathleen's arm in a rare spasm of solicitude and leading her to the end of the garden where a plum tree was displaying a bumper crop of half-grown fruit. Agnes, with remarkable aplomb, swiftly directed the men's attention to some new geraniums, well out of earshot of any possible explosion.

'I really think I shall have to sit down for a moment,' said Ray, as they neared the seat recently vacated by Kathleen and herself. The three sat comfortably, and George White kept up a flow of gentle comment about his surroundings, which allowed Agnes to watch the two distant figures under the plum tree.

They seemed to be in earnest conversation, and Dorothy had ceased to support Kathleen by the arm. However, voices were not raised, no physical assault appeared to be threatening, and Agnes breathed again.

A few spots of rain drove them into the house where Kathleen asked if she could go upstairs for a rest. Two aspirins and half an hour in a darkened room often helped her headache. Not that it cured it completely, mark you, that was too much to expect, but such conditions certainly mitigated the agony a little.

Dorothy led the way with a little too much alacrity to Miss Fogerty's way of thinking, and the rest of the party disposed themselves in the sitting room, awaiting Dorothy's return.

'Well, that's that!' she remarked cheerfully, rather as if she had just posted an awkward parcel, when she reappeared.

She turned to her brother.

'Kathleen has just told me how much you both need a little break. Of course, if we had more room here, and more time to entertain you, then it would be nice to have you here. However, you know how we are placed, but perhaps The Fleece could put you up. Would you like to ring them while you are here? Or call perhaps to select a room?'

Little Miss Fogerty could not help admiring the masterly way in which Dorothy cut the ground from beneath her adversary's feet, presenting him with a firm ultimatum at the same time. Nevertheless, she felt sorry for poor Ray, who looked completely nonplussed. Had he been in ignorance of his wife's plans, perhaps?

'We certainly had spoken of a little holiday,' he said at last, 'but I don't think Thrush Green was mentioned. My idea was a few days by the sea somewhere. Kathleen has been run off her feet looking after me, and you know how delicate she is.'

'Yes indeed,' agreed Dorothy, with some emphasis. 'Well then, you won't want to bother The Fleece, I take it?'

'Not at the moment.'

George White, who had been looking uncomfortable during this exchange, suggested that a turn about the green, now that the rain had eased, might be a good idea while Kathleen rested, and before they set off for home.

'I should enjoy that,' said Ray, getting to his feet.

'Then we'll see you later,' said Dorothy graciously.

The men's footsteps died away, the gate clanged, and Dorothy exploded.

'Well, of all the nerve! Really, Kathleen is outrageous!'

'Please, please!' whispered Agnes in much agitation, 'she may hear you.'

'I don't know that I worry particularly about that,' replied Dorothy. 'A born trouble-maker, that one. I think she simply wanted to rile me. And in that, I suppose, you could say she's succeeded.'

She plumped up a cushion with excessive vigour, and punched it back into place on the sofa.

'But not another word will I say,' she announced, breathing heavily. 'Let us go and get the tea tray ready for when the men return.'

True to her word, the rest of the visit passed in outward harmony. The visitors were attended to with every courtesy, and Dorothy and Agnes waved farewell from the gate with their faces wreathed in polite smiles.

Agnes, following Dorothy back to the house, waited for the inevitable explosion after so much dangerous repression.

'I really don't know,' began her friend, 'what passes in

the minds of some people. Do they never think of anyone but themselves?'

Agnes took this to be a question of the rhetorical kind, and gave a non-committal clearing of the throat.

'Kathleen knows how we are placed *perfectly well*,' went on Dorothy, now in full spate. 'We have no spare room, no spare time, no spare energy, and yet she expects us to take on an invalid and, worse still, herself – a hypochondriac of the first water. It's too much! It really is! Simply because we are lucky enough to live in Thrush Green, she seems to think that we must be available at all times to share our good air and surroundings with all and sundry.'

She paused to take breath in the midst of this tirade, and Agnes managed to insert a gentle word.

'Don't dwell on it, dear. You know she's probably over-anxious on Ray's account, and that's made her thoughtless.'

'Humph!' snorted her headmistress. 'That's as maybe! But we may as well listen to the news, as I see it is time. At least it might act as a counter-irritant.'

And little Miss Fogerty rose to switch on the set.

Across the green, Winnie Bailey was also considering the question of summer visitors to Thrush Green.

Occasionally, she had a twinge of remorse about her refusal to fall in with Richard's plans, although she knew perfectly well that it would have been impossibly difficult to have coped with a strange young mother, a new baby, and an energetic four-year-old.

But she had heard nothing from Richard since his visit, and had received no thanks from his wife for her letter and the roses. It made her rather sad.

She had seen the announcement of the birth of a daughter in the newspaper, and written a little note of congratulation, but that too had elicited no response.

Well, there it was, thought Winnie, she could do no more, and if Richard was still sulking then there was nothing she could do about it but hope that time would heal the rift.

Meanwhile, she decided to go into the garden and collect some geranium cuttings. They could stand in water overnight, and she would pot them tomorrow. A little work with one's hands could be a great comfort when one was worried.

It had been one of Donald's maxims, and Winnie, making her way into the garden, had always recognized its wisdom.

John Lovell too had been gardening that afternoon, and as he was blessedly free from surgery duty that evening, he was studying the paper with his feet up.

His attention was caught by an item concerning car thieves who seemed to be running a lucrative business in London and its suburbs. Only expensive cars were being taken, it appeared, and the police were of the opinion that the cars were stolen to order, disguised in some remote spot, such as a lonely farm with outbuildings, and then fixed up with faked or trade number plates and often shipped abroad.

Doctor Lovell lowered the paper and gazed through the window at his garden. In his mind's eye he saw again the yard at Leys Farm on his second visit.

He had called without warning, simply to check that his patient was progressing satisfactorily. The double doors of a barn had been standing open, and two, or possibly three, large cars were visible. The older men seemed to be at work on them, and the doors of the barn had been hurriedly slammed when the doctor had been noticed.

In front of the house a Porsche stood, and the young man whom John had treated, was busily unscrewing a hub cap.

'Now I wonder?' said John to himself. What would be the best thing to do?

The local police superintendent was a friend of his. The magistrates at Lulling court knew them both well.

Well, he could only look a fool, thought John, making for the telephone. Better that than failing to do one's duty as a responsible citizen.

He began to dial the number.

Down the hill, in Lulling High Street, one light still burned in The Fuchsia Bush.

Mrs Peters had stayed after the shop shut to make up the accounts, and to check an order for one of her wholesale suppliers.

Despite the fact that the café and shop were always busy, and that home-made cakes, scones and biscuits sold briskly every day, there were times when Mrs Peters wondered how long such a business would survive.

Staff wages were a heavy item in her expenditure. Rates and rent added to the burden. The cost of such basic necessities as flour, butter, sugar, coffee and tea had risen astronomically since she first took over the business, and she did not want to price her excellent produce beyond the purse of her loyal customers. It was becoming something of a headache, and short of dismissing one of the staff, or finding some extra way of adding to her income, the worries seemed likely to become more demanding.

She was still studying the accounts when the telephone rang.

'Ah!' said a woman's voice. It was rather a domineering type of voice, thought Mrs Peters, the sort of voice belonging to someone known as 'a born leader'. Could this caller have found a fly in an Eccles cake, and was now about to threaten The Fuchsia Bush with a visit from the Public Health Office? Poor Mrs Peters quailed.

'So glad I found you at home. I presume you live above the shop?'

'Well, no, I don't, but I stayed late to see to some office work,' replied Mrs Peters. 'Can I help you at all?'

'We met at Joan Young's lunch party. My name is Thurgood.'

Light dawned. This was worse than she imagined. Mrs Thurgood, wealthy and influential, could make life unendurable if she had an excuse for complaint.

'I remember,' said she, her mouth dry with apprehension.

'My little party were all most impressed with the catering,' went on the ringing voice. 'I know at least two people who are going to get in touch with you about arranging something similar. That's why I wanted a word with you about a little affair of my own.'

'How kind,' faltered Mrs Peters.

'We are having a christening at St John's church here in Lulling, in about a month's time. The dear rector will conduct the service, of course. He was instrumental in bringing my daughter and her husband together in the first place, incidentally. We are all *devoted* to him.

Mrs Peters knew, as did all Lulling, of Mrs Thurgood's initial animosity to poor Charles Henstock. She had been a great admirer of Lulling's handsome vicar, Anthony Bull, and had made his successor's early days very uncomfortable. Mrs Peters had heard too of the battle of the kneelers, which had taken place before the engagement of Mrs Thurgood's daughter, but naturally said nothing.

'A charming man,' she agreed.

'We shall be quite a small party, somewhere in the region of twenty to thirty guests, and I wondered if you could cater for us?'

'I should be delighted.'

'It would be a tea party mainly, and of course I should like you to make the cake. Perhaps a few little savouries to have with the parting glass of wine? Shall I come down one day to make arrangements, and discuss the budget?'

'Please do. Shall we say on Tuesday afternoon?'

'That will suit me perfectly. I will be with you at two-thirty,' said the lady graciously. 'So glad you can take it on. My friend is envisaging a large buffet lunch, rather like Joan Young's, in aid of the Lifeboat Institute, but no doubt you will be hearing from her. The other person is planning a golden wedding celebration, I gather, for her parents. No doubt there will be other claims on your time.'

Mrs Peters renewed her thanks and put down the receiver. Her hands were trembling, but her heart was light.

Could this be the beginning of a new venture, and a boost for the dear old Fuchsia Bush's fortunes?

PART TWO
Moving In

8 New Neighbours

THRUSH GREEN village school was now well into term time. Tearful newcomers had settled into Miss Fogerty's class and now knew their way to classrooms, lobbies and lavatories, without the guidance of their elders and betters.

Text books and exercise books had been distributed to the older children, desks allotted, monitors appointed, weather charts fixed to the walls and nature tables laden with the produce of a mellow September. Taking it all in all, both Dorothy Watson and her loyal assistant were glad to get back into harness.

It was Agnes who first noticed the removal van outside the wardens' house, at the end of the block of new homes. The name of the firm was emblazoned on the side in a type of Gothic script so fanciful that even little Miss Fogerty, used to all manner of calligraphy, found it impossible to read. But lower down, in large clear Roman capitals, was the word RIPON.

'Ripon,' mused Agnes. 'Yorkshire, surely? And an Abbey or something similar? I must ask Dorothy.'

At that moment, John Todd fell from a low bench, 'meant to be *sat* upon, and not *stood* upon', as his teachers had told him innumerable times, grazed his knee, and set up a hideous howling which drove all geographical conjecture from little Miss Fogerty's mind until later in the day.

Dorothy affirmed that Ripon was indeed in Yorkshire.
'*North* Yorkshire, I think, is the correct postal address.
Why we couldn't keep those nice Ridings heaven alone
knows? A charming place, Agnes. I went there as a girl.
One day, when we have retired, we must go north again.
A coach tour of the Dales should be very pleasant. What
put it into your mind?'

Agnes explained about the removal van, and her headmistress became very animated.

'But this must mean that Mrs Jenner's daughter and her
husband have the post of warden. What good news! I
wonder why we haven't heard before?'

'Betty Bell has usually left the school before we arrive in
the mornings,' pointed out her friend.

'And we have gone when she comes after school on
most days,' agreed Dorothy. 'We don't seem to hear as
much local news as we did when Mrs Cooke cleaned the
school.'

She sounded slightly wistful.

'But how much better Betty Bell does her work,' said
Agnes robustly. 'And she is so honest and cheerful always.
I really wouldn't wish to go back to Mrs Cooke's slatternly
ways, would you?'

And Dorothy agreed, with some reluctance.

The advent of the removal van had been noted by many
other eyes at Thrush Green. Albert Piggott, who never
missed much, commented upon the various items of furniture which he had watched on their way from van to
house, when he supped his mid-morning beer.

'Got a nice bit of carpet, and that'll be in a fine old
muck with them paths still treadin' in,' he announced with
some relish. 'Needs a bit of drugget over it, I reckon, but
folks are too careless to bother with such things these
days.'

'I daresay they know their own business best,' said the
landlord.

'It's the Jenners' girl as has got the job,' continued Albert. 'Name of Jane. Used to be a nurse down Lulling hospital years ago. Mrs Jenner told my Nelly about it at bingo last week.'

'She should be all right then,' said Mr Jones, swabbing down his little sink. 'What's the husband like?'

'Been a policeman,' replied Albert gloomily.

'None the worse for that, surely?'

'Ah, but he was a *Yorkshire* policeman. Not homegrown, as you might say.'

'I've met some jolly nice Yorkshire folk,' said Mr Jones sturdily. 'They tell you themselves they're the salt of the earth.'

'Well, I haven't met one at all. Still, now we'll have our chance, won't we? You'll have to keep to closing hours pretty sharpish, with him living on the doorstep.'

Pleased to have the last word, Albert put down his glass, and departed to his leisurely duties.

Ella Bembridge's front garden was an ideal viewing spot. Winnie Bailey had called with some magazines, and found her friend leaning on the gate, cigarette drooping from her mouth, and eyes fixed upon the activities at the new house.

'Who's moving in, d'you know?' she asked Winnie, as she opened the gate.

'Why, I thought you knew! Jane Jenner that was, and her husband. But there, it's all before your time.'

She stood waiting for Ella to take the magazines and lead the way into the house, but it was obvious that the lady was much too engrossed in watching the removal men negotiating the doorway with a Welsh dresser to attend to Winnie and her offerings.

Resignedly, Winnie sat down on the garden bench, and surveyed a sturdy clump of sedums. They were already changing colour from pale green to pink. Soon, thought Winnie with a pang of regret, they would be a brilliant coral, and autumn would have arrived.

'Ella!' she called. 'Don't you think you might embarrass the newcomers by staring so?'

Ella turned, her face a study of amazement.

'Why on earth? I wouldn't care a fig if people watched me. Come to think of it, they often do. I don't mind.'

Nevertheless, she left the gate, and took her place beside Winnie.

'You know this Jane woman then?'

'Since a child. I'm surprised you hadn't heard she'd been appointed as warden. Mrs Jenner's as pleased as Punch.'

'What's the husband like?'

'A good down-to-earth fellow, I believe. They'll be a first-class pair for the job. I know Charles Henstock was delighted when they were the successful couple.'

'Good! We can do with some fresh blood at Thrush

Green. It'll be nice to have more neighbours. I still miss Dim about the house.'

Winnie handed over the magazines at last. She rose to go.

'Don't hurry away, Winnie. You can see things better from here.'

'I'll call when they have settled in,' Winnie told her. 'They've enough to cope with at the moment.'

Ella followed her to the gate.

Winnie looked back before turning into her own home. Ella had rearranged her bulk upon the gate top, and was watching proceedings as avidly as before.

Charles Henstock was indeed delighted with the appointment. He had not met Jane's husband before the interview, but was impressed, first of all, by his magnificent physique, and then by his quiet confidence.

He was the sort of man, Charles surmised, who would keep his head in any situation. Police training may have had something to do with it, but Charles guessed correctly that here was a particularly well-balanced person, intelligent and kindly, who would be as competent in dealing with a burst water main or an old person's heart attack, as he had been with a riot or a car accident.

The choice of those to live in the homes was being much more difficult, and the meeting of the selection committee had been quite stormy.

The list had been whittled down fairly easily at first. People, like Percy Hodge, who already had a home and were relatively young and able-bodied, were firmly rejected. Some hopefuls from far away, and with no connection with, or relatives living in, Thrush Green, were also crossed from the list, but the rest were dauntingly numerous.

A few general rules had been drawn up. One was that the residents should still be active, and that they should face the fact that minor illnesses such as coughs and colds, temporary stomach upsets and the like, could be coped with competently, with the warden's help, in their own homes, but anything needing sustained nursing must inevitably be dealt with by hospital treatment.

Another rule was that no animals could be allowed, and it was this which Charles did his best to alter. He made no secret of the fact that it was Tom Hardy who was in his mind.

He had broached the subject of a move when he had seen Tom one day, and was surprised to encounter far less opposition to the idea than he had imagined.

'Look at it this way, sir,' the old man said. 'My neighbour's a good sort, and does what she can for me, but I don't like to be beholden, and that's flat. And these meals on wheels I can't eat half the time, and I've had four home helps since you helped me do that form, and not one can I get on with, and that's the truth.'

'You wouldn't miss your garden too badly? And the river?'

'I'm getting past it. It grieves me to see the weeds growing, and the trees needing pruning. And I don't know as the river damp don't make my joints stiffer than they should be. No, taking it all ways, I could up sticks and settle at Thrush Green. I know plenty of folk there, and I'd have Poll.'

The dog looked up and wagged her tail on hearing her name. The rector, the gentlest of men, wondered how best to broach this painful subject.

'At the moment,' he ventured, 'there is a feeling that pets could not be admitted, but I'm hoping to alter that.

A flush crept up the old man's neck and across his wrinkled face.

'No pets, eh? Well then, that settles it. I ain't agoing anywhere without my Poll.'

And Charles knew, all too well, that there would be no budging him from that decision.

'But if we do it for one,' said Justin Venables, who was

chairman of the committee, 'we must do it for all. And suppose someone has an Alsatian, and next door there is a Siamese cat? What then?'

Justin, who was a retired lawyer from Lulling, was a perfect chairman, patient, clear-headed, and cognisant of all the legal difficulties which cropped up. Since his retirement he had, of course, been rather busier than when he was in a full-time profession, but that was only to be expected, and secretly he was rather gratified.

Apart from one day a week in his old office to deal with any aging clients he still served, Justin seemed to spend his time on just such committees as this present one.

He felt considerable sympathy for his old friend Charles Henstock, and knew that no one was more deserving of a place than Tom Hardy, but the 'no pets' rule did seem to be a sensible one.

'Worse still,' put in Mrs Thurgood, who was also on the committee, 'would be a cat of *any* sort next door to budgerigars. I really think we must be firm about this.'

Charles began to feel that he was fighting a losing battle, but persisted nevertheless.

'Let's tackle this another way. Select the residents for our seven homes, see if any have pets, and then decide the next step. I agree that "no pets" is a sensible rule in the long term, but perhaps with these first tenants we might stretch things a bit.'

'I think Mr Henstock has a point there,' said Mrs Thurgood graciously. 'How far have we got?'

'The three doubles are already settled,' said Justin, turning over his papers. 'Mr and Mrs Cross, Mr and Mrs Angell and Captain and Mrs Jermyn. So we are now allotting the four singles, and I think it was generally agreed that old Mrs Bates from the end almshouse at Lulling should be offered one, as that is due to be gutted in readiness for a new laundry room and a store room there. We have her application here. It came in early.'

'So that leaves three?' said Mrs Thurgood.

Justin acknowledged this feat of arithmetic with a kindly nod.

'Let us go on with our selection then, shall we?' he suggested. 'Let's take the case of Miss Fuller, the retired headmistress from Nidden.'

The committee applied themselves to the application forms, among them Miss Fuller's, one from Johnny Enderby, an old gardener, and finally to that of Tom Hardy.

After an hour's hard work the homes were allotted. Now to discover if the lucky ones had pets, and if any arrangements had been made for them.

'Perhaps I could draft a letter,' suggested Justin.

'Why not telephone?' said Charles, who was growing increasingly anxious.

'But there was a note about all this somewhere on the

application form,' pronounced Mrs Thurgood, turning over her papers with such energy that half of them fell on the floor.

John Lovell, bending to pick them up, hit his head against hers and the air was full of apologies.

When things were settled again, it was found that there certainly was an insignificant spot on the form asking for information about any pets already kept.

The Jermyns had put in: 'One Cat.'

Miss Fuller owned 'Two Love Birds.'

Tom Hardy had one dog.

The rest appeared to be without animals.

Justin Venables began to look relieved, and Charles less strained.

'The Jermyns are at one end of the block, and Miss Fuller's apartment is several homes distant, I see, and Tom Hardy's is some way off. And in any case, one imagines that the birds are accommodated in a cage. Well, ladies and gentlemen, what about it?'

'If I may,' said Charles diffidently, 'I should like to suggest that these first tenants are allowed to bring their present pets, on the clear understanding that they may not be replaced and if they cause problems an alternative home must be found for them. Any tenants who come after must realise that pets are not allowed.'

'I think that's an excellent suggestion,' said John Lovell. 'It means that people such as Tom Hardy will not be penalised for having a pet, and debarring them from the homes they really need. I propose it formally.'

'I'll second it,' said Mrs Thurgood. 'So much fairer to the pets,' she added. 'I know I should *never* consent to be parted from my dear pekes.'

'Those in favour?' asked Justin.

All hands went up, and to Charles's mortification he felt tears prick his eyes.

Letters to the successful applicants were to go out during

the week, with the pets' clause clearly stated, but Charles took it upon himself to go beforehand to see Tom.

He had left the old man in some turmoil of spirit, he feared, and wanted to calm him.

He had intended to walk to the cottage by the river, relishing the prospect of gentle exercise in the company of moorhens, willow trees, and the pleasant burbling of the River Pleshey, but at breakfast time the heavens opened, the rain came down in a deluge, and Charles, standing at the window, watched the last of the petunias and marigolds being flattened under the onslaught.

Resignedly, he took out the car, and drove down the main street of Lulling through the downpour. The road was awash, the pavements streaming, and passing vehicles threw up a cloud of spray.

It was still pouring down when he drew up at Tom's cottage, and the rector, collar turned up, hurried across the slippery plank bridge, and gained the shelter of the little porch.

'Why, bless me,' exclaimed Tom, opening the door. 'What brings you out in this weather?'

'Good news, Tom,' said Charles, brushing drops from his jacket.

Polly advanced to meet him, putting up her grey muzzle to be stroked, and wagging her tail.

'You come right in before you tells me more,' said Tom. 'Kettle's hot. Coffee?'

'I'd love some,' said Charles.

He watched the old man moving slowly about his work, taking down a mug from the dresser, reaching for a jar of powdered coffee, making his way deliberately to the drawer where he kept the teaspoons. There was no doubt about it, thought Charles, although he could just about manage when things were going normally, there must be times when a kindly warden would be needed in the future.

'There you are, sir,' said Tom at last, putting the steaming mug before his visitor. 'Get that down you. There's a real autumn nip in the air this morning, and we can't have you ailing anything. Good people are scarce, they tell me.'

'This goes down well,' said Charles. 'Now the news!'

'About the little house?'

'That's right.'

'And Poll?'

'She can go there with you.'

Tom's face lit up.

'Well, that's wholly good news, I must say. What made them change their minds? You, sir, I expect!'

'Only in part, Tom. We all thought it out. It seemed wrong to part people like you from their animals, but I think the long-term idea is still "no pets". That will apply, of course, to the residents who come later.'

He took a long draught of coffee.

'You will be getting a letter in a day or two, Tom, but I wanted to tell you myself.'

'Any idea when we shall move in?'

'In the early part of October, I think. Can you get someone to help you with the move? If not, I'm sure some of the young fellows at my Youth Club could give a hand.'

'I might be glad of that, sir. Most of my friends are as shaky as I am now. More coffee?'

'No thanks, Tom. I must get back, but I'll call again in a few days' time.'

He bent to pat Polly.

'Coming back to Lulling with me again?' he asked her.

'She would too,' said Tom. 'She's as fond of you as she is of me, and that's the truth. But I wouldn't want to part with her, not even to you, sir.'

'Well, there'll be no parting now, Tom. You and Poll can soldier on together. Many thanks for the drink.'

He wrung his old friend's hand, and set forth again into the wild wet world.

9   Some Malefactors

JOHN LOVELL'S TELEPHONE call to the police superintendent had set loose a stream of local activity. He learnt a little from his friend when they met.

'By the time we went to Leys Farm the birds had flown, as you might expect, but we found a few clues, tyre marks, paint scrapings, bits of cloth and so on, which the forensic boys are working on. However, I think these are the chaps directly involved, and it was bright of you to spot them.'

'Not bright enough to twig earlier,' said John ruefully. 'And as for recalling the makes of the cars and colours, not to mention numbers, I'm afraid I'm a broken reed. All I had in mind, of course, was how my patient was reacting to my prescription. He'd had a pretty bad go of sickness and was seriously dehydrated when I first saw him.'

'He must have been in a very poor state for the others to have called you in. I bet that was the last thing they wanted – a visitor to the premises. Obviously, they hid the cars away when you were expected, but were caught on the hop when you turned up unexpectedly.'

'Have you any leads at all?'

'Well, all the other areas have been notified, and we're keeping a sharp watch on the ports which have car ferries, but no doubt they'll lie low for a bit. One thing in our favour, it isn't easy to hide a car. A small packet of heroin can be tucked away quite successfully. A thumping great Rolls isn't so simple.'

He rose to go.

'Anyway, you did a good job by getting in touch. I hope we'll be able to see you in court as a prime witness before long.'

'Heaven help you!' exclaimed the doctor. 'I've always lived in dread of someone asking me where I was on the night of October the fourth three years earlier.'

'Who hasn't?' laughed his friend.

Naturally, John Lovell had said nothing about the affair. All that John had allowed himself was a brief word to Ruth who, as a doctor's wife, was the soul of discretion.

Nevertheless, it was soon common knowledge in Thrush Green and Lulling that something delightfully wicked and illegal seemed to have been happening at Leys Farm over the past year.

Betty Bell was agog with news and conjecture when she went to clean at Harold and Isobel Shoosmiths'.

'Never knew such a carry-on,' she puffed, dusting Harold's study energetically. 'My cousin Alf opened the door, not three days since, to find Constable Darwin on the step with one of them little notebooks. Well, to tell the truth, he's not my *real* cousin, not like Willie Bond, I mean, but Alf's mum and mine used to work up the vicarage when they was young, and they was always good friends even after they got married.'

This sounded to Harold, busy trying to fill in a form for an insurance company which was incapable, it seemed, of expressing its needs in plain English, as a slur on marriage. Did it mean that early friendships usually foundered after a spouse had been acquired?

'So, of course, I always called her Auntie Gert,' went on Betty, knocking an antique paperweight to the ground, 'and Alf was a sort of cousin. When he was born, I mean.'

Harold said he understood that, and watched Betty retrieve the paperweight, luckily unharmed.

'Well, Alf had been ploughing just behind Trotters after

they'd harvested the barley, and the police wanted to know if he'd seen anything funny.'

'Funny?'

'Funny unusual, I mean. Suspicious like. Men with stockings over their faces, holding machine guns. That sort of thing, Alf thought.'

'But surely,' expostulated Harold, setting aside the form for quieter times, 'they wouldn't be got up like that if they were *living* in the place?'

'Who's to say?' said Betty airily, flicking her duster dangerously across a row of miniature ornaments of Indian silver much prized by her employer.

'Anyway, Alf hadn't seen nothin' much, just an odd car or two being put in the barn. That PC Darwin kep' all on about what colour and what make and when was it and that, until Alf said he was fair mazed, and as his dinner was just on the table he told young Darwin one car was red and another was blue just to get rid of him. Alf reckons he'd have been there still if he hadn't told him something.'

'But that is definitely hindering the course of justice!' Harold exclaimed, much alarmed at such behaviour. 'It was very wrong of your cousin to mislead the police like that. For two pins I'd ring the station now and tell them what you have just told me.'

'Oh, I shouldn't bother,' replied Betty. 'Ten to one that Darwin never wrote it down. He's not much of a scholar, they tell me.'

She whisked from the room, leaving Harold confronting his form with severely heightened blood pressure.

At The Two Pheasants the subject was aired with more drama than accuracy.

Percy Hodge said that the way the police handled things was a crying scandal, and it was a wonder more decent people weren't murdered in their beds when you heard how long these Trotters' chaps had been up to a bit of no good. What did we pay our rates for, he wanted to know?

Albert Piggott opined that you could earn more by being dishonest these days, than by sweating day in and day out, as he did, at his own back-breaking job.

And an old man in the corner, toothless and shaky with age, said that no good ever came out of Trotters. It had always had a bad name, and that fellow Archie Something who farmed there before the war – the first war, he meant – had three daughters who all went to the bad, and the local lads was warned about them by the vicar at that time. Not that it stopped 'em, of course.

He would have continued with his reminiscences to the great pleasure of his hearers, but Mr Jones, the landlord, spoiled everything by rapping on the counter and ordering his clients to drink up sharpish.

Even little Miss Fogerty heard something of the affair, for John Todd, capering about in the playground with his hand extended pistol-fashion, yelled that he was a car robber from Trotters and that he was spraying his unconcerned playmates with real bullets, and they ought to be lying dead.

On relating this to Miss Watson later, her headmistress replied:

'Yes, dear, I did hear something about it. Trust John Todd to pick up such news! That boy is not as green as he's cabbage-looking.'

With which statement her colleague agreed.

Nelly Piggott was one of the few inhabitants who managed to ignore the excitement at Leys – or Trotters – Farm.

The truth was that she had a great many other excitements to think about. The first, and most pressing one, was the christening party at Mrs Thurgood's, due to take place in just over a week's time.

She told her friend Mrs Jenner about it as they walked down the hill to a bingo session in Lulling. The two women had struck up a firm friendship. Mrs Jenner, a lifelong resident at Thrush Green, and sister to Percy

Hodge, recognised the good qualities in Albert's wife which far too many local people ignored.

It was true that Nelly was somewhat flighty. She was occasionally vulgar in speech. She dressed rather too flashily for Thrush Green's taste. Nevertheless, she was hardworking, good-tempered, and coped splendidly with Albert's moodiness and bouts of drinking. Altogether, Mrs Jenner approved of Nelly Piggott, and enjoyed their weekly trip to the bingo hall.

'Mrs Peters gets a bit worked up,' said Nelly confidentially. 'Well, I suppose she's a lot to lose if anything goes wrong, and say what you like, that Mrs Thurgood is proper bossy. All teeth and breeches, my father used to say. Tough as they come. She did her best to beat down the price per head when she came to work things out, but give Mrs Peters her due she stuck to her guns, and we've got a fair price, I reckon.'

'She seems to rely on you quite a bit,' responded Mrs Jenner.

'I don't know about that,' replied Nelly, sounding surprised, 'but I don't get in a flap about things, so maybe she talks to me to calm herself. After all, I haven't got the same responsibilities that she has. Stands to reason she worries more.'

'You've got your livelihood to get, and to lose,' pointed out her friend.

'I suppose so,' reflected Nelly, 'but I could turn my hand to pretty well anything, if need be. After all, I did a good spell of cleaning at The Drovers' Arms, and thoroughly enjoyed it. I don't mind a nice bit of scrubbing.'

And that, thought Mrs Jenner, as they approached the hall, was one of Nelly's virtues. She was game to take on anything, even Albert Piggott.

It said much for her courage.

On the way home, Nelly was invited for the first time to

have a cup of coffee at her friend's house along the road to Nidden.

'There's nobody in obviously,' said Mrs Jenner, as the two women surveyed the Piggott establishment which had no glimmer of light in the windows.

Next door The Two Pheasants was glowing with lights, and it did not need much thinking to surmise where Albert was spending the evening.

'Just for a few minutes then,' agreed Nelly, pleasantly surprised by the invitation, and a quarter of an hour later she was ensconced in Mrs Jenner's farmhouse kitchen with a steaming cup in front of her.

She looked about the great square room with approval. The solid-fuel stove gave out a comfortable warmth. From the beams overhead hung nets of onions and shallots, bunches of drying herbs, and some ancient pieces of copper. A blue and white checked cloth was spread cornerwise on the scrubbed kitchen table, and a thriving Busy Lizzie was set squarely in the middle.

'My! I could do with a kitchen like this,' said Nelly enviously. She thought of the small room at Albert's where she cooked, cleaned and lived.

'Come any time you like,' invited Mrs Jenner. 'I like a bit of company, and although Jane and Bill are only down the road now, I don't suppose they'll have much spare time for a bit.'

'How do they like being wardens?'

'Very much. Mind you, they've only got one couple in at the moment, so things are easy. But they're a good pair, though I says it as shouldn't, and to my mind those old people are lucky to have them.'

'So I've heard,' said Nelly, 'and from several people too.'

Mrs Jenner looked gratified.

'Of course, how things will work out when all the houses are taken remains to be seen.'

'They'll shake down all right, I'm sure,' said Nelly.

346 TALES FROM THRUSH GREEN

'That I don't know,' answered her friend. 'I've had a lot to do with old people in my life, and it's my opinion that they can be downright awkward. Worse than children sometimes.'

Later, Nelly was to remember those prophetic words.

During the next two weeks, the new residents began to filter into the homes allotted to them.

Captain Eric Jermyn and his wife Carlotta had been the first to move in. Theirs was one of the larger homes at the farther end of the block. Jane and Bill Cartwright, the wardens, were now comfortably settled at the other end, and were glad to be welcoming the first of their neighbours.

Mrs Jermyn had been an actress before marrying her husband at the beginning of the Second World War. Remnants of youthful prettiness remained, but arthritis had distorted her hands and feet, and the pain made her querulous at times.

Her husband was considerably older than she was, thin, rather shaky, but still very straight-backed and dapper. They had lived in Lulling for some years since the war, and both given a great deal of service to the town.

Their means were small for their savings had vanished when a bank overseas had collapsed. They had lived in army quarters, and later in rented accommodation, and were grateful when they were allotted this present home in their old age.

Their black and white cat Monty was named after the late Field Marshal Montgomery, who was greatly revered by Monty's owner. He was a portly animal of much dignity, and protested loudly at being shut in a basket for several hours while the move was in progress.

The next day little Mrs Bates from the Lulling almshouses moved in, and two days after that Miss Fuller, who had been headmistress of the tiny school at Nidden, took up her abode next door to Mrs Bates. The latter had no pets to add to the usual confusion of moving day, but Miss Fuller's two lovebirds were carried in first thing, their cage heavily draped in an old bedspread.

A week later George and Mary Cross moved into the second double apartment, and Jack and Sybil Angell soon followed them.

Two single homes remained. Johnny Enderby, a retired gardener, was due to move in, and Tom Hardy and Polly the day after.

The rector still worried about uprooting his old friend from the riverside cottage, but when the day came, all was well.

It was one of those translucent October days when the distant hills seemed to have moved ten miles nearer. The sun shone from a cloudless sky, and the vivid gold of the horse chestnut trees vied with the pale lemon of the acacias in the Youngs' garden. It was heart-lifting weather, and the rector was sincerely thankful.

There had been no need to call on the Youth Club members for help.

With surprising efficiency, Tom had organised the move, parcelling up a few treasures, putting out the detritus of years of hoarding for dustmen, the local scrap merchant and the Cubs' jumble sale. It almost seemed, Charles thought, as if he welcomed this new start, despite his age and infirmities.

Polly looked upon the upheaval with a mild eye, seeking out a sunny place in the garden while the turmoil spread around her. As long as she was with her master, it was plain to see, she had no fears.

The last of the residents was safely ensconced by mid-afternoon. Polly explored her new home, found the familiar rag rug, and settled down on it with a sigh of pleasure.

Tom filled the kettle in his tiny bright kitchen, and switched on, marvelling at the speed with which it began to murmur. This was better than the old kitchen hob!

He sat down, his feet beside Poll on the rug, and gazed approvingly at his new abode.

In the end house, Jane and Bill Cartwright were also enjoying a cup of tea. Now all their charges were in residence, and the real job began.

Both were tired, but relieved that the moving in was over, and that, so far, no real problems had arisen.

Jane was perhaps more apprehensive than her sturdy husband.

'I can't help wondering if the hot water system is going to stand up to the demands made on it. Do you think we ought to give a gentle warning to the residents about running their hot taps? After all, Tom Hardy and Johnny Enderby have never coped with hot water straight from the tap. And we must make sure that the emergency bells work in each house. It would be terrible if anything happened, and we knew nothing about it.'

Bill Cartwright smiled at his wife's agitation.

'The bells have been tested time and time again, and

everyone here can cope with the hot water taps. None of them's a fool. You just calm down, and see how easily things will run. Before it gets dark we'll go together to make sure they have all they want.'

Jane smiled back.

'You're right, as usual. Well, it's good to have our family around us. Let's hope they all get on well together.'

'I expect they'll turn out like any other family,' replied Bill, pouring a second cup. 'A good deal of affection spiced with bouts of in-fighting. We'll see soon enough.'

Edward Young, as architect, took a keen interest in the residents' reactions to his work, and on the whole was gratified. All agreed that the houses were light, warm, well-planned and easy to run.

The main objection came from John Lovell one day when he met his brother-in-law, by chance, as he returned from a visit to the Cartwrights.

'All going well there, Edward?'

'No great problems so far,' said the architect.

'There will be,' replied John.

Edward looked taken aback.

'How d'you mean?'

'Well, those outside steps, for instance. You've been extra careful to have no steps inside, but that flight outside could be a menace, particularly in slippery weather.'

'I don't see,' said Edward frostily, 'how you can over-come a natural incline except by steps – and these are particularly shallow ones – or a ramp. As it happens, I've provided both. And an adequate handrail.'

'No need to get stuffy!'

'I'm not getting stuffy,' retorted Edward, 'but I do dislike outsiders criticising something they don't under-stand. You don't seem to realise the difficulties that con-fronted us when facing the problems that this site gave us.'

'I'm not such an outsider that I can't see what a mistake you made with those steps –'

'*Mistake*? What rubbish! You stick to your job, John, and leave me to mine.'

'Unfortunately, I shall have to patch up the results of your mistakes! Mark my words, a few slippery leaves, or later on some snow and ice, and I shall have some old people in my surgery with sprains and breaks. It could all have been avoided with proper planning.'

'Are you suggesting that I'm a bad architect?'

'Not always. But to design an old people's home with a hazard like that, is not only stupid, it's downright criminal.'

By this time, both men were flushed with anger. They took their work seriously, and were sensitive to criticism. The fact that normally the two brothers-in-law got along very peaceably made this present exchange particularly acrimonious.

'The steps are perfectly safe,' said Edward, with considerable emphasis. 'You're getting a proper old woman, John, seeing danger where there is none. I shan't come criticising your healing methods, though I gather that some of them leave much to be desired, so I'd be obliged if you left well alone in my field.'

He strode off across the green to his home, leaving John fuming.

'Pompous ass!' said John to the retreating back. 'You wait till I get my first casualty from the homes! I shan't let you forget it!'

As was to be expected, the new residents soon had visitors. Sons and daughters, grandchildren, and old friends called to see how they had settled into their new quarters.

Miss Watson and Miss Fogerty were greatly intrigued by the coming and goings, and agreed that it would be right and proper to invite Miss Fuller, whom they knew slightly through their teaching activities, to have tea with them.

'I always liked her,' said Agnes warmly, as they carried

the tea things into the sitting room. 'She was always so good with the mothers.'

'Sometimes a little too good,' responded Dorothy, arranging tomato sandwiches neatly. 'I think a headmistress should keep her distance with the parents.'

She began to set out the best cups on the tea tray.

'Such a pretty tea set,' commented Agnes, anxious to turn to a safer subject.

Her friend sighed.

'Mother left a very fine Wedgwood tea service to Katheleen in her will, although she must have known that I'd always hoped for it. But there you are, Kathleen did her wheedling to good effect, and I have to make do with this.'

'And very nice too,' Agnes assured her, as she added teaspons to the saucers. But privately she pondered on the unhappy results following the distribution of the wordly goods of the recently dead.

These melancholy thoughts were interrupted by the ringing of the front door bell, and she hurriedly joined Dorothy in welcoming their guest.

10 Settling Down

OCTOBER, DRAWING TO its close, saw Lulling and Thrush Green in their most vivid colours.

The horse chestnut avenue outside the Youngs' house glowed a bright gold, and the glossy conkers were fast being snatched up from beneath them by the village school's pupils.

Scarlet berries beaded the pyracantha growing over The Two Pheasants, and the virginia creeper clothing Winnie Bailey's house was the rich colour of red wine.

The hedges along the Nidden road were spangled with scarlet hips and crimson haws, while a few late blackberries, glossy as jet, waited for the birds' attentions.

In Miss Fogerty's room, sprays of cape gooseberries brightened the corner by the weather chart, and such seasonal joys as collecting hazelnuts and mushrooms enlivened the children's days.

Miss Fogerty gave her usual autumn handwork lesson on the making of chairs for a dolls' house from horse chestnuts, pins and wool. This involved four pins for the legs, five for the back, and simple weaving of the wool, in and out of the latter, to form a comfortable back rest for the diminutive occupants.

This operation was always accompanied by heavy breathing, enormous concentration and ultimate rapture. Agnes Fogerty enjoyed this annual instruction in the art of miniature furniture making, and felt great satisfaction in watching the children bearing home the results of their labours.

'I suppose,' she commented to Dorothy, over tea that afternoon, 'that they get so much more satisfaction from making a three-dimensional object. I mean, one would far rather have a cat than a *picture* of a cat.'

'Although, of course, a *picture* would be less bother,' observed her headmistress, after due thought.

The tiff between John and Edward still made itself felt. The two couples frequently had an evening together playing cards, but when Joan broached the subject to her husband she was surprised at his response.

'Oh, skip it for a bit! John's in one of his awkward moods. Let him simmer.'

'How do you mean?'

'Oh, he was rather offensive to me the other day.'

'John? Offensive? I can't believe it.'

Edward began to fidget up and down the room.

'Nothing too personal, I suppose, but he was throwing his weight about over the steps at the old people's place.'

'Well, he may be right. Mr Jones mentioned them to me the other morning. He hoped the residents there wouldn't slip on them.'

'Oh, don't you start! There's absolutely nothing wrong with those steps,' exploded Edward. 'The point is I don't particularly want to spend a whole evening in John's company at the moment.'

'Well, calm down,' begged Joan, taken aback at such unaccustomed heat. 'You'll have a seizure if you get into such a state, over such a silly little thing.'

'It isn't a silly little thing to me,' almost shouted her incensed husband. 'It's a criticism of my work, and I'm not standing for it.'

At that Joan shrugged her shoulders, and went out, without comment, to do her shopping.

*

Ruth Lovell, Joan's sister, was also perplexed by her husband's moodiness. She knew from experience that he took everything seriously. It was one of his qualities which his patients appreciated. He was willing to give time, as well as his medical expertize, to their troubles, and this they warmly appreciated.

Such dedication frequently exhausted him, and Ruth did her best to provide a relaxing atmosphere in their home. Their occasional evenings at the Youngs', or in their house, at the card table, were one of John's few outside pleasures.

But he too, it seemed, did not want to spend an evening with his brother-in-law, but said less about his reasons than the voluble Edward.

'Perhaps later on,' he said when Ruth suggested a card-playing evening. 'I'm rather tired these days, and Edward can be a bit overpowering, I find.'

'Just as you like,' answered Ruth. 'And if you're feeling tired, what about a dose or two of that tonic you make up for the patients?'

'That stuff?' exclaimed her husband. 'Not likely! It tastes appalling.'

Ella Bembridge, looking with approval at the bright October landscape, decided to take a pot of newly-made plum jam to Dotty Harmer, and to collect her goat's milk on the same errand.

The air was fresh and invigorating. Three dogs who had escaped from their owners were playing a mad game of 'He' on the green, observed at a safe distance by Albert Piggott's cat sitting on the churchyard wall.

Albert himself, cigarette dangling from his lip, was supporting himself on a hoe, as Ella went by.

'Lovely day,' shouted Ella.

'Ah!' agreed Albert.

'Busy?'

'Always plenty to do,' growled Albert, prodding in a desultory way at a dandelion root.

'That's what keeps you in such good trim,' said Ella bracingly.

She passed on her way, leaving Albert more than usually disgruntled by this exchange.

'*In good trim*,' repeated Albert disgustedly, flinging his cigarette stub over the wall. 'That's a laugh, I must say.'

But Ella was well out of earshot, and by now was traversing the narrow path by the Piggotts' cottage which led to Lulling Woods and Dotty's house.

She found Dotty sitting on the sofa surrounded by various woollen garments which she was busily unravelling.

'Connie and Kit are at the end of the garden,' she said, 'having a bonfire. They'll be here in a minute. How nice to see you.'

'Too good to stay in, so I thought I'd bring you a pot of plum jam.'

'Lovely! I really miss jam making, but Connie won't let me stand for too long, and last time I put in rather too much sugar, and burnt the saucepan. The stove was rather messy too.'

Ella could well imagine it, but forbore to comment.

'And what are you doing with all that wool?'

'It's for a knitting bee in Lulling. Everyone's going to knit squares, for blankets, you know. I thought these old jumpers would do very well to supply some of the wool.'

Ella, who deplored things made from old materials in this way, nobly took hold of a dilapidated scarf and began to unravel it, only to find that innumerable moth holes resulted in lengths of wool not much more than a yard long.

'Better throw this away,' she said after some examination of the material.

'No, no!' protested Dotty. 'Just go on rolling it up, dear, and the knitters can quite well cope with it.'

Luckily, at this moment, Connie and Kit, flushed with exercise and smelling exceedingly autumnal from the

bonfire smoke, arrived to take over, and Ella could sit back and enjoy the rest of her visit.

'And how are your new neighbours settling in?' enquired Connie.

'Pretty well, I gather from the Cartwrights. I bobbed over to see dear old Tom Hardy and his dog yesterday. He's as pleased as Punch with the house. Great relief for Dimity and Charles, who were beginning to worry about getting him to uproot himself.'

I was going to call there yesterday,' said Kit, 'but had to go to the dentist instead.'

'Bad luck! Why is it one always dreads the dentist more than the doctor? After all, there's a lot more to go wrong in the doctor's section.'

'I'm thankful to say,' said Dotty, wrenching madly at a jumper sleeve, 'that I haven't a tooth left in my head.'

'Neither shall I have, at this rate,' observed Kit. 'I must say though, he seems a quiet decent sort of chap. I once had a dentist who had music in the background. I suppose he thought it might soothe his patients.'

'What an idea!' said Connie.

'Exactly! I felt like shouting: "Switch that row off, and attend to your job, man!" But, of course, with all the ironmongery in my mouth at the time, I was helpless!'

'I had a dentist once,' mused Connie, 'who had a tank of tropical fish in one's eyeline. Far from soothing, I found it. I kept worrying about the air flow, and one particularly terrified fish that kept hiding behind some water weed.'

'I heard of one,' said Ella, adding her mite, 'who kept bees in his surgery.'

'In a skep? Surely not?'

'No, in a glass observation case. They had an opening to get out to fly for honey. Quite fascinating really, if you were in any mood to enjoy practical demonstrations.'

'All I can say is,' said Dotty, 'at least you are not shown the tooth he's just extracted, all bloody at one end, as our dentist used to do when we were children.'

'How gruesome!' said Connie.

'He was a friend of my father's,' went on Dotty, dropping half a dozen balls of wool on the floor, much to Flossie's delight. 'They both felt that children should learn to face up to life.'

'And death too, I should think,' said Kit shortly, 'at that rate. Here, what about a cup of tea?'

'An excellent idea,' replied Dotty. 'And we could have some of Ella's plum jam. Unless, of course, you would like to try mine?'

'Yours, dearest aunt, is now making excellent compost,' said Connie gently, 'so we'll settle for Ella's today.'

*

Although Ella had assured her friends that all was going well at the old people's homes, that was not quite true.

To be sure, the residents had enjoyed a little party arranged by Jane and Bill after all their charges had arrived.

Here introductions were made, a glass of wine or orange juice taken, and invitations given to each other's abodes. The atmosphere was cordial. All were thankful to have been among the lucky applicants, and anxious to make friends with those who shared their environment.

Jane and Bill were greatly relieved to see how well their charges settled down, but they did not deceive themselves by thinking that such halcyon conditions would continue for ever. There were bound to be differences of opinion, little complaints, and perhaps ill health to face, but at least, they comforted themselves, the party had gone well and everyone appeared amicably disposed.

The animals, whose inclusion at the homes had so concerned the trustees, gave no trouble at all. The Jermyns' cat Monty, large and placid, was content to sun himself in the angle of a wall at his end of the row. At night time he fraternised with Albert Piggott's cat and the two explored Thrush Green in great contentment. Tom Hardy's Polly they simply ignored.

Polly was equally content. She had Tom, her adored master. The house was warm, her food arrived regularly, and she was getting too old to bother about taking much exercise. A gentle amble about the green, or a leisurely walk at her master's heels along Lulling High Street, suited the old lady very well. She soon forgot the river sounds and smells which had once meant so much to her in her earlier years.

As for Miss Fuller's lovebirds, they twittered together in their cage set in the window, and behaved exactly as they had done for years. If anything they seemed more animated, and according to their doting mistress their appetites had improved since the move.

But although the animals had soon settled in, it was

their human companions who seemed more restless. This, of course, was natural as the first euphoria wore off. People were bound to begin to make comparisons with the homes they had left. Some found a lack of cupboard space. Some found the hot water system inadequate. Some complained that, despite Edward Young's care in sound-proofing, they could hear the next door's television set working.

Jane and Bill did their best to mitigate these little upsets. They were genuinely sympathetic to these elderly people. They persuaded those who complained about the lack of storage space to look again at their possessions and perhaps part with some of them. They suggested certain rearrangements, and put in a lot of time and energy in sorting out a great many articles. Some were much-loved old friends, and it was clear that to part with, say, an ancient corner cupboard, or an occasional table inherited from a grandmother, was going to be a wrench which their owners could not face. Jane was wonderfully diplomatic in these matters, and knew when to stop her suggestions, before agitation took over. But she was successful in helping several of her charges with problems of this kind.

The hot water system was soon remedied by means of a midday boost. The question of noise from neighbouring houses was not so simply answered. Some of the tenants were getting deaf, and automatically set their radios and television sets to a high volume. The fine weather meant that windows, and sometimes doors, were open, and Jane paid several visits to those offenders who were annoying their neighbours in all innocence.

It was soon apparent that the most difficult resident was going to be Carlotta Jermyn. She was a woman who had always demanded attention, and though, as a small-time actress, she had never received national acclaim, she had expected a certain amount of limelight among her fellow artists and even more admiration from the public. As a pretty child and young woman, she had been spoilt, and her husband had continued the process throughout their married life. It was soon common knowledge that her husband took tea to her every morning in bed, and that it took her over an hour to dress and make up her face, before she was ready for the day. Such behaviour occasioned disapproval among one or two of the neighbours, particularly in the case of Miss Fuller, who as a hard-working teacher had always been up betimes, cooked her own breakfast, and never had a meal in bed in her life, except when confined to hospital with broken ribs.

However, all this could have been borne if Carlotta had not taken to calling on her neighbours at the most awkward times. In truth, the poor woman was increasingly bored and missed the daily routine of her life in the little town of Lulling. There she had enjoyed the company of a next-door neighbour whose husband had also been in the army. As his rank had been higher than Carlotta's husband's, a certain amount of deference was shown, and Carlotta was gratified to have the friendship of a senior officer's wife and to exchange confidences over the garden hedge.

She still met her friend in The Fuchsia Bush now and again, and the two couples exchanged visits. But naturally Carlotta was thrown more upon her own resources, and very soon began to turn to her neighbours for company.

As it was usually midday before she began to pay her social calls, several of her victims found them annoying.

It was true that she did not bother Tom Hardy or old Johnny Enderby, guessing that they would not provide the light chit-chat which she so missed since moving from Lulling, but Mrs Bates and Miss Fuller were early among her prey, and very exasperating they found her attentions.

Both these ladies, and the single old men for that matter were used to having their main meal at twelve or soon after, making do with a snack in the evening and sometimes a bedtime drink.

Carlotta was accustomed to preparing an evening meal, and the Jermyns were quite happy with a bowl of soup, cheese and biscuits and fruit at midday.

This meant, of course, that Mrs Jermyn, once her lengthy toilet was completed, was at leisure to call somewhere between half past eleven and twelve upon her neighbours just when they were at a crucial stage of their cooking arrangements, either stirring gravy, prodding potatoes, setting the table, or putting on the sprouts.

Mrs Bates, a humble soul who had spent her active years as a first-rate maid, was flattered at first to be called upon, and was inclined to call Carlotta 'Madam', which pleased her visitor exceedingly. But after three visits in four days, on the last of which poor Mrs Bates had been in the middle of eating shepherd's pie when the imperious knock came at the door, she quite firmly said that it would be more convenient if calls could be made around three in the afternoon when she was not so busy.

Miss Fuller, less impressed with Carlotta's social graces, made it clear on the occasion of the lady's second visit, that she had her lunch promptly at twelve-fifteen, having got used to this over the years of eating school dinners.

Carlotta had laughed merrily in a patronizing way and had commented: 'Oh dear! What a dreadful time to have to face a meal! When do you fit in your little drinkie? I'm usually looking forward to a spot of gin about then.'

'I don't drink,' Miss Fuller had replied shortly, shutting the door smartly upon her visitor.

The Cross pair, George and Mary, and Jack and Sybil Angell had not been hounded quite so severely, possibly because they seemed to be out quite a lot, and also had a number of friends who dropped in.

Jane Cartwright soon became aware of Carlotta's nuisance value and wondered if she should drop a hint.

'A hint?' said Bill, when the matter was discussed. 'Carlotta Jermyn wouldn't know what a hint was! No, my love, just let things sort themselves out. She'll twig before long that her attentions aren't welcome. Our Miss Fuller will make that plain, and if she doesn't, then I'll have a word with the Captain. He's got plenty of horse sense.'

Most of the residents were more than satisfied with their new circumstances, and Tom and Johnny, who had met before on various Lulling occasions, were fast becoming firm friends.

Each little house had a small garden at the back, and a slip of a garden beneath the front windows.

The two old men were soon busy planting their crops in the little plots. Johnny Enderby shared a bundle of fine wallflower plants with his neighbour, and their two front gardens were the first to be prepared, ready for a bright and fragrant show the next spring.

They took to walking along the Nidden road together on fine afternoons, Polly at their heels, and sometimes called at The Two Pheasants of an evening for a pint of ale. It was plain to the Cartwrights that here were two model tenants.

The Thrush Green residents took a great interest in their new neighbours. Winnie Bailey knew most of them from the old days when her husband had been in practice. Ella Bembridge and Mrs Bates were old acquaintances, and Sybil Angell had been to the same craftwork evening classes as Ella.

George and Mary Cross knew the Shoosmiths, and soon there was a good deal of visiting, and being visited, by old and new inhabitants of Thrush Green. Miss Watson and Miss Fogerty's first tea party for Miss Fuller was soon followed by other modest invitations, and the Cartwrights found themselves as busy as their charges in various hospitable engagements around Thrush Green.

'Seem to have settled down lovely, don't they?' said Percy Hodge to the landlord, when Johnny and Tom had departed to their homes across the darkening green.

'Ah! Lovely! Lovelily, I mean,' agreed Mr Jones, twirling a snowy cloth in a glass. He stopped suddenly. Somehow that last word sounded wrong.

He resumed his polishing more slowly, still puzzled.

Say what you like, he mused, English was a deuce of a

language to get right. It got worse the more you thought about it.

'Nearly time, gentlemen,' he said, putting the gleaming glass on a shelf.

That was plain English anyway.

11   Preparing for Bonfire Night

D URING THE LAST FEW days of October, the large
heap on Thrush Green of inflammable material
such as wood, cardboard boxes and paper bags full
of dried leaves, grew daily as November the fifth
approached.

Miss Watson's class had made a splendid Guy Fawkes
stuffed with straw, and dressed in some trousers which
once belonged to Ben Curdle, a jacket of Albert Piggott's
which Nelly had handed over secretly, much to her husband's rage, and some Wellington boots contributed by
Ella Bembridge and destined to smell appallingly when the
fire got going.

The guy was crowned, somewhat incongruously, by a
solar topee which Harold Shoosmith had once sported in
his working colonial days. As Isobel had pointed out, the
sun in Thrush Green, even at its best, hardly warranted
keeping such a piece of head gear.

Once the guy was completed, it had been decided by
Miss Watson that such a great man-sized object would be
best stored in her garden shed. This decision, however,
caused such agitation, and even some tears, in the classroom, that she relented, and the figure hung from a hook
on the back of the schoolroom door, and seriously impeded
anyone going in and out.

It also frightened several of Miss Fogerty's infants who

had been sent with messages to Miss Watson, and one particularly timid child had suffered night terrors as a result.

'It really makes one rather cross,' commented Miss Watson, handing over the letter from the child's irate mother to Agnes, 'when one sees the sort of horrors they watch on the telly. Why, our guy looks positively *benign*!'

Privately, it was not how little Miss Fogerty would have described it. In her opinion, there was something decidedly gruesome in the figure suspended from its hook. Visions of desperate offenders taking their lives in prison cells hovered before her, and she had every sympathy with the young child who had been so affected by the sinister guy.

'Well, it won't be long before we burn it,' she replied diplomatically. 'Frankly, I dread the fireworks far more than the bonfire. At least Thrush Green people seem to have the sense to keep their poor animals indoors.'

'Albert Piggott didn't keep his cat indoors last year,' responded Dorothy Watson somewhat tartly. 'I saw it myself.'

'Oh dear!' cried Agnes. 'The poor thing! Where was it?'

'Sitting by the bonfire washing its face,' replied Dorothy. 'Quite unaffected by the noise.'

'Isn't that just like a cat!' commented Agnes, much relieved.

The celebration of Guy Fawkes's attempt to blow up the Houses of Parliament in 1605 was always a communal affair at Thrush Green.

The schoolchildren helped to build the bonfire and to supply the guy. Fireworks were given by various people who still enjoyed such things, and Harold Shoosmith and his friend Frank Hurst were among the most generous donors.

Percy Hodge always gave a sack of large potatoes which the Boy Scouts baked in the ashes of the bonfire for everybody, and Mr Jones of The Two Pheasants brought out glasses of beer and mugs of cocoa for the assembled throng.

The day before Bonfire Night turned out dank and drizzly, much to the dismay of the children. Would the bonfire light? Would it be too damp? Should they rush over to it and shroud it in a tarpaulin? Percy Hodge'd have one for sure. Could they buy a can of paraffin to make sure it would go? From school funds, say? Or what about firelighters?

Miss Watson dealt with all these anxious enquiries until she saw that a whole hour of arithmetic and geography teaching had somehow vanished, when she became extremely stern and threatened the entire class with Mental-Arithmetic-All-Through-Playtime, which somewhat sobered her pupils.

Over at Rectory Cottages Jane Cartwright decided to put on her raincoat and remind her charges that they were invited to the party on the green at six-thirty on the morrow.

The new steps and paths were slippery in this moist weather, and wet leaves lay like bright pennies wherever one looked.

She completed her tour successfully, and was touched to see how pleased everyone was at the invitation.

'Second childhood, it seems,' thought Jane indulgently, hurrying back to put on the sprouts for lunch.

But they were never to be cooked. Jane's feet went from under her on the top step, and she landed with a sickening crunch.

Lying dazed, Jane's nursing knowledge still functioned.

'The femur,' murmured poor Jane, closing her eyes.

While Jane was still engaged on her rounds that fateful morning, Joan Young and her sister Ruth were enjoying a cup of coffee together, and discussing the odd behaviour of their respective husbands.

'They really are a couple of sillies,' said Joan. 'What

grandmother used to term "mardy babies". What on earth is the matter with them?'

'I'm always anxious about John,' admitted Ruth. 'He works far too hard, and I think this police business is worrying him.'

'What police business?'

Ruth explained about the robberies and John's involvement with Leys Farm.

'Funnily enough,' said Joan, 'Betty Bell said something about it, but I had no idea John was mixed up in it.'

'Well, he's not exactly "mixed up in it" as you say, but the young man whom John treated has been sighted evidently, and if the police can pick him up it means that John will probably have to identify him. I'm sure that's one of his worries at the moment.'

'Poor old boy! Luckily, Edward hasn't anything like that hanging over him, but he's remarkably short-tempered lately. I blame it on a job he's just undertaken near Cirencester. It's an old vicarage which they want Edward to convert into eight flats, and according to him it will only make six. There's a pretty ferocious battle going on at the moment, I know.'

'Never mind. It makes no difference to us,' replied Ruth comfortingly. 'They'll get over it no doubt, and we'll be able to have our card parties again.'

'Maybe they'll be more amenable at the firework party tomorrow,' agreed Joan. 'It's good that it coincides with Paul's half-term this year. He's bringing home a school friend, and Jeremy Hurst has his half term at the same time, so the house will be cheerful.'

'Will Edward be able to stand it?'

'He'll have to,' replied Joan lightly. 'Anyway, I notice that he has an enormous box of fireworks in his study, so that augurs well for all concerned.'

'That's good. Well, I must get back. It's John's half day, and there's lunch to get ready. He comes in straight from his morning round.'

'Not too busy, I hope, with this mild autumn?'

'No, touch wood! It's after Christmas that the trouble begins.'

The sisters kissed affectionately and parted.

Down at The Fuchsia Bush in Lulling High Street Nelly Piggott had been summoned to Mrs Peters's little office.

It was a quarter to twelve. Morning coffee was practically over, and the midday lunch was well ahead, being supervised by Nelly's two competent kitchen maids.

What could this be about, she wondered, taking off her overall? It wasn't like Mrs Peters to interrupt kitchen activities at such a time, unless something urgent had cropped up.

'Sit down, Nelly,' said her employer. 'I won't keep you many minutes, but I thought you ought to know Mrs Jefferson called last night, and she's definitely giving up. The doctor insists, so that's that. You can guess how sorry I am. We've soldiered on here together for many years, and I'm going to miss her.'

'So am I,' said Nelly, with feeling. 'She's one in a thousand. What will you do?'

'That's the question. I shall have to advertise for someone experienced, but the two girls are doing well under you, and can take a certain amount of responsibility.'

She began to fidget with papers on her desk, and Nelly began to wonder what the future would hold for herself.

'If you want me to do more,' she offered, 'I think I could arrange things. Albert's no bother, and you know I enjoy working here.'

Mrs Peters nodded abstractedly.

'Yes, thank you, Nelly. You've been an enormous help, and it's due to you that we're building up this home catering side so successfully. It's plain to me, Nelly, that that's where our living's going to be in the future. That christening party of Mrs Thurgood's has sparked off six, and probably, eight more functions. I'm thinking of investing in a van of our own.'

'Well now, isn't that good news!' exclaimed Nelly. Things must be going better than she had thought. A year ago Mrs Peters had been worrying about the state of the business. Now, it seemed, the outlook was brighter.

As if reading her thoughts, Mrs Peters began to explain.

'We're not suddenly rich, Nelly, or anything like that, but business is certainly looking up and I was left a house last Christmas by an old aunt of mine. It's way up north, at a little town called Alnwick, and as I shall never use it I put it on the market and have a little over twenty thousand from the sale.'

'That must be a great relief to you,' said Nelly warmly.

'It certainly is. But what I wanted to tell you is something I've had in mind for some time. Poor Mrs Jefferson's retirement has brought it to a head.'

She resumed her fidgeting, and Nelly began to wonder if the apple crumble was getting overdone.

'If I get a van and do more of this catering on the spot, I shall need someone who can take complete charge at this end. Would you consider becoming a partner in the firm, and doing that?'

Nelly, for once, was flummoxed.

'Heavens alive! *Partner*? But I could take charge here as I am, couldn't I? I mean, to be a *partner* –'

Words failed her.

'Nelly, I want someone who has the interests of this place at heart. And you have shown that you are proud of The Fuchsia Bush, and willing to turn your hand to anything. All the girls respect you. If you feel you can take this on, I shall be very much relieved. Naturally, your income would be greater.'

She named a sum which to Nelly sounded colossal, and she was about to remonstrate.

'Say nothing,' urged Mrs Peters. 'Think it over. Talk to Albert about it, and let me know before the end of the week.'

She rose and patted Nelly's massive shoulder.

'I'm fair bowled over,' said that lady. 'But it's a wonderful offer, and I'm proud.'

'Off you go then,' said Mrs Peters. 'Something smells good in the kitchen.'

'Well-done apple crumble, I shouldn't wonder,' replied Nelly, making towards her own domain.

The first person to reach Jane Cartwright lying prone on the damp steps was Carlotta Jermyn. She had just emerged from her home and was bound for the Crosses on one of her morning calls.

She was surprisingly calm and competent in this emergency, and knelt down beside Jane, murmuring reassuring words and ignoring the dampness which stained her knees.

'Don't move, my dear,' she said. 'I'll get someone to you immediately.'

But Bill had already arrived and taken charge.

Heads emerged from doorways. Faces were stricken, and lamentation loud.

'If you could go to Doctor Lovell's,' said Bill, supporting his wife's head, 'it would be a great help.'

Carlotta hurried across the green, leaving Bill to comfort his wife, and organize a rug and cushions to ease her position. He was not short of helpers. Everyone, it seemed, was anxious to render first aid.

Within five minutes one of Doctor Lovell's young partners arrived.

'Doctor Lovell's not on duty at the moment,' he explained, as he examined his patient, who was now able to talk to him and to the throng around her.

He made a makeshift splint and he and Bill carefully carried Jane to her own sofa.

'I'll get an ambulance straight away. She'll be taken to St Richard's, of course. As far as I can see, it's a straightforward break, but the X-rays will show up everything.'

He began to dial.

'Those dam' steps are a menace in this weather,' he

remarked conversationally, as he waited for the hospital to reply.

'So it seems,' said Bill, holding his poor wife's hand.

Excitement was running high at the village school, so high indeed that Agnes Fogerty decided to put aside her idea of an autumn collage for the classroom wall that handwork session, and to substitute the theme of Bonfire Night with plenty of well-sharpened red and yellow crayons.

Her class worked industriously. There was rather more chattering than Agnes normally allowed, but occasionally, she told herself, one must give a little licence to young children. The thought of Christmas so soon to be upon them, with all its accompanying trappings of paper chains, calendars, blotters, Christmas cards and rather terrible ornaments made from pine cones, all manufactured in this very classroom, was one to be shelved, at least until this present excitement had gone.

She wandered around the tables admiring guys suspended, black and spider-like, among flaring fires. The red and yellow crayons were working overtime, and Agnes made a mental note to get a few in reserve from the stock cupboard. Red ones always ran out early when Father Christmas hove in sight. And, come to think of, black ones would be needed urgently, after all these guys, for Father Christmas's boots.

It might be as well, mused Agnes as she nodded encouragingly at the upheld masterpieces, to look out that well-tried bookmarker pattern from *The Teachers' World*. A tassel made of bright wool, hanging from the pointed end, would be a useful exercise for young fingers, and would use up the remains of some scarlet four-ply left over from knitting mittens for the church bazaar. Looking ahead has always been one of the attributes of a good teacher, and earnest little Miss Fogerty was one of the very best.

Across the playground, in the top class, peace reigned. Miss Watson, made of sterner stuff than her assistant, had quelled the chattering and the insatiable need, it seemed, to stand up to see if the unlit bonfire was still safely established on the green.

Here handwork on a more sophisticated scale was being done. Embroidery, knitting, single section book-making and paper models were keeping fingers busy, and the most competent reader – and the worst knitter – was sitting in front of the class regaling the rest with a passage from *Three Men In a Boat*.

Dorothy Watson, between marking some deplorable mental arithmetic tests and watching over her charges, was also thinking about Christmas preparations, but in a negative way.

No nativity play, was her first definite decision. Far too much preparation, and really the costumes alone were a headache, despite the help of the parents. If Thrush Green school possessed a proper stage it would be a different kettle of fish, of course, but the heaving about of school furniture was a sore trial. No, a nativity play was definitely out.

And the usual boisterous Christmas tea party seemed rather daunting. Perhaps a simple celebration with carols and some readings would fit the bill? It might be combined with a cup of tea and a slice of Christmas cake for parents and the school's friends after the performance. Something really *simple*, she repeated to herself. She supposed that the cake should really have been made by now. She must ask Nelly Piggott if The Fuchsia Bush had any on sale. Perhaps it could be suitably iced for the school's festivities?

It began to grow murky in the classroom, and the school clock showed that it was nearly home time. She could hear the cries of the infants as they tumbled across the playground to the bliss of freedom.

'Pack up your work, children,' said Miss Watson. 'Thank you for reading to us, dear, but do remember that "Harris" begins with an aitch. All stand, eyes closed. *Closed*, Pat Carter!

'*Keep us, O Lord, in Thy care, and safe from any dangers of the night.*'

'Amen!' said the children with unnecessary vigour. Would school never end?

They streamed out to the lobby, collected coats and scarves, and rushed joyously homeward.

'I shall be glad when tomorrow's over,' said Dorothy to Agnes. 'Guy Fawkes has a lot to answer for.'

While Jane and Bill Cartwright waited for the ambulance to arrive, the elderly folk were persuaded to return to their homes. In this undertaking Carlotta and her husband showed signs of tactful leadership which Bill recognized with much admiration.

As soon as he could see that all were being safely shepherded, he made another telephone call. This time it was to Jane's mother, some half a mile or so away along the road to Nidden.

Listening to the bell ringing in Mrs Jenner's hall, Bill wondered if he would find her in. Probably she had finished lunch by now. He hoped that she had not gone to her bedroom for an afternoon snooze, as sometimes she did.

At length, he heard her voice.

'Mother,' said Billy urgently, 'don't get alarmed, but I've some rather bad news. Are you sitting down?'

'Good heavens, man! Of course I'm not sitting down! There's no room for a chair in this passage. In any case, I'd sooner stand up to bad news. Quickly, what is it?'

He told her briefly.

'Jane says you're not to worry. The ambulance is on its way. Come and see her in Dickie's, she says.'

'Oh, the poor girl!' cried Mrs Jenner. 'That sounds like a long job to me. How will you manage?'

'I was wondering,' began Bill hesitantly, 'if you could see your way clear to coming down here for a day or two?'

'I'll be with you in twenty minutes,' said that noble woman, and hung up.

'Your mother,' said Bill huskily to Jane, 'is an angel. A proper angel!'

'You don't have to tell me that,' said her daughter, as the ambulance swished up to the door.

A CLAMMY MIST engulfed Thrush Green at daybreak
on November the fifth.

The waiting bonfire glistened damply. The hedges
were heavy with droplets, the trees' gold had slipped to their
feet, and the leaves lay thick and sticky in the wet grass.

It was uncannily silent. Distant sounds were muted.
Footsteps, and even the noise of car tyres, were muffled by
the fallen leaves and muddy roads. It was a chastened
assembly that met at the village school, but Miss Watson
did her best to cheer them by saying that the weatherman
had promised a finer afternoon.

'But do 'e *know*?' asked one infant anxiously.

And all that Miss Watson could say in reply was that
presumably he knew better than most.

She hoped it was true.

Across the green, Doctor Lovell heard for the first time
about the accident at the old people's homes, and was
magnanimous enough not to make any comment about
Edward Young's steps in front of his partners.

Nevertheless, he felt a certain satisfaction in hearing that
his fears were not groundless, although he had every
sympathy for poor Jane Cartwright's mishap.

'I hope all the old dears over there will hold tight to the
hand rail,' was his only remark, when he was told the

news, but he said more to Ruth when he went home at lunch time.

'Well, that's the first casualty at Edward's famous edifice. And won't be the last, as far as I can see!'

'What's happened?' asked Ruth, soup spoon suspended in mid-air.

'Jane Cartwright's broken a leg on those idiotic steps. Asking for trouble to put steps like that where there are old people. I told Edward so months ago.'

'But Jane isn't old,' protested Ruth.

'Oh, don't quibble!' snapped her husband. 'I know she's not! All I'm pointing out is that those steps are a hazard, and one which any sane architect would have omitted from his plan from the start.'

Ruth continued to sip her soup in silence. When John was so short-tempered it hardly seemed possible to conduct a civilized conversation.

However, by the time the apple tart stage had been reached, Ruth spoke.

'I'm taking Mary to watch the bonfire just after six. Paul's home and Jeremy Hurst's going to be there as well. Joan suggests we have a drink with them, before or after, just which suits you best.'

'I suppose Edward is attending this bean feast?'

'Naturally.'

'Well, I'll come along for a little while to the bonfire, but don't accept for me later. I'm on surgery duty tonight.'

'Fair enough. We won't be late back. Mary will be tired out with all the excitement.'

'You'll be a lot tireder, I surmise,' said John with a smile.

He pushed back his chair, kissed his wife, and went back to his duties.

Well, he seemed to have cheered up, thought Ruth, clearing the table. But if only he would try some of his own tonic!

*

The weatherman must have known something after all, for by midday a watery sun was trying to disperse the mist.

Winnie Bailey, taking a turn in her garden in the hope of finding a few flowers for the house, was cheered to see the sunshine. She dreaded the winter even more keenly now that Donald had gone. It was not so much the piercing cold of the Cotswold winters, as the short murky days which she found hardest to bear.

She realized, with a shock, that this was the first time she had been outdoors for three days. The rain and dismal weather had turned her attention to a multitude of little tasks indoors. She decided that she would get some exercise during the afternoon by taking some magazines to Dotty, and hearing the news from her old friend.

Meanwhile, she collected four somewhat battered late roses, a few sprigs of hardy fuchsias and two nerines which struggled for existence in the unwelcoming cold of this area, and realized that these were all the flowers to be gathered here in November. It was true that the pyracantha tree which she and Donald had planted years ago was ablaze with scarlet berries, but their prickly stems discouraged any picking, and in any case the berries would soon wither indoors. Better to admire them from the garden, thought Winnie, carrying her rag-taggle posy inside.

Later she set off across the green, admiring the bonfire as she did so. Nathaniel Patten on his plinth seemed to smile benignly on the peaceful scene. Before school ended, as Winnie knew from earlier years, the children would carry the guy across and put him on the top of the pyre, where carefully crossed twigs made a chair for him.

To her surprise, she found Dotty in the garden, throwing weeds over the top of the chicken run to an appreciative bevy of Rhode Island Red hens.

'Should you be out in this damp weather, Dotty?'

'Oh, yes, dear, it's perfectly all right, Connie and Kit are down in Lulling. Do come in.'

She began to wipe muddy hands down her skirt, eyes beaming behind her spectacles.

'Dear things,' she said affectionately to the scrabbling hens. 'You see, I know Connie is most conscientious in feeding them night and morning, but I feel that they miss fresh greenstuff. Now I have just given them dandelion leaves, groundsel, shepherds' purse and some dock leaves. A wonderfully healthy mixture of essential minerals. Have you ever read Gerard's *Herball*?'

'Well, no, Dotty. But I know that Donald had a copy and read it with much enjoyment. He often said that the old boy knew what he was talking about.'

'He was quite right. Dandelion and dock in particular he understood, and I'm sure he would approve of the hens having plenty of them.'

'I must say they seem to appreciate your largesse,' observed Winnie, 'but don't you think you should come in now? Your slippers are soaked.'

She ushered her hostess into the house, and was relieved to see her settled by the fire. Dotty took off her slippers, displaying a pink big toe emerging through a hole in her stocking, and Winnie put them in the hearth to dry. What a time Connie must have looking after this eccentric old aunt!

'Now you must tell me all the news from Thrush Green,' said Dotty, arranging her legs on the sofa. 'Has Mrs Bassett quite recovered? And have you heard about Richard's baby? And is Percy Hodge still courting your Jenny? And how are Agnes Fogerty and Dorothy? And are you going to the Guy Fawkes party? I believe Ella is.'

For one supposed to be out of the swim of village affairs, thought Winnie, Dotty seemed remarkably up to date.

'Mrs Basset's much better, but Joan and Ruth watch her like hawks, I believe. No, no news of Richard, and as far as I know Jenny is free from Percy's attentions. In fact, I gather he has transferred them to Albert Piggott's wife.'

'That won't please Albert, will it?' exclaimed Dotty with much pleasure. 'Go on, dear.'

'The village school is in a state of great excitement,' Molly Curdle told me. George can't wait for tonight when they light the fire. And no, I don't think I shall go, even if Ella does. Jenny and I get an excellent view from the house and it gets rather too boisterous for me with all those fireworks. Donald used to love it.'

'I never did. The poor frightened animals, you know. Which reminds me, Kit and Connie are making plans to go to Venice.'

'What's the connection, Dotty dear?'

'Why, the animals! I went once as a girl and was quite shaken by the callousness of some of the inhabitants, to the cats, in particular. But I'm much relieved to hear that things are greatly improved. Still a lot to be done though, according to the Anglo-Italian Society for Animal Protection. Their report came yesterday. You must borrow it.'

'Thank you. And when are Kit and Connie off?'

'Oh, as soon as possible,' said Dotty somewhat vaguely. 'I tell them Venice gets foggy about now, but I don't think they mind about that. And I have warned them about being taken hostage on these aeroplanes, and advised them to pack a lemon or two to add to the drinking water if they are held up at some rather uncomfortable place like Beirut.'

'It doesn't happen often,' Winnie pointed out.

Dotty gave a little shriek, lowered her legs from the sofa and snatched up the poker.

'Look, dear, a poor earwig on that log on the fire! Can you reach it? Let me get a shovel.'

Winnie followed her gaze, and bent to the rescue with her hostess. Not until the insect was safely deposited outside on the fence was Dotty able to relax again.

'What a mishap! I've always been devoted to earwigs. As children we used to chant a rhyme:

> "*Marco Polo, Marco Polo*
> *His mother was an earwig*
> *His father was a whale.*"

'Now, I wonder what the derivation of that was?'

'I've no idea,' confessed Winnie, her head beginning to spin, as it so often did in Dotty's company. 'But I did hear some children chanting much more topically this morning:

> "*Please to remember*
> *The fifth of November*
> *Gunpowder, treason and plot.*
> *I see no reason*
> *Why gunpowder, treason,*
> *Should ever be forgot.*"'

'And were they begging? With a guy I mean?'

'No, not this time. I wonder what they would expect these days? A penny for the guy wouldn't go very far, would it?'

'A pound probably,' said Dotty. 'Ah! I think I hear the wanderers returning. Stay for tea.'

Nelly Piggott, busy in the kitchen of The Fuchsia Bush, was still unsure about the answer to be given to Mrs Peters.

Her employer was out, chasing up some supplies which a tardy wholesaler had failed to deliver, and Nelly had not had a chance to put one or two queries to her.

Her first, and most overwhelming desire, was to accept the offer with all the delight she felt, but Albert had put one doubt in her head.

To be sure, he had not been much help in discussing this momentous news, when he had returned from the public house next door rather more befuddled than usual.

Nelly insisted on his drinking a cup of black coffee before she told him about Mrs Peters's offer, but she doubted if it did much to clear her spouse's brain.

'Partner?' exclaimed Albert. 'And what pay does that give you?'

Nelly told him. Albert continued to peer sourly into his coffee cup.

'She won't be giving you that much for nothin',' was his comment.

'What d'you mean? It's a fair offer, isn't it? I'll be working harder, that's all.'

'You don't reckon to be a partner unless you puts something into it.'

'Well, I am! My work, my experience, my know-how! And all that,' ended Nelly weakly.

Albert snorted, pushed away the cup, and began to lurch towards the stairs.

'You mark my words, gal, she'll want money before you're taken on as a partner. *Partner indeed!* Don't make me laugh! I'm off to bed, so come up quiet when you do.'

Nelly washed up the cup. Tears joined the water in the washing-up bowl. She did not believe Albert's words, but it had been a long hard day, and what she had needed was some support and comfort in this crisis.

Well, Albert was Albert! Half his trouble was jealousy,

she told herself, mopping her eyes. He acually resented her success, that was part of it, the mean-spirited old toss-pot! She had been a fool to expect anything helpful from that source.

She went to bed in the little back bedroom, and lay awake listening to Albert's snoring next door, and wondering if, just possibly, he was right about having to contribute money to a firm if you were made a partner. She must get things straight with Mrs Peters before she accepted.

If only there were someone to ask! She supposed that she could consult someone like Mr Venables, but that would look as though she did not trust Mrs Peters, and anyway it would cost money.

Suddenly, she thought of her new friend, Mrs Jenner. The very person! Sensible about business affairs, and fair-minded. Tomorrow evening she would walk up the Nidden road, and have a good talk with her!

She had no idea, of course, that her friend was much nearer at hand, sleeping in the spare bedroom of the wardens' house, with the alarm clock set at six-thirty ready for her new duties on the morrow.

A light breeze sprang up round about five o'clock on Guy Fawkes' day, and the children rejoiced. Now the bonfire should blaze merrily, and the guy catch fire without recourse to unseemly proddings with paraffin-soaked rags and such demeaning aids to combustion.

It sat upon its funeral pyre looking splendidly remote. Harold Shoosmith's topee had tilted a little on its way to the summit, and gave the guy a slightly rakish appearance, but all agreed that it was one of the best efforts of Thrush Green school.

At six-thirty sharp the scoutmaster thrust a flaming torch into the base of the pyre and within minutes yellow and orange flames leapt skyward. Cheers went up from the spectators, and the boxes of fireworks began to be sorted out by those in charge, ready for the display.

The scoutmaster, freed from his chief duty, now began to supervise the positioning of the scrubbed potatoes in the bonfire base with the vociferous help of his charges.

What with the shouts of excited children, the crackling of the bonfire, and the sharp reports of a few premature fireworks, it was almost impossible to carry on a conversation, as John Lovell found, when at last he made his way from the surgery to join his family.

Mary was jumping up and down in a frenzy of ecstasy, her face scorched with the heat and her tongue wagging non-stop. Her cousin Paul and his friends were equally excited. It was plain that they would be a long time getting to sleep after such jollifications.

'Marvellous sight!' shouted John to Edward. 'Luckily, I had a short surgery tonight. All my patients are here, I reckon!'

He beamed across at a bevy of old people from the new homes, the Jermyns, Mrs Bates, and the Crosses.

Edward followed his gaze.

'You've got one in hospital, I hear,' he said.

John glanced at him.

'Yes. But I'm not going to say "I told you so", if that's what's in your mind.'

'I should hope not,' snapped Edward, and moved away.

Pompous ass, thought John, turning away from the heat of the blaze. Edward was getting stuffier with every year that passed, the irritating fellow.

At that moment, the first rocket of the evening whooshed skyward, and sent down a cascade of pink and violet stars.

'Ah!' sighed the crowd in great contentment.

'Where's the next?' shouted one wag.

And, as if in answer, the second streaked away towards a black velvet sky.

It was Albert who told Nelly where to find Mrs Jenner that evening. He had heard all the news during the day at The Two Pheasants, and a very pleasurable time he had

had discussing morosely where the blame lay for the accident, and how long Jane Cartwright could expect to remain in hospital.

'It's not so much the surgeon's knifework,' he told his unimpressed listeners, 'as what the shock does to your system. I mean, all them muscles and glands and tubes, they must get in a fine old muddle when the knife goes in, and it's bound to take time to get 'em to join up again.'

He took a gulp of beer.

'That's if they ever do. Did I ever tell you about my operation?'

'Time and again,' said one.

'Too often, Albie! Don't start that again!'

The landlord interposed.

'Jane Cartwright will soon be back. Plenty of spunk there, and a nice healthy woman, like her ma.'

'She's over there now, I'm told, holding the fort.'

'That's right,' said Mr Jones. 'Knows when she's needed, and never been afraid of hard work.'

He looked pointedly at Albert who, by rights, should have been at his duties. Albert chose to ignore the hint until closing time.

The bonfire was at its peak of glory as Nelly crossed the green. As she stepped along the path to the wardens' house, a great cry arose from the watchers round the fire, and she was just in time to see the guy crash through the flames to the inferno below.

'Lot of babies!' was her private comment as she rang the bell.

Mrs Jenner looked tired, but her smile was as welcoming as ever as she invited Nelly to take a seat.

'Bill's just gone along to St Richard's to see poor old Jane,' she said. 'One thing, my duties are pretty light this evening, as about half the people are at the beano on the green.

She told Nelly more about Jane's misfortune and made light of her own help.

'Oh, it's a good thing to be able to turn your hand to what crops up,' she said cheerfully. 'Keeps you on your toes, you know. Now, Nelly, what brings you here?'

Nelly began her tale, diffidently at first, but gradually gaining confidence from her listener's calm attention.

'And so I just wondered if Albert might be right. What do you think?'

'I should say that Albert is hardly *ever* right,' said she robustly. 'Obviously, you'll want to get things absolutely straight with Mrs Peters now this doubt has crept in, but I'm sure she would have said something about it from the start, if that's what she had in mind.'

'That's what I think,' cried Nelly, much relieved. 'She's absolutely straight, I'm sure of that, and I can't think of anyone I'd sooner work for.'

'Work *with*!' corrected Mrs Jenner. 'You see, Nelly, she realizes that you are willing to try your hand at anything. She's had plenty long enough to watch the way you go about things, and believe me, she wouldn't have offered you this if she had any doubts about you being able to cope with it.'

'That never occurred to me,' confessed Nelly.

'You go ahead and accept. You have to look after yourself in this life, even if you are a married woman. And to be frank, Nelly, your Albert's rather more trouble than he's worth, if you'll pardon my saying so.'

Nelly laughed, slapping her hands on her knees.

'You never spoke a truer word,' she replied. 'Thank you, my dear, you've put my mind at rest. I'll be off now.'

'Not before you have a cup of coffee,' said her friend. 'I've still got to find my way around this place, but I found the teapot and the coffee pot before I'd been here five minutes.'

The embers of the bonfire still glowed red when Winnie Bailey undressed for bed.

She and Jenny had watched from the house for an hour

or so, enjoying the children's caperings silhouetted against the bright flames. They watched until the last rocket had blazed its way skyward, and the last Catherine wheel had whirled itself to darkness. The sound of firecrackers went on, and small children waved sparklers until they too had gone and they were herded, protesting, to their beds.

It was very peaceful after the din. Winnie leant from her window to survey the scene. There was a moon showing between silver-edged clouds. It was almost full, and lit Thrush Green with a gentle light.

Nathaniel Patten's statue gleamed opposite, and wet branches glistened as the moonbeams caught them. An owl hooted from Lulling Woods and, high above, the landing lights of an aeroplane winked rhythmically.

Little drifts of smoke wavered across on the air, bringing that most poignant of autumn scents from the bonfire's remains.

Tomorrow morning, a ring of white ash and a few cinders would be all that would remain of the past hours' splendour. The children would scuffle among the debris, hoping for a stray burnt potato, or the gnarled metal of a firework component to treasure. Miss Watson and Miss Fogerty would deplore the state of pupils' shoes, and the yawns which would be the outcome of an evening's heady bliss.

They won't mind, thought Winnie fondly. They've had their fun, and nothing can take away those thrilling memories.

How Donald would have loved it, she thought with a pang, as she climbed into bed.

THE MURKY WEATHER continued. By now the clocks had been put back, and it was time to draw the curtains at around four or five o'clock.

As Jenny remarked to Winnie Bailey: 'No sooner were you up and about than it seemed you were getting ready for bed.'

At the village school the lights were on all day, and Mr Jones's bar lamps, with their red shades, did their best to cheer the gloom.

In Lulling High Street the shops were already beginning to show signs of Christmas looming ever nearer. A large poster in the Post Office window exhorted customers to post early for overseas' mail, and agitated passers-by realized that yet again they had missed surface mail to New Zealand and Australia and would have to send to distant aunts and brothers by air mail. They went on their way toying distractedly with such gifts as silk scarves, handkerchieves and tights – anything, in fact, which could be weighed in grammes rather than pounds, and even then, they thought mournfully, the cost of postage would be devastating.

At The Fuchsia Bush a discreet notice stood in the corner of the window reminding customers that the last orders for Christmas cakes, mince pies and puddings must be put in immediately. The florists nearby requested early orders for holly wreaths and crosses, and the coal merchant's window had a large card saying sternly, 'Order now for Christmas'.

The three Misses Lovelock, Ada, Bertha and Violet, had resolutely set their faces against preparations for Christmas until the beginning of December. They had taken up this stance some years earlier, their reasons being that early December was quite time enough to start thinking about preparations, and there were plenty of jobs to be attended to in November anyway.

'But what about your pudding?' said Dimity, 'and sending off presents to people abroad?'

'We don't eat Christmas pudding,' came the austere reply. 'And we don't send any presents to people who live overseas.'

There seemed to be little to say after this, and Dimity, who had called about contributions to a Christmas bazaar, retired without daring to mention the subject. One Lovelock was intimidating enough. In triplicate they were formidable.

On this particularly dismal November morning, Charles was in some anxiety.

'It seems, my dear,' he said to Dimity, as he ruffled the leaves of his pocket diary, 'that I have promised to go to the old people's Christmas party at Thrush Green, at the same time as the preview of pictures at Janet Thurgood's gallery. Janet *Fairbrother*, I should say now.'

'Just ring one of them and explain,' advised Dimity, who frequently had to cope with such errors.

'But this morning,' went on Charles, becoming even more agitated, 'I had an invitation – well, more of a summons – from the bishop, and that too is for the same afternoon.'

'Then the bishop's must take precedence,' said Dimity, 'and you must telephone to the others. Now, stand away from the table, Charles, while I roll out this pastry, or you will be looking like a miller.'

Charles sat down obediently in a corner of the kitchen, still looking worried.

'I think I shall take a walk up to Thrush Green to see Bill Cartwright and explain. Poor Jane is still in hospital, I hear, but no doubt he and Mrs Jenner are going ahead with Christmas arrangements.'

'A good idea,' responded Dimity, sprinkling flour energetically. She sometimes wondered what her dear husband would feel if she sat down in his study while he was writing his sermons. He probably would not notice, she thought, and would certainly not feel as irritable as she did when he invaded her work room.

'I want to see Mrs Bates in any case. She's offered to clean the church silver at St Andrew's, and it seems a kind gesture. She did all of it here, you remember, and I suppose she misses it.'

'I thought the Bassetts always did it.'

'Mrs Bassett hasn't been able to for some time, and I believe Ruth and Joan have carried on as it was largely given to the church by their great-grandfather. I must call on them and see what they think.'

'Well, dear,' said Dimity, attacking the pastry again with her rolling pin, 'you go and sort out things up there, and I'll see you at lunch time.'

Charles rose with a sigh.

'I do seem to get myself in a pickle with my dates. What should I do without you?'

He kissed her forehead and made for the door. There was flour on his black lapel, but Dimity forbore to comment. The dear man had quite enough to worry him already.

While Charles Henstock was making his way to Thrush Green, Doctor Lovell was just finishing surgery and checking his bag before setting out on his rounds.

The telephone rang. It was the police superintendent.

'I think we may have your man here,' he said. 'Could you get down to an identity parade?'

'What now? No hope!'

'No, probably late tomorrow afternoon. The chief inspector, who is independent of this enquiry, of course, will organize everything. He has to collect several chaps who are fairly similar in looks. It shouldn't be too difficult. Our fellow has no beard, or bright red hair, or anything too outlandish.'

'What happens?'

'We put these chaps in a row, and then invite the suspect to take his place, wherever he likes, among them. Then you – who have been kept away from all this obviously – are brought in and hopefully can touch the right man on the shoulder.'

'It sounds straightforward enough, but I can't tell you how I dread it. Suppose I pick the wrong chap?'

The superintendent laughed.

'It doesn't often happen, so take heart. You are still quite willing to help us?'

'Yes, indeed. When shall I come?'

'Say, five o'clock? If there's any difficulty I will ring you.'

John put the telephone down. His hands were trembling. He picked up his bag and went through the little office towards his car, pausing to tell Miss Pick, the secretary, about the appointment at the police station.

'What have you been up to?' she wanted to know banteringly.

'Nothing yet,' replied John, 'but I might make the most awful hash of things, I can see.'

He left Miss Pick, who looked at the closing door with some perturbation. It wasn't like the doctor to get so anxious about things. Come to think of it, he hadn't looked really fit for some time now. Overwork, she supposed. A dose or two of his own tonic might do him good.

Charles Henstock found Bill Cartwright just about to go shopping in his car. After enquiring about Jane, Charles told him, with genuine distress, about his dilemma.

'Never fear,' replied Bill with a forgiving smile. 'It happens to all of us now and again. You go and see Mother. She's getting a pie ready.'

Charles obeyed, and said he was glad to hear that Jane was making good progress.

'She should be home next week,' said her mother, 'but of course she'll be on sticks for a bit. I'm going to stay on to lend a hand.'

'A sad business,' said Charles.

'And the old people have taken it hard,' added Mrs Jenner. 'They were just settling in nicely, and this accident seems to have upset them.'

'In what way?'

'Well, for one thing they seem to use the steps with quite unnecessary caution, and some will only go down now by the ramp which was really made for cars and vans to use. Then some of them seem very touchy, although I think that's because of Mrs Jermyn, who will interfere with everyone. Bill's had a word with her husband, but it doesn't seem to make much difference. The Crosses were very friendly with them, but since Monty has taken to using their front flower bed as his personal lavatory, things have been a bit strained.'

'Oh dear! Can I help at all?'

'Well, a visit from you is always appreciated,' said Mrs Jenner.

'Actually, I'm going to see Mrs Bates first,' he said, and explained about the silver cleaning.

'That's a good idea. I think she feels a bit useless, and Mrs Young's got enough to do without adding the weekly silver cleaning to her chores. I know the church silver has always been kept at their house as they have a safe, but I expect it could be brought to Mrs Bates on Sunday evenings and she could take it to the Youngs when she had done it. Or maybe she could call there?'

'We'll sort out something,' promised Charles. 'There isn't a great deal of it – not like the splendid old collection we have at St John's – but there is a fine ebony cross with silver decorations, as you know, and the pair of Victorian silver vases, which flank it, are very heavy, if perhaps a little florid for today's taste, and a nice old chalice which I always enjoy handling.'

'Well, I'm sure Mrs Bates will like that little job,' Mrs Jenner assured him. 'Now, can I give you some refreshment before you call on her?'

'No indeed, many thanks. I'll go immediately. I expect you are busy preparing lunch. I left Dimity rolling pastry.'

'And that's just what I was doing,' Mrs Jenner told him, nodding towards the kitchen door, 'when you called.'

'Apple tart?' asked the rector, now on his way.

'What else, after this season's crop?' said Mrs Jenner, waving him off.

After his visit to Mrs Bates, the good rector called on her neighbours. He spent most of his time with Tom and Polly, but was lucky to find Johnny Enderby there too. The two old men seemed fit enough, but were very serious when the question of Jane's accident cropped up.

Only the Angells were out, so that Charles saw practically all the new residents that morning, and was struck by the anxiety and downright nervousness, in some cases, which he had not noticed before. It grieved him too, to hear the bitterness with which the Crosses spoke of the Jermyns next door. Monty had a lot to answer for, thought the rector. It began to look as though the 'no pets' rule was certainly going to be needed in the future.

He was relieved to enter the peaceful sitting room of the Youngs' house. Joan was grateful for Mrs Bates's offer, and promised to go over that afternoon to make arrangements which would suit her.

'Do you think she'd like to come over here to clean the things? We'd love to have her, and it might make a change for her.'

'I'll leave it to you,' said Charles, and set off, more cheerfully now, to his vicarage.

But for the rest of the day, Charles was uneasy. What was amiss at the old people's homes? The residents had settled in so well, had seemed so thankful to be there, so grateful for all the Cartwrights were doing for them. He recalled the happiness at that first party when the new neighbours were warm in their praise of everything, and glad to make friends with each other.

He supposed that a number of things contributed to the present malaise. Certainly, Jane's accident had left them in a state of shock. After all, she was their mother-figure, someone to turn to with their problems, 'a very present help in trouble'. The fact that she had fallen on the ground that they daily traversed was also cause for fear. If she, so comparatively young and nimble, had come a cropper, what might happen to those older and shakier?

And, of course, the first excitement of their new abodes had worn thin. The relatives and friends who had visited them in the first few weeks now came less often. They had seen the old people happily ensconced, and felt that all would be well with them. The coming of short dark days and the onset of winter ills, also meant fewer visitors, and it was easy for some of these old people to give way to self-pity, the most insidious foe of all.

He thought of Mrs Bates. Perhaps she provided the clue to the future happiness of her neighbours. It seemed to Charles that the old people needed to feel part of the life of Thrush Green. Mrs Bates was doing something to be of service, and by doing so was making herself useful in the community. Could the others find help in this way?

The old residents of Thrush Green had been outstandingly welcoming, and he knew that there were real friendships between individuals such as Ella and Tom Hardy and Johnny Enderby who had their love of gardening in common, and Miss Fuller and the teachers at the school who shared many interests, but perhaps more could be done.

But what?

Charles knew how keenly the old people valued their independence, and he himself would have disliked any sort of hearty community activities imposed from outside. No, it would have to be most delicately done, and the residents themselves must show the way. Mrs Bates's initiative might well be the inspiration.

Well, it would be best to wait until Jane was back and strong enough to help him with the problem, decided Charles. For there was a problem here, and one which could grow and cause much unhappiness unless it could be solved with tact and sympathy.

One thing, both Jane and Bill had plenty of those two qualities.

After her talk with Mrs Jenner on Bonfire Night, Nelly had gone to see her employer with an easier mind.

To her relief, all final fears were swept away by Mrs Peters's reassurances. There had been no thought of Nelly putting money into the firm. What she needed, she reiterated, was Nelly's support, expertize, ideas and loyalty.

Nelly threw herself energetically into her new role as one of the partners at The Fuchsia Bush. She revelled in her new-found position, and welcomed the Friday night sessions when she stayed at the office to go through the books with her partner.

Nelly had a natural flair for financial matters, as Mrs Peters soon learnt. There had been periods in Nelly's life when she had been hard-pressed for money, but she had always managed to evade debt or complete penury. She was a saver too, by nature, and she soon saw how certain methods would bring profit to the shop. To her mind, there were some of the wholesalers whose business ploys were suspect. She suggested to Mrs Peters that they should try others, and in this Nelly's hunches had proved correct.

The home-catering side was steadily growing. The van was already on order, and both partners could see that there was a bright future in that side of the business. But it

was Nelly who suggested that fresh rolls with attractive fillings such as ham and tomato, egg and lettuce, cheese and watercress, would find a ready market with many of the office girls and shop assistants who worked so close at hand in Lulling High Street.

'They can't afford the time or the money for a proper sit-down lunch in here,' pointed out Nelly. 'In any case, the single ones are probably going home to something cooked by mum about six o'clock, and the married ones will have something cooking in a casserole to go home to, or a few chops or sausages ready in their baskets. Let's try it for a week anyway. The girls in the kitchen are quick workers and I'll give a hand before putting on the lunches.'

It was a great innovation, and after a week's trial, Mrs Peters agreed it should become a regular service.

'And if need be,' she added when she and Nelly had totted up the books one dreary November Friday, 'we could think of employing a girl part-time, simply to get the rolls ready.'

Hope had already replaced her former apprehension, and affairs at The Fuchsia Bush brightened daily.

A week later, John Lovell bumped into the superintendent in Lulling High Street.

'I hear you didn't have much bother in identifying our friend,' said the latter.

'I was lucky. When I was first called to see that fellow, I noticed an old scar over his right eyebrow, and I remember thinking that he should have had it stitched at the time. It had healed well, but would have been less noticeable. I'd forgotten about it until I saw it at the identity parade.'

'Well, there's no doubt he's our man. He swore he was innocent for quite a time, and said he knew nothing about the other two chaps, but he changed his mind after a bit, and now we're looking up north for his buddies. We should get them pretty soon.'

'And what will happen?'

'Oh, they'll go up to Crown Court without a doubt, with the sort of offences they're charged with. It's been going on a long time, and a great deal of money is involved.'

'I'll be needed as a witness, I suppose?'

'Afraid so. You must hold yourself in readiness.'

'Well, it'll make a change from looking at chickenpox spots,' smiled John.

'Much about then?'

'Quite an epidemic. Nidden School is half empty.'

'I *think* I've had it,' said the superintendent thoughtfully.

'If you had any sense,' responded the doctor, 'you'd have put it behind you before your tenth birthday.'

They parted to their particular duties.

Jane Cartwright arrived home from hospital in good spirits, but woefully wobbly. The old people were touching in their welcome, and Bill had to be particularly tactful in restraining their visits in the early days.

'She's being killed with kindness,' he confided to his mother-in-law, when he had ushered out Miss Fuller who had brought a hyacinth bulb in a glass vase to distract the patient's attention from her ills.

'You'll have to be firm,' Mrs Jenner told him. 'I've said that she has a rest every afternoon, and that's that. I know they all mean well, and Jane's grateful to them, but it's going to be some weeks before she's really fit again.'

'You're quite right, mother,' said Bill, 'but it's difficult when they arrive with bunches of flowers, and little cakes and books, and then beg to see her. I think I'll pass them over to you.'

'You do just that,' said Mrs Jenner firmly. 'I can be quite a dragon if need be.'

One of Jane's early visitors was Joan Young. She gave her news of Mrs Bates and the church silver.

'She comes over to us either on Friday or Saturday afternoon, and stays for tea. She seems to enjoy coming, and we look forward to her visits. Incidentally, the silver has never looked so splendid, and we hear all the news from here as she gets to work.'

'Good news, I hope?' said Jane. 'I think all our people have settled in pretty well. It's a big upheaval for some of them.'

'Oh, I'm sure they all seem very glad to be here,' Joan assured her. 'Molly Curdle usually comes over when Mrs Bates comes, and she gets on with some ironing while the silver's being done. She hears more than I do, I think. They certainly have a hilarious time together and baby Anne gets thoroughly spoilt.'

When Joan had gone, and Jane was alone resting, she turned over Joan's comments in her mind.

Were the old people really as happily settled as she said? Jane was very much aware of all that was going on, and had sensed, since her return from hospital, that some of their charges were a little discontented. The occasional remark had been dropped by her visitors, about the short-comings of neighbours. Monty's reprehensible sanitary arrangements had been mentioned once or twice. The perennial problem of too-loud radios had cropped up. Someone's refrigerator made a bang every now and again in the night. The lavatory flushings were unduly noisy.

And, of course, the paths were slippery, as poor Jane knew only too well.

She supposed it was inevitable, thought Jane, to have these teething troubles. Her mother had often said that old people were worse than children to deal with, and she and Bill had known this from the start. But somehow, there seemed to be more behind these little worries – a general discontent which could not be blamed on the weather, the reaction to initial euphoria, or any other reasons.

Perhaps, she told herself, she was exaggerating things. Her present low state might have something to do with it. How she longed to be up and about again!

Meanwhile, she must count her blessings. Bill and her mother together were coping splendidly with the job, and she was getting stronger and more mobile daily.

Time enough to worry when she had thrown aside her stick, and could scurry about as nimbly as she did before Fate had stricken her down, she told herself.

14   Visitors

To everyone's relief the first few days of December became beguilingly mild and sunny. The last of the apples glowed on the bare branches. The hedges were still beaded with hips and haws, and a few hardy fuchsia bushes dangled bright tassels in defiance of the calendar.

In the gardens at Thrush Green there was great activity as the sodden masses of leaves were raked into piles and late bonfires coped with the outcome.

People who had not been able to face the torrential rain in the latter part of November, now hurried to Lulling High Street to catch up with neglected Christmas shopping, and to purchase Christmas air letters to send to all the people overseas who had been forgotten earlier.

At The Fuchsia Bush a spate of orders came in, not only for cakes and puddings, but also for catering arrangements for local office parties. Nelly and Mrs Peters worked happily overtime.

In the infants' room Miss Fogerty picked her way over mounds of paper chains which overflowed from the desks and deplored the way that so many of the links broke, sending down cascades of coloured paper upon the delighted children below. Certainly paste was not what it used to be, thought Agnes, as she repaired the damage. There was a lot to be said for good old-fashioned paste

made by hand in a pudding basin with strong plain flour.
And it would work out at a quarter the price!

Across the green, Winnie Bailey was inspecting the bowls
of hyacinths which she had planted at the beginning of
September. They were destined to be Christmas presents
for neighbours such as Phyllida Hurst, Ella and Dotty, but
at this rate, she thought, they would be nowhere near
ready.

Certainly, dear reliable Innocence bulbs were doing well,
and Lady Derby too, but why was the bowl of Ostara
taking so long? She carried them into the kitchen, and
decided to give them all more warmth.

Jenny had just put two lamb chops in the grill pan, and
was prodding the potatoes. They always lunched together
in the kitchen, unless Winnie had one of her increasingly
rare lunch parties.

Winnie was just setting the last of the bowls on the wide
window sill, when the front door bell rang.

She hurried to answer it, and to her amazement found
Richard on the doorstep.

'Well, what a surprise! Do come in, Richard dear. Are
you alone?'

A vision of two lamb chops floated before her. Something would have to be rustled up quickly, especially if
Fenella and the children were hard by.

'Quite alone, Aunt Win. I'm on my way to Bath, and
saw a familiar signpost, and thought I'd drop in.'

'You'll stay for lunch?'

'Yes, please. I should like that.'

'Then I shall give you a glass of sherry, and leave you
for a minute to tell Jenny. Then I want to hear all the
news.'

She poured her nephew a glass and left him reading the
newspaper.

Jenny was equal to the emergency.

'Plenty of rashers here, and a few sausages. And there

are eggs and tomatoes, so we can make a mixed grill. But what about pudding?'

'There are lots of apples in the fruit bowl, and cheese and biscuits to spare. He's lucky to get that,' said Richard's aunt, 'if he can't be bothered to ring up beforehand.'

'Shall I set the table in the dining room?'

'Lord, no, Jenny! He can have it here with us.'

She was about to return to the sitting room when she put her head round the door again.

'And he has *my chop*, Jenny, not yours! That's an order.'

'Now tell me about the family,' said Winnie. 'How's the baby?'

'Growing. Cries rather a lot. Especially at night.'

'It's a way babies have. And Fenella?'

'Quite busy with the gallery. There's an exhibition of paintings on glass at the moment. Ready for Christmas, you know.'

'How does she find time with two young children?'

'Actually, Timothy goes to play school three mornings a week, and of course Roger is mainly in charge of the exhibition.'

'Roger?'

'Fenella's cousin. I think it's five times removed. Something like that. I believe their great-grandfathers were first cousins, but I can never work out those things.'

'Nor me,' confessed Winnie. 'And where does he live?'

'Roger has a flat just round the corner. At least, his wife has. I'm afraid they are not on speaking terms just now, and he quite often sleeps in the gallery.'

'It doesn't sound very comfortable,' said Winnie.

'Oh, he has a sleeping bag,' replied Richard, helping himself unasked to another glass of sherry. 'And the floor of the gallery is carpeted. Can I fill your glass?'

'No thank you, dear.'

At that moment, Jenny came in to say that all was ready, and Richard carried his glass with him to the kitchen table.

Winnie noted, with approval, that Jenny had opened a large tin of baked beans to augment the rations. Richard rubbed his hands gleefully.

'What a spread! Do you always eat so splendidly?'

'Only sometimes,' said Winnie, catching Jenny's eye.

'I'm very glad I didn't drop into a pub,' announced Richard. 'It did cross my mind, but I thought it would be so much nicer to see you both and have a snack with you.'

'And I suppose you will spend Christmas in London?' said Winnie, as they set to.

'Fenella will. I shall be on my way back from China.'

'China? At Christmas? But it's the baby's first one, and surely Timothy will be just the right age to love it all!'

'Yes, it's rather a pity, I suppose, but I was asked to go when I was on the earlier lecture tour, and it's so well paid I felt I really couldn't turn it down.'

'Does Fenella agree?'

'She was a bit miffed at first, but she hasn't said anything since, so I suppose she's got over it.'

It all sounded remarkably unsatisfactory to Winnie, but she felt that she could not continue to cross-question a grown man, even if he were her nephew, about his domestic arrangements, and the subject was changed to Thrush Green's news and the doings of old friends.

Later, aunt and nephew walked around the garden. The sun still shone bravely although the shadows were as long at two-thirty this bright December day, as if it were nine o'clock of a summer evening.

Winnie plucked a few late apples from a tree which she and Donald had planted so long ago.

'Take them with you in the car,' she said. 'They're a lovely flavour, and I think they are so beautiful.'

She held the golden globes towards him, and for once Richard seemed aware of something other than his own affairs. He looked closely at the tawny beauty, striped in red and gold, in his hand and sniffed at it appreciatively.

'Ah! That takes me back to my childhood,' he exclaimed. He looked around the garden, the dewy grass marked with their dark footsteps, and a collared dove sipping from the bird bath.

'Do you know, Aunt Win, I should dearly like to live in Thrush Green. I've always felt at home here.'

'Well, Richard, it would certainly be a splendid place to bring up a family, but property's rather expensive. People can get quite quickly now to the motorway, and it has pushed up the price of houses.'

'I suppose so. And Fenella might not like the country. She seems to enjoy the gallery, and of course she owns it, which means we live very cheaply. I couldn't afford to live as we do if we had to pay rent, or we were buying a house.'

'Then you are lucky to be so well provided for,' remarked Winnie, with a touch of impatience. When she had married, it was the man who expected to provide the home, but times had changed, certainly for Richard, it seemed.

He glanced at his watch.

'I must be off. Thank you for the lunch and those lovely apples. They will remind me of Thrush Green all the way to Bath.'

Occasionally, thought Winnie, as she waved him good-bye, just occasionally, there was a nice side to dear Richard.

But what a pity he was not more of a family man!

One golden afternoon in the following week, Charles Henstock went to visit some of his house-bound parishioners at Thrush Green.

He had dropped Dimity at Ella's, leaving the two friends in animated conversation and an aura of blue tobacco smoke from Ella's pungent cigarettes.

His first call was at Ruth Lovell's house where he found Mrs Bassett sitting up in bed, looking very frail but pretty in a shell-pink bedjacket. She was obviously delighted to see him, and Ruth left them alone together.

Later, he came through to the kitchen where she was ironing and commented on the improvement in her mother.

'Marvellous, isn't it? John's so pleased too. As a matter of fact, it's John I'm worrying about at the moment. He's terribly touchy, and he and Edward are being so silly about some tiff they had about the old people's steps.'

Charles said it was the first he'd heard of it.

'I shouldn't think about it,' he advised her. 'It'll blow over. They're too fond of each other to let a little bit of nonsense like that rankle.'

'Well, I hope so. There's such a lot of illness about, particularly this wretched chickenpox which I'm sure Mary will get just in time for Christmas, and John's run off his feet.'

Charles patted her shoulder comfortingly. 'Well, give him my love, or regards perhaps? Anyway, wish him well from me. Now I'm off to see Dotty.'

'Don't eat anything!' warned Ruth with a laugh.

Dotty too was in bed, but not looking as elegant as Mrs Bassett. She had dragged a dilapidated dark grey cardigan over her sensible thick nightgown. There was a hole in one elbow, and the cuffs were fraying.

She must have seen Charles looking at the cardigan's condition for she said cheerfully: 'Connie puts a shawl round me, you know, but it falls off when I'm busy, so I sneak out and get this favourite woolly from the drawer when she's not looking. Violet Lovelock knitted it for me years ago. Such good wool! Sheep seemed to have better fleece in those days. I suppose the grass was purer – none of these horrid pesticides and fertilisers to poison everything.'

'You look very well,' commented Charles. 'Now tell me all the news.'

'Well, the chickens are laying quite nicely for the time of year, and Mrs Jenner has promised me a sitting of duck eggs for one of my broodies later on. Dulcie seems a bit off colour, but goats often do in the winter, I find, and I think Connie forgets to put out the rock salt. Flossie, of course, is in splendid fettle, and is out with Connie and Kit at the moment.'

Charles noted, with amusement, that it was the animals' welfare, rather than her relatives', which concerned his old friend.

'As a matter of fact,' continued Dotty, fishing in the holey sleeve for a ragged handkerchief, 'I think Connie has too much to do with the house and the garden and the animals. The workmen should be gone before Christmas, or *so they say*, but there'll be a terrible mess to clear up. And then, you see, Kit's no gardener, except for manly things like cutting off branches and burning rubbish and chopping

down trees – all *destructive*, if you know what I mean. You never see him *tending* anything, putting in stakes for wobbly plants, or pricking out seedlings. That sort of *positive* gardening.'

Charles remembered Albert Piggott's unaccountable passion for Dulcie the goat.

'Do you think Albert would come regularly to take the animals over?' he suggested. 'Would Connie like that? You know how marvellously he looked after Dulcie whenever you were away, and I hear he's handy with chickens too.'

'A good idea, Charles! I shall mention it to Connie when she gets back. Would that fat wife of his let him come?'

Charles explained about Nelly's new commitments, much to Dotty's interest, and went farther.

'What's more, I think she'd be glad of anything which kept him out of the pub, even if only for an hour or so.'

'Well, I can always supply him with a glass or two of my

home-made wine. So much better for him than that gassy stuff from The Two Pheasants.'

Charles, knowing the catastrophic results of imbibing Dotty's potions, thought that Albert should be warned, if he decided to pay regular visits, but that, he felt sure, could be left in Connie's capable hands.

'Now, I must be off, Dotty. But before I go can I bring you anything? Shall I make you a cup of tea and bring it up?'

'No, no, dear boy! Connie and Kit will be back soon, but do make a cup for yourself. Or better still, help yourself to a glass of my cowslip wine. The bottle's on the kitchen dresser. And please take half a dozen eggs for dear Dimity. They're in a wicker basket Ella gave me last Christmas. The one that's coming unravelled.'

Charles thanked her sincerely and went below, helping himself, as invited, to six splendid brown eggs for his wife, but prudently abstaining from helping himself from the bottle hard by.

He set off across the meadow behind Dotty's house to Lulling Woods, and on his way met first Flossie, Dotty's spaniel, who greeted him rapturously, followed by Kit and Connie looking pink with fresh air and exercise.

'Come back with us,' they begged. But Charles explained that he was bound for an ailing couple who lived in a cottage by The Drovers' Arms.

'And I must get back to pick up Dimity. It gets dark so early.'

'And what did you think of Dotty?'

'Looking very well,' replied Charles. He wondered if he should mention their conversation about Albert, and decided to be bold.

Connie considered the suggestion thoughtfully.

'You know, it might work out very well. Dotty and Albert have always got on like a house on fire. I'll talk to her about it. Thank you, Charles.'

They parted company, and the rector went on to his duties.

It was dark when he emerged from the cottage. There was a nip in the air already, which presaged a frost before morning. Charles turned up his coat collar, and thrust his hands deep into his pockets for warmth.

The path through Lulling Woods was fairly wide and carpeted with dead leaves and pine needles, so that his progress was quiet. There was no need to brush against outstretched branches or clinging brambles, and his footsteps were muffled in the thick covering below.

Although the woods were as familiar to Charles as Thrush Green itself, yet in this sudden darkness he found himself apprehensive. One could quite understand primitive man's fear of forests, and the legends which grew up about the gods and spirits who frequented woodland. There certainly seemed to be a presence here, and not altogether a benign one, thought Charles, quickening his pace.

The trees seemed to press nearer the path than he remembered, like a hostile crowd approaching an unwary traveller. Occasionally, a twig snapped with a report like a gun going off, probably triggered by some small nocturnal animal setting off to look for supper. When a screech owl shattered the stillness with its harsh cry, Charles almost broke into a run.

He was glad to emerge into the open meadow. The lights of Dotty's cottage glowed reassuringly on his right, and in a few minutes he had traversed the alleyway by Albert Piggott's cottage, crossed the road by St Andrew's church, and stood for a moment to take breath.

There were all the familiar shapes he knew and loved. There were lights in the windows of friends' houses, the Youngs', Winnie Bailey's, the Hursts', Harold and Isobel's. There were even lights shining in the village school where, no doubt, Betty Bell was busy sweeping up. The Two Pheasants was as yet in darkness, but a light was on at Albert's next door, and in the gloaming Charles could see the little black cat on the doorstep waiting for its mistress to arrive with bounty from The Fuchsia Bush kitchen.

Calmer now, Charles turned to walk across to Ella's. For a moment, some trick of the light gave him the impression that he was looking at the outline of his old vanished rectory hard by. He thought that he could see the steep roof, the front door, the tall narrow windows that faced the bitter north-east winds.

A great wave of grief for things past swept over the rector. He remembered his study, its high ceiling, its bare look which had secretly pleased him. He saw again the beautiful silver and ivory crucifix which hung on the wall until it had been reduced to a small misshapen lump by the devastating fire. That little pathetic lump was still treasured in his desk drawer at Lulling Vicarage.

And in his heart, thought Charles blinking away a tear, there was still treasured a knot of dear memories of a house much beloved long ago.

The vision faded, and he found himself gazing at the low outline of the new homes, and farther still the lights of Ella's house shone, beckoning him back to the present where Dimity and everyday comfort awaited him.

Part Three
Getting Settled

END OF TERM WAS now in sight, and Agnes and Dorothy were in the throes of rehearsing the children for a concert, in rooms bedizened with paper chains, bells, friezes showing Santa Claus, reindeer, and lots of artificial snow made from pellets of cotton wool which fell from windows, as well as the mural frieze, and was squashed everywhere underfoot.

Miss Watson's children were attempting two carols played by the few who had recorders. The noise produced was excruciating, and Dorothy sometimes had difficulty in distinguishing 'Hark, The Herald Angels Sing' from 'O Come All Ye Faithful'. At times, she despaired. Perhaps straightforward singing would be more rewarding? On the other hand it was only right that the young musicians should be encouraged, and the parents would be gratified to see the expensive recorders being used.

The lower juniors, in charge of a young probationer on the other side of the partition, were being rehearsed endlessly, it seemed to Miss Watson, in some hearty mid-European dances which involved a lot of stamping and clapping. As the stamping and clapping never seemed completely co-ordinated, the resultant racket was hard to bear, but the young teacher, to give her her due, was persistent, and it was to be hoped that all would be well before the great day.

Little Miss Fogerty, with years of experience behind her, opted for two simple songs with actions which she had first tried out with success at several Christmas concerts in the past, blessing the ancient copy of *Child Education*, held together with Scotch tape, which supplied the subject matter.

As always, the children were over-excited and belligerent. Agnes sometimes wondered if the expression 'the season of goodwill' was wholly correct. There was some acrimony between infants fighting over the brightest colours when making paper chains, harsh and wounding criticisms were made about desk-fellows' portrayal of Christmas trees, Christmas fairies, carol-singers and other seasonal matters. Two ferocious little girls, having a tug of war with a strip of tinsel, had to have their wounds dressed before being sent home, and poor Miss Fogerty's head ached with the unusual clamour in her classroom.

On the other hand, as Agnes reminded herself, quite a few children were absent as the chickenpox epidemic took its toll. George Curdle was among the invalids, a dear little boy who gave no trouble, thought Agnes. Now, John Todd, a sore trial and possessed of a voice like a fog-horn, flourished like a green bay tree, and a great nuisance he was. Still, it was an ill wind that blew nobody any good, she quoted to herself, surveying the six or seven empty desks, and certainly there was more room to move about in the bustle of Christmas preparations.

The two teachers were thankful to get back to the peace of the school house at the end of the day.

'I'm amazed at the presents the children are hoping to get,' said Dorothy, removing her shoes, and putting up her aching legs on the sofa. 'I let them make lists this afternoon – a little spelling practice really – and I find they are asking for things like cassette players and adding machines and some computer games of which I'd never heard. They cost pounds, I gather. How parents with more than one child can cope, I cannot think.'

'I don't suppose they'll get all they ask for,' pointed out Agnes.

'I hope not. More fool their parents if they do,' said Dorothy trenchantly. 'At home, we used to be delighted with simple things like jigsaw puzzles, and furniture for the dolls' house, and sweets and a tangerine in the toe of our stocking, and lots of books. Mind you, I did get a pinafore every Christmas from one particular aunt, and that rather rankled, I remember, and Ray used to get a pair of woollen gloves which he detested, saying they were slippery and put his teeth on edge, but on the whole we were well content.'

'I always had a doll,' said Agnes. 'Every Christmas my parents gave me one, and it was usually a dear little thing with a red stuffed body and china head and legs and arms. Usually, my mother had made its clothes. Once it had an evening cloak too.'

Little Miss Fogerty's eyes behind her thick spectacles sparkled at the remembrance.

'And of course, a tangerine like yours, and some sweets, and best of all a sheet of transfers which you stuck on the back of your hand and wetted, and then carefully peeled off the paper backing, and had a beautifully decorated hand – ships and bells and lovely animals! I was never allowed to have them during the year, but at Christmas my parents relented, and I really think those transfers gave me more pleasure than anything!'

'Yes, we were pleased with little things,' agreed Dorothy. 'What games we used to play with natural things, do you remember? The boys always had their conkers, of course, but I was thinking of our girls' games. Blowing dandelion clocks, for instance, and smiting the head off another child's plantain.'

'And holding a buttercup under your chin to see if you liked butter,' said Agnes, 'and making daisy chains, and dear little pipes from acorn cups. Weren't we lucky to live where such things grew?'

Dorothy sighed nostalgically.

'"Where are the something-or-other of yesteryear?"' she quoted. 'What a comfort poetry is, Agnes dear, even if you can't remember it!'

In the week before Christmas, Lulling High Street was chock-a-block with cars, vans delivering extra goods, children on holiday, frantic shoppers and a local brass band which played carols at irregular intervals and with less than perfect notation.

Nelly Piggott enjoyed it all immensely. This was life as she liked it – plenty of noise, colour and movement. Trade was brisk, the till bell tinkled incessantly, and exhausted shoppers queued for cups of refreshing coffee. The savoury rolls seemed to be snapped up earlier each morning by the local office workers and the van drivers, who had soon got to hear of this welcome service and had become regular customers on their way through the town.

Nelly thoroughly enjoyed being in charge, and her exuberance seemed to be infectious. Even Gloria and Rosa wilted less, and almost hurried about the café, and sometimes even managed to smile at the customers.

Mrs Peters was kept busy, running the splendid new van to local business premises where office parties were in full swing. The change in fortune of The Fuchsia Bush was so welcome, that she was too excited to feel tired during the day, but when at last she fell into bed, she realized how close she was to exhaustion.

At Thrush Green, Winnie Bailey and Ella shared their annual task of setting up the crib in St Andrew's church. To the delight of the ladies who decorated the place for Christmas, Tom Hardy and Johnny Enderby had offered to pick holly and ivy on their afternoon rambles, and had supplied them with generous armfuls.

Jane Cartwright, now making steady progress with only one stick for support, was glad to see this interest. If only more of her charges would follow suit, she thought! There seemed to be some slight lessening of discontent with the approach of Christmas, but would it last?

The members of the Lulling Rotary Club, and other good-hearted folk, were busy arranging shopping expeditions for the elderly and disabled, and Christmas parcels were delivered to each of the old people's homes at Thrush Green. These kindnesses were much appreciated, Jane noted, except for some slight bridling by Carlotta Jermyn who muttered something, in Jane's presence, about having no need for charity, and being perfectly well able to buy a Christmas pudding of her own.

Jane, whose hip was giving her some twinges at the time, said that part of the joy of Christmas was the giving and receiving of gifts, and that to be graciously grateful for presents so generously bestowed should be within everyone's power.

At this rebuke Carlotta's face turned pink, and she walked away.

'Perhaps it was wrong of me,' Jane said to Bill later, 'but it really riled me.'

'A bit of plain speaking won't hurt that one,' Bill replied cheerfully.

On Christmas Day St Andrew's church was full, much to the rector's delight. Holly and Christmas roses stood in the two silver vases on the altar. Mrs Bates had surpassed herself, and everywhere the silver gleamed and glinted with the reflected light of candles and a ray or two of winter sunshine.

The flower ladies had dressed a stand by the chancel steps with red and white carnations and hanging trails of ivy, and the brass lectern was similarly festooned. Everyone agreed that the church looked absolutely splendid and as young Cooke, a little befuddled with pre-Christmas drinks, had taken it upon himself to put twice as much coke in the boiler as usual, a pleasant warmth suffused the old building.

Charles Henstock and Dimity had been invited to Christmas dinner at Winnie Bailey's, as the rector was due at the tiny church at Nidden at three-thirty for evensong.

'It's a great problem trying to arrange services for all four parishes,' remarked Charles, neatly cutting his goose into mouth-sized portions. 'I feel quite envious of my predecessors who had numerous curates and lay preachers to help them at such busy times.'

'But you know you enjoy it, Charles,' put in Dimity, passing some extra sage and onion stuffing to him.

The rector nodded slowly.

'Of course I do. I am greatly privileged to serve so many people, and they give me back far more than I can ever give them.'

Winnie, looking after her guests, did not agree with Charles's words, but said nothing. But she thought, as she had so many times, how lucky Lulling and Thrush Green were to have this humble but great-hearted man to look after them.

At three o'clock they listened to the Queen's speech, and then Charles hastened away to his duties, leaving Winnie and Dimity to doze by the log fire.

Dimity, replete with the Christmas feast, fell fast asleep, occasionally emitting a small lady-like snore, but Winnie simply lay back in the armchair, her knitting lying neglected in her lap, while her thoughts ranged over past Christmases shared with Donald.

Mrs Bates had said to her only that morning: 'Christmas is the time of remembering, isn't it?' At that moment, Winnie had construed this as something to do with the giving of cards and presents, but now, in the quiet of the firelit room, she realized that the old lady was probably thinking of Christmases shared with a husband long-dead, or with children now far away. There was an element of sadness in this type of remembering, without doubt, but in fact it was all part and parcel of the renewing of ties between family and friends, and should be considered as something specially dear as one recalled, with gratitude, the days gone by. Nothing, after all, would take those memories away, and they grew more dearly cherished as the years passed.

To say that she still missed Donald was understating things to the point of banality. She still felt that something vital had gone from her, as if an arm or leg had been amputated, and she would never be whole again. But he would have grieved to see her incapable of recovery, and certainly she had been lucky in her home, her friends and Thrush Green itself, to help her through the darkest of the days.

One of her New Year resolutions, she promised, was to give as much comfort to others as she had received. She had much to be thankful for, and self-pity was not going to be allowed to creep in. About that she was adamant.

Her knitting slipped unregarded to the floor. Her head fell forward, and she joined her old friend in a refreshing snooze.

Most of the younger generation at Thrush Green were taking advantage of the dry roads and had set off walking, hoping that the exercise would help their over-taxed digestions.

Edward Young, Joan, Paul and his friends took the path to Lulling Woods. The young ones raced ahead, shouting excitedly, their breath forming little clouds in the chilly air.

Joan was wrapped in her new sheepskin coat, Edward's Christmas present, and chattered cheerfully. As they approached the stile into the woods she took Edward's arm.

'Oh, don't!' he yelped. 'I'm horribly sore!'

Joan looked at him in surprise.

'Have you pulled a muscle or something?'

'No, no. Nothing like that. Must be fibrositis, I think. I've got a sort of itchy burning pain in my right shoulder and back.'

'Too much Christmas pud, I expect,' laughed Joan. 'Would you like to go back?'

'No, I'll be all right,' said Edward, but he certainly looked rather wretched, thought Joan, and she purposely slowed her pace. It was so unusual for any of the Young family to be under the weather that Edward's obvious discomfort was worrying.

The children by now were far ahead, and Joan and Edward stopped to lean over a farm gate and survey the wintry scene. It was very quiet, and in the middle distance they could see eight plump French partridges, standing immobile, their dappled breasts shading to the red feathers above their legs. They were obviously aware of the two scrutinising them, and had frozen into stillness, but as Edward moved along the gate they suddenly took flight, and whirred away across the field.

Already the valley was filling with ghostly white mist, and distant treetops floated as if on water.

'Getting chilly,' remarked Edward with a shiver.

'Yes. We'll be getting back,' agreed Joan, solicitous for his welfare. 'I'll yell for the children.'

There were answering cries from the distance, and soon all the party began to make their way homeward through the early dusk.

'It might be as well to pop over to see John when surgery starts again,' said Joan.

Edward shrugged impatiently.

'Oh, there's nothing really wrong. I'm not going to bother him over Christmas. Probably be gone by morning anyway.'

And with that Joan had to be content.

Mrs Jenner spent Christmas Day with Jane and Bill. There were very few of the old people in their homes. Most had been collected by relatives to spend the day with them, and it was very peaceful in the wardens' new home.

Jane could now get about with much more confidence, often without a stick for support, but to her mother's solicitous eye she still looked pale and drawn.

'Well, I don't get the fresh air and exercise I'm used to,' agreed Jane, 'but that will change when the spring comes, you'll see.'

'I had a visit from Kit Armitage the other morning,' said her mother. 'They've fixed up for a holiday in Venice, but they want someone to live in with their aunt.'

'It's a bit late isn't it, to find someone now? I heard that they were off in a fortnight.'

'They've been let down by the nurse they got through an agency. They asked if I could see my way clear to help out, but frankly I can't face it. She's an amazing old girl for her age, but to live with her for a fortnight is asking too much.'

Jane laughed.

'And you'd have to watch your diet down there, Mum! So what did you say?'

'I said I would try and find somebody reliable, and I thought of Vi Bailey. She nursed with you at the Cottage Hospital, remember?'

'Just the one, if she'd come.'

'Have you got her address? I might sound her out. I believe she went to live in one of the London suburbs when she married, but I don't remember her married name.'

By this time, Jane had hobbled to her bureau and found the address book.

'Here we are! Violet Ellis, and she's on the phone. Ring her now.'

'No, no! Not on Christmas Day, but I will tomorrow, Jane, and I do hope she'll be free. I know the pay will be exceptionally generous. Kit and Connie know they are asking a lot of whoever takes on Dotty, but they really do need a break, and I'm so fond of them.'

Bill now appeared from going his rounds, and from sanding the treacherous steps and paths which had caused his wife's present condition.

'No cups of tea for the world's workers?' he cried. 'Stay there, you girls, and I'll put on the kettle.'

Darkness came early to Thrush Green on Christmas Day. The mist had thickened as night fell, and wreathed eerily about the statue of Nathaniel Patten and the bare branches of the horse chestnut avenue. It was dank and chilly, the birds had gone to roost before five o'clock, and most of the human animals were equally comatose, toasting their toes by the fire, with curtains drawn and lamps lit.

But about seven o'clock the bedroom lights went on at the schoolhouse, as Agnes and Dorothy went aloft to change their dresses ready for a visit next door.

Isobel and Harold had invited them, and their old friends Frank and Phyllida Hurst, to Christmas dinner that evening, and the two maiden ladies were looking forward to a rare evening out.

Little Miss Fogerty surveyed herself in the mirror. She had on her best deep blue woollen frock with a silver locket of her mother's at her neck. The frock was now three years old, but had not been worn more than a dozen times. Her shoes were new, and very daring Agnes felt as she put them on, for they were of grey suede with a splendid cut-steel buckle across the front. She had never owned such dashing shoes in her life, but Dorothy had been present when they were bought, and had egged on her old friend to make the purchase.

It would have been nice, Agnes thought, to have an elegant cape or something really luxurious as a coat, but her everyday camel one would have to do, and she donned it cheerfully. The new blue silk scarf which had been Dorothy's Christmas present was tied over her head. The new gloves, sent by Ray and Kathleen, were put on, and little Miss Fogerty went downstairs to await Dorothy's appearance.

As befitted a headmistress, and one more sophisticated in dress, Dorothy descended the stairs looking quite regal in a bronze silk dress with a matching jacket. A string of amber beads added to the general ambience, and her brown court shoes looked extremely elegant.

'You look truly beautiful, Dorothy,' exclaimed Agnes. 'I just wonder – do you think we should carry our shoes and go in our Wellingtons? It might be rather muddy.'

'Good heavens, no! It's only a few steps, and Isobel has a stout doormat. Shall we go?'

The clammy night air chilled their faces as they emerged from the schoolhouse. Near at hand the light glowed a welcome from the Shoosmiths' porch, but it was impossible to see across the green, and even Nathaniel Patten was a ghostly figure in the swirling fog.

'It really is a most unpleasant night,' commented Dorothy. 'I'm sorry for people who have long journeys.'

'Never mind,' replied Agnes. 'Just think, the shortest day is behind us, and soon it will be spring.'

By this time they had rung the bell and were waiting in the porch, admiring Isobel's Christmas wreath hanging on the front door.

Dorothy, touched by Agnes's resolute cheerfulness, forbore to point out that January, February, and probably March stood between Christmas and the hoped-for spring. But no doubt it would come eventually, and here was Isobel at the door, arms wide in welcome, with Harold behind her, looking handsomer than ever.

'Happy Christmas!' they cried. 'And we hope you are hungry. The turkey is twice the size we ordered, and only just fitted into the oven!'

Later that evening, Bill Cartwright ran his mother-in-law home, and saw her safely into the farmhouse.

She looked tired, he thought, and he hoped that her spell of helping him whilst Jane had been in hospital was not the cause.

'I'm glad you didn't agree to staying with Dotty Harmer,' he said impulsively. 'It would have knocked you up completely. I feel we asked too much of you with our own troubles.'

Mrs Jenner looked surprised.

'It was nothing, Bill. I enjoyed it, and would do the same again, but I suppose I must face the fact that I'm getting old. If only Vi Bailey – I mean, Ellis – will be able to come, I shan't feel so guilty. I shall give her a ring in the morning. If she can't manage it, I really don't know who to suggest.'

'Well, don't offer yourself,' said Bill. 'Some people's hearts rule their heads, and you're one of them.'

He kissed her affectionately, and went out into the mist.

16   Winter Discomforts

THE BELLRINGERS AT Lulling rang out the Old Year, and rang in the New, on the famous peal of St John's church.

The night was still and frosty, and the clamour was heard across the fields and woods, in a dozen little villages within a few miles.

The vicarage hummed and trembled with the noise, but it was a joyous sound, and Charles rejoiced. This year, he promised himself, as the hands of the clock stood at five minutes past midnight, he would work harder, be more patient, and give more attention to dear Dimity who was far too selfless.

There were a number of people making good resolutions at much the same time, but Edward Young was not among them.

He, poor fellow, was being driven to distraction by the pain in his right shoulder. It seemed to have spread to his neck and down the right side of his back.

Joan, over the last week, had applied calamine lotion, witch hazel, petroleum jelly, and had even contemplated using a sinister looking ointment concocted by Dotty, but did not take this final drastic step. Nothing seemed to alleviate the torment, and Edward grew more fractious daily.

When, at last, some nasty little spots began to appear,

and he had spent the last night of the year sitting up in bed and holding his pyjama jacket away from his afflictions, Joan put her foot down.

'I'm calling John in to have a look at you,' she said firmly.

'Oh, don't fuss! Anyway, I suppose I'd better go to the surgery, if I must see him.'

'Not with those spots. You may have something infectious.'

'Thanks. Very reassuring, I must say. What's your guess? Leprosy?'

'Don't be childish. You'll stay there in the morning, and I shall ask John to come after surgery. No arguing now. You need some expert treatment.'

Edward grunted, but forebore to argue. He knew when he was beaten, but it was clear to his wife tht he was still reluctant to be obliged to his brother-in-law.

The distant bells had woken Connie. She and Kit had gone to bed at their usual time, both ready for sleep, but Connie was secretly worrying about Dotty's welfare while they were away.

Mrs Jenner had been as good as her word, and Mrs Ellis was to come on New Year's Day to see the cottage, meet Dotty, and decide if she would take on the job.

Connie had no doubt that she would be a most competent person, particularly if Mrs Jenner and Jane recommended her, but would she want the responsibility of such an eccentric person as dear Dotty? The nearer the time came to going to Venice, the more agitated Connie became. For two pins she would throw over the whole idea, but she knew that Kit was longing to go, Dotty was adamant that she would be perfectly safe on her own, let alone with a companion, and Connie herself realized that she was desperately in need of a break.

Looking after the house and Dotty was a full-time job, and the fact that the new addition to the cottage was still not completed was another complication. It was true that the worst was over, but now the finishing touches had to be done inside, which involved a great deal of to-ing and fro-ing through the house when the weather could be at its worst.

Sometimes Connie had a twinge of nostalgia for the life she had left behind. Then she lived alone, in a fairly remote house, looking after a couple of ponies, ducks and hens, three cats and a dog, and quite often old friends who came to stay for a few days, and whose company she relished. But she enjoyed her solitary life. Any decision she made she could make alone, and stand or fall by the result without too much heart-burning.

Now she had to consider Kit and Dotty, and to wonder if she were doing the right thing. Love them dearly, as she truly did, it certainly made for a more complicated life, mused Connie.

The bells ceased suddenly. Well, tomorrow she must face the interview with Jane Cartwright's fellow-nurse. Meanwhile all her cares must be put aside for a few hours.

She slid down the bed, tucked the bedclothes round her neck, and settled down to sleep.

She suddenly remembered an anecdote about Winston Churchill, who was asked, during the war, if he worried much at night.

'No,' answered the old warrior. 'I think: "To hell with everybody!" and I go to sleep.'

And very sound advice to follow, thought Connie, turning her face towards the pillow.

Not far away, Winnie Bailey too was ready for sleep, but a thought struck her before she dropped off. There had been no word from Richard this year. There was usually a card, true an aggressively non-Christian one usually, such as an abstract painting which looked the same either way up, but this time nothing had arrived.

Of course, she remembered, he had said something

about travelling back from China about Christmas time. That must explain it. Still, it would have been nice to have had a word from him. She was fond of Richard, despite his off-hand ways. Perhaps he would bring his family down for the day soon.

With such comfortable thoughts Winnie slipped into oblivion.

Under the same roof, Jenny was looking forward to the New Year. Life at Thrush Green held all the happiness that she needed.

She thought of her early years at the orphanage where, despite good management, adequate food and a great deal of kindness, life had contrived to be bleak.

The years spent as a foster child with an elderly couple, had been better in many ways, but the work had increased as her foster parents grew more infirm. She mourned them sincerely when they died, but Winnie's offer of a flat in her house, the companionship of her employer, and the pleasant surroundings, were a source of constant joy. It was wonderful to have a real home of her own, she told herself, savouring the warmth of the bed and the luxurious scent of Winnie's Christmas present of expensive soap, from the nearby wash basin.

If the year ahead proved to be as happy as the last, then Jenny was well content.

Vi Ellis arrived punctually at Dotty Harmer's cottage on New Year's Day.

She and her husband had driven down, and the plan was for her to stay overnight with her old friend Jane Cartwright, while her husband took the car on to Lechlade, where he was going to visit an old school friend, recently made a widower. He would pick up Vi on his way home.

She was a small plump woman with dark curly hair and the brightest eyes Connie had ever seen. She seemed lively, willing, and above all, kind. Dotty appeared to take to her, and after coffee, she was shown round the house by Connie.

'I must make it quite clear,' said Connie, when they were out of range of Dotty's hearing, 'that my aunt is pretty self-willed, and often does something rather unpredictable like popping down in the night to see if the chickens are safely locked up. I'm a light sleeper myself, so I usually manage to head her back to bed.'

Mrs Ellis laughed.

'Don't worry. I've dealt with lots of old people in my time, and I promise you I shall be alert.'

'As a matter of fact, I think my aunt will probably be more tranquil about the animals as we have a neighbour, Albert Piggott, coming to look after them, and Dotty has rather more confidence in him than she has in me.'

Connie took her into the spare bedroom which was next door to Dotty's own, and Vi Ellis stood looking with admiration at the view across to Lulling Woods.

'One day,' she said, 'when Ted's retired, I hope we'll be able to come and live in the country. We both miss it badly.'

They sat down and Connie told her about the wages offered, the doctor's treatment, Betty Bell's help in the house, and other relevant matters. Vi Ellis seemed happy with all the arrangements, and it was really now just a matter of finding out how Dotty felt about this possible companion, thought Connie.

As if reading her mind, Vi asked if she might go and walk round the garden for a few minutes and get a breath of real country air.

While she was so disposed, Connie returned to the sitting room and went across to Dotty.

'She'll do!' said that lady before anything was said, much to Connie and Kit's relief.

'I'm glad you like her,' replied Connie. 'I do too.'

'Then you'd better fetch her in,' said Dotty, 'before she freezes to death.'

Joan Young had been as good as her word, and soon after Christmas John Lovell had called to see his brother-in-law.

'Let's have a look at this rash,' said the doctor, helping Edward off with his shirt.

He surveyed the spots in silence, whilst the patient awaited the worst.

'Well,' he said at last. 'You know what you've got, I expect?'

'Far from it! That's why you're here!'

'Shingles. I don't think it will be too bad a dose, but it's a beast of a complaint.'

'I'll endorse that,' said Edward. 'I wonder where I got it?'

'Lots of chickenpox about. It's connected, you know. Have you been in contact with anyone particularly?'

Edward thought, as he did up his shirt buttons.

'Young George Curdle's got it, of course, and I've visited him now and again. Playing snakes and ladders and draughts and other thrilling games.'

'Sounds as though that's it.'

'Am I infectious?'

'No, no! It's one of those things that we think lies dormant, and can flare up if the patient has been under strain or run down. Or, of course, in contact with chickenpox.'

'Well, to tell the truth, John, I am having a devil of a time with a contract in Cirencester. Have had for weeks now. Might be that partly.'

'Quite likely.'

He smiled at his patient.

'We all worry too much,' he went on. 'I've had a few guilty twinges about ticking you off about those steps. No business of mine really.'

'Oh, forget it, John,' said Edward. 'Can you give me something to stop this plaguey itching?'

'Yes. I'll write you a prescription for a lotion and some tablets. And off work for a week at least. Lots of drink – not spirits, old boy – nice healthy stuff like water and orange juice!'

'Thanks a lot!'

'An evening's card-playing might help. Take your mind off your troubles. Come to us on Thursday. It's my evening off surgery.'

Within five minutes he had gone, leaving Edward to try and decipher the hieroglyphics of his prescriptions.

'Why do doctors have such terrible handwriting?' he asked the cat, who had wandered in.

But, rather naturally, there was no reply.

The chickenpox epidemic still raged in Lulling and Thrush Green, and when term began almost a quarter of Miss Watson's pupils were absentees. It certainly made for more manageable classes, and Miss Watson and the young probationer took the opportunity to do a little extra coaching of slow readers.

Little Miss Fogerty always aimed at sending her top infants to the junior school with the ability to read. But, of course, there were some who were slow, and some practically incapable of reading at all, and always would be.

'There seem to be more these days,' she remarked to Dorothy when the matter was under discussion. 'I can't make it out. It can't be only television. Perhaps I am losing my touch.'

'Rubbish!' said her friend. 'I think perhaps we are all trying to do too many things in school time, and the reading gets a little neglected. I intend to have a real blitz this term. After all, the older the child the harder it finds learning to read. We must just put our backs into it for a bit.'

It was while she was doing just this one chilly January morning, that Miss Fuller walked in, somewhat timidly, clutching a large envelope.

'Do hope I'm not interrupting,' she said, surveying the half-dozen children clustered round Miss Watson's desk, forefingers clamped to a line in their readers.

'Not at all,' said Dorothy graciously. 'Go to your desks, children, and carry on quietly.'

'I thought that you might find a use for these Christmas cards,' said Miss Fuller, proffering the envelope.

'Now, that is most kind of you,' said Dorothy, turning over the angels, reindeer, wise men, cats and dogs, all in happy medley. 'With these dreadful cuts in expenditure, it's a very welcome present, believe me. We can make all sorts of good things.'

Miss Fuller flushed with pleasure.

'I must admit, it's lovely to be back in the classroom again, if only for a few minutes. What were you doing with that little group when I came in?'

Miss Watson explained about the backward readers.

'I was rather hoping to get some remedial work when I'd settled,' responded Miss Fuller. 'Just part-time, you know.'

Miss Watson thought quickly, and replied with her usual frankness.

'As things are, I can't see the office expending any more money on extra staff, but we could certainly do with a hand at the moment with this reading effort.'

'Oh, I had no thought of payment,' said Miss Fuller, not quite truthfully. 'But if you really think I could help them I should be more than happy to come for an hour or so during the week.'

'It's a splendid offer,' said Dorothy, and her response was wholly truthful. 'I'll talk it over with the others, and call on you, if I may.'

The ladies parted with expressions of gratitude. Miss Fuller looked quite bright-eyed as she waved at the door, and Dorothy returned to her desk with much to consider.

She must inform the office of Miss Fuller's suggestion, she felt, and then have a word at playtime with her two colleagues.

Not that they would have any objection, she felt sure, to such an experienced teacher as Miss Fuller giving them a brief respite from the efforts of backward readers.

Who would, thought Dorothy, beckoning to the group with a sinking heart?

'There's just one thing,' ventured Agnes that evening. 'Much as I respect Muriel Fuller, I do feel that she can be a trifle – er – perhaps just a little –'

'Bossy?' said Dorothy. 'I've thought of that. She's not going to tell me how to run my school, just because she's been a headmistress. In any case, there were less than twenty on roll at one time at Nidden.'

'How well you sum up things!'

'She could have the staff room for her reading sessions. Five children for half an hour, I thought. If she's willing to give us two hours a week, say, it should fit in very well.'

'Which days does she want to come?'

'I'll have to discuss it with her, but if it fits in with her own plans, I suggest Tuesdays and Thursdays, after morning play. She can have her coffee with us, and then carry on when we've gone back to our classrooms.'

'It sounds splendid.'

'Well, time alone will tell,' said Dorothy. 'But it was most kind of her to bring her Christmas cards. I think we'll ask the children in assembly tomorrow morning to bring theirs too. What a lot we can do with such bounty! It's really rather depressing to have to eke out the painting paper and gummed squares in such a Scrooge-like fashion. Now, we can turn our attention to scrap books and wall pictures, and perhaps a screen. I've always wanted to make a screen!'

Agnes smiled indulgently at such enthusiasm. Really, Dorothy was quite a child at heart. Perhaps all teachers of young children were, she thought, with a flash of insight?

By mid-January the weather had deteriorated into bitterly cold conditions, with an icy north-easter and an overcast sky presaging snow to come.

The last few shrivelled leaves were ripped from the bare branches and skittered about the frozen roads and icy puddles. The birds flocked round the back doors and bird tables, hungry for any largesse that was going.

The hips and haws, the berries of the pyracanthas and cotoneaster were now being attacked ruthlessly, and the half-coconut hanging outside in the playground seemed to have a little posse of tits on it all through the day.

Winter ills now descended upon young and old alike, as well as the wretched chickenpox. Isobel and Harold Shoosmith took to their beds with influenza, managing to stagger in turns to heat soup or milk for each other while the plague lasted.

Jenny had a raging sore throat which John Lovell shook his head over, and spoke darkly about having her tonsils out before long. And Dimity and Charles Henstock found themselves suffering from chilblains, which neither had endured since childhood. They were now stuffing themselves with calcium lactate tablets, and rubbing their afflicted fingers and toes with ointment.

'No good taking calcium lactate now,' their kind friends assured them. 'You should have been taking a course all through the summer.'

'How people do enjoy others' misfortunes,' mused Charles to Dimity, when the third person that day had told them of the uselessness of expecting calcium lactate to work a miracle cure. 'It doesn't give one much hope, does it?'

'Never mind,' said Dimity. 'It makes them feel comfortably superior, and it really makes no difference to us. To be honest, I'm *quite sure* I'm better since we started the tablets.'

'Perhaps it's faith healing,' said Charles.

'And what's wrong with that?' cried Dimity triumphantly. 'You know it is *right* to have faith. And in any case, I don't mind *what* sort of healing it is as long as the chilblains go.'

Ada and Bertha Lovelock were in bed with bronchitis, and Violet did her best to provide rather thin soup, and a succession of depressing 'cold shapes' which were a Lovelock dessert speciality, for the invalids. Luckily, the Lulling doctor, surveying his patients' emaciated frames, suggested that suitable meals might be sent in from The Fuchsia Bush next door.

This, he told Violet, was to ensure that she herself did not succumb, but his advice was taken, and once a day a tray of succulent, but easily digested, dishes appeared, and was borne aloft by Gloria or Rosa to the two old ladies.

'Perishing cold it is in there too,' they remarked to Nelly. 'All they've got in the bedroom is a one-bar electric fire, and a stone hot water bottle apiece.'

Nevertheless, the good food, and their own indomitable constitutions, helped them to recover in record time.

At the old people's homes, the only real casualty was Tom Hardy who also went down with bronchitis, but Jane insisted that he stayed in bed, supplied him with an extra-thick cardigan of Bill's to wear as a bed-jacket, and generally cossetted the old man.

His chief worry was Polly. Was she getting her walk regularly? Was she having the tablets the vet recommended? Had anyone brushed her coat? The ruff round her neck was inclined to tangle.

John Enderby undertook these duties cheerfully, and kept his neighbour company, teaching him to play chess and keeping him informed about all the news of Thrush Green.

He himself had offered to give Ella Bembridge a hand in her garden, and gladly had she accepted.

'Not that there's much to do at the moment,' he told Tom one bitterly cold afternoon, 'but I did the rose pruning for her, and I'm going to spread the muck from the compost on her vegetable patch. She does well enough, for a woman, but don't dig as deep as she should. I'll soon get the place to rights.'

Jane Cartwright had seen this development with the greatest satisfaction. This was what was needed to settle her charges. Mrs Bates was as happy as a sandboy with her little weekly silver cleaning, Miss Fuller had found herself

a couple of hours' teaching at the school, and now Johnny was doing something which used his skills and, even more important, made him feel needed. It looked as if things were looking up at Rectory Cottages after earlier teething troubles, and Jane felt mightily relieved.

The day of Kit and Connie's departure was as cold as ever, but mercifully clear and bright, and the flight was due to go at the time announced, much to their relief.

Harold had offered to take them to the airport, but was still suffering from influenza. As it was a Saturday, Ben Curdle offered to take his place, and Harold knew that he would take even more care of his car than he would himself, and agreed gratefully.

'Well, you're lucky to be going to the sunshine,' said Ben, whose idea of anywhere abroad was of coral beaches, palm trees and continuous sunlight.

'It should be warmer than this,' agreed Kit, 'but we'll be lucky to see much sun in Venice at this time of year. Still, it's such a beautiful city, and with dozens of lovely buildings and pictures to look at, we shall have plenty to do.'

It did not sound much of a holiday to Ben, but people had their own ideas of fun. Look at all those people who went ski-ing in deep snow and ended up, more often than not, with their legs in plaster. Give him a deckchair on the beach with an ice cream cornet, thought Ben, taking the turning to Heathrow.

The place was a seething mass of agitated people, piles of luggage and a formidable block of traffic.

Kit took charge with his usual calm authority.

'I'll get a trolley, Ben, if you could get the cases out of the boot. Connie dear, just mind the hand luggage and stay here by this door. I want Ben to get away as quickly as possible with Harold's car. I can't imagine anything worse than getting it damaged before we set off.'

He hurried away and Ben went to the rear of the car.

Connie gazed despairingly at the throng of people. What an unnerving sight! If only she could go back with Ben to the peace of Thrush Green!

'Oh, Ben,' she cried, 'you will let us know if anything goes wrong at home, won't you? I'm really horribly worried about my aunt. She's not quite – not quite –' she faltered.

'Miss Harmer will be as right as rain,' said Ben, with his slow sweet smile. 'We'll *all* be looking after her, don't you fret.'

Calmed and relieved, Connie returned his smile. One could quite see why Molly had married him. Ben would be a tower of strength in any crisis.

'Here we are!' called Kit triumphantly, piling cases on a trolley. 'Practically there!'

'Yes, they went off all right,' he said to Molly on his return. 'She was a bit panicky at the last minute about Dotty, but I told her she'd be fine.'

'I think she will,' said Molly slowly, 'but I wouldn't want to be in that Mrs Ellis's shoes, not for all the tea in China.'

CONNIE NEED NOT have had any fears, for the two ladies settled down very well together.

It was true that Dotty, with her usual forthrightness, had taken it upon herself to put certain matters straight, but after a day or two's adjustment, harmony reigned.

The first clash had come when Vi, slipping back into hospital language, had said, as she tucked a shawl round her charge's shoulders: 'There, dear, we don't want to get a chill, do we?'

Dotty looked at her with some hauteur.

'When you use the word "we", are you using it in the editorial, or royal, sense? Or are you simply referring to the two of us – you and me?'

After that, Vi was more careful.

She was touched too to get a telephone call from Connie on the night of their arrival in Venice. Although she privately considered it overwhelmingly extravagant, she was proud and pleased to get Connie's appreciation of her services.

Dotty had her own conversation with Connie once the preliminaries were over.

'Oh, we're doing splendidly, dear. So glad the fight was satisfactory and the plane wasn't hi-jacked. It must be so tiresome when that happens, and if people are firing off guns in such a confined space, the noise must be indescribable.

Yes, dear, Mrs Ellis is unpicking my Florentine stitch cushion cover, and I'm doing the crossword. Do you know the anagram of DAIRYCATS? Of course, CARYATIDS! That will help a lot. We're having poached eggs for supper. Goodbye, dear, and my fondest love to you both.'

She smiled across at her companion.

'Now, wasn't that thoughtful of her?'

'It was indeed. It's good to know that they arrived safely.'

Dotty suddenly looked agitated.

'Oh dear! I believe I said we were to have *poached* eggs for supper, but now I come to think of it, I think you suggested *scrambled*.'

'I can cook whichever you prefer,' said Vi.

'Then let's make it poached eggs. You see, I shouldn't like Connie to be imagining us eating poached if we were actually eating scrambled eggs. I should feel rather dishonourable.'

'Then we'll certainly poach the eggs,' said Vi kindly, 'if you would feel happier about it.'

'I would indeed, Mrs Ellis. Incidentally, would you be offended if I called you Vi?'

'I should like it.'

'Then you may call me "Dotty". Most of my friends seem to think it a very suitable name for me, though I can't think why.'

Vi did not enlighten her.

The bitter winds brought a roaring blizzard during the next few days, and considerably added to the usual winter miseries.

The only people to enjoy this weather were the children. Screaming with joy, they rushed about, mouths open to catch the snowflakes, faces scarlet and eyes shining.

Those with sledges found themselves unusually popular with their schoolmates, and after school little bands of children hurried to the slopes behind Harold Shoosmith's garden, and set off on their toboggans on the run down to Lulling Woods.

Only when darkness fell and hunger became acute, did they go reluctantly home, praying that this miraculous weather would hold.

Miss Fogerty and Miss Watson, in company with the other adults in the neighbourhood, were less ecstatic about the weather conditions.

'What a blessing we invested in a freezer,' said Dorothy one evening. 'At least we don't have to go shopping every day. I feel really sorry for people struggling up and down the hill. Willie Marchant said it was like glass when he brought the post this morning.'

'You must be extra careful,' said Agnes solicitously, 'with that hip of yours. They do say that a pair of socks over one's shoes is a great help in slippery weather.'

'You did warn the children, I take it, about the dangers of making slides in the playground?'

'I certainly did.'

'I only ask, dear, because that wretched Todd boy was starting to make one near the lavatories. Just where it wouldn't be seen from the school windows.'

'He really is a *dreadful* child! I fear he will become a delinquent.'

'He's that already,' said her headmistress firmly. 'Mark my words, that boy will either end up in prison, or go on to win the VC if we have another war, which heaven forbid! He's that sort of character, I'm afraid.'

'I shall speak to him tomorrow morning,' said Agnes, looking almost ferocious. 'I can't say that I shall be sorry to see him leave the infants' class, except that he will be one step nearer your own class.'

'You need not worry about that,' replied Dorothy robustly. 'I've sorted out many a John Todd in my time, and I don't think I've lost my touch.'

Winnie Bailey was sorely troubled about Jenny, who seemed to take a long time to recovery from her tonsilitis.

Jenny fretted at the delay, and was impatient of the restrictions put upon her by Doctor Lovell and her employer.

'I don't like the idea of you going out in this weather,' she croaked to Winnie.

'I'm not going out anywhere,' said Winnie calmly. 'The baker, the milkman and the butcher are calling, bless them, and we are managing very well. We've enough provisions in the house to withstand a month's siege, thanks to you, Jenny, so just sit back and relax. You won't get better if you worry so.'

'As soon as she's over this,' John told Winnie privately, 'and the weather cheers up, I think we must get those tonsils out. She seems to get a severe bout of throat trouble every winter, and septic tonsils can lead to a number of complications.'

'Good heavens, John! What do you mean?'

'Oh, trouble with the retina at the back of the eye. Nodes on ligaments here and there. Sometimes infection spreads to the respiratory system. Best to have 'em out.'

'Of course, if that's the case. But surely it's rather a horrid affair, isn't it? Having one's tonsils out at Jenny's age?'

'Oh, she'll be all right,' John assured her. 'Not half as much blood these days. I'll get Pedder-Bennett to do it. He's getting a bit senile, but still manages a very neat little tonsilectomy.'

Winnie, despite having married a doctor, could not help feeling that the profession as a whole seemed remarkably off-hand about their patients' fears.

'Well, I shall say nothing of this to Jenny obviously,' she said. 'It's entirely your business. But I don't want her to have anything done until she is really fit. And if you think that there is anyone better – younger, I mean – perhaps more skilful –' she faltered to a halt.

'Than old PB? Oh, he'll be quite competent. As long as he remembers his spectacles, of course.'

It was that evening, when he had returned from surgery, that John read in the local paper about the court case.

It involved the two older men who had pleaded guilty to stealing cars and selling them. All three had appeared again before the Lulling magistrates who, in view of the number of charges and the large amount of money involved, had sent them to the Crown Court for sentence.

'I see they have given these chaps bail,' commented John to Ruth. 'I'd have put 'em inside.'

'Well, they might be there for months,' said his wife. 'Legal processes seem to take their time, and the gaols are full up, so one reads.'

'That's true. Evidently they've had to surrender their passports, so they can't nip over to their overseas customers, and their sureties will have to find a thousand apiece if they decamp. I wonder when the case will come up?'

'Will you have to appear?'

'I'm not sure. I can't be of any help with these two fellows. I shouldn't know them from Adam, and I've no idea what the cars were that they had in the barn. I could look up my records to establish the two dates when I called, but that's about all.'

'Well, that's one thing you need not bother about,' said Ruth comfortably.

John hoped that she was right. His earlier appearance at court, even in the witness box, had been an ordeal. How he would feel if he were ever to stand in the dock one day, he trembled to think.

During this snowy period, Nelly Piggott was one of the unfortunate people who had to slither down hill to Lulling and struggle up again at the end of the day. It was true that the council men had salted the paths, but nevertheless Nelly wished that there were still a stout hand rail at the edge of the pavement, as old photographs of the steep hill showed in times gone by.

On this particular morning, she was setting off early. Mrs Peters had telephoned the day before to say that she was smitten with the prevailing influenza, and was obliged to keep to her bed. Nelly was off to take charge.

'Don't you fret now,' she had said to her partner. 'Business is slack in this weather, and we can cope easily.'

'Fortunately there are no outside commitments this week,' said Mrs Peters, 'and with any luck I should be back by the weekend.'

Nelly's confidence had grown amazingly since starting work at The Fuchsia Bush, and the necessity of having to make decisions in her friend's absence daunted her not at all.

During the morning the snow took on a new intensity. There was a bitter east wind blowing, and the trunks of the trees lining the High Street were soon plastered with snow on the windward side. The few people who had braved the weather hurried by, bent against the onslaught. Windscreen wipers worked madly to try to cope with the flurries, and the window ledges of The Fuchsia Bush soon bore two or three inches of snow.

Just after twelve, Nelly hurried through from the kitchen. Only two tables were being used, she noticed, as she set a tray of freshly-filled rolls on the counter for the office workers and shop assistants who might be expected very soon.

The windows were steamy, but she noticed a figure studying the name above the shop. Soon the door bell gave its familiar tinkle, and a snow-plastered man appeared.

An icy blast accompanied him. He took off his snowy cap and shook it energetically.

'You get some cruel weather up here, Nelly,' he said.

To that lady's horror, she saw that it was her old paramour Charlie, once visiting oil man at Thrush Green, who had turned her away from his bed and board when he had discovered a more attractive partner.

'And what,' said Nelly, in a tone as frigid as the world
outside, 'do you think you're doing here?'

'You don't sound very welcoming,' replied Charlie, looking hurt.

'I don't feel it after the way you treated me,' responded
Nelly. She became conscious of the interest of the two
customers and lowered her voice. A quick glance had
shown her that this was not the spruce, confident Charlie
that she remembered. Snow apart, there was a seedy look
about his clothes, his shoes were cracked, he had no
gloves, and the canvas hold-all was soaked. Despite herself,
Nelly's heart was touched.

'Well, we can't talk here. Come through to the kitchen,
and I'll put your things to dry.'

What a blessing, she thought agitatedly, that Mrs Peters

was away! How to have explained this unwanted visitor would have been a real headache.

Charlie stood about looking awkward while Nelly hung up his outdoor clothes near the massive stoves. Gloria, Rosa and the two kitchen maids gazed at him open-mouthed.

'Just carry on,' said Nelly. 'I'll be with you in two shakes. Come through to the store room, Charlie.'

Here there was silence. Nelly pushed a pair of steps forward for Charlie's use, and sat herself in the only available chair.

'Well, Charlie, let's hear all about it. Where's Gladys?'

Gladys was her erstwhile friend who had usurped her place in Charlie's fickle attentions. It was Gladys who had caused Nelly's return to Albert a year or two ago. As can be imagined, there was not much love lost between the two ladies.

'She upped and left me. Went back to Norman, same as you went back to Albert. And how's that old misery?'

'You can keep a civil tongue in your head about my husband. He's no Romeo, but he's treated me right since I got back, and we've settled down pretty solidly. Don't think you've any chance of getting me back, Charlie, because I'm not coming. Times have changed, and I'm doing very well for myself here.'

'So I heard. That's partly why I came. Thought you might have a job for me.'

'A job?'

'The fact is things went from bad to worse for me. Gladys was always at me for more money. In the end I sold the business.'

'But what are you living on?'

'Social security mainly. I flogged the furniture, so that brought in a bit. Now I'm looking for a job.'

Nelly took another glance at the cracked shoes and the wet ends of his trouser legs. For a moment she weakened, for she was a kind-hearted woman. But reason held sway, and she spoke firmly.

'Look here, Charlie. There's nothing here for you in the way of work. Lulling's as badly hit as all the other towns, and no one's going to employ a chap your age with no real qualifications.'

Charlie looked down at his hands, twisting them this way and that in his embarrassment.

'Well, if that's the case, I'd better be off. I thought I'd make my way to Birmingham to see old Nobby.'

'Nobby?'

'Don't you remember Nobby Clark? Mary was his missus. They kept the ironmonger's on the corner. Nice pair.'

'Is he offering you a job?'

'Yes, in a way. When his dad died in Birmingham, he left Nobby his shop. A sweetshop, it is, with newspapers and postcards, and all that lark. He said he could do with some help if I needed work.'

'Sounds the best thing you could do,' said Nelly decidedly. 'Does he know you're coming?'

'No. I thought I'd see you first.'

And worm your way into my affections again as well as finding a job, thought Nelly.

'Before you set off,' said Nelly, 'you're going to have a good hot meal, and you can ring Nobby from here to say you are on your way. Where are you staying?'

'With them, I take it.'

'In that case, she'll need a bit of notice to make up a bed. You can use the phone in the office, and then go straight through to the restaurant. I've got to be getting back to my work. We're short-handed with the boss away ill.'

Charlie nodded his agreement, and Nelly ushered him into the office while she bustled back to the kitchen.

'That's an old acquaintance of mine,' she said to the girls. 'Down on his luck, and off to Birmingham this afternoon. Don't charge him, mind. Give the bill to me.'

Within the hour, just as The Fuchsia Bush's regular customers were beginning to struggle in, shivering with cold, Charlie had finished his meal.

He went through to the kitchen to fetch his clothes and to say goodbye to Nelly.

He was looking all the better for his meal, she noted approvingly. There was a hint of the old chirpy Charlie who had first stolen her heart, but she had no intention of succumbing to his charms again.

She was alone in the kitchen, and she took advantage of their privacy to enquire about the state of his immediate finances.

He held open his wallet. It contained two five pound notes.

'I've got a bit of loose change,' he said, rattling a trouser pocket.

'That won't get you far,' said Nelly, opening her handbag. 'Here, take these two fivers. It'll go towards the fare. The bus to Oxford goes in ten minutes, and you'll have to get a train or bus on to Birmingham from there.'

He put them with the other two notes in his wallet, and muttered his thanks, so brokenly, that Nelly looked at him in surprise. To her amazement she saw tears in his eyes for the first time.

Much embarrassed, she hastened across the kitchen to the dresser where the remaining ham and tongue rolls lay in the wooden tray.

She thrust two into a paper bag and held out the package.

'Put those in your pocket, Charlie. It'll save you buying, and you can eat them on the journey.'

'You're one in a thousand, Nelly. I won't forget all you've done today.'

'That's all right. I'm glad to help, but take note, Charlie! It's the last time. Don't come trying your luck again. I hope you get on all right with the Clarks. Don't write, nor telephone. It's the end between us now, Charlie, and best that way.'

He bent suddenly and kissed her cheek.

'That's my old love,' he said warmly. 'Don't worry. I won't embarrass you.'

'If you want to get that bus,' replied Nelly, more shaken than she cared to admit, 'you'd best get outside to the bus stop. Thank the Lord the snow's stopped.'

She watched him cross the restaurant, humping his hold-all, and saw the door close. Much as she would have liked to see him board the bus, and perhaps give him a final wave, she was too upset to leave the haven of the kitchen.

Gloria came in balancing a tray on one hip.

'Your friend nearly missed the bus,' she said brightly. 'Got out there just in time.'

'Good,' replied Nelly huskily. She blew her nose energetically.

'Don't you go getting the flu now,' said Gloria, 'or we'll have to shut up shop.'

She spoke with unaccustomed gentleness, but forbore to make any more enquiries.

Later, she said to Rosa: 'The poor old duck was crying when that chap went away. I bet she was sweet on him once, though what anyone could see in an old fellow like that, beats me.'

'One foot in the grave,' agreed Rosa. 'Must be nearer fifty than forty, poor old thing, *and* going bald.'

'He ate pretty hearty though,' replied Gloria. 'Steak and kidney pie, mashed spud, broad beans, and then the Bakewell tart.'

'Well, she said he was down on his luck,' Rosa reminded her. 'Maybe he didn't have no breakfast. Look out, she's coming back.'

The two girls began to stack plates busily by the sink.

Nelly, now in command of herself, bustled into the room.

'Now, Rosa, you can cut the iced slab into squares ready for the tea tables, and there's some fresh shortbread to put out, Gloria. Look lively now, there's plenty to do.'

The two girls exchanged glances. It was quite clear that things were back to normal.

It was bitterly cold after dark. The wind had dropped, and the snow had not returned, but it was obvious that there would be a hard frost as the skies were clear.

At Thrush Green, Nelly was content to sit alone by the fire and ruminate. She felt completely exhausted by this encounter, and still worried by the pathetic shabbiness of the once dapper Charlie.

A pile of mending waited on the side table and the washing up remained on the draining board, but for the moment these jobs must wait, thought Nelly. Her head ached with thinking, her legs were heavy with standing all day, and her eyes were still sore from secret weeping.

To her surprise, Albert came in at nine o'clock, well before closing time.

'Perishing cold next door,' he told her. 'Got the fire smoking something awful. You're better off in here.'

He bent towards the fire, rubbing his hands.

Nelly stirred herself.

'I'll just get the dishes washed, Albert, and make us a cup of tea.'

'Good idea,' said Albert. 'Did I tell you Miss Harmer give me a pot of jam for you? It's in the cupboard.'

'Thank her, won't you?' Not that we shall ever eat it, she thought privately, remembering 'Dotty's Collywobbles', a common Thrush Green complaint.

'She's not a bad old trout,' went on Albert, now seating himself by the blaze while Nelly tackled the dishes. 'She's promised me a sitting of duck eggs this spring. She's got two broody hens already.'

'But we've nowhere to keep ducks, Albert!'

'I can keep 'em down her place, she says. I'll enjoy that. And I'm to take both the goats to be mated when the time comes. Remind me to get some bran sometime this week. We're getting short down there.'

Nelly thought how much easier it was to live with Albert when he had animals to look after. It seemed to sweeten him somehow.

She put the last plate on the rack and filled the kettle.

'I'll take mine up to bed,' she said.

'Why? You ain't getting flu, are you?'

'No, just bone tired. There's a lot to do with Mrs Peters away.'

'Ah! There must be. Here, you go on up, and I'll bring you a cup in bed. How's that?'

Nelly could hardly believe her ears. She could not remember such a gesture from Albert in all their time together. In her present emotional state, it was too much, and the tears began to flow.

'Here, 'ere, 'ere!' said Albert, much alarmed. 'You've got something coming, my girl. Get you up to bed and wrap up warm.'

Weeping noisily, Nelly obeyed.

She woke some hours later. The bedroom clock said half past three, and the room was bright with moonlight.

She got out of bed and went to the window. Her back room looked across the fields towards Lulling Woods. The larger room, where Albert now snored rhythmically, looked towards Thrush Green.

The whole world was white. The moonlight, reflected from the snowy fields, was intensified. In the garden of The Two Pheasants next door, the small cherry tree cast a circular tracery of shadows on the white lawn.

It was a tree which gave Nelly joy all through the year, from its first tiny leaves, its dangling white flowers, its scarlet fruit so quickly ravished by the birds, and then its final blaze of gold in autumn which it dropped, like a bright skirt, to the ground in November.

But tonight this rare beauty was a bonus. She gazed entranced at the tree's shadow. It looked like fine black lace cast around the foot of the trunk. Snow streaked the fragile branches, and lay like cake icing along the garden hedge. It was a magical night, calm and still, and Nelly, after her stormy day, drew strength from its tranquillity.

She shivered and padded back to bed, content to lie and watch the moonbeams moving across the ceiling.

She hoped that Charlie was somewhere safely asleep, and that he would settle with the Clarks and find a useful job.

Poor old Charlie! It would have been so easy to give way and to say: 'Come back, if things don't work out for you.' But it would never have done, she told herself.

The time with Charlie was firmly in the past, and she did not want to see him again. She was now a settled woman, with a good responsible job and money in the bank.

She thought of Albert, and his unexpected kindness that evening. If only he could always be as thoughtful! Perhaps, it occurred to her, he would be nicer if he had more interests, more animals, a better home. A lot of his moodiness came from too much drinking, she knew. Perhaps, one day, they could afford to move to a more cheerful house, well away from the pub, where Albert could keep ducks and hens, and a dog maybe, and be a happy man.

Who knows? He might even make a habit of bringing his wife a cup of tea in bed!

But at this flight of fancy Nelly's imagination baulked. With a sigh, she closed her eyes against the moonshine, and fell asleep again.

18   A Hint of Spring

AT LULLING VICARAGE Charles and Dimity were congratulating themselves on the gradual improvement in their chilblains.

'I'm quite sure it's the calcium tablets,' said Dimity, beating eggs energetically. 'I don't care what people say. We started to get better as soon as we began to take them.'

'Egg custard for lunch?' asked Charles, watching his wife's efforts.

'Yes, dear, and bottled plums.'

Their little cat Tabitha appeared from nowhere, and gazed up expectantly at Dimity.

'Isn't she clever?' cried her mistress. 'As soon as she hears me whisking up something she comes for her egg and milk.'

She poured a little of the mixture into a saucer and put it on the floor. The cat licked delicately at this bounty.

'Dear thing,' said Dimity indulgently. 'So good for her, all those lovely vitamins.'

The telephone rang in Charles's study, and he hastened away to answer it.

By the time he returned, the egg custard was in a slow oven, and the cat's saucer was immaculately clean.

'Trouble?' asked Dimity, looking at his perplexed expression.

'No, not really, although I can see I shall have to make a

hospital visit very soon. That was Mrs Thurgood. You know she's president of the Lulling Operatic Society, and the wardrobe mistress, whose name I didn't catch unfortunately, has some lung trouble and will have to have an operation which will put her out of action. Mrs Thurgood wanted to know if I knew of anyone who could help.'

'When is the performance?'

'Don't they take the Corn Exchange for a week? Sometime in March or April, I think she said.'

Charles appeared somewhat distracted. Dimity spoke reassuringly.

'Oh, we'll think of someone, I'm sure. Can't her daughter Janet help?'

'Not with a young child.'

'We'll ask all our friends,' said Dimity, 'and something will turn up, you'll see. The only thing is, that our friends, like us, don't have much to do with the theatrical world. But don't worry, Charles, dear. Let's have our coffee early before you go down to the greenhouse.'

The time for Kit and Connie's return had almost arrived, and Vi found herself feeling quite sad about leaving her new friend.

Dotty too had found Vi's stay very stimulating. She had been able to indulge her love of television much more readily, for Vi was as much an addict, particularly of American serials, as Dotty was herself.

Kit and Connie were somewhat scornful of most of the television programmes, so that Dotty did not always see as many programmes as she would have liked.

She said as much to Vi, as they sat amicably gazing at the screen.

'Why don't you have a little set of your own in your bedroom?' suggested Vi. 'You're up there quite a bit, and there are often very good programmes late at night, when you know you are often wakeful.'

'I'll think about it,' said Dotty, watching a close embrace

in vivid technicolor. 'I really don't care for this modern way of kissing, do you, Vi? I mean, it goes on so long, and must be very unhygienic. When I was a girl, one was kissed on the cheek or forehead by relatives and close friends. I can't recall being kissed on the mouth, and certainly not *being eaten* like that!'

Dotty surveyed the couple with some distaste.

'Modern custom, I suppose,' said Vi, busily counting stitches on her knitting needle.

'Something to do with the Common Market, perhaps,' mused Dotty. '"Common" being the operative word. You know, even quite nice men, like dear Kit, have taken to this continental way of kissing on both cheeks! I find it excessive. One tends to bump noses too. I really prefer to be kissed in the English manner.'

'Well, I'm sure Miss Bembridge will give you one of those when she comes,' said Vi. 'You remember she's coming to have tea with you while I call to see Jane and Bill?'

'Yes, yes, of course. Have you put out my sloe jelly?'

'I thought she might prefer the heather honey,' said Vi diplomatically. 'If you recall, you gave her a pot of the sloe jelly last time she came.'

'Quite right. Yes, I'm sure the honey will be better. After all, she's probably been tucking into my sloe jelly all the week.'

Vi forbore to comment on this hopeful remark, but directed Dotty's attention to the screen.

'Oh look! The Indians are massing on the horizon!'

'Good,' replied Dotty. 'Now we should get some good clean fun. Their horses always look in splendid condition, don't they?'

Jane and Bill Cartwright were sorry to be saying goodbye to Vi Ellis. Kit and Connie were due home at the weekend, and Vi was being fetched on the Sunday afternoon.

Naturally enough, the conversation turned to the vagaries of old people.

'I must say I've found Miss Harmer much easier than I
first thought,' confessed Vi. 'She's so absolutely honest –
embarrassingly so at times, but at least you know where
you are with her.'

'Takes after her old dad in that,' Jane told her. 'Matron
at the hospital had some hair-raising tales about him. He
was always very punctilious about visiting any of his boys
in hospital, but evidently the patients were in a fine state of
nerves when the visit was over.'

'We had a headmaster like that when I was a boy in
Yorkshire,' observed Bill. 'I believe he enjoyed caning us.
Youngsters are lucky these days.'

'Now tell me about this job,' said Vi. 'Would it be the
sort of thing that Ted and I might take on later?'

Jane looked thoughtful.

'You've got to have an enormous amount of tact – and
sympathy. I must say that at times I've wondered if we're
doing the right thing. They can be very awkward indeed,
and over such trifles.'

She went on to describe the umbrage taken over Monty's
deplorable sanitary habits, the petty upsets over neighbours'
noises, and Carlotta Jermyn's irritating visits at the wrong
times.

'It all sounds so trivial, I know,' she went on, 'but that's
life here, and we have to remind ourselves how different it
all is from the life they've had before. Gradually, *very*
gradually, I think they are coming to terms with things
here at Thrush Green, and becoming *integrated*, I think is
the word.'

'It's a worthwhile job,' Vi said comfortingly. 'This fortnight with dear old Dotty has been quite hard work, but
I've thoroughly enjoyed it, and I really would like to try
my hand at something like this one day.'

'Well, if ever you do think seriously about it,' said Bill,
'come and stay for a few days, both of you, and see what it
involves. Which reminds me, I must be off to sand the
paths before they freeze.'

When Vi had made her farewells, Bill turned to his wife. 'I wonder if she means it?'

'Vi always meant what she said. I think they'd make a good pair of wardens, and heaven alone knows a great many are needed with so many in their seventies and eighties these days.'

The telephone rang and she walked quite briskly, and without her stick, to answer it.

Almost her old self, thought Bill with relief, setting about his sanding.

The bitter spell of weather abated slightly. The icicles fringing the Cotswold roof tiles and thatch grew shorter. In the middle of the day the puddles, once iron-hard, melted a little, allowing the ice to float above muddy water.

The winter days were beginning to lengthen. Now afternoon tea was enjoyed before the curtains were drawn at dusk, Betty Bell arrived in the light to sweep the school when the children had gone home, and Nelly Piggott found herself mounting the hill, on a good day, whilst the wintry sunset still glowed in the west.

The bulbs had pushed stubby noses through the soil, and the forsythia was in bud. Brave snowdrops were beginning to flower under sheltered hedges, and the signs of spring to come heartened everybody.

The invalids began to emerge, pale but hopeful. Tom Hardy, swathed in a woolly scarf over his overcoat, accompanied Polly and Johnny Enderby on a short stroll across the green. Young George Curdle, and other chickenpox victims, were allowed out for half an hour in the middle of the day to have a breath of fresh air, and very heady stuff they found it after being cooped up.

Even Edward Young, still suffering with shingles, felt more hopeful of recovery as he pottered about the garden, noting the first small leaves of the honeysuckle, and the buds on the lilac bushes getting plumper.

He was now much relieved to have made up the silly quarrel with John. Secretly, he knew that it was one cause of the tension which had helped to produce this most maddening and tormenting complaint of his. The Cirencester worry, annoying though it was, was all part and parcel of his professional life, and he had coped with far worse problems with officialdom in his time. He could overcome this one, he felt sure. But the rare upset with a relative, and one whom he respected as much as John, was something different. He did not mind admitting that it had shaken him.

Another reason for its particular annoyance was the fact that he had a strong feeling that John was right about the steps. Something extra in the way of safety must be done. He had been turning this over in his mind ever since Jane's unfortunate accident, and much as he disliked altering the look of the shallow flight of steps which led the eye gently upward to the line of the building as a whole, he was forced to admit to himself that a central hand rail would be an added precaution.

He felt pretty sure that this extra expense would be met willingly by the trustees, all of whom had been severely shocked by the fact that the youngest and most agile of the inhabitants had been the first to succumb to this unnoticed hazard. Not a word of complaint, with the exception of John's caustic comment, had been levelled at Edward's design by the trustees, which made him all the more determined to put the matter right as quickly as he could. Since making this decision he had felt a lot better.

The occasional card-playing evenings had been resumed, and it was during one of these sessions that Edward made his suggestion.

'A client of mine has a house on the Pembrokeshire coast and has offered it to me if I'd like to have it for a fortnight's holiday in the summer. He's going abroad evidently.'

'Lovely!' cried Ruth. 'And will you go?'

'I think so. Joan and I like the idea, and there's a wonderful beach nearby. We wondered if you would like to join us when the children break up. Perhaps the last week in July and the first in August. What d'you think?'

'Will the owner be agreeable?'

'I'm sure he will. He said: "Bring any friends", and as the house has six bedrooms it seems a great pity to have the place half empty.'

Ruth looked at John. Here, if anything further were needed, was another gesture of Edward's goodwill. The two men's estrangement had worried Ruth far more than it had her more self-reliant sister, and she was anxious to restore the harmony which had always existed until this little rift between the two husbands.

'Well?' asked John of his wife.

'I'd love to go. We haven't been that way for years, and it all sounds perfect. If you really want us,' she added diffidently.

'Then that's settled,' said Edward, rubbing his hands together briskly, and then giving a yelp of pain.

John gave him a quick anxious glance.

'Where did that hurt?'

'One of those dam' scabs caught on my shirt.'

'That all? You'll live!' said his brother-in-law callously. 'Right then, Edward. Pembrokeshire it is, and very many thanks for asking us.'

The telephone call that Jane Cartwright answered was from Charles Henstock who explained that he had had a call from Mrs Thurgood.

Before he could proceed further Jane had said agitatedly: 'Oh, heavens! Mrs Thurgood! What's wrong?'

Of all the people who had interviewed them the redoubtable Mrs Thurgood had seemed to Jane, and to her husband too, the most formidable. Luckily, she had not visited the old people's homes very often, but Jane had felt remarkably apprehensive when she had, expecting some trenchant criticism.

Charles laughed.

'She is rather awe-inspiring, I admit, but this is about a quite different job from your own.'

He explained about the operatic society's problem, and the discussion he and Dimity had had about a temporary replacement for the stricken wardrobe mistress.

'And we came to the conclusion that the only person we knew who had any connection with theatre work was Carlotta Jermyn. Do you think you could sound her out?'

'I will, of course. Shall I tell her to get in touch with you?'

'I think it would be best if she telephoned Mrs Thurgood if she wants to know more.'

'Much the best idea,' said Jane, sounding so relieved that Charles laughed again.

'Well, Jane, I think the two ladies can face each other quite successfully, and we can fade into the background.'

'It certainly suits me to be there,' replied Jane. 'I'll call on her this evening, or at any rate tomorrow. Frankly, I'd like to see her happily occupied. She's the one who is taking longer to settle in than all the others.'

'If she can't settle down with you and Bill as guardian angels, then it's a pity,' said Charles firmly. 'We could do with more couples like you. The trust is always on the look-out, you know.'

Jane had half a mind to mention Vi Ellis's hopes, but decided that it was too early to confide even in such a discreet person as Charles Henstock.

'I'll do what I can,' she promised, and put down the receiver.

Kit and Connie had come back from Venice looking years younger and full of stories of that lovely city.

They had brought Dotty some lace mats from Burano and a pretty pale pink glass cream jug from Murano for Vi.

'I really think I must visit Venice again before I get too old,' said Dotty. 'I rather like the sound of that train that goes from Victoria. It looks very well equipped, and I always enjoyed train travel when I went abroad with Father. We always talked of going on the Trans-Siberian railway, but the trip would have taken up rather a lot of time in the summer holidays, and in any case we were obliged to visit my great-aunts in Broadstairs during August, which made things more awkward.'

'Well, we must think about a holiday for you,' said Connie diplomatically. 'Meanwhile, tell us how the workmen have been getting on.'

'Splendidly, splendidly!' cried Dotty. 'All should be finished by next month.'

'They've been saying that since before Christmas,' observed Kit, 'but let's go and have a look round.'

They left the room, and Dotty looked across at Vi.

'You know, they won't want me to go on that train –

the Orient Express, isn't it? I can see that they think it will be too much for me. Perhaps you would think of accompanying me, Vi? I know they would be quite happy about me if you were going to be there. We have got on so well, haven't we?'

'We have indeed,' said Vi warmly. 'I've enjoyed every minute of my stay here.'

She did not respond to Dotty's tentative invitation, much as she appreciated her trust. A fortnight in Dotty's own home, with a certain amount of support from Betty Bell, Albert Piggott and innumerable kind friends, was one thing. A trip on the Orient Express, and the hazards of the waterways of Venice was another, and resourceful though she was, even Vi's stout heart quailed at the thought.

Much later, when she was safely back in her own home, Vi often thought of Dotty and her proposed holiday. Somehow, she could not imagine Dotty setting off for foreign parts even if Connie and Kit accompanied her, but it was very comforting to think that she had been invited to share the adventures of that indomitable old lady, even if they had come to naught.

As well as the snowdrops, budding shrubs, and melting puddles, there were other signs of spring at Lulling and Thrush Green.

The most superior clothes shop in the High Street had removed the thermal underwear, woolly hats, scarves, and padded jackets from the window, and had a tasteful display of frilly blouses, lightweight suits and pale handbags. A large placard adorned with daffodils exhorted the passerby to GREET THE SPRING, which though perhaps a trifle premature, was certainly hopeful.

At The Two Pheasants at Thrush Green, Mr Jones was cosseting his geranium cuttings and planting trays of lobelia and dwarf marigolds ready for bedding out.

He enthused about his seedlings to Albert, who seemed

to have sunk back into his morose ways now that there was less to do at Dotty Harmer's.

'Seen old Perce?' Albert enquired. 'Hasn't been bad, has 'e? Seems a long time since I bumped into him.'

'I think he's courting again,' said the landlord, twirling a snowy cloth inside a glass.

'More fool him,' grunted Albert. 'Who's he after this time?'

'One of the Cooke girls, I heard.'

'He must be off his onion,' said Albert flatly. 'Them Cooke girls is no better than they ought to be, and their old mum puts 'em up to all manner of mischief.'

'Well, Percy's not a bad catch. Got a farm and a house, and a bit put by I've no doubt.'

'That's as maybe, but them Cookes are proper bad lots. In any case, old Perce is still married.'

'And when did that stop a man running after others?' said Mr Jones, with unwonted cynicism.

'That's true,' agreed Albert gloomily.

He finished his glass and pushed it across the counter.

'Well, I suppose it's the spring,' he said. 'But I should have thought old Perce would have had enough of women by now.'

'Some,' replied the landlord, 'never learn!'

19 Various Surprises

WITH THE END OF February in sight, the countryside around Lulling grew greener. A mild westerly wind held sway, aconites and snowdrops adorned the cottage gardens, the chickenpox epidemic abated, and the village school had its usual quota of pupils.

The three teachers rejoiced as this gentle weather allowed the children to play outside, where they ran off their high spirits and returned to the classrooms slightly more ready for work than in the bleak weeks before, which had kept them confined indoors.

Little Miss Fogerty had discarded the silk scarf which had protected her neck throughout the winter, although she prudently retained her thermal underwear and some fine woollen stockings which Dorothy had given her for Christmas. Dorothy herself, despite her more amply padded figure, felt the cold, and was still ringing the changes with her tweed suits, twin sets and hand-knitted jumpers.

She was engaged in darning the sleeve of one of the latter garments when the telephone rang one evening.

'Drat the thing,' she exclaimed, heaving herself from the armchair, and sticking the needle in the jumper sleeve. 'Now who can that be?'

Dorothy always said this when either the telephone or the front door bell rang, and secretly Agnes found it slightly irritating. After all, no one could know until the bell was answered, could they? However, she had never voiced her annoyance. It might upset Dorothy, and she herself, no doubt, had equally irritating little ways.

She held herself in readiness to go to the telephone if the call should be for her, but she heard Dorothy saying: 'But how kind, Ray! When did you say?'

Agnes relaxed, and studied the crossword. It seemed harder than ever today, and obviously was compiled by someone who knew far more about Charles Dickens's characters than Miss Fogerty did. She wondered about Ray. Very rarely did Dorothy's tone sound so affectionate towards her brother, although Agnes knew that there was a strong bond between the two, but made somewhat tenuous when Kathleen was involved. Perhaps Dorothy was subconsciously jealous? No doubt Freud would have made something of it, but whether his conclusions would be correct little Miss Fogerty had her doubts. Such over-emphasis on *sex*!

Dorothy returned looking pleased.

'That was Ray. They are going to spend a weekend with their Dorset friends, and want us to lunch with them at The Fleece on the Saturday, on their way down.'

'How very kind!'

'He said they had decided to break their journey there as Harrison can be put up in the stables, and have a peaceful lunch and a rest. Really, one sometimes wonders if they are talking about a young child!'

'He is one to them,' replied Agnes percipiently.

'In that case, he and John Todd would have a lot in common,' retorted Dorothy, resuming her darning.

At the old people's homes, Jane Cartwright had cause to be hopeful about the outcome of her visit to Carlotta Jermyn.

It had not been an easy encounter, for Carlotta had become rather haughty at the outset, pointing out that an actress was in quite a different class from a wardrobe mistress, and that the exceptional qualities needed to create a character were definitely more rarified than such practical matters as theatrical costume, which were the concern of lesser minds.

'I think really,' said Jane, 'that they need someone more in the way of a *consultant*. Someone who would know the best costumiers and wig-makers to approach, or perhaps someone who could simply give a hand in adapting costumes.'

Carlotta considered this.

'Well, of course, I have had some experience in these matters when I gave some advice to amateur companies now and again. But I really don't know what to say. I know that the Lulling Operatic people have quite a good name for their little efforts,' she added graciously, 'and I believe they give quite a useful sum to local charities.'

'They do indeed,' Jane assured her.

'And of course I should not want a fee,' went on Carlotta. 'And if they employed a professional it might cost them a tidy sum.'

Jane thought that Carlotta was beginning to weaken, and made a swift move.

'Why don't you ring Mrs Thurgood and see what is involved? You need not commit yourself today. But I know she would appreciate any ideas you have. You might think of someone else that they could approach.'

At this Carlotta's face took on a somewhat obstinate expression.

'I shall ring her as soon as I've had my gin and tonic,' she told Jane firmly. 'This is a Worthy Cause!'

Jane would have loved dearly to hear the conversation between the two autocratic ladies later that morning. No doubt each was a model of frigid politeness. Carlotta would make it quite clear that such an undertaking would not do justice to her true worth, but that if she could assist lesser mortals in the theatrical sphere then she felt it her duty to do so.

Mrs Thurgood would be equally high-handed, gracious in her appreciation of Carlotta's feelings, but not in any way servile in her attitude.

But the outcome was a happy one. Carlotta agreed to give the Lulling Operatic Society the benefit of her expertize, and also consented to help with such lowly but practical matters as altering costumes, should the need arise.

'One must do what one can in this world,' she told Jane. '"We pass this way but once," as someone said.'

On repeating this to Bill his comment was typical.

'"Pass" is about right! Since she's got interested in this lark, she's too busy to bob into our other old dears and annoy them.'

'That's true. Let's hope the Lulling Operatic Society makes her a permanent member.'

It was about this time that Jenny was admitted to Lulling Cottage Hospital for her tonsils operation.

The great man, Mr Pedder-Bennett, came down from the county town once a week to perform straightforward operations at the local hospital.

Tuesday was his day, and the staff of the hospital was extra alert. Castors on the beds were all turned to the exact angle, throughout the wards. Sheets were tucked in so securely that patients were unable to bend their toes. Hair was brushed, dentures put in, noses wiped, pyjamas buttoned and nightgowns adjusted for modesty.

Jenny was obliged to go in on the Monday evening, so that she could be prepared for Mr Pedder-Bennett's ministrations the next morning.

It was one of the longest evenings of her life. She had never before been into a hospital. Her foster parents had slipped away in the comforting familiarity of their own home, some years earlier.

She was fascinated by the variety of women about her, and full of admiration for the bustling nurses. The speed with which they raced from bed to bed, yanking patients upright, pummelling pillows, whisking vases, glasses, pens, spectacles, fruit, talcum powder and scent from bedside tables and putting them briskly below into cupboards which half the patients were unable to reach, fairly took Jenny's breath away.

What energy these girls had! And how tired the patients looked amidst all this activity!

She was allowed a light supper consisting of a bowl of some milky white substance which might have been anything from hot blancmange to thin porridge. It reminded Jenny of her orphanage breakfasts, and like them could have done with a spoonful of sugar. This repast was served at six-thirty which Jenny found surprising as it was called supper.

'Last meal for you, love,' the nurse said cheerfully. 'No breakfast before ops.'

Jenny cleared her bowl obediently, and lay back on the

pillows. It was still only seven o'clock, and she wondered
how Mrs Bailey was managing.

A few minutes later, the nurse came to collect her tray.

'Mrs Bailey's just rung up. Sent her love, and says she'll
be thinking of you. Probably pop in and see you tomorrow
evening if you feel all right.'

'Oh, I shall!' Jenny assured her.

'Well, we'll have to see, won't we?' said the nurse
cryptically. 'Shall we have a bit of shut-eye now?'

Jenny slid down the bed, and closed her eyes, although
sleep, she felt sure, would be impossible.

Dear Mrs Bailey, she thought gratefully! How she longed
to be back with her at Thrush Green!

The pillow was warm against her cheek, the porridge
warm in her stomach.

Jenny was asleep in five minutes.

It was while Mr Pedder-Bennett was at his delicate work
the next morning, that Jane Cartwright went the rounds of
the old people's homes and found all was well.

Polly and Tom were sitting in their porch enjoying the
sunshine. Johnny Enderby was digging in Ella's garden
across the road. Mrs Bates was making herself an apple
dumpling. Miss Fuller was preparing to walk across to the
school for coffee in the staffroom, and then an hour's
reading practice with the slow readers. The Crosses were
changing their bedlinen with the radio on full blast. Jack
and Sybil Angell were away for a few days with friends.
Carlotta was at a sewing session with the other ladies
connected with the Operatic Society, and her husband Eric
was reading the newspaper, as best he could, with Monty
on his lap impeding his view.

After a few words with each, Jane stood at the end of
the building and looked across Thrush Green. The sky was
of that soft tender blue which only early spring can bring.
A hazel bush nearby shook its yellow catkins, the golden
dust powdering some young dandelion leaves below.

Somewhere a lark was singing, and a blackbird winged by, its orange bill carrying a whiskery bundle of dried grass for its nest building.

A beautiful brown and grey snail climbed slowly up the dry stone wall, leaving a glistening trail, and in the shelter of one sunny crevice Jane could see half a dozen ladybirds emerging from hibernation to enjoy this early sunshine.

Nathaniel Patten's benign countenance caught the sun's rays, and pink tipped daisies were already clustered about the plinth.

Jane breathed a sigh of delight. How good it was to be here, to see their charges beginning to enjoy their new surroundings, and, best of all, to be able to move again, perhaps not quite so nimbly as she had when she first arrived, but certainly with more confidence and with less pain as the weeks went by.

A figure loomed up beside her. It was Percy Hodge.

'Oh, hello, uncle,' said Jane. 'And how are things with you?'

'Could be worse,' said Percy cautiously.

'I was going to make a cup of coffee,' said Jane. 'Will you join me?'

'Just off over the road,' responded Percy, nodding towards The Two Pheasants. 'Got to have a word with Albert.'

'Then I won't hold you up,' said his niece, watching him set off, and went back through the dewy morning to her elevenses.

But through the kitchen window she noticed the young Cooke girl pedalling down the road from Nidden.

She got off at The Two Pheasants, propped her bicycle against the wall, and vanished inside.

It certainly looked, thought Jane, stirring her cup, as if Uncle Percy was in the throes of love, yet again.

At Lulling Cottage Hospital, Jenny's recovery was steady, and she was promised a return home within a few days.

'Old P-B', as John Lovell called him, had done his usual

neat surgery, and apart from an irritating little lump which Jenny imagined was a husk from the morning porridge, all was well. Mr Pedder-Bennett, on examining his handiwork, was quite hurt to discover that the irritation was caused by a minute knot in his exquisite needlework, and assured his patient that it was only a matter of hours and then all would be in perfect condition. And so, to give 'old P-B' his due, it certainly was.

When Winnie returned from a visit to Jenny one evening, she was slightly alarmed to see a light on in her sitting room. Could she have forgotten to switch it off? Should she go into the Hursts and ask Frank to accompany her into the house, in case burglars had broken in? As long as they were free from stocking masks over their faces – which Winnie found unendurable – she felt that she could probably cope alone.

But while she stood at the gate, with all these thoughts whirling in her head, the front door opened, and there was her nephew, Richard.

'Oh, what a relief!' cried Winnie. 'I thought you were a burglar!'

'Not quite. I did try to ring you this afternoon,' he said, helping his aunt to take off her coat.

'I must have been in the greenhouse.'

'I had the key you gave me years ago. So here I am.'

'And very nice too,' said Winnie. 'Get yourself a drink, and me too, dear boy, and tell me what brings you here.'

There was silence for a time as Richard filled two glasses and carried them carefully across the room. It gave Winnie time to wonder if Richard were the forerunner of the rest of his family, and if so, was the spare bed made up for him? It usually stood in readiness for just such an emergency, and she was sure that Jenny would have left everything in apple pie order. But more than one person she simply could not accommodate.

She need not have worried.

'I'm afraid I'm homeless, Aunt Win.'

'Homeless?'

'Ever since I came back from China.'

'What happened?'

'When I arrived back I found that Roger had left his wife and moved in with Fenella.'

'What do you mean? Are they living together as man and wife? I thought you said they were cousins, or somehow related.'

'So they are. But very distant cousins.' Richard sounded amused at Winnie's reaction, which made her cross, as well as shocked.

'But what's to be done, Richard? After all, you and Fenella are properly married —'

'So's Roger. The biggest snag of all is that the flat is Fenella's, and she can have who she likes there. At the moment she likes to have Roger, and not me.'

'But what about your baby?'

'That will have to be decided when we get a divorce.'

It all sounded drearily wretched to Winnie, and she turned to more practical things.

'So where have you been staying all this time?'

'With an old school friend. He has a service flat near Marble Arch, but it's much too small for the two of us. I moved into some digs in Notting Hill Gate last week, but there's such a racket going on from a pub next door, I felt I couldn't stand it any longer, and fled down here.'

'But what are your plans, Richard? For the immediate future, I mean? Of course, I can put you up for a day or two, and should be pleased to have you here, but things are a trifle worrying for me too at the moment.'

She explained about Jenny. To her surprise, Richard looked genuinely concerned.

'Poor old Jenny! So she can't make those delicious cheese scones at the moment.'

What a pity, thought Winnie, that he had not told Jenny how delicious they were at the time. But in any case, she would repeat this belated compliment to the invalid.

'The thing is,' he went on, 'I'm having to get my notes together for another tour next month, and I simply can't work in those digs.'

'Well, I suggest that you settle in here for a few days, and we'll look around for quiet lodgings nearby until you set off on your travels again. That is, if you want to be in Thrush Green.'

'There's nothing I'd like more. I can work here, I know.'

Winnie roused herself.

'Well, that's settled. I'm just going to fill a hot water bottle for the spare bed, Richard, and you can take it up and unpack.'

Richard crossed the room and gave her a kiss.

'You are an angel. I can't thank you enough.'

'I'll be glad of your company,' she told him, much touched by this rare display of feeling. 'And while you're upstairs, I will get us some supper.'

'Lovely! I must admit I'm famished.'

'It won't be up to Jenny's standards,' she warned him. 'Scrambled eggs or sardines on toast, and some rather ancient cheese.'

'Delicious!' said Richard, making for the stairs. 'I'll come down for the bottle in two ticks. And, by the way, I brought a pork pie with me, in case I had to pitch camp under a hedge, so we'll add that to the supper table.'

Waiting for the kettle to boil, Winnie pondered on Richard's melancholy news. What a muddle some people seemed to make of their lives! And what would the future hold for this particular four?

More to the point, what would happen to that poor young baby and the unseen, but exuberant, Timothy? Would these marital troubles sort themselves out eventually? At times Richard, despite his brilliant brain, seemed absolutely helpless.

Nevertheless, thought Winnie, he had brought a pork pie with him. One must be thankful for small mercies.

20   Richard's Affairs

A WEEK OR TWO later, on a March day of wind and
sunshine, Dotty Harmer, Connie and Kit celebrated
the departure of the workmen with a particularly
festive lunch.

They broached a bottle of claret from Kit's store, although Dotty had invited them to take their pick of her
own home-brewed variety.

'I really can recommend the parsnip,' she assured them,
'and the wheat and raisin is quite heady stuff.'

'I think Kit particularly wants to try his claret,' said
Connie. 'So let's keep yours for another time.'

'We ought to pour a libation to the household gods,'
Kit said. 'Just to make sure they look after us after all
we've been through.'

'Don't you have to do something dreadful to a chicken
or pigeon, dear, if you make libations?' said Dotty becoming agitated. 'We really can't have anything like that here!'

'You're thinking of foretelling things, Dotty,' said Kit.
'The Greeks used to study the entrails of their sacrifice, if I
remember aright.'

'It all sounds most unpleasant and messy,' replied Dotty,
'and I hope you won't speak of such things when the hens
are present. They understand far more than you give them
credit for, you know.'

Kit held up his glass.

'I promise you that, Dotty. And now, here's to the workmen!'

'And may they never return!' added Connie.

Dotty raised her glass carefully.

'To all of us in this house,' said Dotty.

'I'm not quite sure,' said Connie, 'what we are toasting!'

'Just drink, my dear,' replied her husband, 'and be thankful.'

The news of Richard's arrival had soon reached everyone in Thrush Green. The reasons for his visit were extraordinarily varied.

The old people at the homes were as intrigued as the other residents. Mrs Bates thought he might have been ill, and advised by his doctor to have country air. Miss Fuller had heard that he was studying for an examination. The Jermyns were nearer the mark with the correct guess that Richard's marriage was in jeopardy.

Nelly Piggott told Albert that the rumour going round The Fuchsia Bush was that Richard had lost his job and was now penniless. Winnie Bailey was supporting him until he found work.

Albert, who had spent the day at Dotty's refurbishing the coops ready for broody hens and was in a more mellow frame of mind than usual, contented himself with the rejoinder: 'More fool Mrs Bailey!'

Conjecture was rife in Lulling too. Charles Henstock, who had called at the Lovelocks' house to deliver a parcel from Dimity, was closely questioned, and had to reply, quite truthfully, that he really knew nothing about the matter.

'I fear it may be true that he has left his wife,' said Ada. 'He was never a very reliable character.'

'Do you remember when dear Donald Bailey called here one day when Richard was about six?' said Bertha.

'I shall never forget it,' trumpeted Ada, with a shudder.

'The child fingered *absolutely everything*,' Violet told

Charles. 'And when he asked if he could play in the garden, of course we agreed.'

'But on his way through the kitchen he switched on every one of the burners on the stove,' said Bertha.

'And in the garden he found the hose, turned on the tap to its maximum, and swamped the flower beds,' added Ada.

'And, worse still,' continued Violet, 'he turned it on poor Mrs Jefferson who was pegging out The Fuchsia Bush tea towels next door, and drenched her to the skin!'

'And all in the space of five minutes!' Bertha said.

To Charles it really only sounded a childish prank, but obviously it had been a major disaster remembered, for many years, by the three sisters.

'What a lovely room this is!' he said, trying to change the subject. 'You get all the morning sun.'

'Yes, it is pleasant,' agreed Ada, 'but the whole house is getting too much for us. Far too big, you know. We have been thinking of applying for one of the new homes at Thrush Green.'

Charles was taken aback. No one could say that the Lovelocks were in any need of such accommodation. They had this splendid house already, and a certain amount of domestic help, The Fuchsia Bush next door, and all the shops in Lulling High Street hard by and, above all, far more money than they could ever need.

'I doubt if you would qualify for a place,' said Charles. 'And in any case, the largest of the homes is only for two people.'

'Oh, we really thought of the *single* apartments. One each was our idea.'

'That, I'm sure, would be quite impossible,' said Charles firmly. 'You would be taking up three-quarters of the single people's accommodation at one blow.'

He stood up ready to depart.

'If I were you,' he ventured, 'I should think of closing one or two of your rooms to save work – and heating, of course.'

'We don't have heating much at all,' said Bertha. 'We just put on thicker vests or our winter spencers.'

They waved goodbye to their visitor, and then Ada, who was the most senior of the sisters, turned to Bertha with a reproachful expression.

'There was no need to speak of our *underwear*, Bertha! In very bad taste! Even if he is of the cloth, you must remember that Charles is a MAN!'

At Winnie Bailey's house, upon which so much attention was being focused at this time, affairs were settling down.

Richard was on his best behaviour, helped with the washing up, straightened his bed, and did his best to be unobtrusive.

He worked quietly upstairs for most of the morning, and took a walk in the afternoon. In fact, he was so little bother, Winnie found, after a few days, that she decided that he might just as well stay under her roof rather than go to the bother of finding lodgings for the fortnight or so which remained before he set off on his lecture tour.

The evening before Jenny was due back from hospital, she broached the subject. Naturally, Richard was delighted and grateful.

'But I must stress one thing, Richard. I'm not letting Jenny do any heavy work for a few weeks. I know she'll protest, but I'm going to be adamant. So that means you must pull your weight while you're here. Could you take on the boiler and this fire, for instance? Keep us stoked up, and cleaned out and so on?'

Richard brightened.

'I'd love to. You know I love dirty jobs.'

'You certainly swept the kitchen flue marvellously, I remember, and Phil Hurst still talks of the time you cleaned out her drains.'

'Dear girl!' said Richard affectionately. 'She's wasted on old Frank. I would have liked her for myself.'

'Maybe, Richard, but that time has gone,' said Winnie,

with some asperity. 'Well, if you'll take on those jobs, it will help enormously.'

'I'm a dab hand at vacuum cleaning too,' said Richard, 'though I draw the line at dusting.'

'I can cope with that, and the cooking and shopping,' said Winnie. 'I'm glad you're going to stay, dear boy. We shall manage very well, I'm sure. But what about your family affairs? Do you want to try and meet Fenella before you go?'

Richard looked pensive. He took up the poker, and turned over a beech log on the back of the fire.

'I don't think so. I rang her last night and she was as off-hand as ever. She knows where I shall be for the next month or two, if she wants to get in touch. I think I shall leave it to her for the time being, and try my luck again when I've done this tour.'

'So you think there might be some hope?'

'If Roger takes it into his head to move out, then I think there might be. But not as things are at the moment.'

'Well, you are all four grown up, and presumably sensible people. It's the children, I'm thinking about.'

'So am I, Aunt Win. Now, that's enough of my worries. Tomorrow I start my fire-tending duties, and fetch Jenny from the hospital. Right?'

'From the look of that coal scuttle,' observed Winnie, 'your fire-tending starts immediately.'

Richard obediently collected the scuttle and set off for the coal cellar, followed by his aunt's amused gaze.

The bright March weather continued. The birds were resplendent in their mating finery, nests were being built, and the hedgehogs and squirrels were beginning to stir from their months of hibernation.

Yellow coltsfoot and early primroses starred the banks, and George Curdle found a little bunch of fragrant white violets to present to his adored Miss Fogerty. The trees, so stark throughout the winter, were beginning to grow hazy with swelling buds, and rosettes of young leaves were bursting on the honeysuckle's twining stems.

'It all seems so *hopeful*,' commented Dorothy to Agnes, as they descended the hill to Lulling to keep their luncheon engagement with Ray and Kathleen. 'Somehow I feel we are in for a splendidly hot summer.'

Ray and Kathleen were at The Fleece to greet them, and Harrison was mercifully absent, presumably having his own repast and rest as arranged.

Affectionate greetings were exchanged and the menu studied whilst the four sipped their sherry.

'I wonder what "Sole Veronique" is?' wondered Agnes aloud.

'Grapes on it,' replied Dorothy succinctly. 'I don't think you'd like it, dear. What about these scallops of veal?'

'I can't eat veal now,' said Kathleen, 'after seeing how the poor darling calves are treated on television.'

'I do so agree,' said Agnes. 'That's why I'm having sole, if I may.'

'So shall I,' said Kathleen, 'but I do so hope they can supply plain boiled potatoes. My migraine is so easily brought on.'

'Well, I'll settle for the veal,' said Dorothy sturdily.

'And I shall have a rare fillet steak,' announced Ray, which Agnes thought suitably manly.

The Fleece dealt competently with their order, and Agnes thought how pleasant it was to be sitting with old friends, with good food before them, and the tranquil view of St John's across the green.

At a table in the window, she now noticed young Mr Venables and his wife. She waved to them, and Justin half-rose, gave a courtly little bow, and resumed his seat again. Agnes was touched to see that he was engaged in cutting up his wife's meat, so that she could eat it with her fork, held in her cruelly twisted arthritic hand. Poor Mrs Venables, thought Agnes, almost moved to tears, and she used to do such beautiful crochet-work!

Coffee was brought to them in the hotel sitting room. It was warm and sunny, and for two pins Agnes could have dropped off into a refreshing snooze, but common courtesy compelled her to make an occasional comment on Kathleen's non-stop description of her ailments. At least it gave Dorothy and Ray a chance to have a heart-to-heart talk on a neighbouring settee, she noted with some gratification.

'And my new doctor,' went on Kathleen, 'is taking so much more interest in my case. There were times when I believe my old medical man simply *didn't listen*. I couldn't understand it.'

Agnes knew exactly how he must have felt, but naturally did not say so.

At last, Ray stood up, studying his wrist watch.

'About time we were off, Kath. I'll go and get Harrison.'

The ladies donned their coats and went out of the front door. The air was cool and invigorating.

A frenzied yapping announced the arrival of Ray and his black labrador. The latter leapt upon Kathleen with such impetus that it would have felled any unsuspecting person, but his mistress stood up to his attentions with great indulgence.

'There, there!' she cried. 'Say "hello" to your two aunties.'

The ladies put out their hands civilly and patted the dog's silky head.

'Now, into the car,' ordered Kathleen opening the back door, and the animal leapt upon a rug there spread out, while farewells and thanks were given.

The two ladies waved goodbye, and then set off for home.

'"*Aunties*" indeed!' snorted Dorothy. 'Really, Kathleen takes the biscuit!'

'But what a pleasant party,' said Agnes. 'I enjoyed it so much. And I really think that Harrison's behaviour has improved, don't you?'

'Fat chance of it doing anything else,' said Dorothy, 'when you recall our last meeting with that creature.'

Charles and Dimity Henstock were eagerly awaiting a visit from Anthony Bull. Charles's predecessor had telephoned to say that he was on his way to Gloucester.

Charles hurried to the front door as soon as the bell rang.

'Come in, my dear fellow. What a pleasure this is! Are you alone?'

'Yes, on my way to a conference at Gloucester, and I thought as I was so close, I must call and see you both.'

Dimity now appeared in the hall, and was soon enveloped in a loving bear hug and the delicious scent of Anthony's after-shave lotion. Really, thought Dimity, emerging from the embrace, Anthony smells as gorgeous as he looks, and that's saying something.

'Coffee? A drink?'

'Nothing, thank you. Just a sight of you both, and the dear old church and vicarage. How's it going?'

They spent some time exchanging news, and the two men went out into the spring sunshine to look round the garden. Charles told him about the new homes at Thrush Green, and the alterations to the church almshouses hard by.

'And where is my friend Mrs Bates then?'

Charles explained that she had been the first to be housed afresh.

'She was the best silver cleaner I ever met,' said Anthony.

'She still is,' Charles told him.

They began to stroll back again towards the vicarage. The church clock gave three sonorous chimes, and Anthony, pulling an elegant gold half-hunter from his waistcoat pocket, compared times.

'I don't need to be in Gloucester until six,' he said, 'and I would dearly love to see these new homes and my old friends again.'

'Let me take you up there,' said Charles. 'I know they would all love to see you.'

'Come in my car,' said Anthony, 'and I'll run you back.'

'There's no need for that,' replied Charles. 'I shall visit one or two people there, and enjoy a walk back.'

'In that case,' said Anthony, 'I must make my farewells to Dimity. It has been so good to see you both again.'

Ten minutes later the two men approached Thrush Green. As they came within sight of the new homes, Anthony stopped the car, and looked across to the spot where Charles's rectory had once stood.

'I miss the old house still,' said Charles.

He sounded wistful, and Anthony shot a glance at his sad countenance.

'It was a dreadful shock,' he said. 'But now these new homes have arisen, you see, like a phoenix from the ashes.'

Charles smiled slowly.

'I like that idea.'

Silence fell as the two men gazed at Thrush Green, golden and tranquil in the afternoon sunlight. Both were engrossed with their memories.

'Well,' said Anthony at last, 'it's no good harking back, Charles. We have to go forward, you know. And with hope.'

They got out of the car, and stood a moment, enjoying the fresh breeze.

'Come on, Charles,' cried Anthony, stepping out. 'Let's go and see our old friends.'

Discover more about our forthcoming books through Penguin's FREE newspaper...

Penguin
Quarterly

It's packed with:

- exciting features
- author interviews
- previews & reviews
- books from your favourite films & TV series
- exclusive competitions & much, much more...

READ MORE IN PENGUIN

In every corner of the world, on every subject under the sun, Penguin represents quality and variety – the very best in publishing today.

For complete information about books available from Penguin – including Puffins, Penguin Classics and Arkana – and how to order them, write to us at the appropriate address below. Please note that for copyright reasons the selection of books varies from country to country.

In the United Kingdom: Please write to *Dept. EP, Penguin Books Ltd, Bath Road, Harmondsworth, West Drayton, Middlesex UB7 0DA*

In the United States: Please write to *Consumer Sales, Penguin USA, P.O. Box 999, Dept. 17109, Bergenfield, New Jersey 07621-0120.* VISA and MasterCard holders call 1-800-253-6476 to order Penguin titles

In Canada: Please write to *Penguin Books Canada Ltd, 10 Alcorn Avenue, Suite 300, Toronto, Ontario M4V 3B2*

In Australia: Please write to *Penguin Books Australia Ltd, P.O. Box 257, Ringwood, Victoria 3134*

In New Zealand: Please write to *Penguin Books (NZ) Ltd, Private Bag 102902, North Shore Mail Centre, Auckland 10*

In India: Please write to *Penguin Books India Pvt Ltd, 706 Eros Apartments, 56 Nehru Place, New Delhi 110 019*

In the Netherlands: Please write to *Penguin Books Netherlands bv, Postbus 3507, NL-1001 AH Amsterdam*

In Germany: Please write to *Penguin Books Deutschland GmbH, Metzlerstrasse 26, 60594 Frankfurt am Main*

In Spain: Please write to *Penguin Books S. A., Bravo Murillo 19, 1° B, 28015 Madrid*

In Italy: Please write to *Penguin Italia s.r.l., Via Felice Casati 20, I–20124 Milano*

In France: Please write to *Penguin France S. A., 17 rue Lejeune, F–31000 Toulouse*

In Japan: Please write to *Penguin Books Japan, Ishikiribashi Building, 2–5–4, Suido, Bunkyo-ku, Tokyo 112*

In Greece: Please write to *Penguin Hellas Ltd, Dimocritou 3, GR–106 71 Athens*

In South Africa: Please write to *Longman Penguin Southern Africa (Pty) Ltd, Private Bag X08, Bertsham 2013*

BY THE SAME AUTHOR

A selection of Miss Read omnibus editions in Penguin

Life at Thrush Green

Bubbling with drama, quarrels, gossip and romance, life at Thrush Green is never dull ... This attractive omnibus edition contains *Thrush Green*, *Winter at Thrush Green* and *News from Thrush Green*.

More Stories from Thrush Green

This delightful omnibus edition, containing *Battles at Thrush Green*, *Return to Thrush Green* and *Gossip from Thrush Green*, reveals why Miss Read is one of the best-loved novelists writing today.

Further Chronicles of Fairacre

Four much-loved books – *Miss Clare Remembers*, *Over the Gate*, *The Fairacre Festival* and *Emily Davis* – are collected in this volume.

Fairacre Roundabout

Life in Fairacre ebbs and flows with the seasons. Every face is familiar and each home reverberates with local news. And at the heart of the community is Miss Read, caught up in its joyful festivities – and its minor irritations. This volume contains *Tyler's Row*, *Farther Afield* and *Village Affairs*.

Christmas at Fairacre

In this charming anthology of Christmas tales, past and present, some of the most memorable events ever to occur in and around Fairacre are recalled by Miss Read in the novels *Village Christmas*, *The Christmas Mouse* and *No Holly for Miss Quinn* and in additional short stories.

A Year at Thrush Green is available as a Penguin Audiobook, read by June Whitfield.